THE WORKS OF
FRANCIS BRETT YOUNG

SEVERN EDITION

THE
WORKS OF
FRANCIS BRETT YOUNG

UNDERGROWTH
(with E. Brett Young)

DEEP SEA

THE DARK TOWER

IRON AGE

THE CRESCENT MOON

THE YOUNG PHYSICIAN

THE TRAGIC BRIDE

THE BLACK DIAMOND

THE RED KNIGHT

PILGRIM'S REST

WOODSMOKE

COLD HARBOUR

SEA HORSES

PORTRAIT OF CLARE

MY BROTHER JONATHAN

BLACK ROSES

JIM REDLAKE

MR. AND MRS. PENNINGTON

THE HOUSE UNDER THE WATER

THIS LITTLE WORLD

WHITE LADIES

FAR FOREST

THEY SEEK A COUNTRY

DR. BRADLEY REMEMBERS

THE CITY OF GOLD

MR. LUCTON'S FREEDOM

A MAN ABOUT THE HOUSE

THE ISLAND

FRANCIS BRETT YOUNG

THEY SEEK
A COUNTRY

WILLIAM HEINEMANN LTD
LONDON :: TORONTO

FIRST PUBLISHED AUGUST 1937
REPRINTED OCTOBER 1937, JANUARY 1938
FIRST PUBLISHED IN THE SEVERN EDITION 1939
REPRINTED FEBRUARY 1940, AUGUST 1941
JANUARY 1947

PRINTED IN GREAT BRITAIN AT THE WINDMILL PRESS
KINGSWOOD, SURREY

To
The Earl Baldwin of Bewdley, K.G.,
with the homage and gratitude
of a
friend and neighbour

"They looked for a City that hath Foundations . . ."

CONTENTS

BOOK ONE

FOG OVER ENGLAND

BOOK TWO

STORM OVER AFRICA

vii

PREFACE

THIS long book is the first-fruits of more than twenty years' thought and research and meditation. The work of which *They Seek a Country* is part suggested itself to me originally at the beginning of 1916 when I became, by sheer chance, a humble member of the British Expeditionary Force in East Africa. We were sailing north from Durban to Mombasa in the liner *Armadale Castle,* which had been stripped of most of its contents (with the exception of its live-stock) and had become a cruiser. During that voyage, I found myself seated in the officers' mess—or ward-room, as it was then called—between a brother-officer of the R.A.M.C., my friend Robert Dolbey, and a Boer cavalryman, Major Brink, who later, I believe, became Chief-of-Staff to the Union Defence Force.

Both of them had fought in the Boer War, on different sides. When they discovered this, they immediately began talking across me, recalling the various engagements at which they had been present, the terrain of these remembered fights and the mistakes which had been made by the leaders on either side. The strange form of this comradeship-in-arms and the friendliness of the discussion appealed strongly to my novelist's imagination. It was, indeed, a remarkable thing that these two men, who only fifteen years before, had been devoted to a mutual destruction, should be sailing northward to fight side by side in a savage land against a common enemy; and the spectacle set me thinking on the miracle by which, in so short a time, that hazardous experiment, the Union of South Africa, had justified the political vision that conceived it. On H.M.S. *Armadale Castle*, at that moment, there were, probably a thousand men, Afrikanders of Dutch and English origin, united not only by the ideals they had volunteered to defend, but also by a personal comradeship in which the bitter memories of racial and political conflict had been forgotten. This grey ship, with its cargo of men of both races, many of whom would never return, appeared to me symbolical of that miracle. I was witnessing, it seemed to me, the Birth of a Nation.

An impressive theme—and one which not merely challenged me as an artist but appealed to me as a man who had already given a great part of his heart to South Africa. General Smuts has declared that I am, by nature, an "African"; and even as I write these words, the nostalgia I feel for that fierce and lovely continent, almost persuades me that he is right. All through the East African campaign, which may some-day be realized as one of the most heroic achievements of the Great War, my mind continued to dwell on this subject. When the war was over, I returned to South Africa and spent a year there, saturating myself in the

"atmosphere" of the country and absorbing as much
of its history as my mind could hold.

Yet, when I began to plan the work in detail, I felt
so doubtful of my knowledge and of my powers that
I shrank from writing it. For seventeen years, during
which I produced the long series of Mercian novels,
I continued to brood over a mass of rebellious material
which I still found it impossible to see in perspective
and with the detachment that I deemed necessary for
the treatment of such a huge theme. At last, in 1937,
twenty-one years after the birth of the idea, I made
a final pilgrimage in which I followed the Voor-
trekkers step by step from the Cape to the Limpopo;
and in the following year I began the composition of
this, the first movement of what I had begun to think
of as my "African Symphony."

Every book that a serious artist writes is, in some
degree, an Act of Faith; and this book (or series of
books), the most ambitious I have ever attempted, is,
for what it is worth, my own contribution to a cause
in which I believe most fervently: the Unity of the
South African People. The subject is one which
bristles with thorns as fiercely as the scrub of the Low
Veld. At every step one is compelled to "wait-a-bit."
The whole history of South Africa is beset with
tangles and thickets of distrust, misunderstanding,
prejudice, and (reasonably) bitter memories—so
densely that, at times, it is difficult to see the wood
for the trees. But I have tried to drive a straight path

through these impediments; to maintain an open mind
and to understand, as well as an alien may, the
conflicting motives which have confused—and sometimes stained with the blood of honest men—this page
of history, keeping always in view, however discouraged and bewildered, the great end towards which
South Africa is gradually and inevitably moving, the
high destiny of the land and the folk which, after my
own, I love best on earth.

I have tried, and am still trying, to be fair. If I
fail, as most likely I may, it will not be for want of
good will. That is why, in this preface, I want to
express my profound gratitude for the encouragement
I have received from hundreds of correspondents in
South Africa, irrespective of race and politics, whose
letters have fortified me in the performance of this
perilous task by suggesting that a mere work of fiction,
written by an outsider, may, perhaps, after all,
contribute a little towards a better understanding
between Dutch and English Afrikanders. I am
grateful, above all, to my old chief, friend and
comrade-in-arms, General Smuts, who has declared
his approval of the work of one of his former
subalterns.

In this part of the ambitious scheme, indeed, my
task *qua* historical novelist (as Rhodes would have put
it) has been fairly easy, for the period is so remote that
none of the protagonists are alive. In the second
volume, *The City of Gold*, I have had to deal with

matters more contentious, including the Jameson Raid, which put back the clock twenty years. In the third volume, as yet unwritten, I shall have to deal with the Second Boer War, and with such embarrassing subjects as Concentration Camps. That is a formidable prospect from which bolder men than myself might well shrink; but, even if I fail in the task I have set myself, I know I shall never regret the twenty years of study and thought I have devoted to it; for I still believe in the greatness of South Africa's destiny, and hold an unshaken faith in the future of the land and the people I love.

BOOK ONE

FOG OVER ENGLAND

CHAPTER ONE

AUTUMN JOURNEY

On the first day of October in the year eighteen hundred and thirty-six, fog lay over England. Though fog was the island's natural portion in winter, its inhabitants felt that they had some cause for resentment when the infliction arrived so early; but that summer had been wetter than any in living memory. In June roving thunder-storms had laid the ripening grass. In July rains that seemed as if they would never cease had soaked the cut hay till the swathes lay blackened and rotted. By the end of August corn stood sprouting in the ear, and common folk, who had to think first of their stomachs, shook their heads; for scarcity, they knew, made a speculator's paradise, and the price of wheat, which had fallen from five pounds ten in the Year of Waterloo to less than half that figure in the Year of Reform, was certain to rise. Bitter cold in the air; in men's hearts an equal bitterness: for the Reform Bill was Law—and yet the millennium had not come. And the winter, too, old men said, was like to be cruel cold as well as hungry; for the hedges were heavily berried with hips and haws—God having more thought for the birds of the air than Lord

Melbourne had for the people. In September the farmers scraped together the remnants of ruined harvest, none was left for gleaners; and now, as the first Arctic draughts crept insensibly over the sodden land, the raw, moisture-laden air turned to a mist so dense that even in broad daylight men must grope their way as blindly as if it were already dark, or sit sulkily by their firesides waiting for rain to disperse it or for wind to blow it away. For three days and nights England lay fog-bound, utterly obscured by a blanket of white vapour, uniform and unsullied save where the smoke of hidden cities flawed its sunlit surface with yellowish stains like spills on a soiled tablecloth, or where the summits of wolds, moorlands and mountains, emerging triumphantly, pierced the unsubstantial stuff with high peaks and ridges that lay glittering with the first snow. But these no men, save, perhaps, lonely shepherds, saw.

Over no part of the land did the fog cling and settle more densely than in the valley of Severn where the cliffs of Cotswold and Malvern rose sharply, defining the limits of that ancient firth. Here summer floods had saturated the stiff marls to the depths where the cold clay subsoil held water. The *Hirondelle* coach, whose spanking team of four normally covered the hundred and thirty-six miles from Cheltenham to Liverpool in nine hours and a half, was held up at Worcester. Three times on the Evesham turnpike, where mists rising from the swollen Avon thickened the air, the *Hirondelle* had pulled up to give aid to ditched transport-wagons top-heavy with pockets of hops. When, two hours behind time, the guard slid on the drags and the coach screeched slowly down the hill into Worcester, where the new gas-lamps stretched away in a wan procession, their bleared haloes vaguely indicating the line of the empty High Street but giving little more light than the candle-points flickering like will-o'-the-wisps behind steamed shop-windows, there rose in the hearts of its pair of lonely passengers a feeling of escape and relief.

At the "Star and Garter" Hotel in the Foregate the coach came to a halt and these comrades in distress dismounted. One was a haggard gentleman, with a long, cadaverous face and a skinny nose from which a dewdrop depended, who moved gingerly, as though his limbs were frozen to brittleness. The other, a short, stout, bustling fellow, in a brown beaver hat, with shrewd, humorous eyes, a ruddy complexion, and a figure that strained the buttons of his caped and waisted melton surcoat, jumped out with an air of impatience and accosted the driver.

"How long do you give us to thaw?" he asked briskly.

The man slewed round sullenly. His face, blotched with cold, was ill-humoured, and globules of condensed fog spangled his tousled flaxen wig. One would have guessed he was drunk.

"How long?" he repeated. "That's a fine question

to ask, sir! I can tell you I've had a bellyful! You don't catch me taking the road again afore I can see where I'm going. One thing's certain sure: my cattle and me are stabled in Worcester this night!"

The stout gentleman grunted. "Provoking . . . damnition provoking! Is there any other coach, do you know, running north to Kidderminster? I happen to be in a hurry. Time means money to me."

"I know naught about no coaches but mine," the man answered surlily. "Other coaches are none of my business, *nor* answering questions. If you want information you'ld better ask inside. Mr. Collins will tell you all you want, behappen. Come on, Joe, give us a hand!"

The stout gentleman entered the inn and called for the landlord. A flustered fat man in an apron and shirt-sleeves appeared and tried to be polite.

"We're all at sixes and sevens," he said. "The fog's lying thicker up north. I've five coach-loads of passengers shot in on me unexpected and my wife abed, poor creature, with a heavy cold on the chest, you know what that means, sir. Kidderminster? You'll never get there this day, I can tell you that. There's coaches held up all along the road, and I can't say I blame them. If you care to make yourself comfortable in the Assembly Room, I'll let you know the minute there seems any hope."

"I must get to Grafton Lovett this evening," the traveller persisted.

"Grafton Lovett? But that's nearer Worcester than Kidderminster, and well off the road."

"I am well acquainted with Grafton Lovett. I'm a friend of Colonel Abberley's."

"A friend of Squire Abberley's?" The landlord's tone changed. "Well, I shall have to see what I can do for you in that case. Any friend of Squire Abberley is welcome in this house. I might find somebody willing to drive you to Grafton—that is, if you don't mind paying for it."

"I'm willing to pay anything in reason. But I'm in a hurry. I have parliamentary business waiting for me in London."

"Indeed . . ." The landlord was impressed. "If I might know your name, sir . . ."

"Vizard. Mortimer Vizard. I'm Colonel Abberley's lawyer."

"Then if you'll oblige by stepping this way, sir, I'll do my best for you."

He led Mr. Vizard upstairs and along a creaking passage that smelt of must and fog and stale beer, then ceremoniously threw open the door of a long, dim, barn-like chamber with a vast spread of uncarpeted floor and a high ceiling suspended from which the lights of six candles shone pitifully through the all-pervading fog. At either end of it stood a fireplace crammed with a brisk fire of sulphurous Staffordshire coal; and around these, in two huddled semi-circles, were clustered the unfortunate six coach-loads of wayfarers who shared Mr. Vizard's fate. In spite of the landlord's ceremonious introduction nobody made room for him. They sat there dazed with the fatalistic apathy of two parties of shipwrecked sailors, distrustful of each other and victims of a stupor that made them all dumb. Since there was no chair unoccupied, Mr. Vizard contented himself with a brisk prowling to and fro over the echoing boards of the icy space between the two fireplaces and hoped for the best.

For a quarter of an hour he paced impatiently to and fro, his portfolio under his arm, or gazed hopelessly through the windows into the fog that was so dense that he could not even discern the houses over the street, taking the watch from his fob occasionally and examining it under the candles to check the incredible slowness of the passage of time. At the end of this period the landlord reappeared. Out of respect to Colonel Abberley's friend he had removed his apron and put on a coat. As he entered the two clusters of castaways sprang to their feet simultaneously, each man hoping that the coach in which he had been travelling was about to start.

"Mr. Vizard, sir!" he called.

Mr. Vizard hurried to the door.

"I've done it," the landlord whispered, "I've got a conveyance. You're in luck, sir. There's not many folk that 'ld care to poke their noses out of doors for love or money this day, though the roads in these parts are safe enough, generally speaking—which is more than I could have sworn to, mind you, a few years since, when the rick-burning and machine-breaking was on and a lot of odd characters hanging about and waiting to take their chance. It wasn't harm they was meaning, not even then: only a parcel of 'Brummagem Radicals' got stirring them up and setting fools' minds again' their own interest. All that country folk need—and I speak as one country-born, sir—is a steady hand: the sort of treatment gentlemen like Squire Abberley gives them: a-driving them on the snaffle, but letting them know that you've got the ribbons in one hand and the whip in t'other. I fancy you mentioned, sir, that you were a Parliament gentleman? Well, this Malt Tax, now . . ."

"You say you have got me a chaise?" Mr. Vizard said smoothly, interrupting the spate.

"To be sure, sir. The thought of that there damned Malt Tax put it out of my head. Not exactly a chaise, sir. I found a chap in our tap-room, Jim Hollies by name, with a dray of cider-casks going to Mr. Ombersley's at Chaddesbourne. It won't be not more than a mile or so out of his way to drop you at Grafton; and though he'll go slow, slow is sure, if you take my meaning, and the slower the better on such a day as this and with Jim a bit bosky."

"You mean the fellow is drunk?" Mr. Vizard enquired with alarm.

"Oh, I wouldn't say that, sir, not drunk. He's had about as much as a weak-headed chap can carry comfortable. But drunk or dry, Jim knows his way home right enough; and even if he didn't you can be certain his horses do. Wonderful knowledgeable creatures horses be. I'd sooner trust them than most men in a fog like this."

"And what do I give this fellow?" Mr. Vizard asked cautiously.

"That rests with you, sir. But if you choose to take my advice you'll not overpay him. A carter's wage is round about ten shillings a week. If you spoil these chaps they gets saucy in no time."

In front of the inn the Chaddesbourne dray stood waiting. It was, in fact, a bulky wain with four enormous mud-caked wheels, piled high with hogsheads and drawn by two shaggy-fetlocked plough-horses. Jim Hollies himself showed a stunted, misshapen figure enveloped in sacking that covered his head with a cowl from beneath which, withdrawn like those of a hedgehog, two small, bright, bloodshot eyes blinked at his fare distrustfully. Mr. Vizard regarded the vehicle and its sub-human driver with equal distaste; but it seemed he had no choice in the matter, so, lifting his coat-skirts, he set his neatly-shod foot on a spoke of the near forward wheel and hauled himself on to the fog-damp sacking at Jim Hollies's side. The landlord, bowing obsequiously, wished him a pleasant journey, and with a heavy rumbling and a squeaking of wheels the wagon rolled forward.

At the end of the Foregate, a hundred yards from

the inn, the last gas-lamp winked its good-bye. For another two hundred the ghosts of tall houses defined the street. At this point, with a bump and a convulsive lurch, the unsprung wagon passed from the city's paved road on to the country highway. A phantasmal turnpike-keeper threw wide his gate and waved them on. The empty road was so deeply rutted and so beset with puddled pits and crevasses that the wagon, for all its weight, rolled from side to side like a ship in a heavy sea. Mr. Vizard, still clutching his portfolio, was hard put-to to keep his seat, and the fog grew so thick that he could no longer see the leader's ears. Slow as the horses were, he wished they were even slower. Remembering the hop-wagons ditched on the Evesham road, he was prepared at any moment to find himself flung into the invisible hedgerow. Mr. Vizard regretted his separation from the *Hirondelle's* buoyant springs. He regretted equally the proximity of Jim Hollies, who, accustomed, no doubt, and adapting himself automatically in his sleep to this riotous type of locomotion, swayed sideways with each lurch and leaned, with the most neighbourly abandon, against Mr. Vizard's shoulder, inflicting on his town-bred nostrils an all too rustic aroma of byre and midden. There hung also upon the air a strong odour of pomace or cider, though how much of this was exhaled from Jim Hollies's person and how much arose from the hogsheads and the heaps of empty sacks in which bruised and rotten apples had been stored, Mr. Vizard could not decide. In any case, what with the continued jolting and swaying and the cold which, gradually ascending from his feet, was approaching the more delicate area vulnerable to his hereditary enemy lumbago, he soon reached a stage of suffering and of apprehension so numbing to the sensibility that he almost ceased to feel or to care what happened. Indeed, despite his appearance of drunken stupor, Jim Hollies's hedgehog-eyes were more keenly aware than he judged; for suddenly, with an alarming precipitance which made Mr. Vizard fear an encounter with footpads or desperate poachers or even highwaymen, he leapt from his seat and seizing the leader's bridle led the horses right-handed down a steep pitch of lane that deserted the high road and then through a swollen water-splash, and then, urging them onward with agonized, inarticulate cries, up an even steeper and apparently endless hillside, at the summit of which Mr. Vizard, to his amazement, emerged into a new and relatively fogless air in which an avenue of elms, invisible a moment before, towered like gigantic spectres above and on either side, discovering, through the end of the tunnel their leafy masses enclosed, a range of bright windows enclosed in the sombre shape of a huge stone house with a pillared portico and pediment which he recognized, almost incredulously, as his journey's destination.

CHAPTER TWO

CONVERSATION PIECE

WITHIN an hour Mr. Vizard's congealed blood was beginning to thaw and expand. Though used to the ostentatious entertainment of aldermen and nabobs, and the luxury of their suburban mansions, he could still be thrilled to find himself received in the company and in the homes of landed gentry, the owners of wide acres (there was no possession like land) and the sole repository, in these degenerate days, of those traditions of the ancient regime that were the cause of his country's greatness. Their condition was one to which he himself aspired; and his host, Colonel Abberley, a near spiritual kinsman of Sir Roger de Coverley, his favourite hero in fiction, was as perfect a representative of the type as could be imagined: a little, dry gentleman, with the obvious cut of an old soldier, whose studiously formal manners, combined with his un-selfconscious rusticity (and profanity) of speech, made him a veritable museum-piece. The rest of the cosy company of four was perfectly in keeping and might have been proposed as a conversation piece for Mr. Zoffany. There was the sister of his host, who

13

had long been a widower, Miss Lavinia Abberley, whose antique graces and equally her attire made her nearer to the subjects of eighteenth-century canvases than to the frothy ladies of Regency society. There was also, as there should be in every properly regulated country house, a parson: no mere appanage or dependant, but a man of birth and breeding, a mature younger son of the neighbouring family of Ombersley whose lineage was almost (but not quite) as ancient as Colonel Abberley's own, who could take his part in polite conversation and drink his bottle of wine like a man of the world.

Mr. Vizard smiled contentedly. It was almost worth while to have undergone the uncertainties, discomforts and privations of the last twenty hours for the sake of relishing more richly these contrasting luxuries: the elegance of that spacious dining-room over whose plaster ceiling the candles threw shadows that seemed, as one threw back one's head, to bring the circling rout of opulent nymphs and rude satyrs to life; the warmth of the enormous wood fire that glowed so red and flared so eagerly; the deft movements, around the oval of lucent mahogany, of men-servants in bottle-green breeches and coats with claret facings; the benevolent scrutiny of authentic family portraits, which, having none of his own, he always found exhilarating; and, above all perhaps, the milky excellence of the claret with which this admirable meal of plump roast pheasant had been graced. Mr. Vizard felt not merely in tune with his surroundings but pleased with himself.

"And now," Colonel Abberley said, "your news, sir!"

Mr. Vizard smiled and nodded. "The good news first. Allow me to congratulate you, sir. Our little Enclosure Bill will receive the Royal Assent. I think I may flatter myself, with your permission, that, for a private measure, the affair was managed with unusual smoothness and expedition: two readings without a word of discussion in three weeks. Upstairs, the Committee wasted no time. Your good friends in Parliament, Mr. Ombersley and Mr. Sheldon, were invaluable. Three commissioners are appointed: your cousin, Lord D'Abitot; our reverend friend here, representing the tithe-owners, and Mr. Thomas Collins, who, of course, is one of your tenants."

"Ay, Tom Collins is all right," Colonel Abberley said. "I can answer for him."

Mr. Vizard bowed and smirked in agreement. "The three commissioners," he went on, "will now proceed to meet, receive claims and publish an award. There is a provision that two of them constitute a quorum: so there is really no reason why your cousin and Mr. Ombersley should not settle most things between you to your own satisfaction without calling on Mr. Collins to intervene. Indeed"—Mr. Vizard generously replenished his wine-glass—"from what I have seen of the maps and know of the nature of the land, I think that you, sir, and this gentleman's brother, will have added to your properties two tidy little estates of more than eight hundred acres apiece as the result of a remarkably modest expenditure."

"That is by no means the way, if I may say so," the parson broke in, "in which Colonel Abberley and my brother look at this Enclosure. What they want—and what all right-thinking people want—is to improve the land and eliminate wasteful husbandry for the good of the nation. As things are, sir, the energy of the community is going to waste and the morals of my parishioners are suffering. In looking after a brood of goslings, a few rotten sheep, a skeleton of a cow or a mangy horse, these fellows with rights of commonage lose more than they might have gained by an honest day's work and, what is far worse, acquire the habit of independence and idleness. God did not create the earth, sir, to lie waste for feeding geese, but to be cultivated by man in the sweat of his brow."

"Of course, sir, of course," Mr. Vizard said smoothly, "we are all of the same opinion. Unfortunately, some of the labouring poor fail to realize that it is better to work for a steady two shillings a day for a benevolent employer than to pick up a miserable and uncertain living in that way. The Reform agitation and the last Revolution in France have gone to their heads. To-day everyone talks of 'rights' and nobody of 'duties.' More than one Enclosure Bill has lately been wrecked by misguided sentimentality. The whole country is suffering from an epidemic of morbid sensibility. All this fussing and fuming over the Slave Trade, for instance. To abolish slavery in England was all very well. We are a Christian nation, sir, and should be above reproach. But to lug in the Cape of Good Hope and the West Indian possessions, where heathens are in the majority, is not only unnecessary but foolish. In tropical climes the slave is not a luxury but a necessity. The West Indies, I'm told, will rebel, and none can blame them. Why, even in England members of Parliament allow their reason to be swayed by the sentiments of their constituents. In the case of this little Enclosure Act of ours, I don't mind telling you, we had an anxious moment in committee when one of your self-constituted village Hampdens bobbed up and claimed to be heard."

"A man from my parish? Impossible!" Mr. Ombersley was shocked.

Colonel Abberley laughed. "Control your feelings, George. Mr. Vizard says it's all over. But I think I can guess whom you mean. Was the fellow's name Oakley?"

"John Oakley, sir. That was the name."

"I know the fellow quite well, and I've had my eye on him. He's the grandson, and heir-at-law I suppose, of old Joe Barley whom you buried two years ago, George. He was born and bred over Dulston way, where all bad things come from, and brought up as a nail-maker. When Joe Barley died, this fellow gave up his calling and came to settle down here and loaf in the old man's cottage—you know that very well, or ought to—on the edge of the common."

"I remember Joe Barley quite well: a most respectful old man," the parson grumbled; "but this other fellow . . ."

"Oblige me by passing the port, George. Another glass, Mr. Vizard. I hope the wine's to your taste, it's the year of Coruña. This other fellow is anything but respectful: a regular 'Brummagem Radical,' as we call them down here. But if the Bill's through I reckon we shall soon see the last of him, and a damned good riddance. His 'rights,' as he chooses to call them, are squatter's rights. The cottage was thrown up—you can hardly call it a building—about eighteen years ago, just before I succeeded."

"And encroachments of less than twenty years' date," Mr. Vizard put in, "have no standing whatever nor any claims when it comes to redistribution. The commissioners can pull this man's house down tomorrow if they see fit."

"As they assuredly shall see fit," Mr. Ombersley muttered. "I don't want any Methodists putting ideas into my parishioners' heads!"

"Behold the Church Militant, Mr. Vizard! None the less, I agree with him. The sooner a saucy fellow like this Oakley is brought to his senses the better. As soon as his house is pulled down there will be no difficulty in clearing him out. My parish officer will refuse him a certificate and send him back to his radical friends in Dulston before he does any more harm. These factory-workers will be the ruin of us. The overseer mentioned to me the other day that this fellow actually talked of starting an evening school! What does a labourer who works twelve hours a day for his daily bread want with learning to read? And what will he read when he's learnt? I can tell you, sir: that damned devil Cobbett's *Political Register*! As a matter of fact," the Colonel went on, "these 'encroachments,' as you lawyers call them, are the curse of agriculture. People have the idea that if they can manage to run up a roof and get a fire burning between sunrise and sunset they can stay there till doomsday. I'm afraid that those who have lived in their hovels for more than twenty years may be able to claim an allotment in place of their common rights. That is so, Mr. Vizard?"

"That is so . . . unfortunately."

"But the others will have to go and go double quick, and the first I clear off my common will be Master Oakley. How did the fellow strike you?"

Mr. Vizard deliberated. "On the surface, sir, I must admit, he struck me as a personable young man, tall and dark, one might almost say handsome: much above his station in bearing and dress, if you take my meaning, with considerable powers of expression and force of character which, if properly directed and disciplined . . ."

B

"Ah, there you have it!" Colonel Abberley broke in. "Discipline! That is what this age lacks, sir. But what can you expect when the Court itself sets the Nation such a humiliating example? If I had a fellow like that in my regiment for eighteen months, I could make a man of him. What this unhappy country needs is another war! But if once I start that hare I shall never finish. What had Oakley to say for himself?"

"An oration, sir: a harangue; a positive philippic! Of course, like all fellows of his kind, our village Hampden could never keep to his point, and showed pitiable ignorance of the law. Yet the man has passion and fervour, and spoke as though he were used to it."

"Used to ranting in his conventicles, no doubt. Every Methodist learns to do that," Mr. Ombersley said contemptuously.

"Perhaps, sir. I found myself interested, all the same. It is my business, as a lawyer, to see both sides in other people's cases if I only see one in my own; and if Oakley failed to make out a case for himself—he admitted, hands down, that the squatter's standing was doubtful—he drew an affecting picture—ay, I'll go so far as that—of the general results of enclosure on the commoners in your parish."

"The general results, sir, are obvious," Colonel Abberley said sharply; "they will be to improve the common land several hundred per cent and ensure its being cultivated tidily, without waste. The men who formerly worked for themselves haphazard and

struggled to live from hand to mouth, will now work
for me or Ombersley's brother or Tom Collins for a
regular and generous wage. Why, sir, in England, in
these days the labouring poor are pampered, sir, positively pampered!"

"Oh, no doubt, no doubt! . . ." Mr. Vizard bowed
to the storm. "I am merely defining this young man's
thesis which, naturally, did not dwell on what the
commoner stood to gain but on what he would lose.
First the pride of feeling he had something of his own:
his own cottage, his own patch of soil, his own cow, his
own geese or what not. Then his rights: the right to
cut fern and to glean and to gather manure and firewood . . ."

"And scare every pheasant of mine within a mile
of the common! You might add the right to poach
and the right to pilfer! Ask my head-gamekeeper,
Ballance."

"Mr. Oakley, I hardly need say, did not mention
these. But shall I go on?"

"Ay, go on, go on," Abberley grunted.

"As a result of this, he suggested, the ejected
commoner would have no incentive to thrift or
decency. 'Go to any ale-house,' he said, 'in any parish
lately enclosed, and you will see for yourself the origin
of poverty and poor-rates. For whom are men to be
sober, for whom are they to save? For the parish? If
they are diligent, will they get leave to build a cottage?
If they are sober, will they get land for a cow and milk

for their children? If they are frugal, will they get half an acre of land to plant potatoes and leave to cut fuel? You say they will have wages from the farmers to pay for these things. Two-and-threepence a day, if they're lucky! If they pay for their food, what can the belly spare for the back? You offer them no motives for decency, gentlemen,' he says, 'you take their land and you give them nothing in return but a parish officer and a workhouse. What reason have they to care for anything but a pot of beer? It helps them to forget.'"

Parson Ombersley wagged his head. "I am inclined to think for my own part that even ale is less pernicious than tea. It is excessive tea-drinking that frays the nerves of these unfortunate people and makes them pernickety. As for the practice of gleaning to which you referred: in spite of the oft-quoted warrant of Scripture I have long been convinced that it should be stopped. Any custom that throws together uneducated people of opposite sexes whose carnal passions are apt to be ill-controlled is demoralizing."

Colonel Abberley, brushing aside these reflections, rose impatiently.

"We have heard all this stuff—Oakley's stuff, not yours, George—before. It is the sort of reward any public-spirited landowner must expect to receive. Happily for all of us, it weighed no more heavily with the Committee of Parliament than it does with me. Our Bill has gone through, and no talk will alter it now. What is more, there's no time to be wasted if we are to break up any quantity of land and sow winter wheat this autumn. You and I, George, will have to get busy to-morrow. I'll send Collins word to meet us."

Mr. Vizard smiled. "Mr. Collins, I feel sure, will be at your service, sir. The Act allows each commissioner two guineas a day."

"All the more reason for getting the business settled," Colonel Abberley went on. "What about the other encroachments, Mr. Vizard? I should like to see the last of them."

"Any cottage of more than twenty years' standing carries with it a right to a certain allotment of land but no right to the common. But the cottager, mind you, must pay his share of the legal costs of enclosure and fence his allotment. Speaking from my own experience, I think you are likely to find that most of your cottagers will be only too glad to sell you their land and relieve themselves of legal responsibility. They don't understand it. Offer them five pounds an acre. That is about the usual figure, and by far the most satisfactory way of dealing with the matter."

"Five pounds an acre. . . . Well, it's worth more than that to me. I can buy in the lot for less than two hundred pounds. And what about Oakley? That fellow's insolence sticks in my gizzard still; but I have to keep on the right side of the law all the same."

"Your position in his case is perfectly clear, sir: he has no claim whatever."

"I can eject him and do what I like with the house he is living in?"

"Whatever you like."

"In that case, I'll see that damned hovel pulled down to-morrow. Suppose we join Miss Abberley?" Colonel Abberley moved to the window and gazed out. "The fog's thicker than ever," he said. "I never knew the like of it. And I had hoped to take our visitor to shoot a pheasant to-morrow. . . ."

CHAPTER THREE

BLACK SLAVERY

THE great three days' fog had not throttled and shrouded the land on the day when John Oakley left London and started on the long tramp homeward to Grafton Lovett. He left the stony capital with a heavy heart and a bitter feeling of failure, far different from the enthusiasms with which he had approached it a week before. That visit had marked the first impact of grim actuality on an ardent spirit which, up till now, had been nurtured on dreams and had little acquaintance with reality outside the narrow limits of his own upbringing; and the shock sharply administered to his belief in human justice, together with an increasingly unpalatable sense of his own insignificance and impotence, made him equally humble and hurt and hotly rebellious.

He had been born and bred, as Colonel Abberley was informed, in the sooty borough of Dulston, a conglomeration of mean dwellings, foundries and workshops incongruously encircling the ruins of a feudal fortress, which the fierce draught of the industrial revolution had lately fanned into fervent life: a centre of hot volcanic activity fed by the fuel feverishly dug

25

from the vast coalfield that surrounded and throttled it in the smoke of its monstrous combustion. His mother, an innocent pink-and-white country girl exiled in service at an ale-house in Sedgebury, had loved and married her first courter, a nail-maker who lived and plied his sweated trade in a domestic forge built on to the back of a cottage of smoke-grimed brick indistinguishable from twenty others in the same sordid row.

The life into which Oakley had been born, and which, as a child, he took for granted, was one of unceasing labour amid conditions of brutal savagery and bitter privation. Sixteen hours a day and more his parents toiled in their cramped and sooty cavern forging nails for the iron-shod hooves of the great Duke's victorious cavalry. Twenty thousand horseshoe-nails a week Oakley's father forged, each nail struck twenty-five times with the two-pound hammer: five million one hundred and sixty-eight thousand hammer-strokes of the sinewy spark-scarred forearm—and, as a result of this labour, the nail-maker's grudging pittance of eight shillings a week. In the first ten years of his life, John Oakley's ears never knew peace from the thud and tinkle of hammers; his eyes knew no respite from the spectacle of toil. His father and mother were more like machines than human beings. The moment they ceased working they ate what they could and flung themselves down on the bed they shared with him and slept; when they woke, they ate greedily again and worked till their eyes or their muscles failed them. In the strict economy of this inhuman labour even the strength of a child might count by helping to tip the nice balance between subsistence and actual starvation. Mere hunger was taken as a matter of course. So, as soon as his baby intelligence grew sufficient to grasp the working of that elementary mechanism, the child's frail arms were set to the monotonous task of blowing the bellows that breathed on the forge's gleed. That was a proud day when, six years old and perched on a box to reach the lever, he first set his hand to it, but it was not long before what had seemed an adventure became a slavery. Sometimes his mind wandered; sometimes he fell asleep; and the gleed went black and his father would swear at him fiercely but not unkindly. More than once, overcome by heat or fumes he grew giddy and fainted. Then his mother would run to him, smothering him with anxious tears and kisses. It was a shame, she said, to work the child to death; she would rather work longer herself, she protested, and wear her fingers to the bone; but her husband told her roughly not to be soft and asked her where she thought the next dinner was coming from.

Seven days a week the family worked and sixteen hours at a shift; and the fogger weighed the nails with false weights and haggled over slipshod workmanship and iron wasted, and complained and bullied because more of the carefully-counted shillings were not spent at his tommy-shop.

By the time he was ten John Oakley had not learnt to read or write. A few of the neighbours' children, whose hands could be spared, were "put out" to be kept out of mischief by an unsavoury Dame who "taught school" for threepence a week. Other children of more prosperous households attended the Common Day School or even the brand-new British School in the Sedgebury Road, the dissenters' counterblast to the National Schools which were attached to the Established Church; but these seats of superior learning exacted more than a penny a day, and that, in a week, amounted to more than the earnings of half a day's work: and what was the use of book-learning anyway to a boy whose whole life, in the nature of things, would be divided, like that of his father and mother, between labour and sleep—who had been born to hammer and cut and shape red-hot rods of iron till the day of his death?

By the time he was ten, moreover, John Oakley had scarcely set eyes on a blade of green grass or indeed on any living green save that of the sickly trees which, clinging to the steep on which the Castle crumbled, shook forth in spring, with helpless obstinacy, bright feeble trusses of leaf whose verdure the impalpable dust of carbon that fell from the sky soon tarnished. The town of Dulston stood at the very heart of the blighted zone, marooned in the midst of a slagged and cindery wilderness, and this was John Oakley's world. Beyond its bricky verges, if he had only known, lay as sweet a countryside as any in England, a tangle of green hillsides and flowing streams; but the child knew nothing of these save what his mother whispered to him when warmly huddled beside him in the cold bed shaken by the vibrations of his father's snores, she spoke of the lost paradise of her own not so very distant childhood—of a remote, unimaginable heaven that went by the musical name of Grafton Lovett where the sun, it seemed, always shone, and harsh winds never bit to the bone, and children wandered, without a care in the world, through green lanes and cowslip meadows and bluebell-sheeted coppices, and a gentle old man, his grandfather, kept a cow and hissing geese on the common.

It was for her own pleasure rather than for his that Mary Oakley indulged in this vein of soft reminiscence; but the boy who listened absorbed it eagerly with that craving for fairy tales (her stories were no more real to him) which is natural to the mind of a child. And his mother, indeed, at these times, was little more than a child herself, lying there in the great cold bed and calling on the illusions of memory to trick her into brief forgetfulness of the present misery on which, without knowing why, or even protesting, she had blindly stumbled.

"Tell me more, mam," the child would plead when her whispers ceased. "I don't want to go to sleep yet."

"But we must go to sleep, my precious, or how shall we ever get to work in the morning?"

"Must folk like us do nothing but work for ever and ever?" he asked.

"We must do as God wills," she told him, without much conviction.

"But does God . . . What *is* God?" he demanded.

Mary Oakley was silent. This question was far too complicated to be answered at that time of night, and the spiritual ministrations of the Reverend George Ombersley had hardly equipped her to cope with it.

"Shall we ever go to Grafton Lovett and see that there cow?"

"Oh yes, I reckon we ought to go home some day," she sighed. "And some day you'll go to heaven, provided you'm good."

"I'ld much liever go to Grafton Lovett," the child asserted stubbornly.

She laughed softly. "That's wickedness, that is . . . but so would I. Now come your ways, my pretty, and go to sleep."

There came a time when sleep was none too easy for either of them. His father slept soundly enough. When the monstrous labour of his day's work was done and he had filled his stomach, nothing less than the trumpets of doom could have broken the rhythm of his snoring. But now, when they lay down together, the child's mother could not sleep. No sooner were they warm in bed than a savage cough tore her. It shook him as he lay in her arms, and though a kind neighbour next door gave her syrup of horehound laced with laudanum, nothing could stay it. It was the night air, she said, that caught her breath and choked her, though the gaps of the broken window-panes were stuffed with sacking and the crevices packed with paper. Yet even in the warmth of the forge she coughed as grievously; and that, she said, was because of the dust and the acrid fumes that tickled her throat. Sometimes, at night, when her desperate hacking woke him, the child shrank from the heat of her body which burnt him like a coal. Sometimes he woke warm to feel her icy, drenched in cold sweats. Living with her constantly his father and he grew used to her coughing, and failed to notice how thin and drawn she had grown and how the torn garments hung on her like those of an unstuffed scarecrow. But the neighbours who lived in the row and saw her less frequently noticed the change, and the woman who had given her the syrup of horehound and laudanum came complaining.

"That there cough of yourn, Mrs. Oakley," she said; "it's time you did summat for it. It shakes the wall terrible all night and stops my man sleeping. If I was you, I should go to the chemist and see about it. And if I was your husband I shouldn't be satisfied, that I shouldn't. That's a churchyard cough if ever there was one, you take my word for it."

Mary Oakley smiled wanly. She would try all she could, she assured her, to stop coughing at night. She was always a one for tissicking in winter, she said, but when summer came round she would be as right as ninepence.

The woman shook her head. "Well, that may be," she said, "but I don't like the look of you, neither. You've lost too much flesh for my liking. You put me in mind of a sister of mine that went off in a decline."

The heart of the listening child went cold and sick with dread. His very ignorance of death made the menacing phantom more terrible. He began to watch his mother from day to day. It was true, as the neighbour said, that her face had lost the pink and white of its country roses. It was true that she had grown thin; that by day her peaked face had a bloodless pallor; but at night, when the forge was damped down, he took heart to see her pale cheeks brightened by vivid patches of colour, her eyes sparkling, her manner enlivened by a sudden gaiety which persuaded him that all must be well and that he had no need to fear. But when summer, on which he had been waiting, came, she did not lose her cough. It was on the day of Dulston Wake, when the streets were teeming with colliers and puddlers and nailers and chain-makers who poured into them from every town, village and hamlet of all the Black Country, that suddenly, as she was laughing and coughing together, a blood-vessel gave way and drenched the brick floor of the kitchen with blood. Her husband stared at the red deluge stupidly. It was she who whispered, smiling:

"Fetch the doctor, quick, my pretty. Oh, what a mess!"

The child ran to the corner of the High Street and called the doctor, who said he would come at once. He ran home again without stopping. But too late. His mother was dead.

The parish gave Mary Oakley a pauper's funeral. No bell was tolled—the Dulston Guardians cared little for the living and less for the dead—and the parish "box" was so hastily knocked together that the bearers had doubts if it would hold till the frail body was dumped with perfunctory rites into its anonymous grave. No mourners followed the coffin but John and his father, though the neighbours stood at their doors and gaped as the pitiful procession trudged by. The boy saw their curious faces with hatred in his numbed heart. He was dazed with desolation; there was no place in his empty mind for any emotion but hate of the callous world that had allowed his mother to die. The man by whose side he walked with dry eyes had an even larger share in his blind unreasoning hatred than the gaping neighbours. His father had never been more than a stranger to him and a dreaded rival in his mother's affections; a sullen, capricious tyrant to whom he had only truckled for her sake. He had once seen his mother beaten and had never forgotten it. Now, the last compunction gone, not even sympathy in their common loss could soften the savage dislike which, for her sake, he had concealed.

At the gates of the cemetery whose monstrous bars of black iron seemed to add imprisonment to the other penalties of death, a third mourner silently joined them: a pale, spare, diminutive man with close-cropped iron-grey hair and a stubbly grey beard above a black woollen neck-cloth. Tom Oakley greeted him with a surly nod; but John did not know he was his father's brother Jabez. The two brothers, in fact, had come to words and parted long since; for Jabez was a Methodist and intolerant of Tom's godless ways, and Tom counted the other's piety as softness; but, Death being a solemn peacemaker and forgiveness a brotherly duty, Jabez had left his last (for he was a jobbing cobbler by trade) and come to the funeral. He had a subtler mind than his brother's and a more sensitive heart. As his weak eyes, behind their rusty iron-rimmed spectacles, saw the boy standing utterly apart from his father, dry-eyed and haggard and desolate, pity moved him; and when the rites were over he came to John's side and put his arm round him protectively.

"I'm a stranger to you, lad," he whispered. "I'm your Uncle Jabez. But I know this here loss means more to you than to your father, and I'm sorry for you, if that be any help."

It was no help at all, but rather the contrary. This unexpected touch of warm human tenderness snapped the boy's tense control. For the first time, he burst into tears.

"Be you coming down home, Jabez?" his father said surlily.

"Ay, I reckon I'll come along with you. This lad here wants looking after."

And all the way home he walked with his arm round John's shoulder. He did not speak a word, but the boy knew he was kind.

In the desolate house there was a keg of ale for the bearers. That was part of the funeral ritual in Dulston in those days. Tom Oakley drank more than any of them. The liquor brightened his surly eyes. He glared at his brother, remembering their ancient quarrel. When the last of the bearers had gone, he spat on his horny hands and stripped off his coat.

"Come on, lad," he growled. "There's no call to stand moping about like that. The burying's over. Get out of your coat and look sharp and kindle that gleed!"

The boy started to obey him mechanically; but his uncle checked him.

"What's this, Tom?" he cried indignantly. "You don't tell me you'm going to set the poor child to work within an hour of his mother's burial? Shame on you, brother!"

Tom Oakley slewed round and stared at him, low-browed, like an angry bull. Dusky patches of red suffused his forehead; pulsating arteries stood out on his temples like whipcord.

"And who be you, I should like to know, to say what I should do? The burying's over. The lad's got to earn his living, and so have I. Strip your coat, lad, and do as you'm told!"

"He'll do no such thing," the little man answered firmly.

"So you'll stand between me and mine, will you, you bloody whining Methody? There's no room for idle hands in this house. The lad ates like a man, and he's got to work like a man. He works or he starves."

"He bain't going to work this day, Tom, I tell you that straight. It bain't decent nor proper; and you know that as well as I do."

The boy, listening and trembling, yet too desolate even for fear, was conscious, in the brief interval of tense silence, of a conflict of will. In a physical contest he knew that the strength of this spare, scrubby man would have been no match for that of the angry animal he challenged. Perhaps the strain of the late disaster had tortured and weakened Tom Oakley's spirit more than he deigned to show; perhaps he too had suffered. There was one thunderous moment in which, as he glowered at them both with purple face and clenched fists, it seemed as though the controls would snap and mad violence break loose; till, suddenly, his glaring eyes flinched and fell, his fists relaxed; he threw back his head and burst into a scornful laugh.

"You can have your way this time, Jabez," he said. "It's all one to me. I tell you the lad's a feeble, half-hearted brat and not worth rearing, and a sullen, spiteful young dog at that, if you want to know. A woman's more use to me, and I reckon it won't be long afore I get me another; so the sooner I'm shut of him the better for all on us. One thing I can tell you: he'll never make a nailer; so if you want to make a cobbler on him, you can take him and welcome and do me a good turn for once."

Jabez Oakley looked at the boy with his weak, kind eyes.

"Will you come with me, Johnny?" he said.

The child nodded solemnly. He dared not speak.

"Then the sooner you clear and take the brat out of my sight afore I changes my mind the better," Tom Oakley said.

Hand in hand the small grizzled man and the boy climbed the slope towards Sedgebury. For John Oakley it was the beginning of a new life that was different from any he had known, yet strangely friendly. Not that the aching emptiness of his loss was filled for many months. He still woke with a start in the night to miss the nearness of his mother's body, her warmth, her softness, the tones of her voice and her quiet laughter; to hear, without any reason, certain words which she had always spoken in a way of her own, in a country accent different from that of the Black Country, and which seemed to him, in the consciousness of half-sleep, more exquisite than any imaginable sound. He would cling to their echoes with desperate anxiety until they faded into the silence of night; yet, as time went on, these ghostly visitations grew less frequent and less substantial until, at last, to his disappointment—and somewhat to his shame; for this was disloyalty—they came no more.

John's new state was not merely happier than the old but more healthy. The air that rasped the high Sedgebury ridge so mercilessly had more life in it than that heavy element which, vitiated by the exhalations of crowded chimneys and human lungs, settled low, as in a sump, at the foot of the Castle Hill. From the Sedgebury ridge there stretched open vistas of a wider and as yet unreal world, revealing, beyond the smoke of Dulston, green plains and sombre woodlands and cloud-coloured hills folded range beyond range, dissolved at sunset into a molten flux. All life seemed more airy and neat and clean and spacious; even the cobbling which his uncle set him to learn was a cleanly, a meticulous and even a quiet craft compared with his father's. It involved a series of separate problems, not one changeless mechanical routine performed in a desperate race against jealous Time. There was room for talk in it and quietude for reflection. Though its rewards were meagre enough, his uncle's trade was better paid than the nail-maker's slavery. John never had to go to bed hungry as he had often done in his earlier childhood, and the abundance of coarse but nourishing food and pure air and undisturbed sleep had the effect of making him shoot up sturdily with the strength of a half-starved, hard-pruned tree transplanted into a more generous soil, so quickly that, within a few years, he grew taller than his uncle.

Even more important than this, though he did not know it, was the spiritual expansion that kept pace with this bodily growth. Until now the boy had known no companionship save the almost physical tie that had united him to his mother. In his Uncle Jabez he found his first friend as well as his first counsellor; and this friendship gave as much pleasure to his mentor as to himself. Jabez had lived a bachelor's life, self-centred and lonely, and the joy of watching this almost savage young animal change by degrees into a sentient and civilized human being filled his heart not merely with a sort of paternal solicitude but with creative pride. The boy, his first shyness gone, was quick-witted and responsive. In his uncle's workshop and at night in the candle-lit kitchen, he learnt his letters. Within a year he could read and write. His text-books were the Bible and Wesley's hymns, which Jabez knew nearly by heart, Tom Paine's *Rights of Man* and Foxe's *Book of Martyrs*. The contents of these four tattered, thumb-marked volumes coloured all his childhood. It would be true to say that—reinforced by the infectious influence of his uncle's attitude, which was that of what Colonel Abberley would have called a "Brummagem Radical"—they coloured the rest of his life.

All the visitors who dropped in of an evening for

a cup of tea and a chat with Jabez Oakley were poor
men like himself, yet made of the metal of Cromwell's
Ironsides. All their talk (and the talk to which the rapt
boy listened was endless) was concerned with Religion
—the militant Puritanism of a minority—or with
Politics: the politics of industrial democracy groping
to find its feet. The prophet of the first faith was
Wesley. Those of the second were Paine and Cobbett,
whose *Political Register* was read aloud and eagerly
discussed as a ritual every Saturday night. Those were
days of strong spiritual ferment and bitter discontent.
There were grievous recent wrongs that could not be
forgotten nor forgiven: the suppression of the Lanca-
shire and Nottingham Luddites, the March of the
Blanketeers, the pitiful stupidity of the slaughter of
Peterloo. But "Reform"—the blessed word echoed
and re-echoed continually in his ears—"Reform" was
in the air. A time must come, and come soon, when
the votes of the helpless would weigh in the ballot-box
and their voices, so long suppressed, be heard in Parliament. There was no thought of violence or con-
spiracy in the minds of these men; their religion
countenanced neither; only unquenchable hope and
serene determination and endless patience and faith in
themselves and in each other. When, in mid-June of
the year 'thirty-three, the first Reformed Parliament
met and the Dulston Political Union paraded in
triumph with banners and music and thundered cheers
for Reform and Lord Grey and the King and

Brougham, that grew louder when barrels of beer were broached in the market-place, Jabez Oakley and his friends gathered quietly in his workshop and celebrated the great victory in prayer.

It was the old man's *Nunc Dimittis*. That same week the revelries of the Reform Bill's passing were forgotten: the Russian cholera which, with the first summer heats, had begun to smoulder in the undrained warrens of Worcester where heaped ordure steamed and stank in the sun, swept northward from main-road village to village, like a grass-fire fanned by the wind. In Dulston, where water was scarce and bucketed from shallow wells, the germ found carrion even more to its liking. Within a week twelve hundred folk were taken with it, and one in five died. Whole quarters were stricken. No man dared speak to his neighbour; the streets lay empty. All the shops, save the flaming corner gin-palaces, which did uproarious trade, stood shuttered and lightless. Rumour heightened the fear of the pestilence and an awful uncertainty; for not even the doctors knew for sure how the disease was spread (some saying it was borne by the air and some by touch) or anything more of it save that, like God, it was no respecter of persons, that a man might be hale in the morning and dead by night, and that death by cholera was not only swift and terrible but agonizing. There were no nurses in Dulston to tend the sick but a few decrepit and ignorant midwives, whose foul fingers carried the living poison from one house to the next, and a handful of brave men who counted the sickening and useless service their duty.

Jabez Oakley and the minister of his chapel were among these. For three weeks they went out together doing what they could, which, God knows, was little enough, in the lower town, carrying no medicine with them but faith and cheerfulness. John Oakley pleaded to join them; but his uncle forbade him to stir from the house. The carrying of the dead, he said, was no job for a lad of seventeen; besides which, the cholera had more appetite for the tender flesh of the young, whereas wrinkled, leathery carcasses such as his were not to its taste and would take no harm. The best John could do, he said, was to bide at home and put his hand to such cobbling jobs as turned up, but never, if he could help it, to allow anyone who came from the town to cross the threshold.

Every night the old man returned, his set face reflecting the horrors he had seen. What he did or saw in the lower town, John never knew: when he came home he had no energy left for speech or even for eating; and in any case, the sights he had seen would not bear talking of. He came in with a nod and a cheery smile, but soon his face fell. He slumped down in his corner chair and sat there limp, with closed eyes, till he fell asleep so soundly that John did not dare to disturb him, but left him sleeping. The nights were so stifling hot that he knew he would take no chill. At dawn Mr. Haslam, the minister, called and roused him. Before it was light they had brewed their tea and set out on their grim business again.

At the end of three weeks it seemed as though the blaze had begun to burn itself out. Shopmen took down their shutters and people began to reappear in the deserted streets. But there were courts and alleys in which the disease still smouldered, and, though he confessed that the worst appeared to be over, Jabez Oakley refused to abandon his task while anything remained to be done. One night, when he had left his uncle asleep in his chair as usual, John was wakened suddenly by the sound of a heavy impact in the room below. He hurried downstairs, half asleep; by the light of his tallow candle he saw the spare body of his uncle lying on the floor, his thin knees drawn up to his stomach, his face grey and bloodless, his mouth stretched, teeth clenched in a grinning spasm of pain.

"Go away, lad," the old man gasped. "Go away— don't come nigh! The cholera's got me. There's naught you can do but pray to our merciful Lord and trust in His goodness. Nay, don't touch me! I'm best where I be. Get out into the open as quick as you can: there's death in this air. Run along to the minister's and see if he's taken too. If he be, fetch the doctor to him. Now go, lad, and do what I tell you . . ."

John ran barefooted over the cindery streets and hammered on the doctor's door and brought him back with him. The small house was deathly quiet: not a breath to be heard. The struck lucifer showed them the body of Jabez Oakley huddled on the hearth. He lay dead on his side, like a sleeping child, with his knees drawn up. But his fists were clenched in agony, and his open eyes stared, unseeing.

CHAPTER FOUR

GRAFTON LOVETT

IT was this abrupt severance of the only human tie that held him and the restlessness bred of unwonted solitude that turned John Oakley's thoughts in the direction of Grafton Lovett. His imagination, concerned of late with impressions so much more substantial, had always retained the imprint of those scenes his mother's wistful stories had stamped on it; and in his present state of grief and bewilderment, these childish images, blurred and indefinite as they were, had more actuality and offered more hope of solace than the visible desolation amid which he stood. Nothing bound him to Dulston. It was years since he had seen his father. He neither knew nor cared if he were dead or alive. Though his uncle's friends treated him kindly enough, they were not men of his age. No woman's face had yet troubled or made insecure the self-sufficiency of that bachelor house. He had learnt a craft that should earn him a living wherever he went, but the prospect of pursuing it in Dulston, where life was not only grim enough of itself but also beset at every turn by reminders of death and bereavement, appalled him and urged him to turn his back and escape. And whither, he asked himself, could escape be more right and natural than to the place where the only forbears that he cared to acknowledge had lived and died and been buried for generations?

During his long years of meagre living, his uncle had managed to scrape together a minute hoard of guineas which now were his. Though the cottage and the shop were rented, the goodwill of the cobbler's business, the bench and the furniture were worth a few more. When a customer offered himself he had no hesitation in selling. With a sense of unbounded relief, he packed up his books and his money and set off beyond the hills whose outlines had always tempted him, his tool-bag slung across his back, to find his grandfather.

Over the far hills he walked, out of the grit and smoke of Dulston into lands green past all belief and, as it seemed to him, unbelievably lonely. He had never imagined the country to be so utterly unpeopled as this, one village so distant from another, and the spaces between them so silent. In Bromsberrow, indeed, where he enquired the way to Grafton Lovett, there were nail-shops, and the familiar tinkle of hammers met his ears; but the folk who worked in them looked less grimed and stunted than the nailers of Dulston; life seemed to press on them less heavily in that sweeter, cleaner air.

It was evening, in a hush only stirred by late and lazy bird-song, when he reached Grafton Lovett. He had never tramped so far before, and his feet were blistered. An old man in a smock-frock, cruddled over two sticks, raised one and pointed the way to Joe Barley's cottage. His speech was burred and rustic and barely intelligible, but John's heart leapt to hear it and he laughed with joy, for the accents were those of his mother, remembered in dreams. He was touched to think he was going to see the cottage in which she had been born, and the common on which she had played as a little girl.

So he came to the squatter's door. The house was one-storeyed, built of dab and wattle. Projecting thatch shadowed the door. Inside, it was dark, and the low-ceiled chamber was thick with the pungent smoke of a fire of wet sticks on which Joe Barley was boiling potatoes for his supper.

"Who bi'st thee and what do'st want, young man?" he asked suspiciously. His voice was thin and quavering. He was older and feebler than John had imagined him.

"I be your grandson, John Oakley. I'm Mary's son, grandfather," he said.

"Mary? Mary? What Mary be that?"

"Your own daughter Mary, grandfather."

"I don't rightly mind none of that name. Be her come along wi' you?"

"My mother's been dead and gone of a decline these seven years."

"Poor soul. Well, to think of that now! And you

be her lad? Well, come in and sit you down, then."

John dumped down his heavy tool-bag and straightened his shoulders. He was conscious of his own upright strength and youth, standing above that bowed writhen figure from whose loins, remotely, he had sprung, and whose hands wandered so indeterminedly adjusting the spitting sticks. As the bag fell to the floor the old man gave a jump.

"What's that? What's that?" he asked anxiously. " 'Tis to be hoped you don't mean no harm, young man. I've no money to give you."

It was an unpromising beginning, and the night that followed was even stranger. There was one great bed built into the earth-floored room behind the kitchen, and this he was forced to share with his grandfather; but he could not sleep for the unwonted silence broken only by sounds that were new to him, such as the hooting of owls and the boom of the bittern in the marshy bottoms of the Chaddesbourne brook. Before dawn, the old man woke and began to hawk and wheeze and complain of the rheumatism that gnawed his bones like rats; and John was glad to release himself from discomfort. Outside the bedroom it was lighter than he had imagined, and the beauty that greeted him as he opened the door of the hovel and let out the smoke caught his breath; the furzy heath sparkling in level sunlight with spangles of dewy gossamer; the solemn line of elms that sheltered the village, so noble compared with the smoke-blighted trees of Dulston; the sandstone tower of the church transfigured by golden air; above all, the perfume of that sweet-breathing countryside—of new-mown hay and meadowsweet and almond-scented gorse. In that moment he knew why his mother had loved Grafton Lovett and why he himself must love it as long as he lived.

He was soon to be glad for other reasons that he had come to Grafton. It had been clear, from the night of his arrival, that his grandfather was failing and not long, as they said, for this world. Though he managed to exist and to tend the cow and the flock of geese that grazed the common, it was beyond the strength of his crippled limbs to keep the dark hovel clean, to cut wood for firing, or to till the small plot that, in his prime, he had reclaimed from the wild and in which he grew the crop of potatoes that were his staple—and very nearly his only—food. There was some satisfaction for John Oakley in knowing that he had come to his grandfather's aid at the right moment; to feel he was justifying his own purposeless existence by giving the old man an arm on the downward slope. The accumulations of neglect and disorder in the house and on the land kept him busy well into the winter. It took old Joe Barley a long time to realize who his grandson was; there were days on end, indeed, during which he appeared to forget and regarded John with suspicion as a stranger whose motives were doubtful; but at other times, when they sat together over a fire that no longer filled the cabin with smoke (John had scraped the soot from the chimney with a weighted holly-bush), his failing wits brightened by a jug of hot cider, he would suddenly recall and rehearse the story of how he had built the house in which they sat with an astonishing clarity resembling that of a distant landscape glimpsed through thinnings of mist. He was grateful, too, for the welcome relief from toil John's labour gave him. Sometimes he would stare at John and say: "You be our Mary's boy, bain't you? Ay, I might have knowed it without being told. You do favour her uncommon." When he heard he was like his mother, John's cup of happiness was full.

There was no question, as he had imagined, of his ever plying his cobbler's trade in Grafton. One cobbler, already established, satisfied, in his spare time, the needs of the village, which were small enough— for most of the children went barefoot and many of the labourers made their own footwear with hides and thongs. Until they knew who he was, he found the village people much less forthcoming than Black Country folk, accustomed to the constant influx of floating labour; but when once they had accepted him they were not long in taking him to their hearts and counting him as one of themselves.

The knowledge of their lives revealed by this intimacy appalled him. In his uncle's school of politics he had been taught to deplore and resent the conditions in which the Dulston miners and nail-workers lived. Compared with the Grafton villagers' lives, they were princely. A few of the better-placed had the right to cultivate strips of land in the common field and some rights of grazing, out of which, in favourable years, they could make a living. A few, like his grandfather, had "squatted" and taken in land from the common with the same result. But the bulk of the Grafton cottagers laboured for hire from dawn to sunset on the land of Mr. Ombersley of Chaddesbourne or Colonel Abberley or in the fields that belonged to them and were rented to men like Tom Collins, the farmer; and the average wage each household received was twelve shillings a week, out of which, since they had no land of their own, they must pay for food, to say nothing of clothes and firing. The houses or hovels in which they dwelt were more ancient and therefore more dilapidated than those of the Dulston workers— rain dripped through their thatch and on to their puddled clay floor; nor did they enjoy the comfort of a forging-hearth or a blaze of coals carried from the pit spoil-heap, which made the nailer's or miner's house tolerably warm in winter. There was no school for their children in the village, no religious instruction save Parson Ombersley's perfunctory catechizing, and no place of recreation (if they had had time for it) for themselves. Two ale-houses brewed a turbid fluid from spoiled barley-malt; but little of this was sold; Grafton Lovett labourers had no money to spend on beer. Yet, as drink they must, since only in drink

c

could life seem bearable, they distilled in their homes
a variety of fiery liquors that they called wines,
fermented from a hogwash of crushed turnips and
over-ripe plums and potato-peelings and sprouting
grain, which stupefied at the best and at the worst
made men fighting-mad. They were of a sturdy, good-
humoured race, and at least they breathed pure air.
Otherwise they could not have survived their super-
human excesses of drink and labour. But fatigue and
poison and privation, together with the inbreeding
decreed by the isolation which the Settlement Acts,
by forbidding the labourer to leave the parish of his
birth, imposed upon them, had stamped on the men of
Oakley's own age, or those rather older, the stigmata of
spiritual degeneration: stupidity, sullenness, apathy.

It was the last and most terrible of these that
shocked him, coming, as he did, from the industrial area
of Dulston where his fellow-workmen, for all their
poverty, were quick-witted and independent of spirit.
The Grafton Lovett villagers' acceptance of their condition seemed to him even more sinister than the condition itself. Their state was subdued and frightened.
They lived under the shadow—not of the two great
houses in which the squires of Chaddesbourne and
Grafton preserved (save in matters concerning the
Game Laws) an attitude of mildly benevolent detachment towards the human fauna of their estates, nor
even of the Law, of whose savage penalties they had
heard during the assizes that followed the machine-

breakers' riots—but of that bleak and sombre barrack of brick, the new Bromsberrow Workhouse, and of their natural enemy, the stoat of this hapless warren, Mr. Willets, the parish overseer.

This gross man, the boon-companion and ally in corruption of Collins the farmer, held the unlucky village in his hands. Under the Old Poor Law, when wages were "made up" by rates for the farmers' benefit, he had provided his friends with able-bodied labourers at a few shillings a week, or harnessed his paupers, men and women together, between the shafts of the parish cart to drag muck from the middens and cess-pits to fertilize Collins's fields. Under the New Poor Law, his power became even greater. For no farmer would now give work to a man whose possession of geese or a cow diminished his own share of grazing, while now no able-bodied man who was workless had a right to outdoor relief; with the result that, if he and his family were not to starve, they must toil for a shilling a day from dawn to dark on the roads that were most serviceable to Willets' friends and others who bribed him, or leave their homes and enter the workhouse to pick oakum, like convicts, or crush bones, and fight with other half-starved men for the gristle that clung to them.

Old men who, like the squatter, Joe Barley, until his grandson came, found it hard to fend for themselves, had no choice nor power of protest. To the workhouse with them! The fuller it was, the better.

The more bellies to starve, the more contracts for musty meal and frosted potatoes: the more profits for Mr. Willets' friends, the more bribes for himself! And, supposing the old man were married: then off with his wife to the workhouse as well. But let him not think he would ever set eyes on her again: not even if he had lived and slept with her for fifty years. The New Poor Law insisted on sexual segregation.

All these things John Oakley saw and noted with growing bitterness during his first two years at Grafton. Though he was powerless to remedy them and equally powerless to raise his neighbours' crushed spirits against them, the tradition of service in which he had been reared in his uncle's workshop forbade him to keep silence. He talked radical politics whenever he could to such as would listen to him—without much effect but that of exciting the farmers' suspicious hostility. He offered to teach the children their letters, much to the concern of Parson Ombersley—not so much because Mr. Ombersley dreaded the diffusion of knowledge as because he had heard that Joe Barley's grandson was a Methodist, and therefore an instrument of doctrinal corruption among his neglected flock. He did his duty, as he saw it, to his best; but when the best was done he knew how little of the seed he scattered on the cold Grafton Lovett clay would germinate and take root.

It was only after two years—his grandfather, mercifully, had died of a winter bronchitis, and Oakley

himself, succeeding to what he had left, was contriving
to make a bare living out of the squatter's "encroachment"—that he smelt the first smoulder of resentment
in his neighbours' minds. The spark that fired it was
the news that Squire Ombersley and the colonel, putting their heads together, had decided to improve their
estates by enclosing the common of Grafton that lay
between them: a proposal that affected not only
squatters like himself, but also the more substantial
cottagers who, up till now, had enjoyed rights of
grazing for their pathetic live-stock. Oakley knew all
about Enclosure and its effects; he had not read his
Cobbett for nothing; and because they knew he was
knowledgeable, many of those who stood to lose and,
before this, had used him contemptuously, came
clamouring for information.

There was not much he could tell them, except that
it was rare for an Enclosure Bill to fail; that men
who had land or rights were likely to lose both unless
they fought for them, and that those, like himself,
whose rights were slender and questionable, would
probably waste time—and money, if they had it—in
fighting. The legal procedure was leisurely and in-
exorable. First of all, a notice of petition would be
affixed to the door of the church on three Sundays in
August. . . .

"Can't we tear down them there notices?" asked a
middle-aged cottager named Aaron Sheldon.

"You can tear them down," Oakley said, "but they'll

only put them up again. And if you're caught tearing them down, the constable 'll be after you."

"Ay, he's right, he's right," others said. "It be no good a-puttin' yourself in the road of the Law. What comes a'ter that, John?"

"They'll call a parish meeting."

"And what can us poor folks do, with all the quality settin' there and Tom Collins, damn him, talking a lot of stuff us can't understand?"

"Us can break up the meeting, chaps," an old soldier named Dicketts suggested.

"And that bain't no good neither, George. D'you want your 'ead broken? Didn't you 'ave enough fighting at Waterloo with the Duke when you lost your leg? If there's any parish meetings going to be broke up, I shall keep away from them. Can't you think on anything better nor that to do, John?"

"We can pay a lawyer to speak up for us in Parliament."

"I've no fancy for lawyers—foxes, I call 'em—and where be the money to come from? There bain't no money in Grafton that I've ever heard on to pay 'em with. Nor I wouldna trust him nohow to do his best if Mr. Collins, he went behind of us and give him more."

They trusted nobody. They did not even trust one another. Would they trust him, John Oakley wondered? After all, he was in the same boat as they, or one even leakier.

"I could go to London myself and ask to speak. A

man who's going to suffer has the right to do that for himself, but I'ld do it, and willing, for you chaps as well."

At this most of them looked doubtful. Though they were far too polite or too timid to hint at it, Oakley knew they were asking themselves what he stood to gain at their expense. Only Dicketts, the one-legged soldier, rose to the project.

"Why should John go alone? Let's all go in a body," he cried. "Let's go straight to the Duke: you'll get justice from him, I tell you. If the Duke sees a wrong being done, he'll tell King William of it. John here, having the gift, he can do the talk in Parliament while all the rest of us stands behind him and signify we be of one mind. The more on us goes the better, I say."

"Hold your silly hush, Guy," said Sheldon, "and don't talk foolish. Who be you, with a peg for a leg, to walk all the way to London, and where bi'st going to find fittles to eat, I should like to know. And I'll tell you another thing. If the lot on us went marching in a body, the way you say, we should get no further than Worcester. Mr. Collins would hear on it and ride on ahead and get the police to stop us by warrant. Unlawful Assembly: that's what the justices call it. If anyone's going, I say: let John Oakley go quiet and go alone to speak for us."

"If so be as he don't mention no names," an anxious voice murmured.

"If he don't mention no names nor particulars, what's the good on it, Harry?"

"I bain't going to have my name mentioned, Aaron," the other said stubbornly. "If Mr. Collins he heard as I'd put my name forward against him, like, there'ld be no work for me next week, nor yet for my lads and my missus, and the lot of us 'ld find ourselves cracking bones in Bromsberrow work'us in no time. Let John speak for himself, if he wants to, and leave us out of it."

"Whether John goes or don't go, there's one thing I know," Aaron Sheldon said bitterly, "and that is, if the squire takes the common in and puts me off of it, there won't be one bloody pheasant left in his woods come Christmas that I can get hold on."

NEXT Sunday, the first in August, the sexton affixed the first of the three statutory notices to the board in the church porch, and Parson Ombersley, whose strong point was not his sense of humour, read a sermon, the first that came to his hand, that was based on the story of Naboth's vineyard. After the service was over, a group of cottagers stood and stared at the notices. A few, following the letters with their fingers, laboriously spelt out the portentous, unintelligible words, while others, who could not read, stood gaping and listening.

"If John Oakley was here," one said, "he could tell what this here paper it meant in no time."

Tom Collins, who heard him, passing out with his wife on his arm, turned round with a laugh:

"Master Oakley will know what it means before long," he said. "If it does naught else, it's going to cook his goose, and just about time, too."

There was a parish meeting held in the vestry a few weeks later. Only a few cottagers whom Collins and Willets, the overseer, had cajoled or intimidated came to it. Its purpose was merely to get a petition signed by land-owners representing three-fifths of the value involved; and that was not difficult, for the greater part and the best of the land was already in the promoter's hands. John Oakley watched the pitiful farce without speaking. He saw that Tom Collins had his bleary eyes on him, expecting him to protest. Therefore he kept silence. But he knew, and was glad to know, how many of the men who scrawled their signatures of consent or put their marks to them were acting of their own free will, and how many weakly did what their masters told them. And he knew that his time was not yet; that it would not come until this, together with the contrary petition he had drafted and filled with as many other uncouth signatures, should be presented and perfunctorily accepted by Parliament and passed on to the committee "upstairs," whose bored votes would settle the fate of both.

To find out when that fateful moment arrived was not easy. After the vestry meeting no further public notice was given. Apart from *The Times*, which came to The Hall and was passed on, when the colonel had finished with it, to Parson Ombersley, no London paper with Parliamentary reports ever reached Grafton Lovett; and the sevenpenny Methodist *Pioneer*, which Mr. Haslam, the minister, occasionally sent John from Dulston, was too deeply concerned with the wrongs and rights of industrial workers to record the progress of an obscure agricultural enclosure. To avoid the risk of being caught napping, Oakley trudged twice a week to Worcester, where, at the cost of a pint of beer, he could scan the mangled pages of a London newspaper in the bar of a superior ale-house. There, one day, he discovered that the Grafton Lovett Enclosure Bill had been passed to a committee of the House of Commons for examination in the following week.

He had no time to waste. It was a hundred miles and more from Grafton to London. But he was young and strong and the fire of faith burned in him, and his boots, which he had made for himself, were stouter than any other pair in the village; so, without waiting to ask for money which he knew would be grudged and given suspiciously, he took what was left of his Uncle Jabez's dwindling hoard of guineas and set off southward early on the next day.

It was a fine, dry morning with an unclouded sunrise. The air had a nip in it, and the coarse grass of the common where his cow ran loose (it was a piece of luck she was dry) lay whitened with a silvery bloom so delicate it was hard to guess whether it were mere dew or the earliest rime. As he stepped out of the hovel and fastened the padlock that closed it, John Oakley was suddenly conscious of the affection that now bound him to this place that had once seemed so unpromising. Though he had only lived there two years, it had been his home. There was no spot in the world as he knew it where he would rather live or which he would leave with more pain. He loved the wide sweep of the common with its scattered thickets of gorse and thorn in which nightingales sang; the emerald swards of fine rabbit-bitten turf with its thymy tussocks; the depressions of boggy, undrained land where turf had been cut and water lay and the commoners' cattle came to drink; in the distance, the dark line of coppice called Pritchett's Wood, where his mother had once picked bluebells, and where he himself had been wont to gather his firewood; and, near at hand, the once-neglected vegetable-plot, newly fenced with stag-quicks, in which the orderly rows of potato-haulms grew rusty and ready for digging before sharp frost caught and withered them. Here, humble as it might be, he told himself, was something to lose and something worth fighting for. As he took the Chaddesbourne road, he turned and looked back at it, with love in his heart—and also a sudden, cold disquietude, as though that turning to look had not merely been an act of his conscious will, but the result of some mysterious admonition to make the most and to look his last on it.

That apprehensiveness, so vague as not to be reasonable, kept him company far into the golden September morning. It stayed with him until he had surmounted the Cotswold scarp on the way to Oxford, where corn-coloured roads ran straight between stone-walled downs where men were carting the remains of that year's blighted harvest. But here the hill air was so thin and so sweet and the rolling prospect so free that, encouraged by these, the sheer joy of living and breathing and being young in the pride of his strength dispelled the shadowy disquiet; and when, having bought a loaf of bread in the town of Chipping Norton, he found a soft bed in a barn full of hay, he fell asleep and awoke to the dawn next morning not only with no care in his heart but with a sense of exhilaration and high adventure.

At dusk on the fourth day from Grafton Lovett, he reached the outskirts of London. The approach to the capital excited and awed him. He had no clear ideas of what the city might be, though Mr. Haslam had warned him of the wickedness of this modern Babylon, and his reading of Cobbett, who hated it, had taught him to think of it as a monstrous morbid growth—the "wen," as he called it. Yet at first he saw nothing in London to curdle his blood; it seemed only another, less grimy Dulston, with wider streets and taller houses. For all that, he felt nervously, again and again, for the guineas tied up in his handkerchief, and regarded each man he met as a possible footpad or pickpocket ready to rob him—unnecessarily, as it seemed: for when he wished them good night, in his rustic fashion, they stared with surprise and answered him barely, or surlily, or not at all.

The first things, indeed, that struck him were the hardness of the stone pavements on which his great hobnails rang; the brilliant light of globed gas-lamps, turning night into day, and the hurrying crowds that surged to and fro at an hour when, in Grafton Lovett, all decent folk had long since gone to bed and only poachers were abroad. And then, as the labyrinth of brick and stone grew denser, came buildings which seemed so to soar and impend on either hand that their heaped storeys looked to be in danger of toppling and falling—while, in some, walls were rising still higher, like Babel's tower, with masons clinging like flies to the dizzy scaffolding and climbing ladders with hods of bricks to be laid and plastered by the lantern-light that shone through the smoke-haze like bleared stars. He saw one great mansion darker and grimmer than the rest. It stood back from the street behind a barrier of iron railings, and the windows in its mournful façade were jagged and broken. Oakley halted and stared at it. He guessed it was Apsley House, the abode of the Duke (there was only one Duke in England) whose window-panes, smashed by the mob in the days of Reform, had never been mended but left to await the revenges of Time.

The mere magnitude of these vast masses of masonry was crushing to the spirit and affected him with passive awe, as being something more than human or reason-able; but what filled him with a greater sense of confusion (and even of danger) was the speed and strepitant roar of the torrent of wheeled traffic that thundered past: landaus, cabriolets, chaises and chariots and top-heavy coaches, their horses' wet flanks flecked with splatters of foam. This way and that they hurried ceaselessly with an imperious crack of whips and a trail of sparks struck from iron-shod wheels and hooves, and

the suggestion of something contemptuous if not
fiercely hostile for common folk forced to go on foot
reflected in the blank, bored faces of powdered foot-
men perched high behind.

To John Oakley's eyes and ears, accustomed to the
subdued quality of country sights and sounds, there was
something not merely bewildering but cruel and terrifying in this nightmare of noise and frantic motion.
He was dazed but thankful when, without knowing
where he went, he found himself in a quiet backwater
where street-lamps were farther apart and the roaring
of wheels on stone, though it never ceased, rose and
fell in gusts like a wind that buffets a wood. If the
turmoil was less, the air in this narrower street smelt
foul and lifeless as if it had been breathed and rebreathed by too many lungs. The people who crawled
past him over the littered pavements were decrepit and
malodorous too. They eyed him curiously; and one
aged woman, muffled in rags, put out a skinny hand—
as he thought to stay him, but, in fact, to beg. Here
and there a painted face leered at him under the lamp-
light; street women spoke softly and beckoned him as
he passed. Their shameless words shocked him and
brought the blood to his cheeks and made his skin
tingle; and once he turned instinctively, for the voice
was a Worcestershire voice like his mother's, but the
rouged and ravaged face and the lax mouth that smiled
at him filled him with deeper horror. On and on he
walked, strangely shaken, always looking for some

place where he could sit for a moment and spare his bruised feet. There were no hedgerow-banks to rest on here: only vertical walls of brick and slimy slabs or cobbles. It began to rain drearily. Even the water on his lips tasted stale. He went on and on till the straight street opened upon a square that looked like a market-place, for the stones were littered with vegetable refuse that smelt like a winter cabbage-field, and phantom shapes of empty stalls stood ranged in rows. On one side of the square stood a church with a pedimented and pillared portico; and in the shelter of this, in the company of half a dozen others as homeless as he, he propped himself up against the church wall and stretched out his aching legs and, somehow, fell asleep, his fingers carefully clutching the money in his handkerchief.

Familiar sounds woke him: the cracking of whips, the squeaking of wagon wheels and the cries of carters. A tawny dawn backed the house-tops across the square. He found to his surprise and distaste that he had had a bed-fellow: a young woman who had pressed her body against his for the sake of warmth. She still slept, and her breath smelt heavily of gin when she cursed him for waking her. His other companions in destitution, whose number had increased during the night, still lay scattered under the portico's shadow like corpses; but the square was growing noisy with trampling hooves and grinding wheels, and lanterns moved hither and thither. Men were heaving hampers of green stuff down from the laden wagons and dressing the stalls; and one of them, as John stood watching, called on him to lend a hand. He was a countryman with a broad, whiskered, humorous face; his burly shoulders were covered in rain-soaked sacking and he spoke or shouted in a flat East Anglian accent. When John had helped him to clear his load the carter offered him the alternatives of a penny or a cup of cold tea and a hunk of bread. They sat down on a hamper under the tail of the wagon and munched together. John asked him what the market was called. The carter gaped with his mouth full.

"That's a queer thing to ask," he said. "Why, this is the Garden. Covent Garden the Londoners call it— but I knowed when I first set eyes on your innocent face, lad, you wasn't no Cockney. What be you doing in London?"

John told the man of his mission. He munched and listened without any show of sympathy.

"Well, there's got to be fools in this world, I reckon," he said, "but the softest of all is poor simple labouring men that think they can ever get the upper hand of the gentry. You try it and you'll find out. They may talk of Reform," he said, "but that's one thing that won't never change; and if you want my advice, though you haven't asked for it, it's this, lad: go back where you come from and stay there like everyone else that's got any sense."

John asked him the way to the Houses of Parliament.

The man said he didn't know, and hoped, stubbornly, he never would—because Parliament warn't no business of his or of the likes of him. All he knew of London was the road there from Braintree and back again. It was no doubt out of pity for John's foolishness that he insisted on his accepting the penny as well as the breakfast. "If you *won't* go back home where you come from," he said at parting, "I'll give you another word of advice not asked for, and that is this: you steer clear of policemen by day and false women by night, and if you want another job, you come here to this very place next Monday morning."

John set forth in search of Westminster. There had been no more rain in the night. The pavements though they still offended his nostrils were dry, and had lost their dark terrors. It was still too early for much traffic, and the greater streets, into which he soon found his way, seemed spacious and handsome. Scavengers, equipped with besoms and shovels, were sweeping and clearing away the horse-droppings with which their whole width was felted ankle-deep. At the corner of Piccadilly where the curve of Nash's noble quadrant marked the beginning of the grand new street leading to the Regent's Park, he asked his way of one of them.

The scavenger looked him up and down from his clumping boots to his ruffled hair. " 'Ouses of Parliament?" he said, with a Cockney accent. "Honoured to make your acquaintance, sir." He swept off his hat and winked at his mate. " 'Ere, Jim, hinformation required! The honourable member's come up to Parliament in the new Reformed 'Ouse of Commons and don't know the way to 'is seat! Look you 'ere, my lad," he went on kindly: "just you follow your own bloody nose till you see a column they're building for a sailor with one eye and one arm, and then turn sharp right down W'ite'all till you get to the river, but mind as you don't fall in: there's ten chaps from the country, the image of you, got stuck in the mud there this year!"

John laughed and thanked him. Outside Westminster Hall he accosted a magnificent policeman in a blue frock-coat and tall hat, who scanned him as suspiciously as if he suspected him of being a new Guy Fawkes or one of the Cato Street conspirators.

"And what should you want with the House of Commons, young man, I should like to know?" he demanded, with such severity that John remembered the Covent Garden carter's last words. "The Grafton Lovett Enclosure Bill? Well, I might 'ave guessed it! Now understand this: His Majesty's Commons don't sit on a Saturday nor never have done since Lord Walpole or Orford, who you never heard of I don't suppose, took to beagling. So don't come 'ere 'anging about and asking questions till next Monday, see? Or you'll get into trouble, and don't say I didn't warn you!"

For two days John Oakley tramped London. He loathed it as deeply as Cobbett had loathed it for its vastness, its heartlessness, its huge, remote unconcern;

for its contrasts of wealth and grandeur with an utter squalor which seemed somehow more hopeless and vicious than any he had seen before; for its elegant women of fashion, so exquisite in their varnished chariots, and the bloated tight-waisted bucks who swept off their hats to them or mooned in the windows of clubs; for the diamonds and emeralds that sparkled behind caged windows, and the ordure in the gutters; for the "false women," as the carter had called them, with their whispers and clutching hands and raddled faces, and the drunken men vomiting or prostrate in Seven Dials; for the great houses blazing with chandeliers of cut crystal and the black alleys between Bow Street and Drury Lane where women ran screaming from men with knives in their hands within a stone's throw of the roaring, jostling Strand. For two nights he slept, as best he could, in the company of outcasts poorer than himself, under the pillared portico of St. Paul's Church in Covent Garden, where, at least, there was quiet, and watched dawn tawnily brighten the fringe of chimney-pots, and stretched his cold-cramped legs and shivered and bought a half-loaf of bread and went his way thankful that another night had gone.

All morning John Oakley hung about Westminster Bridge. The tide was out. The oozy foreshore in which the Cockney scavenger had begged him not to get stuck was streaked with black runnels of sewage seeping from the Strand. The River Thames was nothing but one vast sewer serving all London. Gulls wheeled over it with desolate cries. An east wind crisped the ebbing tide with dirty wavelets and the dome of St. Paul's glimmered white and ghostly out of a haze of black smoke. As midday struck in White-hall, John left the bridge and approached the Houses of Parliament.

The same contemptuous constable observed him: "Oh, so *you*'re here again!" He posed magnificently, busily lifting his top-hat to a number of members who drove or walked past on their way to the House, and far too grand to deal with John's questions. As he stood there waiting for an answer, a brisk, youngish gentleman, with abundant chestnut hair and whiskers, and a strong, finely-featured face, to whom the con-stable had vouchsafed a half-hearted salute and who had given John a shrewd glance in passing, suddenly paused in his progress, as though struck by an after-thought, and approached them.

"What does this young man want, constable?" he asked in a tone of authority.

"Oh, he's only one of these country chaps, sir, come up for an Enclosure Bill."

"What Enclosure Bill?" he asked sharply.

"Grafton Lovett, sir, down in Worcestershire," John replied.

"Grafton Lovett in Worcestershire? Your member, Mr. Holland in Baring's Bank, is a friend of mine, though, of course, a political opponent. These Enclo-sure Bills interest me. I am not altogether pleased with the way they are handled. If you like to accompany me, I'll take you straight to the Committee Room. Come along, my friend."

John went with him gratefully to the constable's obvious disapproval. This was the first friendly word he had heard in the streets of London. As they walked, the chestnut-haired gentleman plied him with brisk shrewd, pointed questions as to the conditions of labour in Grafton: how the people were housed, what wages they earned, and what, exactly, their commonage meant to them. "I believed in the benefits of Enclosure once," he said, "and so did Mr. Cobbett; but the more I know of the working of these acts and the more I see of the way in which they are juggled through Parliament, the less liking I have for them. Be sure I will do what I can for you. At least, I'll see that you're heard."

They passed at a surprising pace (his gait was so impetuous) through numerous court-yards and stony corridors and finally up a flight of worn stairs to a small, stuffy oak-panelled room, resembling a court of justice, where he nodded and smiled good-bye and took his seat among a sprinkling of lackadaisical gentlemen who decorated the benches in uninterested attitudes of boredom or of repose. On the right of the chairman, a tall man with a constricted waist and a chest like a pouter-pigeon stood shuffling his papers and loudly clearing his throat and losing his way in the theme he expounded. He mumbled so much and halted so frequently that John, sitting alone at the back of the room, had no idea what he was talking about; but nobody—not even the chairman, who sat scribbling with a quill-pen—appeared to be listening. At the end of a peroration, which seemed to include the words "vexatious and intolerable encroachments," he sat down so suddenly that one honourable member who had been dreaming awoke with a start, and two others, who had been laughing and talking in whispers, looked round with aggrieved astonishment. For a moment it seemed as if nobody else wanted to speak. Then, suddenly, John's companion popped up.

"Sir," he said, "I understand there is present at this moment a witness representing the cottagers of Grafton Lovett who desires to offer his evidence. As I gather that honourable members have completed their observations on Clause Five—*Allotment of Residue*—and seeing that Clause Six—*Encroachments*—is the one in which these petitioners are concerned, the present moment, sir, would seem opportune for the hearing of his evidence. I might add, sir, that this man has walked up to London from Worcestershire for this purpose at considerable inconvenience."

A horsy young man with a brick-red face who sat with his feet on the bench in front of him and was dressed in the outmoded style of a Corinthian, gave a guffaw. "Inconvenience! Well, was there ever?"

The chestnut-haired gentleman bowed to him. "If the honourable gentleman, sir, had ever walked over a hundred and twenty miles in four days, he might possibly fathom the meaning of the word inconvenience."

"What is this witness's name, Mr. Roebuck?" the chairman asked surlily.

"John Oakley, sir."

"And the grounds of his claim to be heard by this committee? Is he himself a cottager?"

"He is, sir, I understand, what is vulgarly known as a 'squatter,' with recognized rights of commonage."

A thin, tall man, with a pale face pock-marked and crinkled like parchment, jumped up angrily: "I feel I must vehemently protest, sir, against the honourable member's phrase. Recognized rights, sir! Recognized when, and by whom? If this Committee of the House of Commons comes here to waste its time listening to any contentious busybody who claims to bear witness on the strength of his possessing a cow and having walked a hundred and twenty miles, sir . . ."

Mr. Roebuck held his ground. "That is for the Chair to decide, sir," he said quietly.

The chairman looked from one to the other. It was clear that the last thing he wanted was any disturbance.

"Is this petitioner represented by counsel?" he asked wearily.

"The people who consider themselves aggrieved by this bill, sir, are not of a condition that permits the enjoyment of such costly luxuries. I myself, sir, fortunately, have some acquaintance with their objections, and am qualified, as I think you are aware, to represent them. With your permission, then, I present myself as their counsel."

The pock-marked member was on his feet again.

"I rise on a point of order, sir," he blustered. "Is the honourable member for Bath entitled to spring this surprise on the committee without proper notice?"

The chairman appeared to be embarrassed. He shuffled his papers and peered at them. "That point seems to be clear. A petition has been presented and referred to this committee: all petitioners to have voices, to examine witnesses, if they please, and to be heard by their counsel. The learned and honourable gentleman is certainly in order. This is only a common petition against a common enclosure, Sir Charles."

"Then for God's sake let's get it over!" the pock-marked member said petulantly. He sat down, rammed his beaver over his eyes and sat with folded arms. The other rose quietly once more and beckoned John forward.

"Your name is John Oakley?" he said.

"That's right, sir."

"You are one of the signatories of the petition against this Enclosure Bill and you live in the parish of Grafton Lovett in the County of Worcester in a dwelling which you believe to be your own property and in the occupation of which you have enjoyed hitherto certain rights of commonage?"

"Yes, sir. My grandfather built it and lived in it till he died."

"Very well . . ."

The manner was so smooth as to seem insinuating, yet so gently persuasive in its quietness that the fear which had made his clenched hands sweat and his head go giddy when first he stepped forward began to evaporate. He believed that this friend, whom sheer chance had precipitated into his affairs, must be trusted, and answered the questions he put to him without reservation, convinced that, even when he did not understand where they led, they must be right and that the words which were written down would not go against his cause. He was conscious, none the less, of an increasing hopelessness. After the little breeze which the horsy young man and the pock-marked gentleman's indignation had raised, the atmosphere of the committee-room relapsed into its former state of doldrums. The clerks scribbled the questions and answers dutifully; but apart from their scratching quills there was no sign of any activity. The chairman, having given his ruling, leaned back, his eyes fixed on the Jacobean ceiling; the member who had slept resumed his heavy breathing, the two gossips their whispers, while the remainder of the committee appeared to have surrendered themselves once more to drowsy boredom.

At last, through the heavy air, he heard his examiner's voice:

"Very well, Mr. Oakley; that will do," he said. "I have finished."

John stared at him in amazement: "What? Is that all, sir?"

He could not believe it was all he was allowed to say: these plain "Yeses" and "Noes" confirming the bare shape of a summary of facts dispassionately marshalled and left to speak for themselves. Could this be the moment for which he had schemed and hoped and steeled himself through all those weeks of waiting, and tramped the hard roads to London? Why, these lounging, smug, indifferent committee-men had not even troubled to listen to him. He would make them listen; he would give them something to think of! They might seize him and throttle him and throw him out of the room, but so long as there was breath in his body, he would speak his mind. The room swam before him. He began to speak rapidly with cold fury: the angry indignation, so long repressed, poured past his lips with such turbulence that he neither knew nor cared what he said. His voice, his words were not longer his own, nor was he his known self, John Oakley, the ignorant squatter from Grafton Lovett, but rather the inspired, unconscious mouthpiece through which, suddenly, the inarticulate bitterness of the remote downtrodden village found speech. As he spoke, blinded by his own passion, he was only vaguely aware of the consternation his impropriety had created: of the distressed face of his friend, imploring him to be silent; of a hubbub of murmurs and protests; of the pock-marked gentleman wildly appealing to the Chair; of the chairman himself, who had risen from his seat and was pointing at him with an accusing arm outstretched and calling on the Sergeant-at-Arms; until, of a sudden, a hand was clapped on his shoulder and another over his mouth and he was forced to his seat. The turmoil subsided, and now the chairman was speaking.

"You are not here," he said, "to address the committee, but to give evidence in a proper manner and to be heard in due course by your counsel. This disorderly interruption is most regrettable. Not even your ignorance can excuse it. It is now for learned counsel for the first petitioners to cross-examine you, if he so wishes."

A stout, ruddy-faced man in a wig and a shabby silk gown, stood up on the chairman's left with a sardonic smile.

"If you please, sir," he said, "I think honourable members will have been able to judge from this intemperate and lamentable outburst how much value should be placed on the witness's evidence. I do not propose to cross-examine."

There were loud murmurs of "Hear, hear!" from the benches.

"Very well, Mr. Vizard," the chairman said. "In that case we will proceed. The witness may go."

CHAPTER SIX

THE JOURNEY BEGINS

HE went, down the echoing corridors, through the solemn, flagged court-yards and out into the dank river-side air. A crowd had gathered on the pavement; they were cheering and surging excitedly about an oddly-shaped two-horsed carriage in which the object of their enthusiasm, a dark man with an ugly, flushed face and a long tip-tilted nose, waved his hand and smiled.

"Bravo, Brougham," they shouted. "Bravo, Brougham! Down with slavery!"

John forced his way roughly through the press. "Down with slavery!" he thought bitterly. "Why, we're all of us slaves!" He was so shaken with anger and disappointment at his own failure that it was not until he had turned his back on Westminster that he realized that his lip had been cut and his mouth was bleeding. He walked furiously westward, seeing nothing of the streets through which he passed, caring nothing for the curses of drivers who swerved to escape running him down, feeling that only through violence or physical action could he release his brain's angry content or cool its boiling turbulence. He walked,

without food or rest, till his legs would carry him no
farther, having no idea how far he had travelled until,
tracing the cut inscription on a milestone, he found he
was forty miles from London and only thirteen from
Oxford. There, staggering into a field where a hay-
stack stood close to the road, he lay down and slept the
death-like, dreamless sleep of utter bodily exhaustion.

During the night the great fog fell. By the time he
woke it was so dense that no glimmer in the uniform
whiteness betrayed the position of the sun by marking
which he might have guessed how long he had slept.
Between emptiness and fatigue John Oakley's spirits
were now in a state of strange volatility. Though he
knew he had failed, the very completeness of his
failure and the futility of regretting what could not
be mended absolved him of any further fruitless
anxiety; and it was better perhaps, after all, to have
failed than never to have striven.

The utter obliteration of the landscape by the fog,
which grew more impenetrable with every mile he
covered, encouraged him in a new sense of isolation
and freedom. Though he was retracing his steps
automatically to Grafton Lovett, bringing home his
bad news, to take one last sentimental look (if the fog
would let him) at the roof that had sheltered him for
two years and to pick up his tool-bag, he knew that he
could not stay there. After the events of the last few
months Grafton Lovett would be no place for him.
The Enclosure Commissioners would pull down his

cottage and uproot his hedges; he would have no
further part or lot in the land his grandfather had recovered from the waste. Yet, oddly enough, in the
exalted mood that had succeeded the other of anger
and humiliation, this did not seem to matter. Let them
do what they would and be damned to them! It was
better to starve and be free, he told himself—though it
cheered him to feel the roll of guineas in his pocket—
than to work on the stolen land at the mercy—scant
mercy, too!—of Tom Collins or Willets the overseer,
with the threat of Bromsberrow workhouse hung over
his head. Yet the world was wide, he told himself; he
was young and strong and could earn his bread by the
trade he had learnt. No tie of blood or duty or even
of affection bound him: and in this he was luckier than
most men. Now, indeed, as, fatigue forgotten, he
swung along, unseeing, invisible, through grey vapour
so dense as to hide not merely the domes and spires of
Oxford but the very parapets of the Cherwell bridge
and the faint-lit shops and colleges on either side of
the High Street, he was as free and detached from life
as a disembodied spirit—more free and indeed more
secure afoot (he smiled to think) than the rich men
who travelled in coaches—it was here that the *Hirondelle*, with Mr. Vizard aboard it, stole cautiously
past, its candle-lamps glimmering like haloed moons
through the mirk—with the prospect of a crashing
collision and a night in a sodden ditch.

He reached Stow-on-the-Wold that night and filled

his stomach at an ale-house with the first food that had passed his lips for twenty-four hours; paid sixpence, although he grudged it, for a warmer night's lodging, and dropped down over the scarp of Cotswold early next day. In the Vale the fog lay thicker; the roads were scattered with ditched wagons and stationary coaches that dared not move. Amid the tangled lanes of the Lenches, he was as good as lost until a lonely carter, huddled in sacks, put him right on the road to Chaddesbourne.

From this point onwards the fog made no difference to him: he knew the road so well that he could have found his way blindfold. This return to familiar surroundings should have encouraged his steps. On the contrary, without any warning, he felt mortally tired. That stormy exaltation, the mere after-swell of the emotional tempest on whose crest his spirits had ridden, fell suddenly to a sullen calm in which the sense of failure, hitherto masked by excitement, returned. The moment approached when he would have to admit his failure to the friends who had trusted him, to defend and excuse himself; and his weakness shrank from confession because he knew that they could not share the freedom in which he had found compensation—that they could not escape but were bound to the soil because they knew no other means of livelihood and had wives and families, hostages in the enemy's hands.

This prospect was one which, in his present state of

fatigue, he shirked facing, though every dragging step brought him relentlessly nearer to it. A dim light diffused through the fog ahead puzzled him—he could not, he thought, have reached the outskirts of the village so soon—till it struck him that it must be shining from the sack-curtained windows of an isolated ale-house kept by one of his prospective fellow-victims, a ruffian named Jem Rudge. He had no fancy either for the house, which had a bad name, or for its keeper; but, by this time, his waning strength was nearly exhausted: he might manage to pull himself together, he thought, if he sat down for a few moments and fortified himself with a mug of beer. He staggered up to the door and tried to open it. It was barred inside with a wooden bolt. When he knocked he heard anxious whispers and a sound of scurrying feet. Heavier steps drew near; the bolt was cautiously shot back, and Rudge's ugly face appeared in a chink of the doorway.

"Who be there?" he asked suspiciously.

"It's me . . . John Oakley."

"John Oakley?" the man repeated. "I thought you was in London. You give me a regular scare. Come in, then: we're all friends here."

"Give us a pot of ale, Jem," John said. "I've been on the road three days and I'm well-nigh famished."

Rudge drew him a mug of treacle-coloured liquor. "That'll soon put some heat in you," he said.

"Ay, good health, lad! And I'll have another pot

too, Jem, damned if I won't, if you'll give me strap!"

The hovel was so dim—the fire that filled it with smoke was no more than a smoulder, and a single tallow-dip stuck in a bottle-neck afforded its only illumination—that, until the voice spoke, John had not been aware of its other occupants. Now two huddled shapes detached themselves from the dark background. One was George Dicketts, the maimed ex-soldier with the wooden leg, and the other Aaron Sheldon, a shady character, but the only labourer in Grafton who had shown any spirit over the Enclosure. John wished them both good evening.

"Well, and how did it go, John?" Sheldon grunted. "What news?"

"No good news, I reckon. 'Tis a hole-in-the-corner business—as good as settled as soon as they set it going."

"What did I tell thee, Aaron?" Dicketts broke in excitedly. "John ought to have gone to the Duke, not to Parliament. The Duke 'ld have seen us righted."

"You and your bloody Duke! He be the same as the rest on 'em," Sheldon answered, spitting contemptuously. "John Oakley, he's got neither more nor less than I knew he would get, and come back with a flea in his ear, the same as I said. My motto's the right one, George: don't go begging for your rights—you might as well ask for the moon for all you'll get—and don't ask for a living neither. Go out nights and take it, like I do."

"You're right there, Aaron: there be no two ways about it. All the same, I say as if John here had gone to the Duke . . ."

Sheldon interrupted him ruthlessly. "What's it like outside, John?"

"You can see a two-three yards. It lies thicker in patches."

"Ay, rare weather for one of my trade, but it's falsified us to-night, and no mistake. Do'st see this here sack?"—he kicked a bundle on the floor—"well, inside that there sack there's a dozen cock pheasants, my hearty, as lovely a lot of birds as Squire Abberley ever r'ared. A'roostin' that snug they was, over in Pritchett's Wood, that George here and me could pick 'em off so easy as blackberryin', and the keepers a-rubbin, their eyes in the fog not two fields off! Old Ballance, I reckon he knew we was after them to-night; but the poor beggar couldn't see a yard before him. Still, it cuts two ways, lad, the same as everything else. When we come along the hedge to the fork of the Worcester road, where the guard of the Brummagem–Bristol mail, who's the poulterer's man, picks 'em up and gives us the money, damn my eyes if there was a sign of the coach on the road. Two hours late, and not a sign of him! A chap who drove by in a chaise, he told me there's half a dozen, not counting the mail, held up between Bromsberrow and Worcester. So here we be, out of harm's way 'tis to be hoped, drinking Jem Rudge's ale and spending the money them there birds has never earned."

"What are you going to do with them, Aaron?" John asked.

"I've give one to Jem here, and you can have one if you like, and I reckon it's just about time I took the rest home with me to hide in the pigsty or burn 'em under the copper. 'Tis a crying shame—such a beautiful lot of birds, too!" He picked up the sackful of pheasants in one hand and a gun in the other. "Come on, George," he said. "It's no good us stopping and bezzling here all night. If the fog lifted up we should look a fine pair of fools. Here's one for you, John. You can shove it in your pocket: there be no blood about it, its purty neck has been wrung."

"Thank you kindly, Aaron," John said. "I'll cook him to-night. What's more, if you like, I'll give you a hand with that sack. It's a two-handed job, and your gun'll be going off if you don't look out, and it's loaded."

"Oh, it's loaded, you make no mistake," Sheldon laughed. "I don't take no risks with Ballance about."

John laughed too. That one pot of Jem Rudge's dark ale on an empty stomach—and even more the charitable way in which Sheldon had made light of his failure—had plucked up his spirits enormously. He was ready to laugh at anything and no longer ashamed of himself. The fatigue had miraculously left his limbs. The weight of the bag of pheasants over his shoulder seemed negligible. As they stepped out into the fog, Aaron Sheldon staggering in front with the gun under his arm, and the one-legged man stumbling behind, he was pleased by the alertness of his senses: his ears were so sharp he could hear a fox barking by Pritchett's Wood. It pleased him, too, to think of himself as the only completely sober member of the party. On the edge of the village Sheldon halted and summoned them with a wave of his arm.

"Now this here's where we've got to be careful," he whispered. "There bain't no saying but what that beggar Ballance won't be back and on the look-out for us. What I ordain is this: you go back of the churchyard, John—if anyone sees that there sack you might just pass the word as you'd bought a stone of potatoes off Jem Rudge. George Dicketts, he'll go through the village as bold as brass—and mind you make plenty of noise with that peg of yourn, George, to show them you've nothing to fear. Then I shall cut round behind Parson Ombersley's wall—I can travel quicker—and meet you two chaps at Monk's Norton cross-road in five minutes' time. Now be that clear, George?"

"Ay, them's the marching orders: bold as brass," George Dicketts bellowed cheerfully. Sheldon clutched his arm:

"Keep your mouth shut, you fool! Do'st want all Grafton to hear us? What's that?" he whispered quickly. "I'ld have sworn I heard steps!"

"Not a sound. You'm a-fancying of it, Aaron," Dicketts chuckled. "If you go on that way, you'll be seeing things next. My God, though, they'm comin'!"

They burst out of the fog with a rush, four spectral figures, Bob Ballance, a giant, leading. He shouted: "Each to his man, lads: there's only three on 'em!" George Dicketts, awkwardly turning to run, went down with a crash, as the foremost keeper leapt on top of him. John Oakley took a straight hit to the point of the chin that knocked him silly. As he staggered backwards and fell with the sack beneath him, he heard the simultaneous report of a gun-shot and a hoarse cry of pain. Then hands gripped his throat and choked him. He tried to tear them away. But the strength had gone out of his body: there was no fight left in him.

CHAPTER SEVEN

COUNTRY ASSIZES

MR. JUSTICE CARLOW, bewigged, in scarlet and ermine, sat uplifted in lonely state above the court from whose crowded benches beneath him the fetid effluvium of sweaty clothes and unwashed bodies rose in wafts of hot air offending his sensitive nostrils. That was the worst of these country assizes. Not one county town in the six that comprised his circuit gave a thought to the dignity and comfort of His Majesty's judges; and Worcester, as he had often complained, was the worst of the lot. The judge's lodgings were dark and dank and musty; the chimneys smoked; the rooms smelt as if they had never been ventilated since the Guildhall was built in the reign of Queen Anne. He could not even be sure that the bed had been properly aired since he slept in it last, in spite of the warming-pans with which it was ostentatiously stuffed. He had written to the High Sheriff, complaining of these discomforts, after his visit earlier in the year, and the High Sheriff had replied that a Bill for the erection of a new County Hall and Courts of Assize had been presented to Parliament. But by the time this was passed, Mr. Justice Carlow reflected gloomily, he would probably have caught his death of damp sheets and been buried: country gentlemen had no conception of the standards of comfort required by civilized folk. There was one thing, thank heaven, they did understand, and that was good living. The pint of port he had drunk with his roast pheasant at dinner last night was a wine of quality. When one got to the age at which one ascended the bench, one began to feel the need of a little stimulation. For one's liver's sake one drank little; but that little ought to be good. And indeed, for a man who by reason of his calling was regrettably denied the modicum of exercise that capricious organ demanded, Mr. Justice Carlow felt himself in tolerably good trim, though at the moment a little impatient with the provincial jury, who, in spite of his clear summing-up, were taking, as usual, an unconscionable time in considering their verdict.

It was not, he thought irritably, as if the facts of the case were in doubt. This was an ordinary poaching affray of the sort with which every criminal court in the country dealt by the dozen: three men caught by a gentleman's keepers *flagrante delicto* with a sackful of game in their hands and armed with a gun which had been discharged and had inflicted a grievous wound in the struggle: a circumstance that rendered them all three liable to capital punishment; and what made these Game Law offences even more simple was the fact that no man committed on a charge of felony had the vexatious right to be represented by counsel who could waste valuable time and draw on a sentimental jury's sympathies and becloud the issue. It was not, he reflected again, as if the accused in this case were by any means prepossessing. The middle-aged man, who appeared to be the ringleader, was a desperate, wolfish type, with hard-bitten criminal written all over his skinny face. It was he who had fired the shot; and that was enough to hang him. The second, the little fellow with the wooden leg, was quite clearly a fool (but a fool, none the less, must take the consequences of his folly)—an old soldier who dragged in the name of the Duke of Wellington. That was not in his favour. The Duke himself had declared that his soldiers were nothing but the scourings of the community. These old soldiers, in fact, were becoming a positive pest all over the country, demanding preferential treatment over their fellow-citizens because they had fought in a war more than twenty years ago. After all, they had been paid for fighting.

The position of the third man in the dock was rather more questionable. Both of the other accused had sworn, and sworn convincingly, that he had actually taken no part in their poaching exploit and that they had merely picked him up in an ale-house on their way home. Admittedly he was carrying the sackful of pheasants; but the other men said he had offered to carry it without knowing what was inside it, which, of course, was rather less credible. He was a much better type than the others: a fine upstanding lad, with a mop

D*

of dark hair, straight eyes in an honest, open face, and good, clear-cut features not without refinement. He was decently dressed and bore himself with a self-respecting air. On the whole, at first sight, the judge had been prejudiced in his favour.

If the fellow had had the sense to hold his tongue he might have got off more lightly. But he hadn't: with a deplorable lack of humility he had actually taken it upon himself to address the bench, and entered, without any excuse, on a long and entirely irrelevant disquisition on the social injustices, as he called them, that drove men to poaching—as if social injustice, imaginary or otherwise, had anything whatever to do with the laws of property. And here, on the desk before him, if there had remained any doubt in the judge's mind as to this young man's guilt, lay a private letter which he had received that morning from a gentleman of family and standing, Colonel Abberley, Lord d'Abitot's cousin, in which, though the spelling was not so good as it might be, he stated in black and white that the prisoner was a "good-for-nothing fellow" and that he hoped the judge would "look to him." Not that Mr. Justice Carlow approved of private communications of this kind: on the contrary, though not unusual, they were reprehensible. On the other hand, the young man had not called any witnesses as to his character, which was suspicious in itself; and this evidence of character, though irregular and unsolicited, was sufficient to explain why he hadn't. What weighed

even more heavily against him was the fact, brought
out in his own evidence, that on the day of the crime
he had just returned from London, where he had been
presenting a petition to Parliament. Working men who
had sufficient assurance to do that sort of thing were,
on the face of it, undesirable members of society,
fomenters of unrest and potential disturbers of the
peace. There were far too many of that kind about in
Worcestershire. Only a few years ago at the Michael-
mas Assizes he had tried and sentenced the Kidderminster rioters. In deference to the sentiment of the
time he had dealt with them lightly. Next year,
encouraged by that lenience, there had been riots in
Worcester and Dulston. It was clearly his duty in
future to prove by exemplary sentences that violence
did not pay. Where *was* that jury?

A panelled door in the wall of the court-room
opened; they filed in, self-consciously.

"You have considered your verdict, gentlemen?"

"Yes, my lord. We find the three prisoners guilty
on all counts, my lord."

"Have you anything to say before I proceed to
sentence?"

The judge fixed John Oakley with an intimidating
eye. His gaze was returned without flinching; but the
prisoner did not speak. Mr. Justice Carlow adjusted
his wig and laid his folded spectacles on the desk in
front of him.

"Aaron Sheldon," he said, "the jury has found you

guilty, and rightly in my opinion, of a capital offence. It does not surprise me that you have nothing to say for yourself. The evidence against you has been only too clear. There is nothing to be said. All men of your condition are fully aware of the penalties imposed by the law for the punishment of armed violence against the person and the protection of property. You need expect no mercy from me or from the offended justice of your country on this side of the grave. I shall pass sentence of death on you when I have dealt with your fellow-prisoners."

Mr. Justice Carlow folded his hands and leant back in his chair.

"Your life, George Dicketts," he said, "is equally in jeopardy. It appears to me, from the way in which you have spoken, that you are foolish and ignorant. You have also, by a visitation of God, been deprived of the use of a limb. Yet you must not imagine that either of these circumstances entitled you to any clemency. You are, or have been a soldier, accustomed to practise lawful violence in the defence of the realm and in the destruction of His Majesty's enemies. Yet you must be taught that this peaceful and happy land to which, by God's mercy, you have returned, does not tolerate the habits of licence which are necessarily accorded to her soldiers abroad and in time of war. I should be justified, indeed, if I imposed upon you the penalty to which, by law, you are equally liable with your associate, Aaron Sheldon. I do not, in fact, feel warranted in recommending that you shall lose your life; yet it is my duty to state that for this violent and disgraceful outrage you shall be sent out of the country, and separated for life from those friends and connections that are dear to you here; that you shall have to employ the rest of your days in labour, at the will and for the profit of another, to show the people of the class to which you belong that they cannot with impunity lend their aid to such outrages against the peace and security of person and property. I sentence you to transportation for life."

Mr. Justice Carlow was warming to his work. He was flattered by the attentive silence with which the court had received a sentence which, he felt, had been framed with dignity and precision in a voice which, as he listened to it, sounded remarkably well.

"You, John Oakley," he said, "are also doubtless aware of the perilous state in which your criminal associations have placed you. You are a young man; you have also been blessed with a higher degree of education and natural intelligence than your partners in crime. This is not in your favour. On the contrary, it is clear that the possession of these gifts which you have misused renders you more dangerous to Society than they. You have taken the liberty and the opportunity of alluding, in evidence, to matters which, although they are irrelevant, must not pass without observation. I do not come here to enquire into grievances. I come here to decide the law. Poverty is indeed, I fear, inseparable from the state of the human race. The Poor, Holy Writ declares, are always with us. But poverty itself, and the misery attendant on it, would no doubt be greatly mitigated if a spirit of prudence were more generally diffused among the people, and if they understood more fully, and practised better, their civil, moral and religious duties. You have stated, impudently and slanderously, that the upper ranks of society care little for the wants and privations of the poor. I deny this positively, upon a very extensive means of knowledge upon subjects of this nature. There is not a calamity or distress incident to humanity, either of body or of mind, that is not humbly endeavoured to be mitigated or relieved by the powerful and the affluent, either of high or midling rank, in this our happy land, which, for its bene-volence, charity, and boundless humanity, has been the admiration of the world. These inexpressible benefits, you, John Oakley, have forfeited. I hope that your fate will be a warning to others. You will leave the country; you will see your friends and relations no more; for though you will be transported for seven years only, it is not likely that at the expiration of that term you will find yourself in a situation to return. You will be in a distant land at the expiration of your sentence. The land which you have disgraced will see you no more: the friends with whom you are connected will be parted from you for ever in this world."

Mr. Justice Carlow, having completed his

judgment, looked round impatiently. The Clerk hurried towards him, carrying the black cap. John Oakley went pale. Aaron Sheldon, smiling, gripped the rail of the dock.

CHAPTER EIGHT

CHAINS

THE convict-ship *Minerva*, a barque of four hundred
and fifty tons burden, ran south-west on the Finisterre
course at ten knots, with studding sails low and aloft.
This was the first fair day she had struck since the
ninth of December, when, weighing anchor off Deptford, she had dropped down on the tide amid flurries
of snow that froze and congealed on her masts and
rigging, and so whitened the desolate saltings on either
shore with their ghostly mantle that it was hard to
distinguish where water ended and land began.

The *Minerva* had spent the last twenty years of her
ageing life on the Van Diemen's Land passage. She
was a ship with an ill name for luck, and this, her
eighth voyage in that grim trade, had begun in keeping with her bad reputation. From the moment when
the last sombre boatload of shivering shackled convicts
had been hurried aboard her from the hulks lying in
the Thames where they had been held in readiness for
sailing, the devil's luck had dogged her. First, swinging in the fairway, she had run foul of a hoy and stove
her in and sunk her. Next, rounding the Foreland and
seeking shelter from the gale that still drove the snow

before it, she had blown on the Goodwins and, shuddering, grounded in the night. Guns booming heavily and masthead lights had summoned the Ramsgate lifeboat, which stood by till dawn, when a great sea lifted the *Minerva* and refloated her. For another week she had lain and strained at a dragging anchor in the teeth of a second sudden fury that swept the West Bay from Portland to Start and caught her taking in water and ballast on the lee shore of Torbay. For two more with naked topmasts and reefed mainsail she rode out an even fiercer gale from the West that hurled the full Atlantic on ironbound Ushant. Now, at last, though the huge afterswell of that tempest still ran abeam, alternately balancing her on its dizzy crests and letting her slide down the face of the wave into sickening troughs, the warm wind that barely filled her sails was a very zephyr.

John Oakley, battened down in the 'tween-decks, knew nothing of the perils and hairbreadth escapes through which he had passed. From the moment when, shivering in his shoddy convict's uniform, he had been taken by road from Worcester jail to the hulk off Deptford and then driven aboard the *Minerva*, his fate had passed out of his own hands so completely that there was nothing more to be gained by speculation; no manner in which he could modify it or change it by the exercise of his own will. The machine into whose cogs he had stumbled had gripped his body. By luck rather than by deliberate intent it had failed to crush his life out of him as it had crushed Aaron Sheldon's; but the moving mechanism still held him helpless and would continue to hold him until the end of his seven years' sentence, unless he died first.

It was now a full month since he had seen the light of day, if that last cheerless glimpse of the frozen Kentish marshes and the low sky solid with snow deserved that name. In the 'tween-decks of the *Minerva* no light glimmered save the lanterns preceding and following the orderly officer who, escorted by soldiers of the guard, twice daily braved the stench of the convicts' barracoon on his hurried tours of inspection, and the tallow-dips that were lit when tubs and cauldrons of food were brought in from the galley; for the scuttles, which must have been closed in any case to keep out the sea, were obscured by the double tiers of bunks or shelves, divided by stanchioned partitions like stalls in a cowshed, that were nailed to the ribs of the ship on either side, and, since the *Minerva* left the Thames, the main-hatch which led to the prison had not been opened.

It was so dark, indeed, in this low-ceilinged noisome cellar, that for some days Oakley found it impossible to comprehend its shape or extent, being conscious of nothing more than the foul suffocation of air breathed and rebreathed to exhaustion by the hundred and forty-four degraded bodies with which it was stuffed. It was only after a week of this pitchy confinement that his eyes, adjusting themselves to perpetual gloom, acquired a new cat-like sense of discrimination in which inanimate forms that had previously been dim and meaningless defined themselves, and even human features (if such features were human) became distinct.

He was lodged, it appeared, in a wooden box or compartment, less than five feet square, in which he and five other convicts, packed close as pilchards in a barrel, were expected to sleep. When the ship pitched or lifted to a head or a following sea, this arrangement had its advantages: the stowage was so snug that their bodies were wedged together; it also afforded heat which, until the animal warmth of a hundred and forty-four human radiators made the air of the prison-deck tepid, had not been supplied by their single threadbare blankets. Yet, in spite of these questionable benefits, the width of the communal bunk was so meagre, that not more than one of its occupants at a time could lie on his back, while the shackled ankles and feet of such of them as were taller than pygmies were perpetually thrust or dangled beyond the edge of their shelf: a convenience to nobody except to the sergeant hurriedly checking the numbers of his charges by pairs of feet when the guard was relieved at the end of each second hour, or to the surgeon making his rounds.

Even on smooth seas, when the main-hatch was open and a wind-sail carried draught downward into the close 'tween-decks, this forced stuffing of six competitive human bodies into a space barely sufficient for the comfort of three was a torture to any creature in whose hardened stomach the normal discomforts of prison life had left the least shred of sensibility or decency; but in stormy weather, when the main-hatch was battened down, enclosing the exhalations of seven score men: when the ship, riding light on huge seas, rose and fell precipitously and staggered and shook and shuddered with groaning timbers under buffets whose monstrous impacts could be felt like the stunning blows of a sandbag; when, to the factor of suffocation and the furious noise of the storm there were added the stink of vomit and sounds of retching and cries of fear—then each of those twenty-four crowded berths with its stifled and suffering human content was as near an approach to hell as man's devilry could devise.

There were few of John Oakley's companions in the *Minerva's* 'tween-decks who, by the time Finisterre was sighted, had not often wished themselves dead. He himself, when he felt that he could bear the torment no longer, had extricated himself from the compact mass in which his body was wedged and lowered himself as well as the leg-irons would let him to the deck in the hope of finding more air and space for the stretching of cramped limbs; but the surface his dangling feet touched at last was awash with sea-water that had penetrated the hatch and swirled to and fro ankle-deep with the drunken ship's plungings and rollings, and slippery with invisible foulness and strewn with the prostrate forms of others who, like himself, had escaped and lay there as if dead, having neither the strength nor the will to haul themselves up again.

In the earlier days of the voyage, when the darkness was still impenetrable to eyes accustomed to light, he had heard plenty of talk and rough joking and snatches of sentimental or bawdy songs; men complained or whined or boldly boasted of their crimes in the cant of the prison-yard, which John could not understand, and in a dozen other dialects from Cockney to Northumbrian; but the sea, that bitter leveller, had soon silenced braggarts and whiners alike. For the next fortnight no voice had been raised save in pain or distress. In the community of suffering all the prisoners fell dumb as a parcel of hard-driven bullocks penned at the gate of a slaughter-house. Even when the sea moderated a little and hunger returned, and the blessing of dazed sleep, rudely broken every two hours by the crash of the opening gate in the loop-holed barricade that divided the prison space from the rest of the 'tween-decks, by the rattle of grounded muskets and the barking words of command—even then the sad herd remained crushed and dumb and spiritless. They sat up in their bunks and grabbed at their food and munched it in silence, or stared out with incurious eyes at their mute companions over the bilge-lapped expanse of deck that separated them.

A more various collection of flotsam than these it would have been hard to imagine. Beneath the grey uniforms there were hidden men of all kinds and conditions and ages: from grizzled veterans of a score of crimes to whom the habit of a convict's life was second nature, to a pair of undersized brats from the slums, peaked and pallid as cellar potatoes, whom offended justice had sentenced to transportation for the crime of filching a loaf of bread; from flashy townsmen who had thriven, for a time, on their wits, and still kept their swagger, to mean sneak-thieves and pickpockets bred in the subterranean warrens of Seven Dials; from hulking ruffians, whose only weapon was brute violence, to effeminate panders and delicate-fingered gentry convicted of coining or forgery, and shady professional men, well-mannered and modest, who had come to grief through being a thought too clever. Yet the bulk of this luckless company was composed not of criminals but of simple and even decent countrymen, like John Oakley himself, who, hard-driven by sheer want or angered by petty tyrannies, had slipped into the net of the Game Laws or were paying the penalty of an unwelcome freedom of speech or action in defence of their vanishing rights. On these—far more than on those others who had consciously flirted with the perils of lawlessness and taken their chances and lost—the misery of transportation lay with a crushing weight. They were men who had been used to living in the open air, to labouring until their thews ached with fatigue and returning to the simplicities of their cottage homes and the company of their wives and families. Here they lay, their legs fettered in irons, in airless darkness, alone, yet cheek by jowl with the meanest scourings of city sewers: men whose quality of mind no less than their unintelligible speech branded them as denizens of another world—almost monsters of a different species: men who were used to living in crowds and to using their wits, not their muscles; quick of speech, ingenious, crafty, and enviably adaptable. When John Oakley saw, through the gloom, the solemn bewildered faces of these pitiful mortals, villagers, like himself, oppressed by their own lonely muteness yet not daring to speak, his heart ached for them.

It was only when the *Minerva* changed her course off Finisterre, the remnants of the Biscayan surges running on her starboard quarter, that the master gave orders for the main-hatch covers to be lifted and, after much hammering of battens, a flood of incredibly white light poured down into the 'tween-decks, illumining their recesses, and what until then had seemed no more than a cavern of vague extent, revealed itself as a quadrangular chamber, roughly forty feet square and less than six feet in height, bounded on either side by the double range of berths and closed at both ends by the loopholed barricades which divided it, for'ard, from a narrower sick-bay, and aft from the more spacious quarters occupied by the guard. The middle of the after barricade was pierced, at the height of a standing man's chest, by a trap-door admitting the muzzle of a small howitzer loaded with grape-shot which, moving on swivels, could rake the whole length of the prisoners' compartment in case of mutiny.

The sight of this ominous weapon's black throat, hitherto invisible, was enough of itself to discount the sense of relief and unreasoning hope that permeated the 'tween-decks along with the unexpected irruption of air and light; yet no sooner were the hatch-covers lifted, than the crushed spirits of the prisoners were obstinately revived. Something had happened at last to break the deadly monotony. The barracoon woke, like a bird-haunted thicket at dawn. Men whose tongues had been suddenly tied for three weeks found speech and addressed their neighbours. They blinked at the light and scratched themselves and stamped and stretched their cramped legs. A babel of confused speech and oaths and even of laughter arose as men recognized the faces of others whom they had known or curiously examined their unknown bed-fellows. In the midst of this turmoil the gate in the after barricade was thrown open with a crash. The sergeant of the guard, a plump man with a fiery whiskered face, and the corporal appeared in the gateway. The sergeant wrinkled his nose and puckered his lips with distaste. "Phew . . . my God," he exclaimed, "if this isn't a stinking shambles! I've seen pigsties in Limerick that looked like a palace compared with this. And the stench of the beggars! No better than animals or niggers, they aren't, not raising as much as a finger to clear the mullock, but set there chattering away like a lot of bloody monkeys . . ." He raised his voice and bellowed: "Stow that blasted noise and keep quiet when the guard comes in and stand to your bunks at attention until you're told not to! Now come on!"

The men shuffled into their places sheepishly. In the opposite rank John became aware of his friend George Dicketts, from whom he had been separated since they reached the hulks at Deptford. The old soldier seemed less the worse for the voyage than most of them. He brought down his peg with a thwack on the deck, cocked his head like a robin and smartly saluted. There was a ripple of uneasy laughter. The sergeant's red face went redder.

"Pretty bobbish customer, eh? Who d'you think you are then?"

"Trooper Dicketts, sergeant. Fifteenth Hussars. Lord Uxbridge's Brigade."

"Oh, that's it, is it? Old soldier and all. Well, you'd better forget it quick. I know your sort, and what's more I'll keep my eye on you. And not so much of your 'sergeant' either: I'm 'Sir' to convicts, and mind you don't forget it!" He turned to the corporal. "Fall in a dozen of these jail-birds with swabs and buckets, the first six on either side'll do, and swill out this deck and scrub it. Keep the dogs to it, mind. Rub their noses in it and see they step lively, and if you catch any one of the bastards shirking, you send up his number and I'll see as he don't shirk twice. I shall look round again in half an hour's time, and if, when I come, this here deck isn't fit for me or the Lord Mayor of Dublin to eat his dinner off, there's going to be trouble for somebody. Go on then, get to it, the first dozen." He spat and retired.

John Oakley was one of them and so was George Dicketts. The work was sufficiently revolting, yet somehow a relief after the days and nights of bored and bitter idleness. They swilled the deck with buckets of sea-water and swabbed the noisome scuppers with clouts of sailcloth. At one moment John found himself scrubbing at Dickett's side. The little man winked cheerily: "Well, John, how goes it? I missed you. I never even knowed you was here. Well, that's company anyway."

The corporal, who stood idly sucking his teeth at the barricade, looked up to see who was talking. "Ho, you again is it?" he said, and sent Dicketts sprawling over the slippery deck with a flying kick. John jumped up and turned round on him with clenched fists and dropped them too late. "What! Another of you? Would you then?" He raised his fixed bayonet threateningly; but John had already thought better of it and was down on his knees, and the corporal turned back muttering to his post. George Dicketts sidled up and spoke in a reproving whisper:

"You didn't ought to have flared up like that, lad," he said. "This here job, it be just like soldiering: the less you say and the less you do, the better. If you acts too willing, the other chaps soon notices it and thinks you be trying to get an advantage over them. And if you acts too bobbish and gets across of the corporal . . . well, then God help your poor soul—for life on this earth won't be worth living. You may be a damned fool like me, and you may be as clever as paint: but the way to get on in the army or prison, I reckon, is to make out you be neither one nor t'other and keep your mouth shut."

In half an hour's time, when the Irish sergeant returned to sniff at it, the prison deck, though still wet, was comparatively sweet and clean, and his humour less violent.

"Now fall in these blackguards," he said, "and let's have a look at them."

The two files of prisoners stood up in front of their berths. It was only when he saw them thus in the mass that John Oakley realized what a ruffianly company they were and how sorely that hellish passage had tried them. Some had suffered so much and were so weak with starvation that their legs could not counter the rolling of the ship; they swayed and clutched at the wooden bunks to sustain themselves. All their features were drawn and scrubby with a three weeks' growth of beard which picked out their teeth and the whites of their eyes and gave them an aspect of hungry ferocity. Their faces, too, had a greyish, light-starved pallor that contrasted with the soldiers' well-fed ruddy complexions. The sergeant walked down the deck between the files, examining each man as he passed with the contemptuous eyes of a farmer considering an ill-fed parcel of cattle. Opposite one, a man with a sparse white stubble of beard, a thin, shaggy chest and hot, black beady eyes, he stopped.

"Hello . . . I've seen this ugly mug before now."

"Yes, sir."

"This isn't the first time you've been through the passage?"

"No, sir. Transported last time in the *Minerva*. I done seven years at Macquarie."

"And turned up again, like a bad penny! Well, mind you behave yourself. I want none of your old hands' tricks. What's your name?"

"Tim Kelly, sir. Born and dragged up in the parish of Tipperary."

"Tipperary, is it?" The sergeant laughed. "Well, don't forget there's another Irishman got his eye on you!" He turned to the corporal. "All correct. Where's that farrier got to, damn him?"

"Where's the farrier?" the corporal shouted. A hatchet-faced, shambling figure of a soldier appeared with a blacksmith's leathern apron over his singlet. He carried a bag full of what might have been implements of torture which he let fall on the deck with a metallic crash.

"Now get on with it, Jones. I don't want to stay breathing this stench all day," the sergeant blustered.

The farrier produced a steel gad and a three-pound hammer with which he methodically proceeded to drive out the rivets that closed the loops of the convicts' leg irons. His hands were brutal and clumsy. Sometimes the gad, which a second soldier held, slipped from the head of the rivet and ripped the skin of a bony ankle. Once the hammer slipped too and struck the soldier's forearm a numbing blow. The man rubbed it and glared at his comrade. The hatchet-faced farrier grinned; the sergeant laughed and swore at the victim: "Call yourself a soldier? Get on with it, you white-livered son of a bitch!"

John Oakley stood sixth in the row. This time the aim was better: the farrier was getting his eye in. The rivet shot out with a single blow; but the hammer's dull impact shook the bone and bruised it. John clenched his teeth and his fists, awaiting the next; and once more, with a sickening thud, the rivet shot out, and the two men passed on.

CHAPTER NINE

SHIPMATES

HE was free. At first his legs, unaccustomed to liberty, seemed useless, deterred by the habit of being frustrated, from moving. When he came to examine his ankles he found that the shackle had rubbed and inflamed the skin, though in this he had got off more lightly than others who had ulcers to show: but indeed, in the exhilaration of this astonishing freedom and in the new joy of light and of air, which, now that a wind-sail had been set in the hatchway, swept the length of the prisoners' pen and dried the newly-swabbed decks, such trifles were not to be dwelt on, and life, by contrast, seemed tolerable.

It appeared even more so when, on the following day, the order was given that convicts were to take two hours' exercise, in three equal batches, in the waist of the ship on the main-deck. John Oakley and Dicketts, both of whom were berthed aft, found themselves in the same detachment. John waited with his friend till the last to give him a hand up the ladder—unnecessarily, for the one-legged man swung himself up with surprising agility. As he reached the companion top his unaccustomed eyes blinked; he was dismayed and

almost blinded by the fierceness of light beating down
from the flawless sky and reflected from the sun-
bleached deck and surrounding sea. No such crystalline brightness had ever pierced the soft canopy of the
Midland skies that he knew; he had never known that
the glory of light could be cruel. For a time, unable
to bear its assaults, he sat on the coaming of the main-
hatch, his head in his hands. The sun pierced the
texture of his shoddy grey uniform and warmed his
back.

At length, daring to open his eyes, he perceived
that the pen in which he would now be permitted to
breathe fresh air twice a day resembled in shape—apart
from the ranges of berths and the impending main-
deck—the prison below. Here, as there, the enclosure
was bounded, fore and aft and on either side above the
level of the bulwarks, by wooden barricades that
separated it from the fo'c'sle, the quarter-deck and the
sea. For'ard and aft those members of the crew and of
the guard who were not on duty diverted themselves.
Beyond the quarter-deck, in inaccessible grandeur, rose
the poop, from whose railing the master of the ship
and the captain commanding the detachment of redcoats looked down on the forty-odd convicts who had
emerged from the 'tween-decks with the interested
remoteness of spectators on the brink of a bear-pit.

John Oakley was not aware of their scrutiny. When
he lifted his light-blinded eyes from the deck he was
overwhelmed by the dizzy height of the *Minerva's*

tapering masts; her towers of crowded canvas belly-
ing against the blue sky; the white wings of birds that
soared and wheeled or seemed to float without effort
on the dazzling air; by the immensity of the surrounding sea disclosed on either hand as the vessel lifted
and solemnly rolled this way and that on the long
Atlantic swell; and above all by a sense of the smallness, the loneliness, the helplessness—not only of himself and of his unhappy comrades in exile but of the
ship and all her company afloat and detached from all
human-kind and all familiar sights on that trackless
waste of waters.

Though it had used him so savagely, this was the
first time he had actually set eyes on the ocean; and
somehow this vast expanse of indigo translucent deep-
sea sweeping slowly, rhythmically eastward in an endless succession of summits and troughs, on whose glassy
surface the great ship rose and sank like a floating spar,
seemed more terrible, in its implications of strength
unexerted, in its sinister quietude, than the thunderous
fury into which it had lately been lashed. In the evening, when he came on deck for his second turn of
exercise, its aspect was even more solemn; for then the
declining sun swept the great swell abeam. It burnished
the crests of the waves with lurid light and magnified
the depth of the troughs between with gigantic
shadows; until, as the spent sun reached the horizon
and sank into layers of vapour that took from its contact the semblance of mountainous land dissolved in a

fiery flux of their molten substance, the whole waste grew black as ebony and cold and threatening, and the small floating speck of hapless life of which he made part seemed so feeble and pitiable that he was thankful when the bugle sounded and the guard, with their bayoneted muskets, drove him and his shivering comrades below.

That night, for the first time John Oakley slept soundly. Even the cramped berth irked him less, for two of its occupants had removed themselves with their blankets and dossed down on the deck, and the wind-sail set in the main-hatch brought into the prison-pen not merely a constant flood of soft, sweet air, but the soothing whisper of the bow-wave rippling along the *Minerva's* sides. Indeed, now that the turmoil had subsided, he found that the ship (like all other ships) had, apart from such gross sounds as her bell's clapper notes, the tread of the sentry and the pattering bare feet of the watch, a voice of her own, compact of a multitude of minute sounds: the singing note of taut shrouds and standing-ropes; the creaking of blocks; the dull flap of a filling sail; the seething and slapping of wavelets; and, beneath all these, in a sort of continuous bourdon, a complex sound that was even more integral and proper to herself, in which every component timber of her structure responded in turn to the strains the movement of the waves imposed on it. Sometimes, when the rhythm was set, the *Minerva* creaked like an enormous basket; sometimes the note

E

gathered impetus and deepened to a monstrous snoring with which were mingled strange overtones that resembled the ringing of chimes or the solemn clangour of great bells tolling and humming in caverns under the sea. When, at times, in the middle of the night the relief of the guard or the change of watch aroused him, John would lie and listen to this strange concert until he fell asleep.

It was no stranger than all the rest of the circumstances in which he so incredibly found himself. Yet youth is adaptable and hardships are relative; and when once the convict-ship had escaped the region of storms the condition of life aboard her was hardly more brutal than that to which he had been used as a child in Dulston. It was its unfamiliarity rather than its harshness that at first had bewildered him; and now that the geography of the ship and the routine in which life proceeded to the call of bugles and striking of bells had become familiar, there was not much—apart from the loss of freedom which the crew and the soldiers shared—to grumble about. The very narrowness of his surroundings made them comprehensible. Though the food had, so far, been abominable, it was sufficient. The quarters, though overcrowded, were now moderately clean. His human relationships, of which his solitary upbringing had made him instinctively chary, were all that he needed.

His principal companion, naturally enough, was George Dicketts, who, after their happy re-discovery of each other, clung to him. At home, before common misfortune threw them together, they had been no more than acquaintances. Now friendship soon ripened between them. At first John had felt the appeal of the maimed man's physical handicap: it was not long before he realized that in spite of it Dicketts was hardier and more adaptable than himself. This short, sturdy, broad-faced man with his blond beard and wide-set merry blue eyes had not marched with the Duke's battalions in Flanders for nothing. His body, maimed though it might be, was that of an athlete, combining with huge physical strength and iron muscles an agility that matched the quickness of a shrewd, untutored mind whose reactions were swift and determined. It was no wonder that poor Aaron Sheldon, long since hanged outside Worcester jail, had chosen Dicketts as a companion in his poaching exploits. The man, though he joked and made himself out a buffoon, was as full of ready instincts and apprehensions as any wild creature with an equal share of cunning, courage and resource. Though Dicketts affected to give him credit for his superior intelligence and generally deferred to him, John Oakley knew that the lame man's experience of rough living was wider and his fibre tougher than his own. He guessed that in any physical emergency involving both of them, George Dicketts would probably treat him as a child and take the lead and endure to the end, never losing for one moment the resolute cheerfulness which puckered his smiling eyes and widened his mouth with dry humour. Indeed, any man who could find matter for joking in the ghastly earlier days of the *Minerva's* passage was well worth cultivating as a friend.

A third convict soon attached himself to them: in the beginning by reason of mere proximity, for now that the berth had happily been vacated by two of its original occupants, he was John's nearest bed-fellow; but later by the natural attraction of like to like. He, too, was a countryman and another victim of the Game Law's savagery. His name was Job Radway, and he came from a Warwickshire village on the northern edge of Cotswold, where he had worked as a plough-man like his father before him. It was no wonder that John had felt cramped in his berth and that two others had left it: Job Radway's bulk was enough to fill half of it. He was an enormous fair-haired man, at least six feet three in height, with a vast spread of shoulder and unwieldy, ponderous limbs. He had a large craggy face with rough-hewn features that would have been noble but for a contradictory softness which gave them the look of a child's. All his bodily movements were cumbrous and slow and ungainly. His great hands had no purpose; he lifted his feet as though the weight of the furrow's clay still burdened them. His speech —and he spoke but rarely—had a rustic ponderousness; and his eyes, deep-set beneath shaggy blond eye-brows, were large and hurt and puzzled, yet so gentle in their bewildered solemnity that John could not help

likening him in his secret mind to the pair of great
shire horses, Bloom and Vic (named after the heir-
apparent, the little princess), which, together with
Katie his wife and a dog called Flash (that was a
terror on rabbits), and his five small children, were
the staple subjects of his talk, to judge from it, the
only other inhabitants of the minute, sequestered world
from which he had been torn.

His story, as he told it clumsily, lying by John's
side at night, was pitiful in its simplicity. He had
worked, from the age of six when he was set to pick
stones and scare crows, on the same farm near
Moreton-in-the-Marsh, and risen by degrees to the
proud position of carter; but the farmer who employed
him had died and his horses had been sold, and the
man who succeeded him had brought with him a carter
of his own. Week after week Job Radway had tramped
the countryside and offered himself for work of any
kind. There was none, as he knew, to be had in his
parish; if he went to a distance, he was told to go back,
since a man with five young children—one at the breast
and another on the way—might burden the rates. So
back he came to the village where he had been born,
and there the parish gave him eleven shillings a week
to spend his huge strength on road-work from light till
dark, out of which he must pay three guineas a year
for the hovel he dwelt in. He spoke of this misery
without any resentment, accepting it patiently, it
seemed, as man's natural lot. It had been a prime year

for potatoes, he said, and the children never went short; and sometimes he picked up a turnip or two that had fallen in the road from an overloaded cart. It was his wife rather than he who suffered. She was expecting her sixth, and worried herself, as women did, with fancies. Then, one evening, on his way homeward, he came on a wounded pheasant fluttering in the road. It was well-nigh dead, its plumage plastered with blood and dust; so he picked it up and wrung its neck and carried it home to make a soup for his wife.

"I didn't reckon there was no harm in that," he said. "If I hadn't a'picked 'en up the fox would have had 'en. And none would a'been the worse or the wiser, mark you, if so be that just as I stood there a'wiping the blood off the poor varmint on the grass of the verge, that new farmer what turned me off hadn't happened to ride by. 'What have you got there, then, Job Radway?' he says. It was a cock pheasant, I told him, as I'd picked up out of the road well-nigh blown to bits. 'In the road?' he says. 'So that's it, is it? Not off my land? How does it happen,' he says, 'that I never see'd him when I came past just now? And whose do you reckon it be?' You could tell by the way he talked he were turning wicked. 'Well, farmer,' I says, 'if so be as you want him, you take him and welcome. Whoever it was as fired that shot made a mortal mess of him.' At this he jumps down from his horse in a fret. 'Less of your "farmer,"' he says. 'My name's Mr. Burman,' he says, 'and I'll see as you don't forget it!

I've had my eye on you this long while, Job Radway.
You and your litter of brats are naught but a damned
lot of poaching vermin, but I've catched you red-
handed now. I've been waiting for this. You come
quiet along with me to the village,' he says, 'and we'll
see what constable have to say about it.' " The big
man sighed. "It'ld have been all right," he went on,
"if so be as farmer had 'na lifted his whip to me. I
reckon he got scared on a sudden, being a small, feeble
body himself and seeing the size of me. When I felt
the sting of the whip, I loses myself like—only a
moment it were—and ups with my fist and dropped
him one on the jaw, and down the poor beggar went
like a bullock, he did! At the go off I reckoned I must
ha' killed him, not knowing my own strength, as you
might say. If I had, they'ld ha' strung me up for a
murderer, and there would have been an end of it.
But after a bit he comes round and I hoists him up on
the back of his horse and leads him home quiet as any
lamb to the farm. 'Thank you, Radway,' he says, 'for
bringing me home like this'; and you'ld have thought
as that was the end of it, him knowing how he'd
tormented me. But it warn't. The next I knew was
the constable come with a warrant when we was abed.
And the next was Warwick Jail, and the next the
'Sizes. And now here I be . . ."

He still gave the impression of not quite knowing
where he was or how he had come there. It was this
helpless bewilderment, this abrupt and arbitrary, this

almost surgical severance of a huge and patient body from the native earth to which it was so near and from the minute and dear familiarities of a life governed more by instinct than by thought, that made Oakley and Dicketts feel kindly towards him. And Job Radway clung to them with a pitiful eagerness because he knew they were country folk like himself, because they understood his uncouth speech and listened, without impatience, when he spoke to them endlessly of his horses, Bloom and Vic, his dog, Flash, and his wife and children. "There'll be six on 'em now, bless their poor little hearts," he said.

CHAPTER TEN

DOLDRUMS

THEY seemed certainly, all three of them, of a different breed from most of the prison-deck's herded humanity. No doubt there were other countrymen in that hapless cargo. From every county assize there poured forth at that time a steady stream of common folk sentenced to transportation: the healthiest, the most highly-spirited—and, in that, perhaps, the best—blood of rural England drained away by this brutal and drastic phlebotomy to be lost in the thirsty sands of Botany Bay. Weeks passed before many of them stirred from the dumb paralysis with which separation had stricken them. When they found their tongues they gathered themselves automatically into groups made natural by community of dialect or of experience.

One such group—the noisiest and the only one that quickly adapted itself to the prison's routine with assured bravado—found an obvious leader in the old convict Tim Kelly, who had been "through the passage" before and seemed likely, given the chance, to go through it again. They were most of them, old hands and youngsters, clearly destined for various degrees of eminence in the career of crime. They made

light—or more often vied with one another in boasting—of the offences for which they had been lagged.
They were generally Londoners, and John Oakley,
hearing of their exploits (for he could not help listening), was fascinated and appalled by the pride they
took in them and by the glimpses vouchsafed of the
nightmare world they inhabited and seemingly enjoyed: a world of mean crime, of pimps and prostitutes
and forgers and cracksmen and pickpockets in which
nothing on earth or in heaven was held to be sacred
in life—or even, for that matter, in death, since one of
the most popular of their company, a benevolent-look-
ing old man with a lardy bald scalp and a long grey
beard, had been sentenced for life for body-snatching.
Even in their new surroundings Tim Kelly's gang
practised their crafts, if it were only in evading fatigues
or filching their comrades' rations of food and water
and contriving to fasten the blame for their subtle in-
discipline on innocent shoulders.

Job Radway, because of his enormous bulk and his
rustic simplicity, became the chosen butt of their tricks
and depredations, while John Oakley and Dicketts,
because they protected (or tried to protect) their friend,
had a share in their spite, until suddenly, roused by the
petty guerrilla to an access of fury of the kind in which
he had "dropped one" on Farmer Burman, the blond
Titan picked Kelly up by his skinny neck, and but for
the guard rushing in with their bayonets, would have
hove him overboard. Even then his tormentors had

the laugh of him; for Job Radway, overpowered by the soldiers, was clapped into irons and shut up alone for a week in a pitch-black airless hole reserved for delinquents—a shackled Samson with hatred as well as bewilderment in his childlike eyes.

"It wasn't the being alone as I minded," he told them later, "so much as the company. A sick cat or summat had left a plague of fleas there; and the rats— by Jiminy, George, they was as big as rabbits sniffing all round your nose and lips and a'chewing your whiskers. If I'd had my dog Flash to that lot he'ld have enjoyed himself more than a bit!"

After that, for fear of the carter's strength, Tim Kelly's gang prudently left him and his friends alone. Yet still John listened to their talk and their noisy boasting. He listened because it was only from the foul lips of Kelly and one or two others that he could gather any idea of the kind of fate that awaited him in Van Diemen's Land. Tim Kelly talked freely enough of his own experience. It was his pleasure to curdle the blood of his audience by telling them of the hardships and the brutalities he had undergone, and to prove himself a hero by making light of them. He told them gloatingly how, when the ship arrived at Hell's Gates, the fun would begin: they would be sorted out into classes in keeping with the character of their offences. The small fry of the criminal world—mere forgers and pimps and pickpockets and passers of flash money like himself—would be clothed in grey and set to light labour on the shipbuilding slips, and might even, with luck, aspire to the liberties of "good conduct" men. But the larger criminals who had been sentenced for crimes of violence (such as John and Radway and Dicketts) would wear yellow. The authorities took no risks. Their regime was planned to break any violent spirit that remained in a convict as quickly as possible. From the first they wore irons: a ring round either ankle and the slack of the chain between picked up by a leather thong attached to the waist-belt. It was one thing, he said, to lie quiet on shipboard in irons, but quite another to work in them. At every movement the metal chafed the skin and sooner or later wore its way through. Chain-galls had a way of not healing, particularly when men worked, as the yellow man worked, up to their waists in foul mud or water, hewing timber out of the King's River swamps and launching the massive trunks and floating them down-stream. And, to make escape more difficult, these convicts were chained in twos, so that the movement of each inflicted pain on the other. Escape? Well, some men did escape: nine or ten every year. Most of them were found sooner or later dead in the swamps or the bush. The prison smiths knew their job too well to forge chains that could be ovalled to slip an ankle or hammered apart with stones. Sometimes, when a couple escaped, one popped off before the other; and *that* was a nice go (he said) for a chap to wake up and find the other chap cold and himself too far gone to hoist the corpse on his shoulders and carry it back with him! There was one couple he knew who took it into their heads to get out of it by murder and suicide, and that was a nice go too, because the chap that did the job first thought better of it when it came to himself, and found himself regular dished. He couldn't get rid of his irons nor yet of the other one; and he knew if he dragged the other chap back to Hobart he'ld be shot for the murder, and if he didn't carry him back he'ld have to stay there till the corpse swelled up, so there it was, anyway! And there was another chain-gang, too (Kelly said), that got off with an axe. There were six of them when they started, but only one when they finished. How was that? Why, that axe came in remarkable handy: there was one of them coves that happened to be a butcher and a smart man at his job, and he kept his pals in fresh meat till there was only two on 'em—himself and another little, small chap named Higgins—left. When it come to the last, Higgins pinches the axe when the butcher he wasn't looking and gets him fair from behind; but although he was used to the diet by now, he couldn't touch him. Then the bloodhounds came up and grabbed him, and the guards behind them; and he comes back to Macquarie quiet as any lamb and grinning all over his face and gives himself up, stark staring gibbering mad!

What was there, John asked himself, behind these ghastly stories with which Tim Kelly entertained his rapt, gaping audience: the panders, the sneak-thieves, the pickpockets, the two wizened children whom he had claimed as his own from the first? What was it in Macquarie that could drive common men like himself (for not half of the convicts in his own batch were criminals) to murder, to suicide, even to cannibalism? The answer was not far to seek. It was fear of the cat and the triangle. The only recognized form of punishment in the penal settlements was flogging. It was meted out, in varying degrees of savagery, from a dozen strokes of the cat to a hundred, for every kind of offence, from a trivial mistake or lapse of memory or mere sullenness to sporadic or organized violence and insubordination. In the settlement known as Hell's Gates, not one convict in ten escaped in a year the cat's savage scarifications. In the prison yard, as a reminder (if that were necessary), stood two wooden triangles of seven-foot beams set up like a gipsy's trivet, to which the naked victims were strapped by their wrists at the apex and by their ankles below. The daily floggings in public were the convicts' regular evening amusement.

The warders themselves were experts, taking care to disentangle the knotted thongs from their clots of blood before every stroke, making patterns by crossing the cuts on the pulped white flesh. When they grew lazy or bored with their butchery, they would call on one of the other convicts to take a hand, maliciously pleased to pick out one whom they knew to be no friend of the victim. If the new torturer tried to "cut light," he knew what to expect: when the flogging was over, he, too, would be strapped to the triangle. More than once, in Tim Kelly's time, men had been beaten to death, and were thankful to die, knowing that they could not be beaten again. When he spoke of these devilries, John Oakley saw that the mere recollection of what he had seen and suffered himself was sufficient to shake his nerve and make his features go grey. His eyes narrowed, his lips twitched back like a snarling dog's; he had the wary look of a trapped animal that smells death, or something indefinite even worse than death. And John shivered, too.

"Why do you hark to that jail-bird's rubbidge?" George Dicketts reproved him. "He be only trying to scare us. If you'd knowed so many Irish as I have when I was out with the Duke, you'ld take no count of it. They be liars, every damned one on 'em."

But John knew from the look of Kelly's grey face when he spoke of the floggings that the man was not lying. As he lay in his berth at night listening to the voice of the ship, kept awake by Job Radway's enormous flounderings, his mind helplessly pondered, again and again, on the possibilities of attempting escape.

Escape . . . Kelly's stories of escapes from Van Diemen's Land were generally more grim in their sequels than those of life patiently endured in the settlement, and even to dally with the idea of escaping was profitless for a man enclosed in a floating prison a thousand miles from dry land (for all he knew) in mid-Atlantic. Yet day by day, insensibly, and as it almost seemed miraculously—so often did her course appear to a land man's eyes to be set with a freakish disregard for her destination—the *Minerva* stole southward over the curve of the watery globe towards the Equator. John Oakley guessed this only from the increasing heat and the way in which the sun, once welcomed as friendly, became an enemy. No sooner had it blazed above the horizon at dawn than the great ball seemed to shoot to the zenith in one savage leap, and to hang there, malignantly triumphant, until, at noon, the dome of bleached sky poured down heat like a salamander—until melted pitch in the seams of the deck became scalding to the feet, and metallic objects such as the glistening binnacles, the soldiers' brass accoutrements and the barrels of their carbines, seared the skin that chanced to touch them like a cautery. And by noon the tepid breeze which at dawn had crisped the sea with wavelets and given to the eyes at least an illusion of freshness had faltered and died. Not a cat's-paw ruffled the surface with patches of scaly snakeskin. Only, here and there as the bowsprit lifted to the swell and the hull rolled over, a shoal of flying-fish shot out like spray spattered from a seething crucible. But the sea itself was like dark molten glass, translucent, foamless, olivine, and so profound that the huge shapes vaguely moving in fathomless glooms that no eye could reach but for the sun's penetration, seemed phantoms of a lost world, a forgotten creation, that when the revealing light slanted westward would sink once more into obscure oblivion and never more be seen.

Though the teak planks blistered the soles of their feet like the bars of a gridiron (for only the officers on the poop and the guard on the quarter-deck were sheltered by awnings), the prisoners were still driven on deck to take air and exercise. Even that scorching midday glare was preferable to the oven heat of the 'tween-decks, where, gasping for air and stripped to the waist, they sweated through the rest of the day and the sleepless stifling nights. For the first time in their lives, these men, who had lived in a well-watered country, knew the torment of thirst. The regulated allowance of water for each was half a gallon: a portion meagre enough in a temperate climate. The stuff was tepid and turbid; it stank like bilge-water; some casks had been washed by the Biscay surges and salted. If men drank they were drenched with sweat; if they did not drink their mouths and throats grew foul and dry as kilns; if a drop of the precious liquid were spilt it could not be replaced, and much water was spilt in the reckless confusion of animals mad with thirst who jostled each other like pigs scrambling with their feet in a trough of swill. They watched each other's pannikins with gloating, envious eyes, and schemed to steal them from the strong or to take them by force from the weak. In this struggle for water Tim Kelly's predatory gang of desperadoes became an organized terror. It was fortunate for John and George Dicketts that their leader had learned to fear Job Radway's strength.

For a week they lay parched in the doldrums. Now, when the convicts went above, there was no talk or laughter or movement. Each man kept to himself: some sitting helplessly on the hatch-combings with bowed heads; some lying huddled in the scuppers, seeking the bulwarks' shade. There was no sound on deck but the rhythmical slappings of lifeless water and the flapping of slack canvas as the inert ship lurched and wallowed. On high, the sails that were set in the hope of catching the faintest waft of wind hung gleaming in rigid folds like the marble draping of statuary. Even when the sun sank, plunging into the sea like a red-hot plummet and turning the shadows of rigging on the bleached deck peacock-green, there was little relief, no movement in the water-logged air. For now, as it seemed, the expanses of wood and metal that had been baked all day exhaled the heat that had entered them, and the upper sky, from which cooler air might have fallen, was blanketed with steamy volumes of vapour that ringed the horizon with anvil-shaped masses of thunder-cloud whose purple bellies dry lightning ripped or illuminated with ceaseless flickers.

In the 'tween-decks a dozen convicts lay prostrate with heat-stroke, and many of the rest were in so poor a case that the surgeon, moved less, perhaps, by humanity than by the prospect of losing a number of the half-guinea fees that were paid to him as a gratuity for every man landed alive in Van Diemen's Land, prevailed on the captain to grant permission for any man who seemed on the verge of collapsing to sleep on deck.

Job Radway was one of the first he chose. Half a gallon of water was no sort of ration for that bulky body with its vast evaporating surface, accustomed to sweat like a horse ploughing clay-land and make good its huge losses instantly. Such powerful louts, the surgeon knew by experience, were often the first to go under. He lay gasping like a stranded fish; when the sergeant ordered him on to his feet he could barely stand till John Oakley lent him a shoulder, and with the excuse of helping him up the companion-ladder, found his way to the main-deck with him.

By this time, though the livid lightning still washed the horizon, the sky above the *Minerva's* swaying top-masts had cleared to a velvety indigo so calm and high and spacious that, gazing into its depths, and lying alone for the first time in many weeks, John Oakley experienced a strange and delicious lightening of the spirit, a sense of compression lifted, almost an illusion of freedom. A heavy dew drenched the deck: as he lay with lifted knees, the sensation of cold moisture was kind to his blistered feet. Though the sky was clear, it seemed to him unaccountably empty and spangled with constellations of strange shape. Charles's Wain, the one he knew best, was missing: he could not think why. Even the stars, it seemed, must be different in this alien world! Ah, well . . .

He grew drowsy watching them, and slipped into a dreamless sleep, that was broken in the middle of the night by a sudden shout in his ear. John jumped up with a start. The deck gleamed white with moonlight. It was Job Radway who had disturbed him. The giant was tossing from side to side. As he lay there, heaving, there issued from his cracked lips a continuous low muttering of words hard to distinguish. John shook his shoulder to waken him. But Radway was not asleep. He lay there with eyes wide open but unseeing. He was driving his plough through the heavy Ditchford marls and shouting to his horses Bloom and Vic as they turned at the headlands. He was angry, and lifting his fist to drop Farmer Burman a clip on the jaw, and laughing as Flash, his dog, scratched back the soil from a rabbit-hole. He was calling his children by name and hoisting one of them to his shoulder. He was drinking water in greedy gulps like a horse and smacking his lips and shouting and singing, and then falling to unintelligible mutters again. But never, for an instant, ceasing.

Other men who had been sleeping on deck grew angry at being wakened. "Stop that blasted row over there!" one called. "Can't you let a poor beggar sleep?"

"Give him a kick in the ribs, mate, and wake him. He's got the nightmare."

"Give him a kick on his bloody head!"

"That's no nightmare, that isn't, that's rambling. The chap's off his chump."

"Ay, that's what it is. He've gone balmy lying in the moonlight."

"How's anyone going to sleep with that row going on? Who is it, anyway?"

"That big chap what grabbed Tim Kelly. If anyone's going to tackle that great beggar it won't be me!"

"Call the guard, then, and tell him to fetch the doctor. That's his pal by the side of him. He ought to do it."

John walked to the barricade where the sentry was standing.

"There's a prisoner ill over here," he said. "We want the doctor." The soldier stared at him sullenly without answering. "Can't you hear what I say?"

"I can hear what you say, all right; but I'm not supposed to answer you. No communication with convicts. I oughtn't by rights to have said what I have."

"Then for God's sake call the corporal. You can't leave this poor devil raving like that and do nothing."

"I'm not calling no corporal for you nor anyone else. I know better than that. The guard 'll be changed in a few minutes' time at four bells, and then you can tell him yourself."

At four bells the guard changed. The corporal reluctantly opened the gate in the barricade and stared at Radway's prostrate figure with surly eyes. The big man's clumsy fingers were tearing at his chest. From his lips there still poured an unceasing flood of wild words.

"If I fetch the doctor," the corporal said, "he won't half thank me for it; but if this here beggar popped off and he hadn't been told, it'ld be just as bad. Mind you chaps keep an eye on him, and see as he don't chuck himself overboard. They do that sometimes."

The doctor came, with a coat slipped over his calico nightshirt. His eyes blinked with sleep; he breathed heavily; and his breath smelt of gin. The corporal and the sentry each carried a lantern—unnecessarily, for the moon shone light as day. The convicts, who were all now awake, stood round in a curious circle as the doctor knelt on the deck and uncovered the sick man's torso. Radway continued to stare at the sky; his clutching fingers moved; his lips muttered unceasingly.

The doctor was talking to himself: "High fever . . . Muttering delirium . . . No rash to be seen . . . It isn't typhus, thank God . . . that's a good thing, anyway." His fingers searched Radway's groins and then his armpits. In the right armpit they hesitated, palpating, and stopped. He looked up suddenly and spoke sharply:

"Corporal!"

"Yes, sir."

"Clear the deck. Get these convicts below. Don't let anyone go near the bunk in which he was sleeping. Pick out the fellows who share it with him and have touched him. Get them to carry him to the sick-bay, and keep them clear of the rest. Do you know which they are?"

"Yes, sir. This convict here, name of Oakley, is one of them, and I'll soon find the others. I heard you say it's not jail fever, I think, sir. That's one good thing."

The doctor laughed harshly. "A good thing, is it? That's all you know about it. It's twenty times worse than typhus, you fool. This chap's got the Plague."

CHAPTER ELEVEN

LANDFALL

THE ring of convicts standing in the moonlight shrank back. There was no need for the corporal to order them below. They melted away of their own accord and vanished, eagerly carrying with them into the sleeping 'tween-decks the horror of that dreadful word. "We've got plague aboard. D'you hear that, boys? We've got plague!"

The corporal followed them, searching for the rest of Job Radway's berth-mates, leaving Oakley and the doctor, grotesque in his coat and night-cap, alone on the moon-white deck where Radway lay, his great fingers still clutching and tearing at his chest, his lips still muttering.

They carried his dead weight of fifteen stone down the main-hatch companion and stowed it in the black hole of a sick-bay, immediately in front of the for'ard barricade, ruthlessly turning out the five heat-stroke patients who had already been placed there. They rigged up a curtain of sail-cloth between the sick-bay and the prison compartment, which made a pretence of isolating infection and certainly excluded the faintest breath of fresh air. This barrier, flimsy as it was, seemed better than nothing. It did give, at least, an illusion of physical protection and veil from his comrades' eyes the spectacle of Radway's sufferings. But it did not shut off from their ears the sound of his ravings: that perpetual stream of words, now savage, now tender, now shaped into sense and now incoherent, that flowed from his unconscious lips. A few bolder than the rest, such as Kelly and his crew, pretended to find Radway's ravings amusing. They laughed when they heard Job shouting to his horses and mimicked his uncouth speech. Yet beneath their bravado, they must have felt, like the rest who listened in silence, the neighbourhood of something imminent and dreadful behind that sail-cloth. It was the uninterrupted persistence, day and night, of that sinister sound which played on the drums of their ears like a Chinese torturer's devilish water-drops, that gradually frayed their nerves and made even Kelly lose his self-control.

"Why can't that damned doctor give him a dollop and finish the noisy swine and give us some peace?" he asked angrily. "If I could fix him myself without catching the plague and without being nabbed, I'ld do it!" he boasted.

In the middle of the second night of delirium, Radway's shouting and muttering suddenly ceased. For an hour they heard stertorous breathing; and after that silence—though whether he were mercifully dead or merely slept, none could tell. The dropped sail kept his secret until the doctor appeared next morning and lifted it and peered inside for a moment and departed without a word. A little later the ship's carpenter was heard on the fo'c'sle, hammering planks. In the middle of the forenoon a huge oblong box was lowered through the hatch to the 'tween-decks, and Radway's berth-mates, already exposed to infection, were ordered to enter the sick-bay and lift the body into it, and, when the lid was nailed down, to hoist it on to the deck where it lay white and vast in the sun, until the sail-maker sewed it into a pocket of canvas and weighted it at the foot with a thirty-pound shot.

No exercise-men were allowed on the deck that morning until noon, when, once more, the gates in the barricade crashed open and the sergeant com-manded them all to fall in and troop up for the funeral. They stood waiting there, wilting for half an hour in the vertical sun, till the master—there was no chaplain aboard—came down from the poop with a tattered prayer-book. He held the book at arm's length and mumbled the burial service so clumsily that John Oakley caught only a word here and there. "*This our brother . . .*" he heard, "*to be turned into corrup-tion. . . .*" He was standing, with Dicketts at his elbow, beside the hatch-cover on which the coffin was balanced, and gazing down through the gap in the bulwarks at the sea. And the sea was glassy black, as it had been for more than a week. Not even a spurt of flying-fish flawed the oily surface of a sullen tropical swell that lifted the ship and passed on unbroken. Then he heard the bo's'n's sharp word of command. The hatch-cover tilted. There was a grinding sound as the coffin slid, a great splash as it dived and sank. John Oakley closed his eyes and shuddered, for, as the pale shape plunged dimly into the hyaline deeps, it seemed (or was it but fancy?) that vast living shapes pursued it, nosing it this way and that, like hungry minnows scrambling for a sunken crumb. And, at that moment, startling the horror out of his mind, came another sound. The boom of the idle mainsail swung over with a clap that made the ship stagger as a sudden squall struck her. The crew scattered to their stations. The captain had dropped his prayer-book and was bawling commands:

"Take a reef in those topsails, quick! Get aloft, and look to your royals!"

The sullen sea was awake and streaked with running foam; the ship shuddered and heeled and strained and plunged through the broken water like a live thing suddenly freed from her death-like catalepsy by that pitiful sacrifice.

Not only on the busy deck, but down in the prison, it seemed as though with the burial of Job Radway and the coming of that breeze the threat of death had been blown away for ever. Yet the doctor, mindful of his half-guineas, was taking the matter more seriously. The berth in which Radway had slept had been boarded up, and his bed-fellows were ordered to sleep on deck by themselves, examined daily, and isolated from their companions; for it seemed too much to hope that all of them should have escaped infection.

Apart from the loss of George Dickett's cheery company, John Oakley did not resent this forced segregation. In a way he welcomed it. Though he was not unacquainted with death, there was an element of arbitrary injustice and cruelty and pitifulness in Job Radway's end that inclined him to a lonely and savage fatalism. Was there so much to choose, he asked himself, between plunging feet first to the sharks in a canvas sack, and spending seven years (as well say eternity) in chains within reach of the cat and the triangle?

In a few days it came to look, indeed, as if he were not likely to be offered the choice of these grim alternatives. Three of his companions in isolation went down, one after another, with the plague; and three more, from a berth on the opposite side of the 'tween-decks, followed them. Of the six, only one recovered, to save the doctor his ten-and-sixpence. Five times—and each time, he perceived, with diminished emotion—John Oakley stood by the bulwarks and saw the hatch tilted. There was less horror in these funerals than in Radway's; for the brisk trade-wind now steadily ruffled the sea's bright surface, and, even if he had wished to, he could not have seen what happened beneath it. And somehow, again, with the vessel's escape from those latitudes of steaming air and their melancholy glassy seas, so sullen even in sunlight, there had come to him a strange, unreasoning lightening of the spirit which, bred of sheer physical relief, filled his heart with obstinate courage, almost with hope. There was communicable zest in the breath of the south-east trade gaily rippling a sea that sparkled clear as sapphire under a sky no longer ringed with brooding thunder-cloud; zest, too, in the mettlesome strength with which the ship danced on the waves; in her creaming wake and the iris of fine mist sprent from her cleaving bows; in the untiring strength of wide-winged albatrosses that wheeled and soared round the dizzy spars and kept the ship company day after day. Then that soft trade-wind died, and another wind took its place that braced the sinews and crisped the skin with the chill of Antarctic ice; and the ship changed course and flew from the setting sun into seas more noble that sheeted her starboard quarter with drenching spray; and, out of the dawn, one day, there arose a phantom of land with a flat-topped mountain behind it which some said, with bitter irony, was the Cape of Good Hope.

It was evening when the *Minerva*, having rounded Cape Point, dropped anchor in False Bay. Other craft were lying off Simonstown; an East Indiaman putting in to revictual on her homeward voyage, a frigate of fifty guns, the *Southampton*, and a fleet of scattered fishing-boats manned by Malays. To the north-west the bulk of Table Mountain rose black; its precipices and forest-clad knees lay in shade, but the flat top cut sharp as a knife-edge across the crimson sky. Beyond the verge of this monstrous shadow stretched a dazzling curve of coral-sand and of surf, each as white as the other; and beyond this, again, a peaked range of tawny mountains flushed blood-red in the sunset. The soft air was so still in the placid interval between the diurnal breezes of sea and land, that John Oakley, on deck, could hear the voices of sailors laughing in the man-of-war; it was so clear that the shore of Simonstown seemed only a stone's throw from where he stood.

The mere sight of land after so many months of watery monotony excited him. He yearned to set foot on it, for itself no less than for its freedom. A strong swimmer, he thought, dropping quietly overboard, could reach land without much difficulty and escape, in the night, to those mountains. But he was not a strong swimmer. The most he had ever done was to float and splash on hot Sundays in summer in the shallow pools of the Chaddesbourne Brook. When he looked at the deep blue water yearningly he could not forget the foul, swirling shapes that had butted at Radway's sinking coffin. And in any case, as it proved, such adventurous speculation was vain; for no sooner had the *Minerva* dropped anchor than an order was given to clear the deck, and the soldiers drove the men who were on it below and crashed-to the door in the barricade and shot the bolts.

"They'll batten us down for a couple of days," the old hands explained, "while they take on fresh food and water, and just about time! And belike they'll let them young bulls of redcoats ashore to have a look at the women and blue their month's pay. The best wine costs no more than beer in Capetown. Them lucky beggars has a gentleman's life, and no mistake! Hark, now! They're launching the boats. They don't lose no time!"

In the 'tween-decks none could guess what was happening above, for the main-hatch was closed. They heard only a stamping and trampling of feet, a grounding of muskets, confused with the rumble and scraping of boats slung out to be launched. Between these, in the absence of the other, watery sounds to which they were used, the motionless ship seemed strangely silent, though sometimes they heard the rhythmical plashing of oars or the wail of "Ship ahoy!" carried faintly over the water as boats from the shore approached.

But no boat from the shore came alongside that night. The *Minerva* had sailed into Simon's Bay with the yellow flag flying. At sunset a single light was hoisted to her main topmast-head. She was a ship with a "foul bill," as they called it. But for the urgent shortage of water—by now the slimy tubs stank and the convicts' half-gallons were barely drinkable—the captain would not have dared to put into Simonstown with a tale of five deaths from bubonic plague in a convict ship packed to suffocation. Convict-ships, as he knew to his cost, were always suspect. There was no question of anyone landing, and no more than a slender hope that the quarantine regulations might be relaxed sufficiently to allow of his loading a few thousand gallons of water.

But the Capetown Authorities were taking no risks. They knew all about plague-ships—or rather knew nothing about them, apart from the sinister fact that plague—and even more, small-pox—had a way of escaping from ships on the East India passage, and that a single case flaring up on dry land was a deadly peril not merely to the verminous warrens of Hottentots and Malays that lined the foreshore and the old slave compounds on the farms, but to the inhabitants of the stately Dutch houses that crumbled along the Heeren-gracht, to the soldiers in barracks, to officers and their wives, to His Excellency the Governor, Sir Benjamin D'Urban himself.

No sooner had the *Minerva* dropped anchor and hoisted her signals than a long-boat, bristling with carbines, shot out from the shore and scattered the fishing-craft crowding about her to sell their catch like a barracuda harrying a shoal of mackerel. She lay at a quarter of a cable's length from the ship, while the quarantine officer aboard her stood up in the stern and bawled at the *Minerva's* captain. What was the sickness aboard, he asked, and what was she wanting? How could she take on water without breaking quarantine? Not a cask, not a drop! There were plenty of desolate places east of Cape Hanklip, he shouted, where rivers ran into the sea and a landing-party could get all the water they wanted without carrying the risk of the pest to innocent people. Why, with wind blowing off the land, even the frigate was in danger! A sanitary patrol would be set. If a single boat left the ship during the night, it might look to be fired on. If the *Minerva* herself had not weighed and set sail by dawn, there would be the devil to pay. And he meant what he said.

It was the plashing oars of the patrol rowing round the ship that puzzled John Oakley listening through the night. He woke to find that the old, rippling sound of water had returned. The *Minerva* was under way and lifting to meet the Agulhas swell. When the hatches were raised, the ship lay abeam of Cape Hanklip; a line of surf broke and misted the gleaming shores of False Bay, behind which the Hottentots Holland range rose vast and arid. Past Hanklip, not only the swell but also a savage south-easter faced them. Plague or no plague, no human being could stand on the wave-swept deck. Once more the main-hatch was closed and battened down. Ten days passed before it was opened. The water the convicts drank gratefully was green with slime. But there was one thing for which all—and John Oakley more than most —were thankful. There were no more cases of plague.

So the gale died down. Once more with vain surmise they heard the slow thunder of the anchor-chain running out and a new stir of mysterious activity on deck. This time the old hands could offer no explanation: their African geography began and ended with Capetown. Then the sergeant, who, since the plague scare, had rarely appeared in the 'tween-decks, came bustling below. For once, he spoke good-humouredly.

"Any sea-faring man that knows how to handle an oar want a job?"

There was silence. "That's right!" he said contemptuously, "don't all speak at once! I might have known that the sound of work would scare you, you damned lazy dogs! All right, then. Fall in the first six, and look smart about it!"

John Oakley, with Dicketts and four others, stepped forward. The sergeant's eye lighted on Dicketts malignantly:

"What do you think *you're* doing? What's the use of a one-legged man in a boat, I should like to know?"

Dicketts grinned and saluted. "My arms be all right, sir," he said, "and I know how to handle an oar. If you don't reckon I'm fit to row, I know how to steer."

"Come on, then. Fall in the next man as well."

They trooped up on deck. Three boats had been launched and lay heaving alongside, the two hindermost laden already with empty casks and attached by a tow-rope to the first, in which the mate, the corporal and two armed soldiers were sitting. From the rail of the poop the master surveyed the sergeant's selection scornfully.

"Well, you've picked out a rare lot of scarecrows," he said. "You might have done better than that. What's the use of that peg-legged beggar?" (But before the sergeant could answer, George Dicketts had slung himself ape-like over the side and dropped to the boat.) "Mr. Taylor!" the captain shouted.

"Ay, ay, sir?"

"Don't waste any time. The weather-glass don't look too good, and the sky's too white for my liking. You know what this blasted coast is."

"Ay, ay, sir! I'll keep 'em to it. All aboard, there? Give way, then!"

They rowed for the shore. It lay low and girt with barren sand-hills and a backing of grey-green scrub, its line divided in the midst by an intrusion of gleaming water that might well be the mouth of a river. The ship lay much farther from the shore than they had imagined. Between the rowers and the coast stretched a broad belt of angry breakers, impenetrable, as it seemed, save in the one spot for which they were steering, a zone of diminished fury where the river silt heaped on the rocks smoothed a bar of sand. They pulled steadily towards this gap, with the boats in tow behind straining this way and that and wallowing so deeply that at times they were lost to sight, while the roar of the breakers on either hand grew nearer and more deafening. No craft but a flat-bottomed boat could have lived in those zones of broken surf. Even in the relative smoothness of the channel between, the boat was confronted by a glacis of water which, as they approached, rose high overhead, obscuring the land. The face of the mate in the sternsheets looked grim but unperturbed. He was watching the run of the surges and waiting his time. A greater wave caught the boat astern and tossed it upward.

"Now . . . all together!" he shouted. "Four strokes! Ship your oars!"

The tumult on either hand drowned his voice; the oarsmen ducked as a solid sheet of white water came hissing over their heads; it blinded and drenched them and filled the bilge ankle-deep, as the long-boat shuddered, hung poised for one moment, and then shot forward, running on and on down the face of a wave that flattened itself and ran creaming in shallow water.

They were through. Though the roar of the breakers behind still deafened them, the face of the lagoon in which they now floated lay smooth as a mirror: a wide estuary girdled by low banks of barren sand-dune, its surface scattered with multitudes of water-fowl, wild-geese and duck and teal, flocks of rosy-breasted flamingoes and stilted cranes, all so fearless of man that this sudden invasion of their sanctuary did not disturb them. The crew beached the long-boat and brought the others alongside a spit of soil that had escaped the encroachment of blown sand and made a natural landing-place; and there, in the midst of a thicket of grey-green bushes, the mate found the spring of sweet water that was set down on the charts. The men drank of it as eagerly as if they had never tasted water before. They laughed, stretched their limbs and stamped their feet. It seemed strange and blissful to feel living earth beneath them again.

But there was no time to waste, as the captain had said, and the corporal soon set them working. Their muscles, long unaccustomed to labour, had grown soft; there was no strength in their bodies; the heat, radiated from the white dunes of sand and cruelly reflected by the white sky, seemed terrific. Yet the heavy casks must be hauled up the slope and filled and bunged and rolled down again, and all against time. It was no wonder that the cunning old hands had not hurried to volunteer for this brutal labour. The six convicts worked stripped to the waist and streaming with sweat. Only George Dicketts, whose peg, sinking deep in the sand, made his flounderings ludicrous, had been set to the pleasanter task of bucketing water from the spring; and even he sweated. The lagoon steamed with heat; the air quivered above the white sands; the flats of scrub between it and the rising land swam with streaks of mirage as though the desert were flooded. There was no sound on the air but the bar's continuous thunder; no breath of wind stirred it; yet from the soil's surface, where glaucous succulents and wiry dwarf shrubs were trampled, there rose to the nostrils hot wafts of a pungent smell, neither of mint nor sage nor vervain, yet partaking of all three: the tang which is, above all others, the smell of Africa.

For five hours they toiled without ceasing, and half of their task was not done. The veiled sun made the northward sky incandescent. The dry brush crackled with bursting seed-pods that made a noise like that of a kindling fire. And suddenly, pouncing out of the sky, a single gust of wind smote them. It blew the sand into their eyes and their open mouths.

"Come along, hurry up, get on with it!" the mate cried. "I don't like the look of it. That's how a south-easter begins."

He ran to the crown of the rise and gazed over the sea. It was white as the sky and covered with a faint haze. The white sea joined the white sky without any horizon. The *Minerva's* black hull against it seemed to swim uplifted on air. She looked smaller, as though she had drifted away from the shore. The wild-fowl which scattered the estuary were disquieted. The wild geese rose together and flew over his head with necks outstretched and creaking wings. Flocks of teal and duck left the water and gathered in wedges, flighting inland. Flamingoes soared in circles and were lost in the sky.

"I don't like it," the mate shouted. "Those birds, they know what's coming, and she's on a lee shore."

Another gust came. Behind it, beyond the bar, the width of the bay was streaked with spatters of running foam, the *Minerva's* shape blurred. Yet another: the wind leapt on them with the spite of an angry animal. They stooped, but could barely hold their ground, while sand and pebbles peppered their faces like a blast of small-shot. The wind roared through the grey-green trees of the bush and blanched them, it lashed the calm estuary white. It was so loud in their ears that they could no longer hear the surf save between the wind's buffets. The mate, crouched on the rise and still watching the *Minerva,* saw a hoist of flags run up. He saw a puff of white smoke spurt from her side, and heard, faint, but distinct above the roar of the breakers, the dull thud of a gun. He ran down from his ridge and called to the corporal:

"Come on, quick, man! The ship's going to run for it. Make your convicts shove off the boats and get 'em aboard. Leave them casks: they don't matter," he shouted. "If it comes up much more we shall be lucky to get back with what we've got." A second gun boomed. "My God, she's not half in a hurry!"

They were all in a hurry. By now the force of the south-easter was frightening. Between gusts, its violence remained as fierce as that of the first blast that had struck them. Sand was stripped and spouted and swept from the seaward dunes in solid sheets; spray bodily torn from the water lashed them like hail. Between sand sinking below and sand flying above and the pressure of air hurled against them in monstrous buffets, the men hurrying towards the boats could not run—they were hard put to stand. They bowed their heads, closed their eyes and floundered forward in a straggling file. All but Dicketts. With only one leg at his service, it was all he could do to hold his ground. John Oakley thought of him suddenly, and looked back to see him, a pitiful, bewildered figure, forty yards behind, beckoning violently. He turned round and ran back—it was easy enough to go with the wind—to help him.

"Give us a hand, George. We'll manage it yet if you stick close to me," he said.

Dicketts smiled. "It's not all that bad, John. I'ld get there, you trust me, if I wanted. What about going the other way? Shall us run for it, lad?"

"Run for it?"

"Why not? Them beggars 'll never follow us. They be scared to their marrows. What's more, if it comes to that, I'd liever be shot than drownded. Come on . . . Even if they runs after us, they've got to run through the sand, while we're on firm land. We've a hundred yards' lead, don't forget, and they'll never fire steady in this wind nor yet find a target when once we be past them bushes. Come on, lad, it's now or never. Keep your head low if they fires."

He laughed as he spoke with an old soldier's zest in the escapade. In a moment he was off, his head bent low. He went skipping down the wind with amazing agility. John could hardly keep up with him. As they ran, an angry cry reached them:

"Hi! . . . Two beggars have bolted! They're off! It's the soldier and Oakley. Hi! . . . come back or I fire!"

"Let the beggar fire!" George Dicketts chuckled. "Come on, lad! Come on!"

John turned for a moment. The red-faced corporal and the two soldiers were stumbling after them, ankle-deep in sand. They dropped on one knee and took aim and fired. John only heard the reports of their muskets. No ball whistled past. If it did, its whine was lost in the sleet of sand. Again they ran forward and fired. Another figure joined them. It was that of the mate. He was pulling the corporal by the shoulder, shouting in his ear and gesticulating and pointing to the boats. The corporal turned sullenly. John saw the four men fighting their way backward against the wind. But by this time he was lying on his belly among the grey-green bushes, his temples bursting, his lungs pumping for breath. And beside him, George Dicketts lay rocked with uncontrollable laughter.

"They'll never come after us now, lad, not in this world!" he panted. "It's as good as soldiering, this is. By God, it makes a young man of me!"

The boats were afloat. The last four tumbled into them. Once more, in the distance, the urgent gun boomed down the wind.

BOOK TWO

STORM OVER AFRICA

CHAPTER ONE

WELGELEGEN

THE south-easter which had sent the *Minerva* running for her life blew inland with undiminished fury, harrying man, beast and tree. It caught Jan Bothma and his convoy of two heavily-laden wagons in the last lap of his month-long journey from the Cape to his Uncle Adrian Prinsloo's farm of Welgelegen, at the point where the coastal road emerged into the arid belt that lay between it and the Assegai River. It was a road by courtesy only, being nothing more than a track worn on the face of the land by the hooves of driven herds and scored by the traffic of wagons. Where the ruts had worn too deep and rain-storms had turned them to quagmires, many wagons had swerved and made parallel paths in the bush, so that the "road," in fact, resembled the path of a hurricane, a strip of churned earth and sand driven straight and as far as eye could see, through a waste of thorn and aloe and candelabra trees. Over this track the two wagons, with their augmented spans of sixteen oxen apiece, appeared to crawl onward with the deliberation of centipedes. The thrust of the wind against their tilts was so fierce that the wagons pitched in the gusts like ships in a squally sea. That was why Jan Bothma had hitched a fore-span of two oxen to each of them; yet even so, the poor beasts lurched and stumbled; and at a steeper pitch the leaders fell to their knees.

Bothma cursed them, urging them onward with whip and *sjambok*. There was nothing like a south-easter to fray a hasty man's temper. Each suffered the sting of the lash and the blows of the *sjambok* in silence. Their red coats were darkened with sweat and spattered with foam; their great eyes looked blank and resigned; one by one they slumped down in the dust, their heads turned from the wind. Bothma knew that he could not move them until they had rested. And not only the oxen were grateful for this respite. He could see that his Hottentot servants were equally spent. They flopped down on their bellies, panting, their arms shielding their heads, while the two naked children, the *voorloopers* who led the teams, lay shivering, their skins, the colour of faded leaves, caked with sand and sweat, under the lee of the fore-span oxen.

Jan Bothma regarded them with contemptuous eyes. It was not in his nature to accept defeat like these meaner creatures. He left them without a word, and stalked forward stubbornly in the teeth of the wind to the crest of the rise, from which, as he thought (though one mile of this veld was no different from the last or the next), the white buildings of Welgelegen should almost be visible. He stood gazing, an immense hand

shadowing his eyes, but no such welcome sight rewarded him; nothing more than a uniform waste of
thorn and grey-green bushes cleft by the wagon-track
rolling on and on to be lost in a haze of suspended
dust and atomized spray blown inland. Though the
sun could not be seen, he knew it could not be far
from setting, and the prospect of approaching the farm
after sunset displeased him, for there was still a drift
to be crossed and it was hard to gauge the depth of
water in darkness.

"Ten minutes. . . . I will not give them more if it
breaks their winds," he told himself.

Standing there on the ridge, silhouetted against the
white sky, Jan Bothma's still figure resembled some
tall, rough-hewn monolith. Many men of his race
were cast in that Anakim mould—almost as though
unlimited freedom of air and space, together with the
virgin strength of the African soil in which the old seed
was sown, had endowed its cells with fabulous powers
of growth. He stood six feet four in his heel-less veld-
shoes of bullock's hide. His massive thighs, sheathed
in trousers of bark-tanned sheepskin sustained by a
draw-string and fitted with a great flap in front, were
pillars fit to sustain the heavy abdomen and torso. A
check shirt and a waistcoat of dappled calfskin, open
at the neck, showed a column of throat more massive
than the head it carried, above which the tapering
crown of a broad-brimmed hat appeared slightly
ludicrous. And the face beneath the hat was, again,

somewhat disappointing: as though the sculptor whose fancy had modelled that tremendous frame had grown careless or wilfully freakish when he reached the throat and scamped his work on the rest. The cranium itself was small and narrow at the temples; the pale blue eyes set too close together, the nose, lips and jaw peremptorily moulded without any attempt at refinement, producing the kind of face that a child might have contrived out of clay: an impression enhanced by the layers of red dust which, coating the man's gigantic figure from head to foot, gave the whole the appearance of a statue in terra-cotta. It was a rudimentary face, and yet, when one came to examine it, neither unkindly nor brutal: rather the expression of a spirit profoundly childlike, informed by habit and instinct rather than by thought, slow to mirth or anger, enduring, endlessly patient, and, above all, obstinate.

It was this quality rather than the others that showed itself in his set jaw and protruded lower lip when, at the end of the ten minutes' respite on which he had decided, he returned to the wagons, and wielding the bamboo whip-stock with its thirty-foot thong, set the foremost team in motion, abusing and encouraging them by name.

"Trek, you devils," he thundered. "Trek, you *schelms! Trek, you lazy troop of mares! Ay, Blauwberg, would you?" (The long lash curled in the air like a salmon cast and stung the off-leader's muzzle.) *"Loop, you devils, loop!"*

The great wagons lurched forward, sinking half-way to their axles in sand. The *voorloopers* tugged at the reins attached to the leaders' horns, lifting their lowered heads to the slope. Klaas, the Hottentot headman, slashed at the after-oxen's flanks with his six-foot *sjambok*. In a cloud of dust, stumbling, they breasted the rise. Now the going was easier. Jan Bothma was well pleased with himself. He vaulted on to the driving step, cut a plug from a rope of tobacco and rubbed it into his pipe. The spans plodded forward now at their usual pace of three miles an hour, as though the savage impetus that had set them in motion still carried them on, as though they knew that this rhythm, once broken, could not be recaptured. And suddenly, in spite of their tiredness, they quickened their steps. Though he could not see it, Jan Bothma knew they smelt water. He smiled to himself with satisfaction. If the river could be smelt already, he had not guessed his position so badly. How deep would the water be?

They gradually shelved to the drift. Two Hottentots, tugging and throwing their weight against it, checked the skidded wagon's progress. Without need, it seemed; for no sooner had the leaders' feet touched water than they halted and plunged their parched mouths in it. Then came shouts of alarm from behind. The rest of the span, equally eager and not to be cheated, swerved sideways, twisting the trace into a loop and swinging the *disselboom* round to a right angle, dragging the wagon itself across the slope till it lay balanced broadside-on and in danger of over-turning. Jan Bothma jumped down into the drift and snatched the leading reins from the *voorlooper's* feeble hands. The leather snapped with the strain. Then he seized the horns of the ox called Blauwberg. He lifted the massive head by sheer force against its straining neck-muscles and pulled Blauwberg with him deeper and deeper into the stream, until the great beast, beaten and bellowing with fright at the tug of the current, came plunging on of itself, till the *trek-tow* straightened, the twisted axle swung round and the wagon came after, lurching from stone to stone.

The drift proved to be deeper, in fact, than he had expected. In mid-stream water flowed over the floor of the wagon. Bothma's calfskin waistcoat was soaked to the arm-holes, and when he waded back, without the support of the sure-footed oxen to steady him, there were moments in which it might have been safer to swim. Yet the sudden emergency had not in the least perturbed him. Such escapes and alarms, though not out of the ordinary, gave spice, indeed, to the drudgery of trekking on and on, twenty miles a day for week after week, through an unending monotony of dust. The soaking refreshed and cooled his baked skin; the struggle stimulated him. It was for mastery in such contests with natural forces that his vast thews had been made. His heavy face brightened; he laughed to himself, remembering the ticklish moment when the ox whose horns he had held had lost its footing. That would make a fine story to tell when he came to Welgelegen, an occasion for a little innocent boasting that would show him up as the hero he liked to appear in his cousin Lisbet's eyes.

Yet, even in exultation, the habit of caution did not forsake him. Before he started to water the second span and lead it into the drift, he looked to his sawn-off buffalo horn to see that the powder was dry, and, finding the granules sodden, refilled it. In those times and in those parts a prudent man took no risks. Ever since he had emerged from the forest-belt Jan Bothma had kept his eyes skinned, his ears alert, his gun loaded; and a moment since, on the farther side of the drift, he had become aware, through the promptings of that subtle supplementary sense which hunters and hunted develop, that he was not alone and that his movements were being watched. There, too, looking up sharply in the direction from which the warning vibrations came, he had picked out a group of Kaffir women in mission clothes standing motionless in the bush with baskets balanced on their leather caps. And he did not like it: when Kaffir women appeared so far from their frontier it meant, as a rule, that messages were being carried and that trouble was brewing. What with vagrant Hottentots and Bastards and liberated slaves, the country through all his journey had swarmed with black mischief. As soon as the other wagon was through, he would ask to see their passes.

other, high as the roof, rose a moulded hillock which resembled the dump of refuse dug from a mine, but was, in fact, composed of dry dung collected from the cattle-kraal and was an index, if more were needed, of its owner's prosperity.

At the foot of the garden Jan Bothma off-saddled his horse, knee-haltering it and allowing it to stumble away in search of grazing. Then he unfastened the leather thong that secured the wicker gate and moved, with ponderous steps, between the clipped hedges of pomegranate to the stoep. From the dim interior of the *voorhuis* there came to his ears a monotonous murmur which told him that this was the hour of evening prayer. His uncle was reading a portion of Scripture. Jan Bothma took off his hat and stood with bowed head while the murmur ran on and on, no more than a word here and there distinguishable. But Jan Bothma had no need to listen. With a single phrase as a clue he could have continued the recitation; for the text of the Bible was in all such men's memories and its words on their tongues.

It was a savage portion that Adrian read that evening: the story of the civil war against Benjamin in the Book of Judges and the slaughter of Gibeah: how the men of Israel inclosed the Benjamites round about and chased them and trod them down with ease over against Gibeah toward the sunrising, and gleaned of them in the highways five thousand men, and pursued hard after them unto Girdom and slew two thousand men of them, so that all which fell that day of Benjamin were twenty and five thousand men that drew the sword, and all these were men of valour. When the numbers of the slaughtered rolled off his tongue, the voice of Adrian Prinsloo rose in a savage ecstasy, for the cause of that war, as he knew, was the unforgivable betrayal of a guest, and the bloody vengeance just.

CHAPTER TWO

DUTCH INTERIOR

JAN listened until the roll of the last word died away; he heard the familiar flap as his uncle closed the great brass-bound Bible and clasped it. Then he stepped to the doorway, his huge bulk filling it, the sun's last rays casting his shadow across the floor of ant-heap darkened with bullocks' blood. The interior of the *voorhuis* lay dim in the failing light. It was a large room, nearly thirty feet square and twelve feet high, rudely furnished with a single table, straight-backed chairs seated with thongs, and painted wagon-chests, all stained glossy black by perpetual fumes of wood-smoke that spread from a deep-set hearth on which an iron cauldron now bubbled. Overhead, within reach of a tall man's arm, ran rafters of rough-hewn yellow-wood, sustaining the shelf-like floor of a rudimentary attic in which soap and candles and ropes of tobacco were stored; and from the beams themselves hung *sjamboks* of rhinoceros-hide, pelts of lion and leopard, blown ostrich-eggs and feathers, spare leather reims and whip-stocks and calabashes, long strings of dried fruit and fringes of Indian corn-cobs.

At the head of the table, the closed Bible before

him, sat Adrian Prinsloo. He was a massive man of sixty. In his youth he must have been as tall as his nephew, but now he drooped, as though the weight of his limbs had become a burden. A white beard straggled over the table in front of him and his face, though deeply scored by premature age, had, apart from the grossly-modelled nose, a greater distinction than Jan's. There were remnants of power and ruthlessness in the line of the rigid mouth, the high cheekbones, the noble forehead, the craggy orbits within which his deep-set eyes of steel-blue appeared shrewd and fearless, yet oddly old. At his right hand sat his wife, Jacoba, a woman of fifty. It is possible that in the days when her husband had courted her Jacoba Celliers had been slim and beautiful. Even now, discounting the ungainly deposits of fat which made her figure, slumped on the rest-bench, shapeless, her face had a saddened, placid sweetness. Her mouth was serene with the smile of a primitive Demeter, and still her voice was soft and melodious as that of a young girl, betraying, in tones of a surprising refinement, an origin more gentle than her husband's, a warmer, more generous blood—the blood, in fact, of her Huguenot ancestors at French Hoek, infused and modified by a ruder northern strain, yet still unsubdued.

That strain, submerged and well-nigh lost in his mother, declared itself obstinately in her second surviving son, Barend: a tall boy of twenty, dark-haired and sanguine-complexioned, with clear-cut, proud, mobile lips and eyes like a falcon's of smouldering amber, who sat by her side. His body had neither his mother's benignant placidity nor his father's ponderable force: it was graceful, yet tense and resilient as a bent blade of steel—and perhaps as hard. There was swiftness and courage in it as well as strength.

The French blood showed itself again in his elder sister, Lisbet, who with the younger, Anna, sat facing him. She was a slim, vivid girl, a couple of years younger than Barend, with the same Latin regularity and refinement of feature, the same air of tension in repose, of swiftness in movement. Her skin, like Barend's, was dark, but more finely-textured: not reddened, as his, by sun, but rather warmed from within by the translucence of lively blood that glowed beneath it, and delicately dusted with its own bloom like a ripe fruit. It was this delicacy of surface softening the fugitive colour that made Lisbet's hair, smoothly parted in the middle and drawn back about her small head, and her eyebrows, too bold for beauty and tapered like a swift's wing, seem blacker than Barend's. Her eyes, too, were gentler than his and did not smoulder, hidden hues of olive cooling the amber to hazel.

Though more slightly made, Lisbet seemed in every way more nervously potent, even more alive than her sister. Anna Prinsloo looked much as her mother must have looked at the time of her marriage: solidly built, yet not without grace; slow-moving, yet sure of purpose; long-limbed, yet sturdy. If she lacked Lisbet's immediate nervous energy, she had reserves of endurance and the phlegmatic composure of the blond north. In contrast with her sister's raven darkness her skin and the thin-spun gold of her hair seemed dazzlingly fair. Her eyes, like her father's, were steely-blue, contradicting the superficial impression of softness derived from features less definite than Lisbet's, moulded rather than chiselled. Anna's face was still that of a child, but of an obstinate child; its placidness had an intense and brooding quality. That innocent mouth, those cold eyes, were capable of passion, less fiery, less generous perhaps, than her sister's, but more sustained. Nor was she less sensitive than Lisbet in her seeming quietude. It was she, indeed, who when Bothma's shadow darkened the doorway, became first aware of it. A wave of quick colour mounted from her white neck to her hair. "It's Jan," she cried. "Cousin Jan!"

Jan Bothma stooped to enter the *voorhuis*. The height of the lintel had not been planned for men of his mould.

"Good evening, uncle, how goes it? Good evening, aunt . . . good evening, cousins," he said. He lumbered forward, shaking hands with the old man and Barend and kissing the three women in turn on the cheek. When he kissed Lisbet, his heavy face flushed in the dark and the hands that touched her trembled.

Mevrouw Prinsloo's eyes watched him though her body did not turn.

"Quick, Hendrik," she said gently, in her calm melodious voice. "Quick, what are you thinking of? Call Ayah to wash your cousin's feet!"

"What, Hendrik?" Bothma exclaimed, "too grand to shake hands with me?"

A boy of ten, the youngest of the family, rose from the shadows in which he had been sitting unseen. He touched Bothma's hand with a surly formality. He was an odd, secret lad, too old for his years. He admired his cousin and envied his strength, but disliked him, for Jan could not resist teasing the child for his solemnity with the roughness of an overgrown puppy that plays with a kitten and teases it till it spits. Hendrik escaped from Jan's bearish clutches and ran to the screen to call Ayah, and a moment later, the old woman staggered in with the foot-washing tub. She was a Madagascan slave who had nursed the whole Prinsloo family one after another: an ancient crone with lashless, wicked eyes and pendulous breasts like bags of wrinkled leather. With hands like claws she unfastened the thongs of Jan's veld-shoes and bathed his hot feet. Lisbet watched with lowered eyes, the ghost of a smile on her lips.

"A sup of peach-brandy, Jan?" his aunt suggested.

"Give him food," her husband grunted. "I'll wager he's famished."

Jan laughed: "Not a bite have I had since noon but

a chew of biltong, uncle; but more than a bellyful of dust. This wind is a devil," he said.

Anna rose quickly and moved to the tripod pot and ladled him out a platter of victuals. It was the standard frontier dish: a stew of ragged mutton highly peppered and swimming in sheep's-tail fat. Jan took it from her without thanks. He put his hand to his forehead and murmured a blessing; then began to eat greedily, smacking his thick lips. The grease glistened on his chin.

"Now, what news?" said his uncle, lighting his pipe and filling the room with puffs of yellow smoke.

Jan Bothma spoke with his mouth full: "The drift was up to my chin. They must have had rain on the Berg. If my eyes hadn't been sore to see you—" he glanced shyly at Lisbet "—I should have outspanned for the night and slept on the other side." He told how the oxen had swerved at the drift and the wagon tilted; how he had plunged in water up to his eyes, and lifted Blauwberg's horns and dragged the span through by main force. His boasting excited him to lyrical exaggerations. While his uncle listened sceptically, puffing at his pipe, the water grew deeper, the current stronger, his own feat of strength more remarkable. "That ox has a neck like a buffalo bull," Jan declared. "It was like lifting half a ton. And a lion's shoulders! I tell you, never in my life . . ."

He stopped suddenly. His flushed face went blank and fell. He slewed round angrily. In the dusk he had heard a laugh, a low, woman's laugh. Anna nudged her sister impatiently; but when Jan turned round, Lisbet's face was demure and attentive, her eyes met his angry eyes without a quiver. Yet he knew it was she who had laughed and humbled him. He thought of David bringing the Ark of the Covenant out of the house of Abinadab at Gibeah, and of Michal, his wife, looking down through a window and despising him in her heart. At that moment he would have hated Lisbet, had he not loved her.

"Why do you stop, cousin Jan?" she asked meekly.

But the magnificent story was broken. He could not go on.

"There is no more to tell," he said gruffly. "I am here, and the wagons will follow."

"And it is good to see you, nephew," his aunt purred comfortingly.

"But what news?" Adrian Prinsloo repeated. "How goes it at the Cape?"

"My mamma is well; but the old *baas* grows feeble." He tapped his head. "And all things go badly . . . badly. From bad to worse. To see the fruit and the wine-farms would break your heart. All falling to rack and ruin: water-furrows clogged or broken and the land going dirty everywhere for want of labour. As soon as the slaves are freed and are called apprentices, they grow wild."

"Now that," his aunt said, "I do not understand. Here our slaves are part of the family. When I told our Ayah and her husband they were free they threw themselves down and cried at my knees, begging not to be sent away."

"Ah, the slaves at the Cape are different. They have sharp ears; they know the English are against us, and the missionaries get at them. They can go where they will. They sit on the banks of the furrows and smoke *dakka* and joke when they see the harvest unreaped and grapes rotting on the vine. Try to tempt them to work for wages, and they only laugh at you. They have tasted idleness; nothing short of starving will make them work. And why should they starve, when they can wander about in bands and steal all they want, while the missionaries encourage them and the English look on and protect them? And where can the farmer find money to pay them in any case?"

"There is the Government compensation. That, surely, will be paid," Adrian said.

"That fine compensation! I can tell you more about that. That's the dirtiest joke the English ever played on us. Go back to the beginning. Who brought ship-loads of slaves to the Cape and made fortunes out of them? The English. What next? The missionaries are getting to work. Their God will not allow slavery."

"Then their God is not ours," said Adrian sternly. "Is it not written: 'Cursed be Canaan: a slave of slaves shall he be unto his brethren'? Did not the children of Israel have slaves?"

Jan laughed. "In the Englishmen's Bible they are

careful to call them 'servants'; and the English can always become religious when it suits them. 'What?' they say, 'do you mean to tell us these damned Dutchmen actually keep slaves? Under our beautiful English flag, where all men are free and equal? We must look into this. But don't be afraid,' they say: 'an Englishman's word is his bond. We only act in the sacred name of Humanity!' That's the way they talk. 'Just put down your claims on paper,' they say, 'and everyone shall be satisfied.' So the claims go in. Three million English pounds' worth. It is not so bad to screw eighty-five pounds a head out of a Government that robs folk whenever it can, even though you may have paid the best part of a hundred for each of them. Then, just about the end of the year, the award comes from England. That three million pounds has shrunk on the voyage to twelve hundred thousand. The slave you have paid the English a hundred pounds for is worth thirty-three. A sacrifice in the sacred name of Humanity. Humanity? A sacrifice in the name of barefaced fraud and robbery!"

Adrian Prinsloo shook his head. "That is bad news indeed for those who have many slaves. A loss . . . a big loss."

Jan Bothma rose and spat in the plated spit-box. "Ah, but wait!" he laughed bitterly. "The best of an Englishman's joke is in the tail, like a scorpion's sting. You know what these Cape Boers are, packed so close together that every man of them can see his neighbour's smoke and they've almost forgotten how to stand on their own feet. 'Well,' they say to themselves, 'thirty pounds is better than nothing, and money is money.' So down they go to the Castle with their drafts in their pockets expecting to be paid. The clerks look at them as if they were dirt. 'If you'd taken the trouble to read what's written,' they tell them, 'you'ld have seen that these drafts can only be cashed in London. We've nothing to do with them here!' Well, what can the Boer do? Must he charter a ship and then wait another six months for his money? There are men, I tell you, who have torn up their drafts in a rage. But others, who have more sense, take them round to an English merchant and beg him the favour of cashing them, which he does, out of the kindness of his heart, at a discount of twenty per cent and in paper-money that is worth no more than half what it ought to be. And now, if you get twenty pounds for your hundred-pound slave, you're a lucky man."

"It is not just," Adrian Prinsloo said. "No, that is not just."

"It is what the English call justice; and as long as the English government stays and rules us it is all we shall get. If our cousins at the Cape had any spunk in them, they'ld have raised a commando and marched on the treasury and taken all they wanted."

"No, no, nephew. That will not do. Rebellion is useless. Remember Slachter's Nek."

"Shall I ever forget that butchery? Will our grand-

G

children ever forget it? Didn't the English hang my own cousin Stephanus, ay, and hanged him a second time when their rotten rope broke? I tell you, these English . . ."

Lisbet's voice interrupted him. It was melodious and light like her mother's.

"It was Colonel Cuyler who hanged them, cousin," she said. "He was Dutch, not English. And every one of the judges who sat and condemned them was as Dutch as yourself, and you know it." Anna clapped a hand on her mouth. "Let me be! Why shouldn't I speak? Let him tell the truth!"

Jan Bothma threw up his hands in despair, his face red, distorted with rage. "That is what you *would* say!" he cried. "You, your father's daughter, my cousin. Just because you have been to school at the Cape and hob-nobbed with these government toadies and cheese-faced Hollanders, your Cloetes, your Truters, and danced at the Castle and flirted with English monkeys in uniform, and gone gadding off to the races on Green Point common in an eight-horse coach—why, you're no better than English yourself. You put us to shame! Why don't you go back to them?"

Adrian Prinsloo brought down his fist on the table with a thump. "Peace, peace, children," he said. "Why must you two always be bickering?"

Lisbet sat with her soft lips tightened. There were tears in her eyes; she breathed quickly; her cheeks glowed crimson. Jan turned his back on her, glowering over the ashes.

"You are both right, and you are both wrong," Andrian Prinsloo continued judicially. "The judges and Cuyler were Dutch, but the power behind them all and the hand that wrote the sentence was English. It is a tragedy of twenty years ago, and better forgotten." (Barend clenched his fists and shook his head: his lips silently shaped the word "Never!") "The trouble with our people has always been the same. We do not change much. I suppose we are a turbulent people by nature."

"A strong-spirited, independent people, father," Barend protested.

"A people that likes to go its own way, my son. In the Dutch Company's days, before you were born, many farmers banded together and fought the Government."

"There was no Slachter's Nek," Barend muttered.

"That Government was not strong enough. That was the reason. But government there must be. So Stephanus Bothma said at the foot of the gallows. I was there, and I heard him. Dying lips speak wisdom. 'Do not resist the Government,' he said, 'even though it be one of foreigners. Obey the law of the English while you live in their land.'"

"In *our* land," Barend whispered. "We were here for a hundred years before they ever set foot on it."

"That is true. And the Bushmen and Hottentots and Kaffirs were here before us, my son, and others may come after the English, if God so wills it. But my word is Stephanus Bothma's: obey them while you live under them."

Jan turned from the hearth. His quick blaze of anger was spent, his face sullen but calm. He picked up the last word.

"While you live under them, yes," he said. "But why should we live under a law we detest? Is not Africa wide enough? Do the English rule the whole world, then? That is how men are muttering on the *stoep* of every farm I've off-saddled at between here and Capetown. A man can have any farm he wants in exchange for a span of good oxen. In the Winterberg they don't even trouble to sell: they strip the houses and stow what they can in their wagons and abandon the land for any who like to take it. Who can blame them for trekking, with the English treading on their heels and the Kaffirs burning their toes, the English stealing their slaves and the Kaffirs their cattle?"

Adrian shook his head obstinately. "I say that a man who abandons land he has paid for and a house he has built is an improvident, hot-headed fool. No man of age and judgment would play such tricks with his property."

"Yet, father," Barend broke in eagerly, "old Jacobus Uys is not young or foolish, and he is trekking."

"And Pieter Retief of the Winterberg," Bothma persisted, "is a solid man."

Adrian laughed. "Retief, solid? You don't know what you're saying. I know the man well. A bankrupt. He cleared out of Grahamstown more than ten years ago and left debts."

"A man may have ill-fortune."

"Men should pay what they owe."

"Well, then: Gerrit Maritz of Graaf Reinet. Isn't he solid enough?"

"You mean rich enough, nephew, and slim enough. I know that man too. No doubt Maritz would try to persuade every Boer in the district to trek. He knows what he's doing. The man is a wagon-maker. I say once again: let young men without ties do whatever they will. If they pay for their folly, it's their concern, not ours. But it is no light thing for a man of my years who has built a house and planted a garden and begotten children and buried them at his door, to be torn up by the roots and transplanted God knows where just because his neighbours grow restless . . ."

"And harder still for his wife, nephew," Jacoba said. "A woman's home is more dear to her than a man's."

"Yet, auntie, wherever I go," Jan Bothma persisted, "it is the women, I hear, who are more eager to trek than the men. And why so? The answer is easy. Women's memories are longer than men's. They remember what happened two years ago: four hundred and fifty farms burnt to the ground and more than three hundred gutted. They are afraid of the Kaffirs swarming over us again; and I say they are right, uncle."

"Pray Heaven they are wrong," Vrouw Prinsloo wagged her head and shuddered.

"Never fear, ma!" Her husband patted her fat arm. "Never fear. The worst of them, Hintza, is dead, and the Kaffirs have learnt their lesson."

"Ah, the war was a good war to start with," Bothma agreed. "At least it taught them something. But it did not give us back what the devils had stolen. There are still thousands of our horses and hundreds of thousands of our cattle and sheep in their kraals; and whatever good our commandos did the English have undone. What can one say of this Government that calls us wild beasts and tells the chiefs that the Kaffirs were justified and gives them back the land they stole and lets them keep our cattle? The Kaffirs are no fools, uncle, and one thing that war has taught them: they know now that the Government is against us and ties our hands behind our backs and will leave them next time to do what they like with us."

Prinsloo shook his head slowly. "Your ears are too big, Jan. They mop up alarms like a sponge. The frontier is quieter to-day than I've ever known it."

"Then why does old Jacobus Uys leave Olitant's Hoek? Why are the English in Albany putting their farms up to auction? Why is the whole of the Winter-

berg, the whole of the Zwartruggens, trekking? There
is no smoke without fire, uncle. You sleep here at
Welgelegen. One day is the same as the next and the
one before it. For months at a time you have no speech
with any living soul but yourselves. But some day,
suddenly, you will wake up and discover that, while
you were sleeping, your neighbours have stolen away
like an elephant herd in the night. You will ride to
the north and the south and find the land empty, and
Welgelegen will lie well enough then—alone on the
open veld with all Kaffirland swarming in front of it,
and yourself like an aged wildebeeste bull driven out
of the herd and left for the lions to feed on."

"Enough, enough of this talk, nephew," the old
man said irritably. "What can you know of these
things? You have been away three months on trek
and stuffing your head with wild rumours. It is always
the same. Folk who live at a distance know more about
Kaffirland than we do. I have eyes and ears, and I tell
you, the frontier is quiet."

"The frontier, perhaps," Jan Bothma persisted.
"But what is happening behind it? Who can tell when
a veld-fire has started three hundred miles away? Yet
before you can see or smell the smoke of it, you know
that the grass is on fire from the game that is stampeding in front of it. That is what happens each winter
in Kaffirland. First, the young men of the Amazulu
need blood to bathe their spears. They make war and
eat up the Kaffir tribes beyond the Kei River; and

they, in their flight, must swarm on the lands of the Ndhlambi and drive them out, and the Ndhlambi, flying, must fall on the Fingoes and drive the Fingoes on us. Wave on wave! And who will protect us with our neighbours gone? The English?"

The old man was silent. Bothma pressed his advantage:

"Wild rumours I may have heard as I trekked; but I have eyes as well as ears. Again and again I saw parties of Kaffir women coming and going: there was one at the drift this evening. They have passes the missionaries give them. They say they go to the mission-stations to see their friends. I know better than that. I have seen the same thing before. They are carrying messages. When trouble is brewing there are always these women on the road. A bad sign . . ."

Adrian Prinsloo sighed. "It is dark," he said. "Light the candle."

Lisbet rose. Stooping low at the hearth she blew on the embers and kindled a straw with which she lit a thick sheep's-tallow dip. She set it on the middle of the table, where the flaring wick illumined the faces of those who sat round with an unflattering light: her mother's, sweet and unhappy; Barend's, flushed with eagerness; her father's, lined and haggard and anxious and terribly old. It was clear that, for all his obstinacy, Jan's dark warnings had shaken him.

"That is better," he said. "When Sarel comes home from the fort to-morrow, you shall tell him your stories, nephew. His thoughts are rather like yours. He is the head of the house in these days. I grow tired and old. Sarel has gone to the kraal at the fort to pick out some cattle of ours that were stolen a month ago."

Bothma laughed triumphantly. "Ah, so it seems that cattle still vanish on this quiet frontier?" he was beginning to say when a glance of fierce appeal from Lisbet's eyes checked him. "Good, uncle," he said, "I will talk with Sarel to-morrow. I am glad he thinks as I do. There is something that must be decided, and soon. My thought is that there is no time to waste."

Anna's voice spoke quickly: "I hear them . . . the wagons."

"At last! I was getting anxious." Bothma moved towards the door. Now the sounds of arrival grew nearer: shrill inarticulate cries and a cracking of whips like pistol-shots. There was a swift patter of steps up the path. On the *stoep* there appeared the dust-reddened figure of Klaas the Hottentot, his eyes blinking at the light, his yellow triangular face transformed by excitement. He spoke rapidly in imperfect Dutch, excusing himself for the delay. Bothma listened, frowning.

"What? Two of them? Where did you find them? What were they doing?"

"In the road, *baas*. They heard the wagons. They were so faint that they could go no farther. We helped them into the wagons. Now they can walk."

G*

Bothma turned round with a laugh. "Do you hear that?" he said. "Two damned English! Even here we cannot be rid of them!"

Two bedraggled figures in grey climbed the steps of the *stoep* laboriously. The taller clutched at the post, breathing heavily. The shorter swung himself up with difficulty: he had a wooden leg. Bothma stared at both of them sourly. There was an unfriendly silence until the old man at the table spoke.

"*Dag!*" he grunted. "*Kom binnen.* Come in, strangers, whoever you be. Come in and be seated."

The taller man staggered forward. He put out a groping hand to steady himself, and pitched forward, full-length, with a thud on the ant-heap floor. Lisbet ran to his side with a cry.

"Brandy, brandy . . . quick, Anna! Quick . . . what are you doing? He may die!"

Anna Prinsloo moved slowly, reluctantly. She was watching Jan Bothma's sour face.

CHAPTER THREE

STRANGE AWAKENING

JOHN OAKLEY, gradually emerging from profound
nescience into that borderland in which dream and
reality mingle and are confused, stirred feebly, winced
and lay still. He did not wonder where he was or what
had happened to him; he did not care. The first effort
to reclaim himself, to lay hold on thought and control
it, was so painful and so futile that he was glad to
abandon it. His thoughts were huge, vague and
shadowy, rising slowly, turning, sinking, lost past
recovery in unfathomable depths. He had seen such
vague shapes before, looking over the *Minerva's* gun-
wale. He had watched them swirling and butting at
narrow oblongs of sailcloth that went down and down
unvexed by their molestation. His mind was as heed-
less now as those sailcloth bundles. The monstrous,
swirling thoughts pursued it in vain. It sank down
and down, untroubled, insensate, through green
glooms into absolute darkness. And darkness was most
welcome of all.

It was always a watery darkness. Even in those
kindly depths he felt the wash of the sea. A soundless
swell still lifted his body and rocked it. Though the

surface on which he lay seemed cold and solid, oddly
different, somehow, in substance from the wooden
deck, he supposed he was still aboard the *Minerva*,
convinced and yet puzzled—for in that case the
medley of impressions, so vivid and yet so strange,
which troubled his clouded consciousness in sudden
flashes of revelation and faded as swiftly, must surely
be the figments of a disordered brain. He remembered
with fear poor Job Radway's disjointed ravings, and
wondered, in one astonishing moment of clarity, if he
were sick of the plague. Perhaps he was dying; perhaps
this confusion was death. But a dead man, he told
himself, could not move and feel pain as he did. No
dead man could be aware of a temple swollen like an
egg, of a blood-caked wound, of a skull that seemed
ready to split. No dead man could move his tongue
or lick his cracked lips and taste in his throat the burning bitterness of brandy. The problem was too hard, too
painful to be solved. It was better to relax, to abandon
this useless effort of thinking; better still to sleep.

Yet how could one sleep with an iron wedge splitting the skull and so many restless noises vibrating in
the ears: the noise of that devilish wind that was never
silent, the torment of human voices that would not be
still? What was the meaning of this ceaseless chatter,
this strange speech from which, now and then, familiar
groups of syllables detached themselves to be lost, no
sooner than the mind grasped them, in unintelligible
babble? Many voices there were, subdued or excitedly

competing. Some were voices of men: one harsh and, as it seemed, violent; another calm, reassuring. Voices of women, too: and one of these, for all the unknown words it uttered, had a honeyed sweetness, a light melodiousness that did not wound the bruised brain like the rest, but rather soothed it. If that voice and no other would speak, John felt, he might sleep.

But not only sounds kept him awake. There was a brutal light that constantly flared and flickered and made his eyes wince beneath their closed lids—unless, indeed, its flickers were not external but part of the lightning-play that throbbed and broke into jagged flashes inside his head with each new pulsation of pain. It was an effort even to distinguish one from the other and far better not to try, though there were moments when the light and the voices became so intolerable that if his tongue had not been swollen and sticking in his parched mouth he would have forced himself to cry out and bid them be quiet and have pity on him and take the light away. But even these gusts of unspoken anger fatigued him. By slow degrees the contest of voices grew faint. He heard movements and whispers. A shadowy form bent over him; and he was aware that this presence, whatever it might be, was benevolent, that the unseen eyes that scrutinized him were kindly. And, suddenly, the light which had tortured his shut eyes wavered, grew distant, went out. The world was dark and silent. He sighed and fell asleep.

When he woke, the pain in his head had gone: his

mind was no longer confused but cool and clear, every sense at once exploring the astonishing circumstances in which he found himself. Though still, when he closed his eyes, he felt the motion of the ship, he was certainly no longer at sea, but lying full-length on a smooth floor of pounded earth beneath a high-raftered roof festooned with things shaped like gigantic cobwebs. Some person unknown had pushed a saddlebag under his head and drawn over his body a rug of skins, long-haired and stiff to the fingers and charged with an unfamiliar smell which vaguely suggested that of a fox. On his left, a faint glow revealed the presence of a fire, not of wood or coal but of some smouldering peaty substance which, when the wind swept down the chimney and fanned it, as it did from time to time in gusts that shook the whole building like a rat in a terrier's teeth, blew out puffs of acrid smoke that made him catch his breath. In spite of the rug and the fire his limbs were stiff with cold; the chill of the earth drew up into his bones; he had not felt so perished since the days when his seasick body was rolled out of the Bay of Biscay. It was not only the odour of the rug or the smoke that puzzled him; the whole atmosphere of the place was permeated by foreign scents: a reek of tallow and strangely aromatic tobacco-smoke commingled with a hot smell of fleeces which made him wonder if he had found his way into a shearing-shed.

But how had he come there at all? The process of

memory was more painful than that of perception. He feared to force it; and yet, by slow degrees, as he lay there putting a brake on his too-active mind, there emerged, with an odd effect of unreality, a series of disconnected sensations and visions: the remains of what his mind's surface had rejected and retained during the last twenty hours, whose shape and continuity had been broken and jumbled, like fragments of a shattered mirror, by the violent blow which had finally knocked him senseless.

A great wind was blowing: the same wind as that which now howled down the chimney and shook the house. It sucked the breath out of his body. He would have called on Dicketts to stop, if only for a moment, but could not, for lack of it. Every standing grey-green bush, every wiry trailer, was spined or clawed or bristling with clumps of spears. They caught at him as he passed, tore his clothes to ribbons, drove their spines like red-hot needles into his flesh. The soil itself was sprinkled with crystals that cut like splintered glass and blistered his feet with heat. There was no end to this wilderness of thickets through which he scrambled. Its awful, eternal sameness made him feel as though his dwindling strength were wasted, as though the wind-swept bush were keeping pace with him as he ran. And that sense of continual frustration turned in a while to fear—panic fear of this growth that was always the same and would not let him escape unless he ran on and on . . .

The wind dropped of a sudden, or rather vexed them no more, rushing overhead with a malignant swish as the clouds of sand and spray swept inland. They had come, as the sun began to decline, to the dip of a valley which that demon took in its stride, a sandy slope scattered with tufts of bleached grass and dark green clumps of the plant whose fleshy leaves were broad-bladed spears lifting, here and there, a spire of blood-red blossom. There were other growths of shape unimaginable: tall angular trunks sheathed in what looked like a warty hide rather than bark, which broke overhead into clusters of leafless, stiff candelabra, like the arms of dead men, desiccated, and stretched upward in vain appeal to the pitiless sky.

At the foot of the slope loose sand checked Dicketts' headlong pace. John caught up with him as he pitched forward and fell at the edge of a belt of grasses taller than a man whose stiff stems, bent to the draught of the wind overhead, made a rustling sound that suddenly aroused in John Oakley a passionate lust for water: a desire not so much of the mind (for by this time the process of logical thought was suspended) as of the whole body in which every drained cell demanded the refreshment of moisture; a yearning not of cracked lips and dust-parched throat but of the hidden tissues; an inward urgency, more potent than conscious will.

Constrained by this he found himself crawling forward past the prostrate body of Dicketts, who lay on his face with no sign of life save the pumping of his brawny chest, towards the grasses from whose watery rustling the stimulus came. He thrust his body through them; then shrank back, gasping with fear at the thud of stampeding hooves as a herd of startled buffalo thundered past with lowered heads and lashing tails. The plunging black bodies hurtled by in a cloud of dust and vanished. John Oakley crawled on, his heart pounding and fluttering. It flashed through his mind that perhaps the beasts had been drinking; and this frantic hope was encouraged, for here the sand was smooth and firm and, a little farther on, moulded in sharp-cut runnels where surely water had flowed. But no water flowed or lay in the runnels now. The spruit was dry; the sand, caked with moisture, had set, its glistening surface scorched his hands as they touched it.

With this new frustration an animal frenzy seized him. In a burst of unaccountable fury he found himself scrabbling with his nails at the sand. His hands were tearing into it and scratching and scooping and throwing it backward with the eagerness of a dog that tears at a rabbit-hole. The caked sand spattered behind him in a continuous stream till at length his bleeding finger-tips felt the sand they scooped growing cooler. It was darker too, and the grains, cohering with moisture, stuck to the skin. He was breathing hard and laughing hoarsely to himself; and now from the bottom of his pit he scooped muddy water which he lapped, sand and all, as fast as the tiny well filled. He smeared the muddy stuff too on his burning eyelids, his neck, his hair. It was as though not merely his gullet but the whole surface of his skin craved moisture. When he had finished this orgy he rose and staggered back through the belt of grass, on legs that no longer seemed to belong to him, to the place where Dicketts still lay. His tongue shaped the word "water," but the noise he made was grotesque. "Over there," he said, "through the grass. I've found water." Dicketts sat up and blinked. They reeled through the grass side by side like two drunken men. The little well had filled up. The sand had settled; the water was milkily turbid. Dicketts drank his fill, and then John drank again. They looked at each other's dabbled faces and laughed.

"I was well-nigh finished, lad," Dicketts confessed. " 'Twas the want of use in the limbs. Not having stirred a leg, as you might say, for three months and then running ten miles. I reckon that's what we've covered, to judge by the sun. Well, we'd best be moving on."

John shook his head. "No more running for me just yet. Where d'you reckon we're going, George?"

"God knows. Away from the sea. If we go on long enough we be sure to get somewhere or other. All right, lad. Half an hour of easy, as we used to say when they marched us off our feet in Flanders."

They were lying side by side between the grey

bushes. Though the sun had now passed the zenith and slipped down the sky with the trajectory of a white-hot ball whose flight is spent, the heat of that windless kloof was almost unbearable. The baked earth released the reserves it had gathered all day. In intervals between the buffets of wind that still hurled the sand above them, it seemed to John Oakley as though the earth audibly simmered and hissed like a frying-pan; the dry bush was thrilled by sudden spits and fizzles above the perpetual singing note of unseen cicalas. The air was dense with aromatic wafts: those minty, pungent odours, exhaled on the motionless air like hot gusts from some savage beast's throat, which had struck his nostrils when first he set foot on African soil; and over the glaring earth that he idly watched through half-closed eyes (the light seemed less cruel now) he saw a thin moving streak of black which he took for some trick of his sun-dazzled sight, but which resolved itself at last into an endless procession of gigantic black ants, far larger than any he had seen in his life, with long legs and questing eyes and savage mandibles. As they neared they seemed to be making straight for him. He jumped hurriedly to his feet, recalling some vaguely-remembered missionary tale of armies of ants that would strip a man's flesh from his bones; but the ribbon of black swerved suddenly to avoid one of the clusters of red-spired spears, and trailed on with dreadful intentness; and when they had passed there was yet another foul waft on the air, which made Dicketts, who had lain sleeping like a tired dog, sit up and sniff.

"My God, lad," he cried. "The wind must have changed. That's a smell I know. I smelt it at Quarter Brass when the battle was over. There's a dead horse stinking somewhere hereabouts, you take my word for it. And dead horses signifies live men in the neighbourhood. Come on, let's be moving afore it falls dark and the lions get after us. There be plenty of them ugly varmints in these parts from what I've a'heard."

They crossed the spruit, and again the bush unrolled its uniform desolation. But now that the sun declined the waste grew golden: a new liveliness sharpened the air and quickened their waning strength. The white sun deepened to apricot. All around them that which had seemed dead came to life. The noonday din of the cicalas grew faint. In a sweet and temperate silence they heard the songs of wakened birds, subdued chuckles and whimpers and flutings and bold, clear whistles. Clouds of insects powdered the air with a dust of gold; each gauzy wing made a quivering flake of light, and among these floating myriads strange birds made havoc. They were more richly coloured than any John had known, some had golden bodies barred with black and some were scarlet, and one small bird which haunted the reedy spruits was like a green flame. It was not only the evening light and the cooler air that made the bush seem more friendly. All this part of the waste was richly nourished with water draining underground to a swamp and so to the river. The spruits were fringed with taller trees that were leafy and living, and some of them actually held pools of stagnant water. It was cheering to feel that here, at least, a man need not die of thirst.

"We be getting on fine," Dicketts said.

That was all very well, John agreed, but what were they getting on to?

"Well, surely to goodness, lad, this bloody old wood can't go on for ever," Dicketts answered, "and we're better out of it. Sooner or later we be certain to come to a turnpike, and once you set foot on the high-road all you need do is to follow it. There's no road that ever I heard on that didn't lead somewhere."

They tramped on in silence. The apricot sun sank faster and faster. Soon the sinking disc turned blood-red, and the golden bush grew tawny-red like the soil. It set; the sky dimmed and darkened so quickly that within a few moments they could no longer see where they went or avoid the thorns that lay in wait for them; and by this time every cautious step was an agony of effort.

"It's no good, George," John Oakley said. "I'm just about done."

Dicketts halted reluctantly. He still reckoned they couldn't be far from that there road. "How so be, if we bide here a bit," he said, "the moon'll come up, and then we can move on again."

But no moon rose. The night fell pitchy black without even a glimmer of starlight; so dark that they could not even see each other's faces.

"Well, there's nought to be done but stay where we be," Dicketts said. "This has properly done us. If we're here for the night, as it seems, I wish I'd thought to take a good drink at that puddle we passed just now. Let's turn back a bit and find it."

John followed him wearily. When once they had stopped walking it was as much as he could do to move his stiff legs. He could not compete with the maimed man's untiring strength; and their quest was fruitless in any case, since, stumbling in the dark, his guide soon lost all sense of direction.

"If I could see one bloody star," he grumbled, "I could steer by the beggar."

John was thankful there were no stars to steer by. "Give it up, George, for God's sake," he pleaded.

They lay down on the banks of a dried-up spruit mercifully free from thorns. John's limbs were no sooner stretched than he fell asleep from exhaustion. It was chill that woke him. The earth, which a few hours before had scorched his body, now radiated an icy cold; and the air, though still tepid, had condensed to a dew that drenched his torn garments. He huddled closer to George Dicketts, who still slept soundly, in search of warmth, and lay listening to the sounds of night. The bush was far noisier now than it had been in the heat of day. A louder cicala fizzed and crackled in the trees; the frogs in the stagnant puddles of the spruits and the more distant swamps gave forth a shrill ringing note as of toneless bells or chattering castanets; and above this perpetual din which he could not understand but came to accept, so constant it was, as the African equivalent of nocturnal silence, he distinguished sounds that startled because they were sudden and mysterious. The whole bush was alive and rustling with stealthy movement, with sounds of stirred leaves, cracked branches and snapping twigs, with grunts, snorings, snorts and stampings. At times, as these sounds grew nearer, his strained ears distinguished the dull, regular impacts of a heavy tread, as though some vast monster moved past; and once, with a shudder, he heard a sniffing and felt what seemed like a puff of hot breath on his cheek. In the distant swamp a bird called all night with a monotonous wheezing note, and from time to time overhead he heard the swish and creak of invisible wings. There were other sounds: faint barks like the bark of a fox, that shrilled of a sudden to a bedlam chorus of wailing, and remote, dismal howls, and, suddenly, drowning these, a hollow roar that shook the air with vibrations and silenced the rest— so that, hearing it, it seemed, the bush went mute and checked its restless rustlings and held its breath, listening. And after that there was no other sound for a while but that of the frogs' ringing castanets which rose and fell as though a fitful breeze wafted it, though no breeze moved, till, once more, the hushed bush found courage, and the noises of snapping twigs and stirrings and stealthy footsteps began all over again.

This night was not kindly, as other nights John Oakley had known. It was full of mystery, restlessness, vague apprehensiveness. He envied George Dicketts for being able to sleep through it. Not even the gnats whose bites covered his face and arms with itching weals and blisters had power to wake the old soldier. But what, after all, was the profit of tiring one's mind with incalculable terrors? Whatever ill might befall him next, he was better off shivering there in the bush, a free man, than as a prisoner in the *Minerva's* stinking 'tween decks, bound for the calculable hell of Van Diemen's Land, for the toil of the chain-gang, the pain of the cat and the triangle. He huddled even closer to his comrade's comfortable warmth. The ringing note of the frogs' castanets grew fainter and fainter. By a miracle he slept.

George Dicketts wakened him. His broad, cheery face, burnt lobster-red with sun, was glistening with water.

"Here, what did I tell you?" he said. "I knew I was on the right road. There we are, the two of us, with mouths as dry as a bone, not three yards from this blessed water. Get you up and fill your belly, lad. You'll need it afore the end of this day by the look of it. That devil of a wind's still blowing."

John crawled to the puddle and drank. The sand on its verge was scarred with imprints of hooves and clawed pads of creatures that had supped it in the night. It was all very well for George to look so cheerful. His own stomach craved more than water—it was twenty-four hours since last he had tasted food—and his legs had so stiffened during the night that he could not move them an inch without pain.

"That'll soon work off when we get moving," George told him. "We may have a good step to go afore we strikes that there road."

They set off as the sun enlivened the bush with a paler fire. The trees that had burned with gold in the sunset were silver now. It was true that movement loosened his limbs a little; yet the first spurt of the energy which sleep had renewed exhausted it; what he lacked was neither will nor courage but mere strength. And no sooner were they afoot than the sun shot up and drank such life as was left in it out of his body. They trailed on and on, George Dicketts holding on yesterday's northward course, till John Oakley felt he could drag his steps no farther.

"I can't do no more, George," he said. "You'd best leave me here. Go on till you've struck that road of yours and then come back for me."

"Not likely, lad. If once I lost touch with you, I'ld never find you again. No, no. Howsomever it goes we must hang together. But I'm beggared if this bain't the most unaccountable queer country I've ever set foot in, although I've been in foreign parts before, mind. There be neither meadow nor plough to it. Not so much as field-track or bridle-path, let alone a turn-pike in thirty miles; not a sign of a rick or a barn or a cottage nor even a church-tower like what you'ld expect! Set you down and rest for a bit, and then we'll get going again."

And what next? It was from this point in his journey that John Oakley's memory failed him, that the fragments of his mind's shattered mirror became disconnected, refusing to fall into any order of time or place. Lying there on the hard ant-heap floor of Welgelegen with eyes closed and the reek of smoulder-ing kraal-manure in his nostrils, he could see himself sitting hopelessly in the sun with his swollen hands pressed to his eyes. After that he found memory neither of word nor of thought; nothing more to be grasped, indeed, than a nightmare of mere sensation: of a blinding light that bored into his eyes; of most cruel heat; of a thirst that not merely consumed his throat, but obsessed and tortured his mind; of fiery pains that lanced him with every stumbling step; of a mortal, numb weariness that would have welcomed death. Yet, somehow or other, it seemed that they must have struggled on in these confused agonies through the greater part of the day; for there came again that moment of relief and transfiguration that marked the hour of sunset. He could feel himself, momentarily, halting and raising his eyes to a gentler sky; he could feel cooler air in his throat; he could hear George Dicketts begging him to try once more, and to take a grip of his arm if he thought that would help. He could see himself shaking his head, and reeling and falling. And then, in a gleam of fuller illumination, he suddenly saw Dicketts starting away from him, hopping on through the bush like a maniac and shouting hoarsely as he went.

"He's seen water," John thought. "That's it: he must have seen water. There's nothing but water could make him go mad like that; but it's no use trying to follow him; I couldn't; I must wait till he comes." And then Dicketts was tugging at his shoulder, trying to rouse him and pull him on to his feet. There was another figure beside him: a small yellow man who danced in the dusk and made clicking sounds with his tongue. He supported John on one side and George on the other; they dragged him forward between them, though he would rather they had left him alone. And George Dicketts chuckled insanely as they walked.

"What did I tell you, lad?" he said in a thin, choked voice. "Didn't I say all along that if we kept on we should come to a road?"

CHAPTER FOUR

DARK ENCOUNTER

IN the sleeping-room on the opposite side of the *voorhuis*, in the vast trellised cartel bed with its feather-stuffed mattress which she shared with her sister Anna, Lisbet Prinsloo, too, lay awake. It was rare for her not to sleep soundly. In the flat, uneventful life of Welgelegen, she sometimes thought, there was little enough to choose between sleeping and being awake, save that, when one slept, there was always the chance of dreaming.

But to-night she could not sleep. This was partly the fault, no doubt, of that demon wind which had blustered and roared and shaken the house for two days without reaching the end of its spite. It made her light-headed and restless; it quickened her temper, and when it had blown for so long she felt ready to quarrel with anyone, if only to let off steam. There was nothing at all unusual in her quarrelling with Jan Bothma. Their two natures had always been as flint and steel; sparks flew whenever they met. This was one of the reasons, Jan oddly explained, for his being in love with her. Why hadn't he the wits to see for himself how much better it would be for all of them if he would fall in love with Anna, who was obviously made for him, and adored him and hung on his words; who yearned to be trampled on by his clumsy feet, and asked nothing better of life than to sit listening to him? Why couldn't he realize that Anna, with her splendid white body, her shapely limbs, her spun-gold hair, was not only more beautiful than herself, but also more richly endowed with the very qualities that the woman he loved should possess; physical strength to match his heroic build and to bear him the brood of lusty sons on which every frontiersman counted; placid fortitude to sustain the stress of a pioneer's life; a nature equally constant in its hates and loves; a hard core of steadfastness that was sometimes no more than obstinacy and at others (Lisbet admitted it grudgingly) sheerly stupid?

Yet in spite of all these comfortable virtues— some of which she admired, if she did not envy them, because they were unattainable by herself—Lisbet loved Anna, not merely out of the natural warmth of a generous heart, but with the protective affection of an elder sister for a younger (though so little younger) and the compassion of a complicated nature for one more simple. Though she knew that Anna could never quite understand her, and did not know it, her own complete understanding supplied the deficiency. The divergencies of their temperaments were superficial compared with the common tie of blood and racial experience; and when they quarrelled—as they had quarrelled that evening—Lisbet felt an aching, an almost physical disquietude, as though some part of her living body had been severed and torn away. This sense of incompleteness was one of the things, no doubt, that kept her awake; and she resented even more the cause of it, the antagonism between Jan and herself. From the moment when she had laughed at his boasting she had seen Anna's face cloud over and known that a storm was due. In the distraction of John Oakley's dramatic arrival she had forgotten those clouds. But Anna never forgot. No sooner had they entered the bedroom and pulled the curtain of tanned zebra-hide over the doorway than she had opened fire:

"Why did you laugh at our cousin like that?" she asked fiercely.

"Because he was ridiculous, Anna. How could I help laughing? A great man of his age to brag like a schoolboy! He never grows up."

"Why shouldn't a man tell the truth? Is it his fault that he's stronger than others? You hurt him. You're always hurting him and making him look small."

"I could never do that. He grows like an elephant. His hide ought to be thicker."

"It isn't a question of thickness. Your arrows are like the Bushmen's: they're dipped in poison. You know you can hurt him more than anyone else, and you take delight in it."

"Oh, that isn't fair, Anna. Just a little innocent laugh!"

"'Innocent, indeed! And even that didn't satisfy you. When he spoke of Slachter's Nek . . ."

"Slachter's Nek, Slachter's Nek. . . . Oh, how tired I am of this endless Slachter's Nek. You can't be in Jan's company for an hour without hearing about it. It's only the horrible name that keeps it alive. If it had happened to be any other sort of tradesman's nek —say, a grocer's or tinker's or tailor's or candlestick-maker's instead of a butcher's—everybody would have forgotten all about it by now! And what's more, it *was* Colonel Cuyler who hanged them: you know it was."

"We shall never forget it. We have no right to forget it. It was justly named, even if it was named by accident. God knew, when somebody named it, what was going to take place. A butchery. An English butchery."

Lisbet sighed. "There you go again! As soon as ever Jan Bothma enters this house you become a mere echo. You no sooner hear the word 'English,' you two, than you arch your backs and bristle like porcupines. Yes, darling, you do! Let's settle it once and for all. Let's agree that there's nothing horrible between here and Capetown—neither rust on the wheat nor drought nor locusts nor Kaffirs—that isn't the fault of the English. Will you be satisfied now?"

Anna flushed. If there was one thing she hated it was Lisbet's trick of joking when she was most serious.

"I'll agree about the Kaffirs," she answered sulkily. "Everyone knows that the English egg them on secretly against us and call us tigers if we lift a hand to protect ourselves."

"But, my little one, think! When the Kaffirs broke through two years ago, wasn't it the English settlers they fell upon first? Didn't they burn far more of their farms than ours, and kill more of them, too? And didn't the English officers lead in the war to punish them?"

"That means nothing at all," Anna declared, "except that the Kaffirs are not to be trusted. Any more than the English," she added, with venom.

She stepped out of her blue cotton gown and let down her hair. She swept the comb viciously through its fine-spun threads which, stiffened by the electricity which the south-easter breeds, flew out rebelliously, encircling her head with an aureole of light. Lisbet saw her lovely shoulders, so milky-white, and her angry eyes and her lips, that held the hair-ties, pouting like a sulky child's, and a wave of tenderness rose in her. She held out her arms.

"Oh, Anna, Anna," she said. There was a smile in her voice that partook of its tenderness; but Anna read it differently.

"I will not be laughed at!" she cried. "You laugh at Jan, you laugh at me, you laugh at everything and everybody." She turned her back.

"No, no, it's not that kind of laugh," Lisbet pleaded.

She took Anna in her arms and held her and kissed her white shoulders. Anna suffered the caress without yielding. She stood cold and obstinate. In silence she went on combing her hair, then plaited it tight and tied the ends with the hair-rags and jumped into bed and lay with her back towards Lisbet. And when Lisbet again would have fondled her, she stiffened and moved away from her in the vast feather-bed that would have held half a dozen sisters if there had been so many. Nor did she answer when Lisbet wished her good night.

And Lisbet lay sleepless, lonely, staring up at the dark thatch, where the white ants stirred and the fat tarantulas made their nests. There was always some contest of misunderstanding like this, she reflected, the moment Jan Bothma arrived; and it wasn't Jan Bothma's fault nor even Anna's, but the fault of that blundering Providence (if that were the word) which made such a stupid hash of simple folks' love-affairs. What was more, though she would gladly have taken back every word she had said if that would make Anna come round (and she knew it wouldn't), she knew she had spoken the truth: Jan Bothma and Anna —and Barend too, for that matter—were unfair to the English. If they had lived at Capetown, as she had for more than two years, they would have realized how unjust they were. At Capetown the English and Dutch lived side by side in perfect friendliness. If they quarrelled, they quarrelled amongst themselves,

H

and not with each other. Of course, the two races were different. That only made the relation more interesting; and the difference didn't prevent English officers falling in love with Dutch girls and marrying them and being happy with them. She herself had been fluttered more than once, though not very seriously, by young Englishmen who had flirted with her at the Castle dances.

She liked Englishmen: that was the awful truth of the matter. Their touch was lighter; they knew how to laugh and to play; their outlook on life was less grim, and nearer her own, than that of her Dutch relations who were always brooding and looking for grievances. They were more civilized (if only Anna could hear her thoughts!), and, even if they were vain, that was the fault of their splendid uniforms, and it didn't prevent them laughing at their vanity when a pretty girl teased them. Imagine Jan Bothma ever laughing at himself!

And she liked their language too: partly, no doubt, because she was flattered by being able to speak it and understand it, but not only for that—it was not merely less harsh, but richer and subtler than her own. That childish vocabulary was all very well for frontiersmen like her brothers or Jan Bothma, for talking about flocks and herds and crops or swearing at oxen and Hottentots. But there were many complicated thoughts in her mind that this rustic tongue simply could not express; and, since thoughts cannot live without words, she often thought in English and talked it whenever she could—particularly with her only cultured friend, Mr. Blair, the predikant, who, because he was Scotch (what a specious distinction!) and a Presbyterian, had been adopted, for want of a Dutchman, as pastor of the Reformed Church, and counted, in that jealous community, as one of the family. Even Anna and Jan, those hot irreconcilables, accepted Mr. Blair. Yet what was the difference between him and the hundreds of other English settlers whom the Government had planted (and deserted, some said) on the Kaffirland border? The whole attitude of Jan and Anna was illogical and childish and indefensible. She was a fool, she told herself, to take it so seriously, to lie there worrying over anything so ridiculous.

And now, as her indignation cooled, Lisbet's mind returned to what—but for this wretched tiff with Anna —it would naturally have been thinking of: the coming of the two exhausted wanderers whom Jan Bothma's wagons had picked up in the bush. The sudden appearance of that tall, dark wraith in the doorway was, in fact, the most exciting thing that had happened at Welgelegen for months. When he staggered and fell, it was she who had called for brandy and been first at his side. Anna would say she had done so because the stranger was English. But that wasn't true. She would have done as much for a Kaffir, a Hottentot, for any human being who looked as pitiable. She had knelt beside him and spilt brandy over his lips while the others looked on. She had asked for the *huisapotheek* in which medicines were kept and salved the wound on his forehead and bathed his dust-caked face.

It gave her fingers an odd sensation, to bathe the face of this unconscious stranger. It was like washing the face of a sleeping child; his helplessness had filled her with pity, his stillness with awe; for, although his faint breathings showed that he was alive, he lay still as death. It was the first time in her life that her fingers had ever touched a man's face or that she had examined a man's features so closely without his knowing, and without danger to her modesty; and the face of this stranger, so pale and so passive, had affected her with a tenderness that she could not have foreseen—not only because he lay there so pitifully at her mercy, but also because it was so different from the faces of men that she knew. There was an unusual refinement, it seemed to her, in the chiselling of those bloodless features; the long dark lashes of his closed eyes were such as a woman might have envied; his skin was softer than she had imagined a man's could be, and the line of his still lips, though not unmanly, gave an impression of sweetness, of gentleness, almost of innocence, that was appealing—not merely to her compassion, but to something else in her that she could not name. As she had bathed his face and salved with balsam the red wound that streaked his forehead and, reluctantly helped by Jan Bothma, had lifted the limp body from where it had fallen to the front of the hearth, and stowed a saddle-bag under his lolling head and thrown a kaross of leopard-skin over his shoulders, she had been moved, she could not tell why, and oddly tremulous, as though she herself had somehow been shaken by his fall.

His companion, the sturdy man with the blond beard and the wooden leg, did not interest her. The sup of brandy that Anna had given him soon brought back the colour to his weathered, good-humoured face. Her father and Jan Bothma were asking him questions which he appeared not to understand, though their English was good enough. They called upon Lisbet to interpret; but even then she had the impression that he was slyly evading her, trying, by making himself stupid, to keep something back. They had come from the sea—so much he admitted. The boat in which they had landed had left them behind because the ship to which it belonged was dragging her anchors and had been forced to run by the wind. They had struggled inland for two days and a night through the bush in search of a friendly roof. By the mercy of Providence he had heard the cracking of the Hottentot's whip and managed, by a despairing effort, to catch up with the wagons. When she asked where the ship had come from and whither they were bound, he pretended not to understand. When she pressed him, he looked so embarrassed that she had to take pity on him. Was it Capetown, perhaps? she suggested. Yes, perhaps it was Capetown, he agreed, though what with one thing and another he couldn't remember rightly; he was that famished for food, he said, that his mind was all in a muddle. They gave him a dish of the mutton stew from which Jan had already eaten. He fell on it ravenously, bolting it like a dog; and when he had filled his stomach (for now it was getting late) they sent him out to doss down in Bothma's wagon. Lisbet saw how thankful he was to escape from her questioning. She knew he was trying to hide something. What was he hiding?

That question still puzzled her active, wakeful mind as she lay staring into the dark thatch, reconstructing the scene. Capetown . . . Capetown. . . . That was the word to unlock his secret. She saw suddenly, in an unaccountable flash of inspiration, Table Bay, with the low outline of Robben Island lying across it like a stranded whale, and, in the lee of the island, a single ship. She had been taken out for a pleasure-sail in the bay, with a cousin, and an aunt for chaperon, by one of her cousin's admirers, an ensign of the Fifty-fifth, who, like all the young English officers (and no Afrikander), fancied his seamanship. She remembered how she had idly asked the name of that ship, and how Ensign Fellows had told her it was the *Minerva*, outward-bound with convicts from England for Van Diemen's Land.

"If you like," he had said, "we'll sail round her and have a look at them."

Lisbet's aunt, who was no sailor, and had already made discreet sacrifices on the altar of romance, was not anxious to sail any further; but her cousin Katjie, eager to show an adventurous spirit, accepted the proposal with enthusiasm. "Why, we might even see a real live murderer, Mamma," she said; and young Mr. Fellows had laughed: "Hardly that, I'm afraid, Miss Celliers. We don't transport murderers. We treat 'em far more kindly: we hang 'em—but you may see some pretty tough criminals, all the same." Miss Celliers was enchanted.

The skiff danced on the glittering water; the brisk breeze made her easy to handle, and the young soldier did what he would with her, encircling the *Minerva* with the grace of a wheeling gull.

"If you'll look on the main-deck, Miss Celliers," he said, "you'll see some of the villains at exercise. The red tunics, of course, are the soldiers on guard— I don't envy them!—but the convicts are all dressed in grey."

The convicts were all dressed in grey. . . . And so were both of these wanderers—though their clothes were so ripped with thorns and caked with red dust that but for this flash of revealing memory she would not have remembered their colour. And they had come from the sea—so much, cautiously, the one-legged man had admitted—and, now that the clue was given, she remembered another thing that her eyes had seen but her mind had not troubled to interpret:

a purple scar embracing the leg of the man who had fallen, above each ankle. She could guess what they signified now: they were the scars left by chains.

These deductions shocked her. She found it hard to believe that a face so refined, a mouth so gentle and innocent that the memory of it still haunted her, could be that of a hardened criminal—not of a murderer, indeed—they hanged murderers, Ensign Fellows had said—but of a man entangled in meaner if less terrible crime. The man with the wooden leg might fit into the picture, though his simple face, for all his evasions and wariness, looked honest enough. But the other stranger, her stranger? No, no. . . . She could never accept a conclusion so monstrous! The victim of some cruel mistake; the innocent accomplice of some crime of which he knew nothing; the associate, by accident or sheer chance, of lawless men: any of these he might be, perhaps, but never a hardened criminal! It might even be possible, this eager advocacy persuaded her, that, in this wakeful mood, imagination was playing her tricks: that the grey uniforms which both of the men appeared to have been wearing were not what she thought she remembered; that the circular scars had some other explanation than the chafing of chains—or even (for this uncertainty cut both ways) that the face and the mouth which had moved her with feelings that were not merely painful, were neither so innocent nor so appealing as in faint candle-light they had seemed.

There was only one way in which these dubious questions could be answered, as answered they must be before her mind could be set at rest, and that was by seeing for herself. After all, there was nothing wrong in that. Wasn't it almost a duty, seeing that she was awake, to find out how the stranger was faring? If he still slept, well and good: no harm would be done. If he had wakened, then surely he might need some small attention: a draught of water, perhaps warmer covering, for these autumn dews were cold (she was chilly herself) and those grey rags of his (were they grey indeed?) would give little warmth to a man who lay next an ant-heap floor. If he were still unconscious, she could pull a sheepskin over him without his knowing; and, asleep or awake, she could solve, once for all, these problems that pestered her: the question of hodden-grey clothes, of the chain-galls, of whether the face her fingers had touched were innocent, as she had imagined, or depraved. When once this—the last and the most important of the three—was determined, she would be able to sleep, but not, she felt, before.

It was an easy matter for once to steal out of bed without her sister being aware of it. Anna slept with the usual dreamless composure of the healthy, uncomplicated animal that she was, in the separate trough of the feather-bed she had excavated for herself. It would have been wiser, Lisbet decided, to slip on her *veld-schoens*. Though it was late in the year, there was always the chance of treading with bare feet on a scorpion, or even on a night adder that had swarmed into the house for warmth. She was African-bred and wary by instinct of such terrors; yet the fear of being heard and discovered was even stronger than they; so she went bare-footed over the slippery springbok-pelts with which the earth floor was strewn, carrying with her, as a plausible excuse for her mission, a sheep-skin kaross.

To her eyes, inured to the bedroom's darkness, the *voorhuis* seemed embarrassingly light. The table, with the great Bible upon it, the empty chairs and the rest-bench stood clearly outlined against the glow of the kraal-manure fire which had by now burned through to red. On tiptoe she stole towards Oakley and bent over him. His clothes confirmed her memory; they were of convict-grey. His ankles, thrust out from the torn trousers, were ringed with livid scars. She hardly dared look at his face for fear of what it might show her. A faint colour (unless they were merely tinged by the flush of the embers) had returned to his wax-pale cheeks; he breathed gently, regularly. But what flooded her heart with joy and thankfulness was not so much his recovery as the knowledge that memory had not deceived her. One glance was enough to assure her: this face was the face she remembered. Whatever other damning evidence might be brought against him, she was prepared to believe in his innocence and ready, from that moment, to stand by him and to protect him at all costs. As she looked down at him, he opened his eyes and returned her gaze with mild wonder. He sighed deeply and spoke in a dry whisper. "Where am I?" he said.

"This is Welgelegen," she said. "Do not trouble yourself. You are safe: that is all that matters. Lie quiet and go to sleep."

He was silent for a while. His eyes still regarded her steadfastly.

"My throat is so burnt and dry," he said, "that it hurts me to speak."

"There is no need to speak. I will give you some water."

"Yes. . . . Water."

She brought an earthenware pitcher. He stretched out his hands for it eagerly; but when his fingers closed on it the weight was too much for him and he would have dropped it and spilt it had she not hastened to help him. She knelt beside him and propped his head and held the pitcher to his lips. He drank slowly, luxuriously, washing his mouth; but the exertion tried him; when she let down his listless head he breathed heavily.

"Don't take it away," he said. "I can do with some more."

"It is bad to drink too much all at once," she warned him. "Better wait a moment."

Once more he was silent. Outside, the south-easter had spent itself and the night was still but for the distant wailing of jackals. She felt oddly happy to be kneeling alone beside him in that wide silence. Then he spoke again:

"I asked you something," he said, "but I forget what it was and what you answered. It hurts me to think. My head . . ."

He put up his hand to the broken forehead. Lisbet stayed it gently. "Don't touch your forehead," she said. "I put a salve on it. You cut your head when you fell."

"When I fell? Yes, that must be it. The pain is easier. I don't remember falling. That's funny, isn't it?"

"Don't try to remember." His fingers still clutched the hand that had stayed them. They clung to it pitifully, like a baby's, vaguely prehensile. And she did not unclasp them. It seemed to her as if this contact, unconscious as it was, were a means of support to him; as though the fingers clinging to her hand were clutching blindly, instinctively, impersonally, at something stable in an unsteady world and finding mysterious comfort. She felt as though, through this tenuous physical channel, her own vital strength were flowing into him; and she was happy in this, for all she wished was to give. It would have hurt her, she thought, if he had let her hand go.

"Yes . . . I must have fallen," he said. The conclusion appeared to satisfy him for a while. Then suddenly, as though the idea were a new one, he asked her again where he was.

"At Welgelegen," she patiently told him again. "It is a farm on the edge of the Assegai Bush. It belongs to my father, Adrian Prinsloo; and I am Lisbet."

"Lisbet . . ." he repeated faintly. "I know your voice: I have heard your voice before . . . unless I only dreamt it. There were others, too. Words I couldn't understand."

"We were talking in Dutch when you lay there. You must have heard."

"Dutch? But you are English, surely?"

She smiled. "No, I am Dutch, too. I speak English, not very well. Now try not to think any more. You ought to be sleeping."

"If I could drink again I might go to sleep," he said solemnly.

"Then if you promise to go to sleep I will give you more water. But you must let go my hand first, you know."

She disentangled his fingers gently and gave him another draught of water from the pitcher; but when he had drunk his fill and she had put the pitcher aside, she saw his hand groping for hers and could not refuse it. Indeed, as their fingers met he gave a long sigh of content that touched and rewarded her; and soon, by the faint slackening of his clasp and his measured breathing, she guessed he had fallen asleep. With her free hand she spread over him the kaross she had brought with her from the bedroom—it covered the scarred, pitiful ankles, the torn grey clothes, and for this she was glad; but she dared not disentangle the other hand for fear of waking him and robbing him of that mystical support which she felt he still needed and she was anxious to give. She wished she had brought another kaross for herself; for the glow of sods from the *mest-kock* was fading; the night air seeped in to the hearth beneath the wicker door, and it grew mortally cold.

A strange vigil, stranger than anything that had ever happened to her before, and enthralling not merely in its unexpectedness but in its secrecy: for she knew that if she were discovered—which God forbid!—she could neither defend nor explain herself. Apart from the ritual of the "upsitting," as it was called, during which engaged couples sat solemnly facing each other on either side of a table until the candle between them burnt down to a line of pins stuck in its tallow to mark the end of the time allotted to courtship, young men and women of her race were never left to themselves. For a girl to be found sitting in the dark and holding a stranger's hand would be enough to convict her of looseness. She could imagine her mother's concern, her sister's contempt, her brother's and Jan Bothma's rage if they guessed what she was doing at that moment; yet to her it seemed not merely natural and right but a matter of duty. If she freed her hand from his fingers, the movement would almost certainly wake him; he might even cry out as he woke—and that would be disastrous, for the partition walls of the house fell short of the roof and every sound from the *voorhuis* penetrated the three bedrooms. When she moved her cramped fingers to ease them, ever so slightly, the muscles of the hand that clasped them tightened—even as he slept it seemed as if he were loth to release her—and this half-conscious action touched her as evidence of the fact that he still needed her and, in some obscure way, depended on that innocent contact.

And, even without these specious pretensions, Lisbet Prinsloo's honesty compelled her to confess that she did not want to leave the stranger. Though the night air chilled her body, her heart was thrilled by an unfamiliar, unaccountable warmth, a novel emotion of a surpassing sweetness, maternal in tenderness, protective, yet also fiercely possessive. Whatever darkness his past might conceal, whatever threats or dangers the future might hold for him, this poor bedraggled creature who had fluttered in out of the dark and fallen like a stunned moth was hers to protect by right of the impulse which had brought her first to his side: doubly hers in the trust, the dependence implied by his hand that clutched her and would not let her go.

So the night wore on. The dung fire settled to powdery ashes. She had no means of measuring time. There was only one clock in the house, an elegant ornament that had come from France with her mother's ancestors, and its frivolous chime had never tinkled at Welgelegen. Now that the wind had died down, the house was alive with many minute sounds: the stirring of termites in interstices of the mud walls; the restless fluttering of bats in the reed thatch; the heavy breathing of sleepers. Outside on the veld, hunting jackals squealed to each other or burst into a shrill querulous chorus fighting for food; sometimes a hobbled horse stamped, or sleepy moans came from the cattle-kraal: sounds that quickened rather than broke the silence of the African night, and so familiar to her ears that on any night but this she would not have heard them. John Oakley slept soundly now. His breathing was unhurried and gentle; and, as sleep deepened, the pressure of his fingers almost imperceptibly relaxed.

"In a moment I must try to leave him," Lisbet thought; "for Anna may wake and miss me."

And then, suddenly, she became aware of a different sort of sound: a sharp gasp, as if somebody were choking. Lisbet held her breath. Silence followed that sound; and yet it was an uneasy silence. The cattle in the kraal were restless; they were moving about or stamping; there was a soft, continuous thudding of many hooves, as though they had suddenly smelt danger—perhaps a lion—and huddled together not knowing where to turn. The sound of hooves grew nearer and then, again, faint. She heard a quick burst of laughter; then shouts and a shrill devilish whistling. She snatched her hand quickly away from John Oakley's and ran to the door of the room where her brother Barend slept and tugged at his shoulder.

"Kaffirs, Barend," she said. "The cattle are out of the kraal, and I heard them whistling. Quick, run to the wagons and wake Jan. But don't go without a gun . . . are you mad?" She picked up the weapon that lay beside his bed and thrust it into his hands.

And now the whole house was awake. In one bedroom door there appeared the white figure of Anna in her shift; from the other her father emerged. He was fully dressed in the shirt and trousers in which he had slept, and carried an elephant-gun with a four-foot barrel.

"What is it? A lion?" he asked.

"Kaffirs, father. They're raiding the kraals. I heard them whistling. Barend has run to call Jan."

"The damned Hottentots must have been drunk."

"I think one of them tried to give an alarm. I heard something . . ."

Adrian Prinsloo hurried out; for a man stiff with age, he went quickly.

Anna shivered. "I didn't hear anything. Were you awake, Lisbet?"

"Yes, I was awake. But they've gone by now. Don't stand shivering there like that, foolish child. Go back to bed."

"Not until I know what's happened."

"Then fetch a kaross from the bed and wrap it round you."

They stood on the stoep together, enveloped in the

same dressed sheepskin, that still smelt of mutton. The sky was as luminous with starlight as if the moon were shining; the horizon, fringed with bush, the shapes of the garden trees and of Bothma's wagons stood out inky against its dim background of powder-blue. Lights moved silently hither and thither and men shouted. Lisbet's arm was round Anna's waist. They huddled closely together for warmth. It comforted Lisbet to feel that their quarrel was forgotten.

"You're still cold," she said. "Let's go back to bed."

Anna shook her head. "I must know what's happened," she said. "Thank goodness Jan's here."

Lisbet smiled to herself. "She wants Jan to see her with her hair down," she thought, "and it won't make a bit of difference."

"Look! They're coming back now."

Four figures slowly approached the stoep: their father, Barend, the man with the wooden leg, and Jan Bothma towering above them. Jan was holding forth violently as usual.

"The best Hottentot I ever had! And my new span of Zuurveld oxen that cost me three hundred and fifty-six dollars less than two months ago! Then you say that this frontier is quiet and fit to live on."

"What is it, then, nephew?" Jacoba's calm voice enquired.

More ponderous in movement than the others, she had only just reached the doorway, where she stood with a sun-bonnet framing her large pale face.

"What is it? More devilry, aunt! My best Hottentot, old man Klaas. One must have crept up behind him while another held his attention by moving in the bush at a distance. Then a reim pulled tight round the neck. K . . . k . . . k! *Kapot!* Not a squeak, and his yellow face purple as a pickling-cabbage. The other boy ran and they speared him through with their assegais: five wounds, like our Lord Jesus Christ. But that is nothing. My new span of black Zuurvelds: three hundred and fifty-six dollars, and Lord knows how many others."

"We must make a plan. We must turn Sarel back and ride to the Fort to-morrow and report to the captain," the old man said wearily.

Jan Bothma gasped; his huge shape seemed to swell with suppressed indignation.

"Make your plans!" he cried. "Mine are made. If the Government fails to protect me, I act for myself. How many men are we here? There's you, uncle, and Barend and Sarel and myself, and this Englishman here, if he knows how to sit a horse and handle a gun . . ."

"Can you ride and shoot?" Lisbet asked.

"Can I ride and shoot, miss?" Dicketts answered indignantly. "You hoist me atop of a horse and put a gun in my hands and see! I'm a soldier, I am. Fifteenth Hussars, what used to be Light Dragoons, Lord Uxbridge's Brigade."

"Yes, Jan, he can ride and shoot."

"As well as most Englishmen, I suppose, and that's not saying much. Well, that makes five of us—or four and a half," Bothma went on scornfully; "and we'll send boys running to Nelsrust and Keurfontein to inspan the Nels and the Oosthuizens, so that should make ten guns, which is all we need. The Nels and the Oosthuizens ought to be here by dawn, and it's no good starting before we can see the spoor. We may not get our sheep and our cattle back—they've got three hours' start on us—but by God, if we don't, we'll make the black devils pay for it! That new ox of mine, that Blauwberg, the one I pulled through the drift, uncle, he's worth half a dozen of any of yours or mine: the heart of a lion, the neck of a buffalo! I forget if I told you . . ."

This time Lisbet did not laugh.

"Come inside, come inside, children," her mother said. "Come, father, there's still time to sleep. Why, Hendrik, what's the matter with you?"

The small boy was sitting perched on the rest-bench, crying to himself. When Jacoba fondled him he only cried the more.

"They've taken Slingveld. . . . They've taken my little black bull that was my own . . . my very own," he cried disconsolately.

CHAPTER FIVE

CONFESSION

LISBET PRINSLOO still slept, lying close to her sister for warmth, when the ten men rode off at dawn. She slept on till the sun was well up and the old slave Ayah roused them, telling them that the coffee was ready.

Their mother had already established herself on the rest-bench from which she would probably not move for the rest of the day, with a charcoal brazier comforting her feet and, on the table before her, a steaming coffee-kettle and the volume of Willem Sluiter's Sacred Songs lying open beside the clasped Bible. In the background the two old slaves and the Hottentot house-servants stood waiting with bowed heads. Little Hendrik sat fidgeting at her elbow, hungry for his breakfast.

But neither human impatience nor even such an excitement as the riding away of armed men could break the devotional routine of Welgelegen. In that house no day was begun or ended without the singing of a psalm or a hymn, no food ever tasted without the saying of an elaborate grace. As Lisbet and Anna took their appointed places, Mevrouw Prinsloo rose ponderously and began to sing the psalm she had selected.

The two girls and the child joined in. The four treble voices, singing in unison without any self-consciousness, sounded weak and pathetic, yet touching in their simplicity. Though the book, as a matter of form, lay open on the table, none of the singers had need to look at it; for the words they sang had been part of the minds of all four since their earliest childhood.

For Lisbet, in spite of her reverent air, they had no significance that morning. From the moment when Ayah had wakened her, her mind had been full of her stranger, giving shape, with new energy, to the plan of action in which sleep had crystallized the vague thoughts of her vigil. This was no time for dreaming. She was convinced by now that the unknown man was a prisoner escaped from a convict-ship. How or why he had come to that pass, she neither knew nor cared. It was enough for her to know that he needed the protection which only she could give him; for, even if he were as innocent as she chose to fancy, she knew that, so long as he remained within reach of the law, his liberty—and perhaps his life—were in danger. It was true that the remoteness of Welgelegen gave him a certain security: in the "outer districts" the officers of the law were not usually on the alert; the Land-drost, a friendly and easy-going Dutchman, rarely passed that way. The only immediate danger lay in the chance of the farm being visited by soldiers of the frontier patrol. In the ordinary way, even this would not have been likely; but the fact that the kraals had been raided and cattle stolen made a visit of enquiry almost certain as soon as the news reached the Fort. And that would be disastrous. Although she was the only member of the family who had noticed the fugitive's clothes and guessed what they signified, the eyes of soldiers recently stationed in Capetown would be more wary. It was part of their duty to keep count of strangers and question them; and a stranger in convict grey who could not account for himself would be snapped up as soon as seen.

Her first problem, then, was to get Oakley out of the house; the second to rid him of his tell-tale clothes, which, unobtrusive enough in the dusk of the previous evening, might betray him at once in the brutal light of day. So she thought and schemed as her lips moved mechanically shaping the words of the psalm, not daring to lift her eyes in the direction of the hearth where, she supposed, he still lay.

The long psalm came to an end, and Hendrick, as became the youngest of the family, raised his hand to his forehead and gabbled through grace. The excitements of the night had sharpened the child's appetite. He was still eating greedily long after the others had finished, pestering his mother, as he ate, with innumerable questions:

"Can I go and see Klaas's head, ma? I should like to see that. Jan said it was swollen up like a purple cabbage."

"That is not a sight for children, and I am sure they have buried him by now."

"Well, can I take a pony just a little way into the bush and see if I can follow the spoor?"

"In the bush, indeed! You'll do nothing of the sort. If you take the pony you must keep within sight of the house. Now mind what I say."

"Then may I take Barend's little gun and shoot at an ox's knuckle-bone? Barend says I ought to be able to hit one at eighty paces before I can say I've learnt to shoot. And I *must* learn to shoot, ma. Supposing the Kaffirs came back again. Supposing I saw the Kaffir who stole my little black bull, and I didn't know how to shoot him?"

"I don't like your shooting with Barend's little gun when he isn't there. You might put too much powder in and burst it, and that would be a fine thing!"

"But wouldn't it be rather a good idea," he persisted, "just to let off a shot now and then, so that if any of the Kaffirs come back they'll know there's a man in the house? I'm sure Barend would say so."

"There's no need for that. The men will soon be home again. Be a good boy, now, Hendrik, and do what your mother tells you."

The men would soon be home again. . . . Jacoba Prinsloo sighed. While she answered the small boy's questions her mind was as busy as Lisbet's. These days when men rode away into Kaffirland, though common enough, were always full of anxiety. Though they took the adventure so lightly, one never knew how many of them would return. On occasions like this she always thought of her three strong sons, Gerrit and Hans and Pieter, who had lost their lives two years ago in the last Kaffir war, and of Paul, whom a buffalo had gored to death in the Assegai Bush, and Theunis, whose head had been blown to bits by a bursting gun-barrel. When once she began to brood on these losses, all the others came back to her: little Katjie, who had been drowned in the dam while the wretched Hotten-tot girl was making love in the bushes, and Teda, and the first Anna, her eldest, who had wilted away with the summer dysentery. Twelve children in all she had borne, and only five of them living, and the other seven buried decently, thank God, in the little white-walled graveyard.

It was on anxious days such as this that she thought so wistfully of her early married life at French Hoek, surrounded by friendly neighbours and numberless cousins, and no more than half a day's journey from the settled security of Capetown, where there were neither savage men nor savage beasts. She might have been there at this moment, she thought, with all her twelve children around her, if Adrian had not been cursed, like all the Prinsloos, with this maggot of rest-lessness, this lust for far wandering. And now, just as if the anxieties of life on the frontier were not enough for them, her sons Sarel and Barend must always be talking and talking of going farther, of packing the wagons and trekking northward again over the mountains into unknown lands, unknown perils. It was their youth, she supposed, just youth and the accursed Prinsloo blood in their bodies that drove them. Yet surely even the most wayward and thoughtless might understand that a woman of fifty who weighed sixteen stone and had borne twelve and buried eight was not likely to hanker after uncertain adventures? Couldn't they see for themselves that she and their father had come to a time of life when all they asked was to be left where they were, to enjoy such quiet as God gave them, to sleep and eat and be thankful, and watch the fruit they had planted blossom and ripen, and walk slowly on Sunday evenings to visit their dear ones' graves? They said that the Kaffirs were coming over again. So be it. If they came, let them come. Forewarned was forearmed. There were forts on the frontier; there were soldiers. And were there no Kaffirs, then, in those wastes beyond the mountains for which Sarel and Barend were yearning, in those desolate wastes where men had no neighbours to succour them? A vain question. One might as well reason with a stone as with these headstrong men. If they had set their wild hearts on trekking, nothing would stop them. And where Boer men went, their women always went with them. She shook her head slowly and sighed. She heard Lisbet speaking.

"The stranger who came in last night, ma, that poor

in-blown Englishman: we have not even thought of him."

"Never fear. Half an hour ago, when I came, he was still asleep. I looked at him."

"But he must be famished; he has tasted no food, ma."

"Sleep is better than food. Perhaps the singing has wakened the fellow by now."

"I will go and see."

"Go, then. If he is wakened you can find out how he is. He will understand you."

Anna moved away scornfully to the sunlit stoep. She hated to hear Lisbet speaking English. Lisbet crossed the room to the hearth. John Oakley lay exactly as she had left him. He gazed up at her with mild, submissive eyes, and smiled faintly.

"So it wasn't a dream," he said. "I was beginning to wonder."

Lisbet put her finger to her lips and shook her head.

"You must have slept more than twelve hours," she said. "How are you this morning?"

"I don't know. I think I'm all right. Yes, I'm sure I'm all right. Only a little bit dazed. And hungry. My throat is so dry."

Jacoba approached them slowly. "What does he say?" she enquired.

"He says he's hungry."

"Dear Lord, I should think the poor fellow was hungry! Give him coffee and bread, Lisbet."

Lisbet gave him an earthenware cup of the black decoction and a slice of bread. John Oakley sat up, without difficulty, and ate. The two women watched him. Never in all his life had he tasted food so good. He ate dreamily for a time; then suddenly spoke:

"My friend. . . . Where is he?"

"Your friend is safe and well. Do not think of him," Lisbet said.

"Is he here . . . in this room?"

"No, no. But he'll be back before long."

"It was that crack on the head. It must have knocked me out properly. How kind you have been! I'm afraid we have no money to pay for our lodging."

"Money? Money?" That, at least, was a word Mevrouw Prinsloo understood. "What is the poor *kerel* raving about? Tell him this house is the house of a Boer, not a store-keeper. Any man who off-saddles at Welgelegen is welcome to sleep by the fire and to eat such food as we have. Tell him that! I am sorry they lost their horses, though. We have none to spare."

"My mother says you are welcome," Lisbet told him. "In this country you must never, never speak of money. We only do what all others would do for us. It is the custom. Can you eat any more?"

Oakley shook his head. "Not just yet. My stomach is feeble. But I would like to see my friend. If you tell me where he is, I think I could walk and find him. It's better I should try to walk. We have a long way to go."

"Where are you going?" she asked.

"I can't say until I have spoken with him."

"Then why worry? You'll need more than one night's rest before you are fit for a journey. If you'll trust me, as I want you to trust me, I think you should be safe."

"Safe?" he answered quickly, suspiciously.

"Don't speak of that now. We will talk of those things later. Your clothes. . . ." (He went hot with alarm) . . . "your clothes are all torn. We must find you some others, rather more respectable; and when you have washed yourself you can sleep in the wagon with your friend. Lie still, now, and trust me to do what I know is best. There is plenty of time."

He nodded submissively, and lay down once more with a sigh.

"What is all this story?" Jacoba asked. "You speak so quickly." Though she trusted Lisbet, she did not altogether like these mysterious whisperings in a foreign tongue.

"He remembers nothing, ma," Lisbet explained. "They were lost in the bush, as Klaas said. His clothes are torn to ribbons. The man is half naked. Couldn't we find him a shirt—an old shirt—and some trousers somewhere? A white man should not look like a Hottento, mother."

"You are right," she said. "Poor thing! We will see, we will see. *I was a stranger, and ye took me in: I was naked, and ye clothed me.* Yes, so is it written."

She turned her back on them and waddled away to the sleep-room where the wagon-chests filled with the clothes of her dead sons were kept. As soon as she was out of ear-shot, Lisbet leant over and whispered:

"These clothes must be burnt. That's the first thing. Do you understand? After that we will make a plan. Until then, be careful to say no more than you can help. Understand, you have lost your memory: you remember nothing. My mother is good and simple; but there are others who have sharp ears and suspicious minds. Here is one of them. Do not answer."

Anna hurried in from the stoep:

"Lisbet! Lisbet! Where are you? Hendrik has got Barend's little gun."

"Then for heaven's sake run and take it from him."

"What are you doing down there?" Anna asked distrustfully.

"The wound on his forehead. It's healing well. He's fallen asleep again, poor thing." The sound of a shot rang out. "Oh, go, Anna, go! Don't let him out of your sight, or that wretched child will kill himself!"

Anna turned and ran as Jacoba came panting back from the sleep-room. "I heard a shot, Lisbet," she said.

"Yes, yes. It was Hendrik. He's got Barend's little gun. Anna's gone out to stop him."

"That child will be the death of me. What a breed, these Prinsloos! Thank Heaven it's nothing worse: on these days when I hear a shot I see nothing but terror. Look, child, what I have found." She unfolded a pair of sheepskin trousers and a check cotton shirt. "He will be lost in them," she said. "All our boys were so tall. These things were poor Pieter's. He puts me in mind a little of Pieter, Lisbet, this young man: Pieter was dark, like you and Barend and my poor dear father. But Pieter was more of a man than this one. Now that he sleeps he looks nothing but a child. It is a nice face, Lisbet, an innocent face. This is a boy one would like to take care of."

Her long gaze had a brooding, an almost greedy tenderness. The mere sight of John's youth and helplessness moved her maternal heart which had so much affection to spare. "But these Englishmen," she went on, "are always more gently made than us Afrikanders. They must come of a richer soil and a kinder climate. That is why Jan and Barend dislike and despise them: our boys are born hard and daring and old and impatient, and think that everyone ought to be like themselves. The English are different from us, but they are as God made them and have done no harm. I am sorry for them: it was a crime of the Government, I say, to dump these poor settlers down in the bush like cattle to starve and be eaten up by the Kaffirs: men who had never handled a gun and women who had never moulded a bullet. How anxious his mother will be! We must send her a message to let her know the poor fellow is safe. Has he told you where he was going?"

Lisbet shook her head. "He has told me nothing . . . nothing. Let us put Piet's clothes by his side, ma, and leave him alone. When he wakes again he will see them, and put them on. And then, if we find he can walk, he shall go to the wagon with his friend. It will be better for all of us that he should be out of the way when Cousin Jan comes home. If Jan finds him still here, we shall never hear the last of it."

"That is right," Jacoba agreed. "Jan is hasty and violent. Yet Jan is a good boy, too. I wish you would be more kind to him. Why, when I was your age I was married and had two children: our first little Anna and Sarel. Yes, those were the days of happiness."

"I am happy enough as it is, ma. I like Jan, but I do not love him, and never shall."

"Ah, love, love. . . . That is another thing. But a woman ought to have children, plenty of children. If you start too late you won't have enough to keep your mind busy when you grow old."

Lisbet laughed and kissed her. "Hendrik keeps my mind busy enough as it is," she said. "I had better see what he's doing now. I expect he and Anna are up at the dam; but the child is as wily as any baboon. If she isn't sharp, he'll get hold of that gun again."

She put on her pleated cotton sun-bonnet and stepped out into the white, still glare of the morning sun. Jacoba heard her singing as she ran down the path to the wicker gate. "What a blessed thing to be young and to sing for no reason!" she thought. The vast woman moved heavily to her rest-bench, the station from which, like that of a pale, benevolent spider, sitting day after day immobile yet always conscious of the faintest vibration that troubled her web of fine-spun consciousness, her acute mind controlled and directed the life of Welgelegen. She placed her feet on the charcoal comforter under the dome of her skirts and folded her placid hands on the table in front of her. She closed her eyes dreamily. One would have said that she slept.

But Jacoba Prinsloo did not sleep. As the sound of Lisbet's singing faded away she became aware of a faint rustling over by the hearth where John Oakley lay. She rose and approached him cautiously, so quietly that he did not hear her. He had dragged off his thin grey trousers—there were only a few rags of them left— and pulled on Pieter's. He sat, stripped to the waist, taking breath, and Jacoba saw that he was not the frail boy his face had led her to suppose, but a well-built young man, with powerful muscles under the satin skin of his wide shoulders. "But the boy is thin as a vulture," she thought. "They must surely have starved him; a fellow of his size ought to carry more flesh on his bones. That was why he fainted. We must take him in hand and make a man of him." It pleased her to watch him thus, without his knowing. His unconscious nakedness touched some chord of maternal tenderness, reminding her (or was it, perhaps, the clothes?) of Pieter, the boy she had lost, and made her feel even more kindly towards him. But she was curious, too, as all Boer women are curious of strangers. She wanted to know, in the usual way, the details that every stranger should furnish when he came to take shelter at a farm: his name, his age, his business and where he had come from, and how he had lost his horse, the names of his parents and all their family history—all those things over which, a little suspiciously, she felt that Lisbet had purposely evaded her. As she stood there in silence John Oakley became aware of her scrutiny. He started and looked round. She nodded her head and smiled encouragingly.

"Go on," she said, in her halting English. "Take no notice of me. I am an old woman. I know what a naked man looks like."

He laughed and pulled on the check shirt. It was much too big for him; the cuffs hung over his hands. He laughed. She was glad of that. There was not much wrong with a man who could laugh.

"That's better," he said. "I begin to feel more like myself."

Jacoba began her catechism: "What is your name?" she asked.

He hesitated, suddenly remembering Lisbet's cautions. It was difficult to lie to this motherly woman. "My name's John," he said.

"So . . . John is like Jan. And how is your father called?"

"His name was Thomas." The keen, placid eyes still

fixed him; there was no evading them. "Thomas Grafton," he said, and felt that she knew he lied.

"Thomas . . . Hrafton." She formed the "g" as if it were aspirated: "Thomas Hrafton. Well . . . and your mother?"

"Her name was Mary. She is dead."

"Poor soul, poor soul. . . . And brothers and sisters?" she pressed him.

"I have none, ma'am."

Jacoba threw up her hands. "So you are your father's only child? What a misfortune! Yet so God wills it, no doubt. And where have you come from?"

"From the sea. Where the river runs out."

"Ah, the Kouwie River." She nodded and seemed to be satisfied. "The Kouwie River: I know. There are many English there. And where were you going?"

"We are looking for work," he told her.

"Work? What kind of work can you do?"

"I am a cobbler by trade, ma'am. I can make shoes and boots."

"Men can make *veld-schoen* for themselves, and a woman's shoes last a lifetime. Still, a fellow who can work with leather is always useful, though that is a woman's business rather than a man's."

Lisbet fluttered in; her cheeks flushed with alarm when she heard them speaking. She looked anxiously from one face to the other, and was thankful to see that her mother's was still kind.

"He has found his tongue . . . and part of his

memory," Jacoba said. "And Piet's clothes are better than nothing. These rags of his are not fit for a Hottentot. Give them to Ayah to burn. . . ."

"I will burn them myself."

Lisbet bundled the tell-tale garments together and carried them eagerly to the untidy group of huts at the back where the slaves and the Hottentots lived in a compound of their own. With a handful of sticks she livened the fire that always burned there and watched the shoddy material sink to ashes. It filled her with fierce satisfaction to see the end of them. The first and most urgent part of her programme was performed. When she returned to the *voorhuis* she found John Oakley on his feet. He was taller than she had imagined, and less frail, though, as soon as he moved, he winced with pain and seemed uncertain of his balance.

"Take him out to the wagon," Jacoba told her, "and make him lie down again. One sees that he has no strength to spare. Go slowly; do not hurry him."

Lisbet led the way and Oakley followed cautiously. The scene through which he had staggered in darkness appeared strange to him and tinged with the enchantment of an invalid mood. The fierce African sun burned through the still, pellucid air; but the heat was no longer a torment, and the air itself had a vinous exhilaration that filled him with zest and hope as he breathed it. They passed through the garden's green close to the scarred patch of veld outside where Jan

Bothma's two dusty wagons stood like abandoned hulks, the *disselboom* of each propped up on the first yoke, the other empty yokes and the *trek-tow* stretched out in a long line in front of them. Lisbet led him slowly. He could not see her face for the flaps of the *kappje* that shielded it from the sun; but his own feebleness made him aware of her body's vitality, and he marked the grace of her movement. In his shy and solitary life he had had small acquaintance with women; and this woman, it seemed to him, was more vivid and resolute than any other he had known. There was something in her eagerness that reminded him of his mother; yet that was not all. She was the only woman he remembered with whom he had felt no shyness; the only human being, perhaps, with whom, from the first moment, he had been unreservedly at ease: and though this might be no more than the result of the unreal and strangely intimate circumstances in which he had clung to her hand in the dark, at a time when his instinctive timidity was masked and his natural defences were down, he could not help being aware of an emotion towards her unconnected with gratitude or even admiration, a desire to recapture the tones of her voice, to examine once again the face that the sun-bonnet hid, to touch, in broad daylight, the fingers whose warmth and softness had comforted him so mysteriously in the night. In all his life John Oakley had known no friend; and this girl, it seemed to him, was more to him than a friend. They were strangers; and yet their relationship (on his side at least) had a mystical element in it that puzzled him and vexed his heart with a sense of incompleteness, of unexplainable yearning that resembled physical hunger and yet was so sweet that he wished for it to continue rather than to be assuaged.

Lisbet mounted the step of the wagon in front of him; all her movements were swift and precise. She gazed down on him, smiling. There was an anxious eagerness in her face: though she would not press him, she could not feel secure until he was safely concealed from inquisitive attention by the wagon's tilt. And John Oakley gazed up at her, spellbound, awed by what was for him a new revelation of beauty: her smiling lips with a hint of impetuosity sharpening their sweetness; her cheeks, with the delicate bloom that veiled their rich colour; her frank hazel eyes, so deep, so grave, yet so softly compassionate, beneath the black brows whose heaviness gave them, despite their softness, a look of firm resolution. He gazed and was lost in wonder—so long, so intently that Lisbet became sensible of his rapt, immediate absorption and grew suddenly so confused that the quick blood mounted in her neck and spread to her cheeks, and an unwonted embarrassment compelled her to speak more harshly.

"Come along," she said, "you mustn't stand there in the sun or it will make you feel faint. Give me your hand, and climb up slowly."

It was more than he could have hoped for; yet the

hand that grasped his and steadied him, though delicately shaped and soft to his touch beyond belief, was not the hand he remembered. The clasp was firm and nervous, and the strength behind it by no means frail or ethereal. In his weakness he wondered at it and was glad of it. The effort of mounting the wagon, indeed, taxed him more than he had expected. His heart fluttered, and he was thankful to lay himself down breathing quickly on the wagon-bed strung with crisscross leather reims.

"You see," she reproved him, "you are not nearly so strong as you think."

She busied herself, to hide the remains of her confusion, in stuffing an empty saddle-bag under his head, and her eyes, which he sought continually, were averted.

"There is no time to lose," she said. "I dare not stay here much longer. My mother spoke to you while I was burning your clothes. She said you had recovered part of your memory. What did she mean?"

"She asked me my name. I lied to her."

"Good. What did you tell her?"

"I said my name was John Grafton. My real name . . ."

"You need not say it. John Grafton is a good enough name. And easy to remember."

"I would rather tell you my real name."

"No, no. Better not. You shall tell me some day. What else?"

"I said we came from the coast. It was true."

"Yes, yes. That is fortunate. And then?"

"That we were wandering looking for work and that my mother was dead."

"Ah, that is good too. Her heart is so large and tender. You said nothing more? Nothing about . . . the clothes that I burned?"

"No. I only answered her questions. Most of them truly."

She was silent for a moment, as if it were hard to find words.

"Those grey clothes . . ." she said at last, "I have seen some like them before. We sailed out to a ship in Table Bay: I think I know what they mean."

"I am glad you know. If you hadn't known, I should have had to tell you. I lied to your mother, just once, but I could never have lied to you. My friend and me, we've escaped from a convict ship that put in for water. Is that what you guessed?"

"Yes, that was it. Your ankles too. The marks of the chains."

"I had forgotten all about those." He paused for a moment. "Why didn't you tell your mother what you had seen? Why didn't you raise an alarm? Why do you help me like this?"

"I don't know. I can't say. I think first of all because you were English, and all the rest are mad against the English and I am contrary by nature. And then, when I saw you again in the night, I didn't believe . . ."

"What?"

". . . that you could be so very wicked—I mean a real criminal."

"Would you take my word if I told you I wasn't, or would you think I was trying to shield myself by lies?"

She looked him solemnly full in the eyes. For a moment, a tense and endless moment, she did not answer. He shook his head:

"Ah, you'ld rather not answer," he said hurriedly. "Let us leave it so."

She smiled at his hasty sensitiveness. "No, no," she said gently, "you are wrong. I would surely take your word for it. I will believe whatever you tell me."

"And before God I swear I will tell you nothing but the truth. Listen now: I have done nothing, nothing of which my conscience accuses me. Can you believe that is true?"

"I told you I would believe you. That is only what I believed before, without your telling me. Now will you be satisfied?"

"Satisfied? It is almost too much for me!" His eyes filled with tears. "I had come to think there was nothing but cruelty in this world—only hatred and cruelty. I did not want to live any more. My feelings were dead already. I had almost ceased to believe in goodness or mercy. Now all that is changed." His

I*

voice broke—"and it isn't easy to . . . to come back to life again."

She laughed nervously, tenderly. "Don't even try to forget. You are still weak and tired. Just lie there, close your eyes for a while and be quiet. In an hour or two Ayah will bring you more food. It is much better that I should not come. I have stayed here too long as it is. To-morrow, perhaps . . ."

As she went, with a swift, half-timid gesture, she laid her hand on his brow.

CHAPTER SIX

THE PREDIKANT

THROUGH the heat of that afternoon the Reverend
Andrew Blair rode northward to Welgelegen along the
fringes of the Assegai Bush. Apart from his costume—
a frock-coat of rusty black broadcloth buttoned tightly
to the neck, with trousers to match, and a felt hat with
a wider brim and a lower crown than Jan Bothma's—
there was nothing in Mr. Blair's appearance to proclaim his calling. He was a tall, spare, middle-aged
man, with a long face, heavily scored by wrinkles, and
deep-set blue eyes beneath bushy brows divided at the
root of the nose by two vertical furrows which gave his
shaven (but not very well-shaven) face a puzzled air.
His brown hands tightly grasping the reins and his
feet thrust determinedly into the long-girthed stirrups,
looked all knuckle and ankle; and his features, beneath
the leathery skin sun-scorched and furrowed like the
African soil, showed the same quality of bony pro-
tuberance. He rode clumsily, by faith rather than by
sight, without any pretensions to horsemanship, pre-
cariously poised on the back of his elderly cream-
coloured mare. Beneath these harsh externals he looked
what he still was essentially: a shrewd, serious, studious

cottager from the moors of Angus who, nearly thirty years since, had tramped in from Kirriemuir to St. Andrews to study divinity and achieved his ambition by becoming a minister of the Presbyterian Church.

If variety of experience were ever likely to change the essential Mr. Blair, it would have done so by now. Seventeen years before this, at the age of twenty-four, inflamed by the example of others of his countrymen whose names were already legends in the mission-field, he had attached himself to one of the state-assisted parties of emigrants to whom the colonial government had allotted land on the Kap River frontier of Kaffirland. He had played his part in that forlorn and brutal experiment in which batches of hopeful men, like himself unprepared and unqualified for emergency and privation, had been callously dumped and abandoned in a tract of virgin bush so remote and savage that not even the boldest of born colonials had ever attempted to tame it. He had shared in his party's bewilderment and disillusion. He had watched their hopes wither, as the wheat they sowed was stricken by rust and parched by drought and stripped by locusts. He had toiled with them, starved with them, prayed with them, married them, buried them, and seen, with amazement no less than with pride and thankfulness, the miracle by which, with the passage of time, their fortitude and their stubborn ant-like toil were rewarded, creating, in the midst of the waste, an oasis of orderly life, in which, out of hardship, despair and ruin, hope sprang anew.

This was not the kind of mission his young enthusiasms had foreseen. It had been more seriously concerned with his comrades' mortal bodies than with their immortal souls. He had found the smattering of medical science with which he had fortunately armed himself at St. Andrews of more avail than the Shorter Catechism; the elements of husbandry he had picked up on his father's fields as a child of greater use than doctrinal erudition, and human comradeship even more valuable than either. Yet if his mission was different from what he had imagined it would be, and his position had become less that of a pastor than of a companion in endeavour and distress, he had the satisfaction of knowing that he had contributed in works as well as in faith to the life of the little community to which it had pleased God to join him.

For fifteen years he had been their servant and friend as well as their teacher. It had been his privilege, under Providence, to see the righteous flourish as a green bay-tree and the wilderness blossom as a rose. As time went by and the scattered parties of settlers began to find their feet, as the first rude buildings of daub and wattle and huts of reeds became homesteads, regarded not merely as temporary shelters but as the permanent centres round which their lives and the lives of their children revolved, as the area of tilth expanded, as their cattle gave increase, and orchards and gardens embosomed the raw house-walls in fruitful and vigorous green which made them look as though they had been lived in for half a century, the memory of those early struggles became less a reminder of past bitterness than a measure of present content. And with this new sense of settled security, the things of the spirit, which were Mr. Blair's proper concern, emerged from the material preoccupations which had necessarily overlain them.

Though there was as yet no church, and no spare money to build one, on the Kap River Frontier, there arose, in the settlers' minds, a hunger for religious instruction. Though he still had his small allotment of land to till, his house to keep clean and his livestock to tend, Mr. Blair became the spiritual guide and pastor of all the isolated communities of settlers that lay scattered in the bush from the springs of the Kap to the mouth of the Great Fish River. It was a parish of four hundred square miles, a cure of seven hundred souls, and the mere physical labour of covering it was sufficient to tax the strength of one man. But this man was tireless, not merely by virtue of his stern Scots upbringing but because of the ardent missionary zeal, so long suppressed, which now found its justification.

His flock was not only immense but heterogeneous. It comprised men of many different races and faiths. In the north, by the pits of red clay where the Kaffirs came for their war-paint, lived a turbulent community of Roman Catholic Irishmen; to the south he found

Anglicans; in between lay a number of farms inhabited by Boers of the Dutch Reformed Church. Mr. Blair, in spite of his strong Calvinistic prejudices, made no distinction between them and was welcomed by all. To one group he was priest, to another pastor, to another predikant. It was sufficient for him to know that they were all his brethren in Christ. He loved them as such, in his grave, dour way, and was loved in return.

In the fourteenth year of his ministry, when he was no longer the ardent young student of divinity who had sailed in the *Brilliant* for South Africa in eighteen-twenty, but a hard-bitten man of forty who looked older than his years, Mr. Blair fell in love—or, at least, perceived the disadvantages of celibacy and the desirability of a minister's being a married man. The woman of his choice was the daughter of a Dutch farmer named Grobler, who had brought up a swarming family in conditions of primitive squalor on one of the frontier farms near the Kap River's source.

Mr. Blair had known Hannie Grobler (her full name was Johanna) since she was a child. The promiscuous conditions of life at her father's farm Graskop had always distressed him, and it is possible that the contrasting innocence of Hannie and her livelier intelligence appealed to him more than her beauty, which was in no way remarkable. As for old Grobler, he was only too glad to get rid of his daughter: in his two-roomed house there were already eight of them to house and to feed. The enormous disparity in age—Hannie was only sixteen—did not trouble him: it was no uncommon thing for Boer widowers of sixty to marry girls younger than she. He gave Hannie his blessing (and nothing more) and celebrated the occasion by getting drunk and extremely lubricious on *brandewyn*. Next morning, while he still mercifully slept, Mr. Blair left Graskop on his cream-coloured mare and rode over the hills, with Hannie astride behind him, to get married in Grahamstown.

This odd marriage shocked Mr. Blair's friends in the English settlement. Apart from the indecency of a mature man's marrying a child less than half his age, it would have been more becoming, they thought and said without hesitation, if he had chosen a woman of his own race: they were as proud of their blood, these English, as they are to-day. Yet Scotch missionaries, as everyone knew, were not over-fastidious: the celebrated Dr. Vanderkemp had actually married a stinking Hottentot, and Hannie Grobler, however dubiously coloured some of her father's progeny might be, was certainly white: dazzlingly white, in fact, with fine flaxen hair and a delicate pink-and-white skin and chicory-blue eyes. The men in the settlement were far less critical than their womenfolk. It was high time the pastor married, they said, in any case, and if he liked his meat tender, well, more luck to him!—though, of course, in a year or two his wife would grow fat as a pig.

And his marriage, odd though it seemed at first, was beyond doubt successful. It made a woman of Hannie and a young man of Mr. Blair, and, apart from all else, brought an enormous addition of comfort to his bachelor home. There was no problem of frontier life with which his wife was not better qualified than he to deal. She understood the care of livestock; she was good-humoured and physically strong and precociously canny; she could talk with the Hottentot servants click for click and speak her mind in his own tongue to an insolent Kaffir; if things came to the worst (and one never knew) she could load and handle a musket better than her husband. If she was younger than he in years, there were many things in which she was Mr. Blair's elder; and one of these was the intimacies of married life. She knew far more about that than this shy man had ever dreamed of, and if he had not loved her when she rode on the cream-coloured mare behind him to Grahamstown, there is no doubt that within a short time of their wedding his long-repressed manhood found a liberation that exalted him to serene heights of rapturous (and fortunately legitimate) love.

The warmth of this generous emotion was sufficient to neutralize the frigid disapproval with which many of his flock regarded his marriage. With this delightful child in his arms and by his side their censure did not affect him. A strange, but surely a justifiable gaiety lightened his step; it brought smiles to his rather dour lips and humorous twists to his tongue which were misunderstood—not because they were unbecoming but because they were unfamiliar. The Pastor, folk said, was making a fool of himself over his little Dutch brat. But Mr. Blair, though their gossip came back to his ears as all malice will, was not perturbed by it. A minister of the Lord was not, to his mind, the less godly for being a happy man; and to this new, gay serenity there was shortly to be added an even greater happiness. Within three months of their marriage God blessed their union: his wife was with child.

Her confinement was due to take place towards the end of December and Mr. Blair so planned his journeys that he would return from the northern settlements a few days before Christmas. On the afternoon of Sunday, December the twenty-first, as he left his father-in-law's farm at Graskop, the first wave of the Kaffir invasion was breaking on a front a hundred miles long. Over all the drifts of the Great Fish River the black hordes surged in a savage spate. From the Winterberg to the sea the frontier was swept by flame and bathed in blood.

Four days later, famished and bedraggled, he rode into Grahamstown. As he reached the west door of the church where the Committee of Safety were serving out muskets and ammunition, a woman recognized him and hurried to meet him. She was the wife of a neighbour named Page. If he had looked at her face

Mr. Blair might have read what was in it; but he was so elated and dazed with relief at having reached the place where all the refugees from the frontier were congregated that he saw nothing. "Where is she? Where's Hannie?" he asked.

Mrs. Page put her apron to her eyes and burst into tears. "Poor thing," she said, "poor child!" She shook her head hopelessly, unable to speak. Mr. Blair, white as death, scrambled down from his horse and shook her by the shoulder. "Tell me . . . tell me," he said. "What is it? For God's sake tell me!"

Her story, broken by sobs, was simple and pitiful enough. The settlers of the lower Kap River settlements had been warned and had taken to flight as soon as the first of the raiders had crossed Kaffir's Drift. The men lagged behind as a rearguard, while their women and children, forty or fifty of them, set out on the thirty-mile walk to Grahamstown. No sooner had they reached the church than Hannie's pains had come on. A bad time—but what could one expect after such a strain?—and the baby still-born: such a beautiful boy! And then, just as all seemed well over, the flooding had come on. The doctor had done all he could, but nothing would stop it . . . nothing! Poor child . . . poor child . . ."

"You mean that my wife is dead?" he cried.

Mrs. Page had no need to answer.

This catastrophe had marked a turning-point in

Andrew Blair's life. At the moment of its impact he was too utterly numbed and overwhelmed to realize how much his spirit was bruised and twisted. In those early tragic days of the First Kaffir Rising there was more than enough forced activity to engross his mind and mercifully keep him from brooding. Already more than seven thousand refugees were herded in Grahamstown. Many had suffered a devastation as tragic as his, and had need of an example of fortitude no less than of spiritual consolations. Four hundred and fifty homesteads had been burnt to the ground and three hundred pillaged; more than a quarter of a million head of live-stock had been lifted; not merely were their homes wrecked, but their sole source of livelihood was gone.

Nor did his function end with religious exhortation. In an emergency such as this it was the duty of every man who could carry arms to take his part in the just retribution. Though regular troops had been summoned from the Cape to reinforce the frontier's scattered garrison, it was on the English settlers themselves and on the Boer commandos that the brunt of the fighting fell. This time it was not enough to clear the bush and the forests as far as the Great Fish River and to recapture the driven cattle. Now, after so many years of half-hearted official vacillation, the men of the frontier were determined to act for themselves. If the law would not help them, they would take the law in their hands, riding into the heart of Kaffirland and dictating peace at last in the only language the chiefs understood: flame for flame, blood for blood, and pillage for pillage. For seven months Andrew Blair rode with them, taking his part in their hardships and perils, until the black tide that had overwhelmed the Eastern Province was rolled back beyond the Keiskamma, the Buffalo River, the Kei, until, at last, there was peace in the land.

But there was no peace in his heart. It seemed to him there could never more be peace in it. When the soldiers had built their new forts and the Boer commandos were disbanded and the settlers of his flock returned to the fire-blackened shells that had once been their homes and set themselves, with incredible faith and patience, to start their lives over again, Andrew Blair's war-worn eyes could not share in their courageous illusions. Beneath his surface of native dourness and shy sensibility he was a lonely, a bitter, a sensitive, suffering man, with an attitude towards life which he found hard to reconcile with his calling. He had not the heart—ay, that was the word for it—to continue his work in surroundings that only spoke to him of desolation and death. The wound, which the warlike, intense activities of the last six months had deadened rather than healed, was deeper, in fact, than he had imagined. And beneath all this (though he hardly knew it himself) he was now a man with a grudge: a grudge against the colonial government which, smugly, meanly and callously secure in Capetown, had sacrificed him and his by using them as a helpless living buffer between themselves and the Kaffir hordes; a grudge (and one that was even more deeply grounded and of which he was ashamed) against his own people who, when she was alive, had been shocked by his marriage and turned up their noses at Hannie, and now that she was dead, embittered him with empty condolences. These were no longer his people, he told himself savagely; he had neither part nor lot with them. He would be happier (though still how deeply unhappy!) out of their sight— out of sight of all faces and scenes that recalled his disaster.

He found he had more in common—unnatural though this might seem—with the folk of his dead wife's race than with his own countrymen: perhaps a community of hate forges stronger bonds than a community of love. Like himself, if for different reasons (though some were the same), the Dutch farmers hated the government with a deep, implacable hatred. Like himself, they were Calvinists, bred in a creed that had more of the Old Testament in it than the New: a harsh, vital, uncompromising religion that was nearer to that of his rugged youth in Angus than the mild piety of the Southern folk with whom his lot had been cast. What was more, his wife's kinsfolk accepted and welcomed him, not merely because he had married a woman of their race and spoke their language, but because, in those days, there were few Dutch pastors available, and congregations of the Dutch Reformed Church were eager to profit by the presence of Presbyterian pastors, the ministers of a sister church, and adopt them as their predikants. So it came about that, as time went by, the gulf between Andrew Blair and his original cure grew deeper and wider. A year after Hannie's death he had left the Kap River settlement, abandoning the house he had built and the land he had cleared, attaching himself, with a convert's enthusiasm, to a community more to his taste, and starting life over again with new vigour if not with new hope.

Even so, as he rode towards Welgelegen that afternoon on the cream-coloured mare which was now almost the only remaining relic of his life at Dyke Head, Mr. Blair's mind was troubled. Once more, it seemed, he approached a parting of the ways. Riding from farm to farm and receiving the confidences of lonely men and women to whom, in the intervals between quarterly communions, his visits constituted a solitary link with the outer world, he had become aware of a pervasive restlessness of body and spirit, puzzling if only because it appeared to arise of itself at the same moment and to develop in the same way among families completely divided from one another and scattered over an area of hundreds of square miles: a phenomenon resembling in its nature as in its unanimity the mysterious impulse which, on the same day and at the same hour, compels migrant birds to take to the air or ants to expel from their nests the flights of winged drones.

During the first year of his roving ministry he had often listened to grievances. To say that the frontier Boers were contented would not have been true. But during the last six months their vague discontents had crystallized with an astonishing rapidity. From the Winterberg to the sea, a morbid excitement thrilled the scattered community. On every farm stoep at which he off-saddled, instead of hearing the usual placid family gossip, the old talk of locusts and drought and crops and live-stock, he found himself plunged into an impassioned debate: one burning question excited and exercised every mind: *To trek or not to trek?*

The answer, he saw, was not to be dictated by reason. The springs of the movement lay far deeper than that. Racial feeling, resentment, righteous indignation, might serve as excuses; but the impulse beneath it was not very different from that which had set the ancestral wagons rolling west over the plains of Asia, breaking forth again, after a lapse of settled centuries, to drive folk of the same vagrant blood five thousand miles overseas to the farms of the Cape, uprooting them thence, in the space of three generations, to pause, for a while, on the eastern frontier, and now, reawakened, urging them to break loose and pass on once more.

Towards what? This important question did not

seem to trouble them, though rumour answered it with glowing encouragements. Already small parties, driven by drought from the Winterberg, had crossed the mountains of the north in search of new pasture, and found such a paradise as graziers might dream of: vast rolling steppes of lush grassland, well-watered by huge, quiet rivers and uninhabited: a new, boundless, empty world to be had for the asking, where a man with a wagon might wander for months and camp where he chose without meeting another, and sleep soundly, no longer haunted by the fear of predatory savages; a country, moreover, where men could live as they would, unvexed by the laws, the taxes, the pin-pricking regulations of foreigners, subject to no control but the promptings of conscience and the written Word of God.

And supposing a man grew weary of this Eden, or restless for adventure, why, then, at will, he might strike his camp and load his wagons and roll on again over the sea of waving grasses, north, always north, into warmer air and richer land, until, on the horizon, new shapes of blue mountain arose, the Berg of the Salt Pans, and welling at their feet the source of the sacred Nile. These things men knew for certain: Janse van Rensburg and Louis Trigardt of Graaf Reinet had seen them, trekking north with nine wagons and nine armed men through an empty land strewn with the bones of some ancient slaughter. "Long Hans" van Rensburg was dead, so the rumour ran, his skull beaten in by the *kerries* of the knob-nosed Kaffirs. That was his own fault for quarrelling with his partner. In strange lands men should stand together. But Trigardt, a more prudent fellow of middle age, had settled for good in the rich and watered valleys of the Salt Pan Mountains. A man who had won the wages of daring. A man to be envied.

And not only these. Even before Trigardt and Van Rensburg had crossed the great Yellow River, two new parties were following hot on the spoor of their wagons: one led by that grim, lanky man Hendrik Potgieter of the Tarka, whom folk nicknamed "Blauwberg" and the other by Sarel Cilliers, with a medley of Britses and Krugers and Liebenbergs from the Colesberg district. When they joined forces beyond the Orange they could count, between them, on more than sixty armed men, of whom, before long, they had need, when the exiled hordes of the Matabele broke on them and fell round the laagered wagons in drifts of dead five deep.

Even in the wide grass-lands of the North, it seemed, men must take their own part if they wished to hold what they seized. But that, after all, the young men said, was part of the game. It was one thing to sit on the frontier waiting for Kaffirs to creep out of the bush and raid your kraals in the night while you lay with one of your hands tied behind your back by the malicious English: quite another to face the devils in open country, where they could not approach to attack without being seen, where a man with a gun-trained horse could make rings round them, firing into the brown as often as he wished, and gallop away unscathed. Unforeseen disaster might fall on men who took foolish risks, as, by all accounts, some fools of the Liebenbergs had done, trekking away from the rest of the party, as soon as Blauwberg's back was turned, and leaving their wagons in Moselikatze's country unlaagered and almost unguarded. No wonder the Matabele swooped down and made mincemeat of them! But when Blauwberg Potgieter and Cilliers came back and the savages who had given their spears a bath in the blood of the Liebenbergs (children, too: that showed the sort of monsters they were!) tried their tricks again on the main camp at Vegkop, there was a different story to tell! Forty men, with a spare gun apiece, and a woman to load it with nicked bullets and slugs, inside a circle of fifty wagons lashed wheel to wheel with trek-chains and stuffed with thorn-bushes between. Outside, a wider circle of Matabele, more than five thousand of them, squatting down on the ground like vultures waiting for a death. But that would not do for Blauwberg: no use wasting good shot and powder before they came within range. A red rag waved on a whip-stock: a red rag to a bull. They jumped to their feet and hissed and on they came. One hundred yards . . . fifty . . . twenty . . . Blauwberg held his fire. One could smell the grease on their bodies. Thirty paces . . . Now rapid fire. Powder and shot rammed down the hot barrels in handfuls, blazing away point-blank at the mass of shining bodies, the open mouths hissing and howling, the hands that tore at the chains and the thorn-bushes and tugged at the wagons till the dead lay in drifts and the black wave broke and drew back. Once more, indeed, they charged; but this charge was the last. If they wanted more they could have it. They did not want more.

The lesson was clear enough: from this moment onwards—even more when Potgieter, reinforced by the parties whose wagons toiled over the mountains from Graaf Reinet and crossed on the pontoons of the Orange with Maritz, had followed the Matabele to the Molopo and burned Moselikatze's great place to the ground—men knew that on the grassy plains of the rolling high-veld the assegai could never be match for the musket nor the running savage for armed and mounted men, and that a rich land of unending promise and hope and freedom awaited those who had spirit enough to break with the past and take what was offered them.

Such were the stories Mr. Blair heard on the stoeps of the farms where men smoked their carved stone pipes and talked and spat in the evening and women sat anxiously listening. Men made up their minds and acted so swiftly that more than once when he rode to a farm expecting shelter for the night he had found it abandoned, and Hottentot families squatting in the empty *voorhuis*. If people continued to trek at this rate, the time would soon come when he would find himself left as a pastor without a flock; and at this prospect his conscience pricked him, for he counted himself a good shepherd, and if his people persisted in drifting away in this sheep-like fashion, he supposed that sooner or later it would be his duty to follow them.

Among his colleagues, the Scottish-born predikants of the Dutch Reformed Church with whom he took counsel, there was little difference of opinion. They were most of them settled men with wives and families, comfortably situated, and not in the least in love with adventure. Apart from their inclination to stay behind, this new ridiculous passion for rushing off into the wild was, if not precisely illegal—though even this seemed in doubt—by no means approved of by the colonial government. It was the duty of a pastor, they said, to stand by the civil authority, to render unto Cæsar the things that were Cæsar's.

Andrew Blair remained unconvinced by their arguments, and least of all by the last. He could not pretend to respect a government that never knew its own mind and had failed, with such terrible results to himself, to protect its own subjects—a distant government of smug officials too stupid to learn the lesson the Kaffir incursion should surely have taught them, too lazy to take the trouble to understand what people on the frontier were thinking, too callous to care. And still his folk went on trekking. What six months ago had been no more than a spiritual restlessness had become a mass-migration that gained strength and speed as it grew.

That afternoon, as he rode towards Welgelegen, the fierce debate which had divided Mr. Blair's mind for so long was drawing to a bitter end. He had reached a point at which he owed it to his conscience to take a decision, and though he already knew what the decision must be, he had deferred the moment of taking it until this visit—probably the last he would ever make to the Prinsloos'—was over.

Among all the farms he was in the habit of visiting, Welgelegen was that in which he had always felt most at home. Though it was no older than many others—and no farm on the frontier was older than himself—it had about it an air of permanence and serenity, proceeding less from the place than from its inhabitants. Old Adrian himself had struck him from the first as a man of exceptional character and intelligence, uniting with the customary Boer virtues of kindliness, courage and simplicity, a grave balance of mind, a judicial lack of prejudice and breadth of outlook, unusual in a man isolated from civilized converse. If he had need of an unbiassed judgment backed by experience and tempered by sympathy on any human problem of African life, there was no man living from whom he would sooner seek it than Adrian Prinsloo. He liked and admired Jacoba, too— not merely because she was gracious, serene and motherly, but because she, too, possessed a quality of spirit settled and stable, successfully defying the haphazard conditions of frontier life and subtly pervading them, infusing into the air of Welgelegen a sense of good breeding, an aristocracy not only of manners but of thought, in comparison with which the atmosphere of other farms he frequented (including that of his father-in-law, Grobler, at Graskop) appeared not merely uncouth and slovenly, but mean.

He had the feeling, in short, that these older people at Welgelegen, while adapting themselves to the wild, had refused to abandon or even to relax the standards of self-respect established in their blood by centuries of civilization; that essentially they were more civilized, if no better educated, than many of the English settlers who affected to despise them. He reckoned it as a misfortune that he had not known such folk as the Prinsloos in his earlier days.

He had found the qualities of Jacoba and Adrian reflected to a certain degree in all their children. The three youngest, Barend and Anna and the little boy Hendrik, were less true to type than their elders, Sarel and Lisbet. That was natural enough, after all: they had been born on the frontier; their nerves had been subjected in infancy to the strains and uncertainties of pioneer life. But Sarel had inherited much of his father's gravity and firmness of character as well as his physical distinction. Wherever he went he was known as an upright and serious man, somewhat reserved by nature and slow of speech, yet just and reliable and sound to the very marrow; while Lisbet . . .

Ah, Lisbet. . . . Mr. Blair shook his head and sighed heavily as he thought of her. From the first moment when he had set eyes on her, nearly three years ago, he had felt that a new experience had entered his life. This discovery had shocked him, for, like most silent men, he was seriously concerned with his own reactions, and the mere fact that the presence of any woman could move him profoundly and instantly, at a moment when he regarded himself as a devoted widower inconsolably shattered by the loss of his young wife, appeared to him not only extraordinary but shameful.

And yet, as soon as he saw her, he knew he loved Lisbet Prinsloo, and was ashamed to confess it, for the state implied a fickleness and a humiliating levity of which he could never have believed himself to be capable, and which, had he observed it in a member of his own congregation, he would have felt it his duty to discountenance or even to reprove.

Still, there, to his shame and confusion, it was. There were evidently more varieties of love than he had imagined. It had taken him forty years to recognize (or, at any rate, to admit that he recognized) the most obvious of them; and here, without the least warning and at a most inappropriate time, came a second which, in any other circumstances, would have been considered more becoming than the first. There was nothing in the customs of the society to which he had now attached himself to prevent his proposing immediately for Lisbet's hand: it was not uncommon for a Boer widower to set about remarrying in a business-like way as soon as his wife was buried; for the economy of a frontier farm could not be considered complete without a mistress. The only impediments to his paying his addresses to Lisbet existed in Mr. Blair's own mind; and the fact that they appeared insuperable suggested that this new passion was of a nature entirely different from his first.

He had hardly regarded Hannie Grobler as a creature of finer clay than himself, even less as one whose delicacy he must approach with circumspection and almost with awe. He had never doubted his qualifications to marry her or considered it possible that she could reject him. Nor, when he had decided to marry Hannie, had it ever struck him that their disparity of age made their union ludicrous to some and to others distasteful. Though he had been more than twice as old as Hannie, he had not, in those days, been conscious of it; he had felt himself young in years as in innocence. But now he was neither young nor innocent. The woes of the last two years had weighed upon him and broken him and changed him into an old and tired man, still capable, alas, of suffering the pangs of love, but no longer justified in asking a woman so young and exquisite as Lisbet to share his declining days or daring

to risk a rebuff. He had lived his life, he told himself, and now nothing was left to him but the
melancholy delight of a noble resignation.

Yet, though he resigned himself to this state, Mr.
Blair could not keep away from her. He was always
able to satisfy his conscience with some specious excuse
for riding out of his way to call at Welgelegen. He
called there so often, indeed, and the Prinsloos, pity-
ing his loneliness, made him so welcome, that he had
begun to think of himself as one of them and of the
farm as a second home. It was an easy and pleasant
relationship: the nearest thing to a normal family life
he had ever experienced. They welcomed Mr. Blair
not only because they liked him and were sorry for
him, but also because he constituted their principal link
with the outer world; and Lisbet, who had more
acquaintance with that world and more interest in it,
was even more glad to see him than the rest of the
family. He was the only person she ever met with
whom she could talk English, the only visitor who had
any pretensions to the kind of culture she had enjoyed
in Capetown and missed at Welgelegen.

He was her friend, her counsellor, her confidant.
She found it easy to speak to him of things that meant
much to her, but which the rest of the family—even
her mother—would have regarded with misunderstanding if not with contempt. He lent her books
from his small and precious library: they made a con-
venient excuse for his frequent visits. There were

none at Welgelegen save the brass-clamped family Bible, which they knew almost by heart, and Willem Sluiter's Spiritual Songs, an annotated Heidelberg Catechism, and the *Donderslag der Goddelozen* and Bogatsy's Golden Treasury. But the English books that Mr. Blair brought—though there were collections of sermons among them in which, out of kindness to him, she professed an interest she did not feel—were not only religious: there were historical works which she absorbed with eagerness and volumes of poetry which enraptured her. And when she had read his books they would discuss them, sitting alone on the stoep in the twilight, in a tongue which the others did not understand and which, of itself, gave their quiet talk a quality of intimacy, almost of secrecy that made it even more precious. Mr. Blair loved to listen to Lisbet speaking English in the soft melodious voice she had inherited from her mother—in the precise, clipped accent her sharp ear had mimicked from the speech of officers at the Cape, quaintly delicate, as it seemed to him, compared with his own Angus Doric. He was taken, too, by the quickness of her virgin intelligence and by a sensibility which, because he had never before known an educated woman, amazed him.

These sessions of quiet converse were sweeter than any other moments in Mr. Blair's lonely life. Yet their sweetness always seemed to him precarious. Of all the qualities he adored in Lisbet, the most precious to him was her childlike frankness. She was ready to open her heart to him as to no other living soul, harrowing his feelings and making him fiercely jealous as she spoke to him of the uncouth advances of Jan Bothma and of other eligible young men (so much younger than he, alas!) who had haunted Welgelegen from time to time and asked her to "sit up" with them, exalting him to an access of selfish thankfulness when she confessed how distasteful to her these advances were. There was no coquetry in these confidences. Her candour of itself made it clear that she regarded him as a kind and elderly friend whose interest in her affairs of the heart was detached and unemotional; and though there were times when he felt he must tell her he loved her and throw himself on her mercy, the fear not only of being humiliated but also of shattering this delightful intimacy and losing even as much of her as he had been blessed with, checked the impulse and fettered his tongue.

But he knew, all the same, he could not live without Lisbet; and this knowledge had lately begun to complicate his life by confronting him, for the first time, with an insoluble conflict between love and duty. It was his duty, as he believed, to leave the Eastern Province and follow his vagrant flock over the berg into the new lands where, rightly or wrongly, they had decided to cast their lot; yet if he crossed the berg he would probably never see Lisbet again, for her father had always set his face stubbornly against the idea of migrating, and Adrian Prinsloo was not a man who changed his mind easily, but rather prided himself on his resistance to mere public opinion.

There was no excuse acceptable to his conscience by which Mr. Blair could convince himself that he had a right to stay behind. If his colleagues in Albany persisted in their resolution to remain, there would be predikants enough, and more than enough, to minister to the needs of the dwindled community. Married men, such as they, with established churches and homes, had some semblance of a pretext with which to salve their consciences. But he was unmarried and homeless, a free man, to all appearances in the full vigour of middle age, unhindered by any family tie or material responsibility; if he did not trek with the rest, or even wavered, he knew that the reproach of faithlessness would remain with him inwardly all the days of his life.

That was why, as he approached Welgelegen in the cool of the evening, having ridden since noon, his face was so grave. Every step of the cream-coloured mare was bringing him nearer to the unbearable moment of meeting and of farewell. That was why, dismounting at the garden foot, and noting, with dissatisfaction, Jan Bothma's outspanned wagons, his heart beat so tempestuously and his lips trembled. For he knew that when he set eyes on Lisbet the resolution in which he had steeled himself would be strained beyond human endurance. And Mr. Blair was only too human.

So little prepared was he for that momentous meeting that he felt almost relieved when, entering the *voorhuis*, he found it empty but for Vrouw Prinsloo, who, during the daytime at least, was part of its permanent furniture, sitting with folded hands, like a statue of the benignant Buddha, at the head of the table, with the comforter under her feet and the coffee-urn before her. Anyone who did not know her habits would have thought her asleep; yet no sooner had the predikant's shadow darkened the doorway than she was ready to welcome him with the slow smile that made her massive face so sweet.

"*Ach, predikant,*" she said. "*Kom binnen, kom binnen. Hoe vaart gy?*"

"*Gezond* . . . well, Tante Jacoba. I am always well. I have no time to be otherwise," he told her, pressing her hand.

"But ready for coffee?" She poured out a cup of the black decoction of scorched grain and gave him a crystal of sugar-candy to suck as he sipped it.

"You are alone, tante," he said. He was wondering already where Lisbet might be.

"Alone, yes. Anna has taken Hendrik to the dam—that child must be watched continually!—and Lisbet . . . ah, Lisbet has taken tea to the Englishman."

"The Englishman?"

"Yes, you might know him perhaps. He comes from the coast and his name is Grafton . . . Jan Grafton."

Mr. Blair shook his head. "The name is new to

me; but that's not surprising; I've quite lost touch with the English settlers. I am almost a Dutchman now."

She smiled:—"Never, never, my friend. A man with one eye could be sure of that if he saw you a mile away. But this poor in-blown Englishman, as we used to call them when I was a girl at the Cape, had the foolishness to get lost in the Assegai Bush. When he came to the door he fell flat. One would have said he was dead. Now he rests in Jan Bothma's wagon."

"And Lisbet is looking after him?" A faint jealousy tinged the enquiry. Mr. Blair was quick to dissemble it. "I will go and see him later when I have heard all the news."

"The news. Ah, what news!" Mevrouw Prinsloo shook her head in despair. "The old story again. We were raided by Kaffirs last night. They broke into the cattle kraal and drove off our nephew's oxen, two splendid new spans, as well as sixty of ours. The old baas and the boys rode off at dawn to spoor them if they could. But who knows? By the time they started they'll be lost in the Kouwie Forest, and who can follow them there? A bad business, and there is no end to it, no end to it. Ah, here she comes! A surprise, Lisbet!"

Mr. Blair rose clumsily to greet her. It was strange, he thought, how much lovelier she always seemed than he had imagined her; so cool, so clean, so maddeningly self-possessed compared with himself. As she smiled and held out her hand, her hazel eyes met his with their innocent, confident frankness, knowing nothing of how their beauty made him tremble.

"No surprise," she said. "I thought you were coming and knew you had come. I saw the old mare."

"You have another guest?" he said stiffly.

(Was it possible that she blushed, or was this rich hue a trick of the sunset light?)

"Yes, yes, but my young man is better," she said, recovering herself. "He won't need a nurse any longer, thank Heaven. But you, Mr. Blair . . ." she changed the subject eagerly, almost too eagerly. "You are late this evening: much later than usual. Although I expected you, I had almost given you up."

"I was delayed all morning," he said. "A call from the coast, from Hans Strijdom, of Meerlust. A sad business. A funeral."

"What? Not Hans' father?" Jacoba enquired.

"No, no. None of our folk. It was a wreck. That wild south-easter."

"Ay, we felt it even here. Poor fellows, poor fellows! Who are they?"

(Why was Lisbet's body so suddenly tense? Why did she clench her hands? Why did she seem to gasp when she begged him to tell them more?)

"I don't know who they were. We shall probably never know. I can only tell you what young Hans told me. Three days ago—three or four: I do not remember—just before the gale started, a ship put in and dropped anchor off the Bushman River mouth. Hans didn't notice her himself—he is not observant—but from what the Hottentots told him, he thought she was an Indiaman. I think he was wrong—but that part of the story comes later. She must have put in there for water; and that is odd, too; she might easily have chosen an inhabited spot like Port Frances or Port Elizabeth. However, apart from the surf, it's not so bad a place, with two rivers, the Bushman and the Kariega, running out together. So she launches a boat —the Hottentot says there were three—and lands a party to fill up her water-barrels. Then up comes the gale. The big ship gets anxious—no wonder, either, on a lee-shore fringed with breakers—and ups with her anchor and fires signal-guns for the landing-party to come back. Easier said than done, when once the south-easter starts blowing; the surf on that shore is no joke at the best of times. The Hottentot saw the boats riding it bravely one moment. The next, they were gone. The men on the ship must have seen what happened too, for she took no further risks—she just cut and ran for it."

"Almighty, what lives sailors lead!" Jacoba sighed. "I have never been on the sea, and I pray that I never may. So the Tottie gave the alarm?"

"Not he! The Hottentots do not value human life; and what could he do, in any case? The boats were gone, and no man could fight with that surf. He went home and said nothing about it till two days later, when he came and told Hans Strijdom there were white men lying on the sand who badly needed burying, and Hans, who's a godly man though not over-bright, sent a message for me to give them Christian burial."

"Poor fellows! How many of them were there?"

"Eight in all. One was dressed like a sailor, and two were redcoats in uniform."

"A troop-ship, then?"

"I have my doubts." (Mr. Blair was enjoying his little mystery: it flattered him to see how intently Lisbet listened; but why was she so pale?) "I doubt it. As I say, there were only two redcoats and one seafaring man. But the rest were all uniformed, in a manner of speaking. Though half of their clothes had been torn and stripped—the sharks had been busy—what was left was all of a piece: the material was grey."

"All alike. To think of it! That puts me in mind of something. Now where have I seen grey clothes?" Vrouw Prinsloo meditated.

"Ah, Mother, the English always wear cloth rather than leather," Lisbet broke in quickly. "It is what they call hodden."

"But this, niece, was different. It was shoddy, not good Scots hodden. I knew what it meant the moment I saw it: the vessel was a transport ship, and the dead men were convicts."

"God is just," Jacoba said. "Supposing that they

had escaped! The country is full enough of such desperate folk already."

"Mother, how can you speak such words?" Lisbet cried. "Is it true, Mr. Blair," she asked, "that all the poor souls you buried there must have been criminals?"

"They were all of them convicts: they must all have transgressed the law."

"Our own folk transgress the law every day, but they are not transported. I have heard at the Cape that the English law is cruel."

"It is severe," Mr. Blair admitted, "severer than ours."

"And sometimes mistakes are made?"

"No doubt. Even judges are human."

"Daughter, daughter, what has come over you?" Jacoba mildly protested. "What have we to do with such things?"

"I want to know something, Mother. I want the predikant to tell me if his thoughts are the same as yours. Was it God's will that these men should be drowned?"

Andrew Blair was silent. He could not understand this intensity, and he could not seek an explanation for it in her face, for the light was failing rapidly and the *voorhuis* grew dim.

"The will of God is in everything, Lisbet," he said. "You know that well."

"Then . . . if one of them had been saved, Mr. Blair—if one had escaped from the waves?"

He smiled. "You are supposing a thing that could not have happened, my child. No human being could possibly have lived in that sea. The boats must have been smashed to matchwood; those poor men's bodies . . . I have seen death often enough in my life, but nothing quite so terrible."

"But, *if*, Mr. Blair?" she entreated. "Answer me that!"

No wonder that Anna stood gaping at them from the doorway, astonished, bewildered by the passionate vibrations that thrilled the darkness out of which only the face of Lisbet, who stood facing her, could be seen, strained, eager, preternaturally pale. What was the meaning of this dark drama, this electric intensity? Anna asked herself. Were they quarrelling, or had Lisbet taken leave of her senses? With Lisbet in her present inexplicable mood, almost anything seemed possible. She heard the predikant's voice:

"In that case," he was saying, "I should also consider it God's will that this man should be saved."

"And forgiven?"

"That only God knows. Say, rather, reserved by His Grace for some other use—maybe one more merciful."

"Yes, yes. . . . That is what I wanted you to say: that is what I believe. . . ." Her voice broke on the words. Then she put her hands to her eyes. She knelt at her mother's side and buried her streaming eyes in Jacoba's ample bosom. Mevrouw Prinsloo bent over her tenderly. Her fat pale hands sustained and caressed Lisbet's sob-shaken figure.

"Take no notice of her, predikant," she said in her calm, sweet voice. "The poor child is sensitive and over-wrought. And no wonder in such days as these. We live in the midst of strain and anxiety and horror and never, never know what is coming next." She sighed. Although her hands still embraced and comforted Lisbet, her mind was already far away with Adrian and her sons in the Kouwie Forest. "It is late. Bring the candles, Anna," she said. "It is better to show a light, for the men should surely be riding home by now. And tell Ayah to bring the wash-tub for the predikant's feet."

CHAPTER SEVEN

RIDE INTO KAFFIRLAND

THEY were nearing the boundaries of Welgelegen at that moment, a slow cavalcade of ten grim men and fagged horses. They had most of them been in the saddle for more than fourteen hours, which is more than is good for any man or beast, and not merely riding but straining ear and eye and keeping awake that sixth sense of apprehensiveness which sniffs danger before it draws near that, born of the habit of unremitting caution, became an essential part of the frontier Boer's equipment. They were all armed, with a variety of weapons, from flint-lock, shot-guns charged with buck shot and smooth-bore military muskets to grooved eight-pounders, every piece primed and ready for a snap-shot at leaping savage or blindly charging rhinoceros.

Yet through all that day not a single shot had been fired nor had the horses moved faster than a light canter. In the twilight, when they had foregathered on the march of Welgelegen where the Prinsloos' next neighbours, the Nels and the Oosthuizens, had joined them, it had been mortally cold. The horses' breath fumed in the air; dew darkened their fetlocks, and

George Dicketts, who was not, like the rest, protected from head to foot by garments of bark-tanned leather and mole-skin, but still wore his shoddy grey, felt chilled to the bone and sighed for the face-cloth uniform he had sported in Flanders.

This was not his idea of a military enterprise. This motley collection of uncouth and bearded ruffians, with powder-horns slung on their shoulders and pipes stuck in their hat-bands, who growled at each other in short bursts of guttural speech and rode with slovenly stirrups sweeping the grass, would have made a poor figure beside a patrol of the Dutch irregulars, whom the troopers of the Fifteenth Hussars had always despised. And their mounts were no more presentable than their riders: stocky, shaggy beasts, unshod and ungroomed and harnessed with strips of leather whose clumsiness would have put any village saddler in England to shame. Could he ride, indeed! With a cob such as the one they had given him, the shabbiest of the whole mangy bunch, it would have been impossible to show them what riding meant even if he had wanted to. These chaps didn't ride at all, to his way of thinking: they just slumped in their saddles and let the beasts do the rest. He would have given anything for a rousing gallop to set his blood flowing. But not a bit of it.

When they had lingered freezing for half an hour in the dusk, the last of the party joined them: a tall, well-set-up man of the same pattern as the rest, whom

George guessed to be the son of his grey-bearded host, for he rode at the head of the straggling column by the old man's side.

Even then the mean pace did not quicken. They were following, it seemed, in the steps of a fantastic naked creature whom George took at first for a little boy, but who was, in fact, an old man, a tame Bushman expert in tracking. This grotesque figure ran in front of them with swift pattering steps, pausing here and there and changing direction like a running partridge and turning from time to time to encourage them with inarticulate cries. If Jan Bothma's murdered Hottentot Klaas had seemed ugly, this diminutive, sub-human creature was more hideous still, with his hollow back and bulbous protruding belly, his flat face, decorated with a porcupine quill that pierced the bridgeless nose, his slanting eyes that glittered like those of a wizened, wicked child, and his bossed skull dotted with peppercorns of wool like those that are left on the rump of a fly-blown sheep. Yet, hideous or no, the small monster knew his business. Not a scratch on the hard sun-baked soil missed his wicked eyes. Though the party seemed to be moving slowly, they were covering the ground. Even his shabby mount, whose appearance Dicketts had despised, had a trippling pace, between a walk and a canter, that made riding so easy that a man could have slept in the saddle, and a sureness of foot that absolved him of watchfulness.

They rode on and on in silence through dry, open mimosa-bush of the kind of which Dicketts had had his fill the day before. He recognized the pungent smell of it. Sometimes they encountered patches of denser thicket, through which the leading horsemen must hack their way. Remembering the thorny torments of yesterday, George thanked Heaven he was no longer on foot. He felt even more thankful when suddenly a scorching sun burst forth and turned the icy morning air to a furnace blast so fierce that he no longer envied his companions' moleskins and leather. It was a relief, indeed, when they came at last to a silent, swollen river and a drift so deep that the turbid flood washed the cob's belly and the bushman was forced to swim.

George slipped his foot out of the stirrup and let his leg dangle luxuriously in the water's delicious coolness; and on the further side the arid bush gave place to a forest-belt of tall trees with tawny or silvery shafts shooting up as straight as the *Minerva's* masts, their branches bearded with tufts of grey-green lichen and festooned with vines that hung in loose ends and loops like a wrecked ship's rigging. The air in these woods was mercifully cool and yet somehow flat, as though all the life had been sucked out of it by the interwoven masses of foliage that drank the light above and made a moist gloom beneath. Their silence, too, was oppressive. It seemed to him that hours had passed since a word had been spoken. He would have been

glad, if he had dared, to sing or whistle a marching-
song to keep up his spirits; but he had not even the
heart for that, all the rest of the grim cavalcade seemed
pledged to silence, riding stubbornly on in the wake of
the bushman's grotesque, childlike figure which stooped
and peered and halted and clicked its tongue and
gesticulated and then pattered on like a running
partridge. There must be rich landlords in these parts,
George thought, with all this here timber, and good
roosting for pheasants, but not so much as a feather
did he see till the tall trees ended on an edge sharp-
cut as a fifty-foot wall, and they came to another
river.

He was glad to drink of the water, and so was his
horse, but by this time he was famished. They must
have been riding for five hours by his reckoning, and
he had tasted nothing but a cupful of bitter black
coffee since his gorge of mutton last night. His companions, it seemed, felt no need of food, though the
man who rode next to him was slicing what looked like
a plug of tobacco and stolidly chewing. A quid of
tobacco would be better than nothing, he thought,
though he doubted his stomach would stand it. He
made signs to his neighbour, a shaggy, blond-bearded
man with hot blue eyes, who took his meaning and
nodded and handed him a plug. It wasn't tobacco after
all, but a strip of sun-dried meat. When he chewed it
the savour was gamy, but not unpleasant, rather like
that of the broth they made in Grafton from the re-

mains of a pheasant, and in spite of the smallness of the
portion he had been given, his hunger was relieved.

As they splashed through the drift—it was shallower
than the last—he felt a miraculous revival of energy.
In any case, he was thankful to be in the open. Them
there woods had got on his nerves. When he reached
the further bank he became aware that something had
happened. The tracker had stopped and lay prostrate
on his belly, and the men who had crossed before him
were gathered in a bunch round Adrian Prinsloo and
talking excitedly. On the ground he saw signs of a
bivouac: the remains of a fire of charred sticks and
recent droppings of cattle. The men nodded and
smiled and looked to the priming of their flint-locks
as though they expected to use them. The small-
headed giant, in whose wagon George had slept, gave
the bushman a flick with the tapered *sjambok* that
swung from his saddle-bow. The tiny monster jumped
up with a cackle of laughter and hurried on, tracking
again.

Now they moved much faster. The bush was a
scattered parkland of sandy soil on which even George
Dickett's unpractised eye could distinguish the spoor
of the driven cattle. The bushman was running now—
he skimmed the ground so fast that the trippling horses
barely kept up with him. The thudding of their forty
hooves on soft sand made a new exhilarating rhythm.
There was a feeling of subdued excitement and hope in
the air; he was conscious of the old exaltation, half

gay, half tremulous, of a squadron riding into action, expecting, at every moment, to hear the first shot.

But no shot was fired, and suddenly the loose sand ended. The sound of the trippling hooves rang sharp and brittle. They had come to a treeless ridge of water-worn stone streaked with glistening veins. Not a vestige of green, not so much as desiccated lichen could find hold on that wind-scoured, sun-baked surface. It was as smooth as a bleached human skull, and so hard that nothing less than an iron-shod hoof could have left a scratch on it. Nor was it an isolated patch of barrenness. From the point they had reached, the area of denudation extended for miles: a great dome of shelving hill-top over which the air, quivering with heat, swam in silvery streaks of mirage that made it seem as though thunder had lately broken and rain lay in pools. The sunlight danced back from its glittering crystalline particles as though it could not penetrate it, yet the stone was so hot that the horses felt its fierce radiations and lifted their feet uneasily as though the heat scorched the frogs and hurt them.

The bushman had come to a halt and appeared to be puzzled. He went down on his hands and knees, crawling hither and thither, scrutinizing the smooth stone, making casts in every direction, like a feathering hound who has lost the quarry's scent. Jan Bothma stood over him, threatening him with his *sjambok* and spurring him on to new effort; but the monster was utterly thwarted; there was no more spoor to be seen than if the stony plateau had been the watery waste that it seemed. The men moved back to the sand for the sake of their horses' hooves. They gathered in a group round old Adrian in an anxious debate, not a word of which George Dicketts could understand. Jan Bothma, it seemed, was for riding on and making another cast; but the rest shook their heads, and finally the old man turned his horse's head towards the declining sun, leaving the bushman to fend for himself, and set off at a canter.

The line they took was different from that by which they had come. It lay through more open country, and George Dicketts was surprised to find that the Boers were better horsemen and their sorry mounts better cattle than he had imagined. After two hours of hard riding, in the heat of the afternoon, they came to a dip in the downs and looked down on a village of low whitewashed houses, and a church with a zinc-roofed nave and a square tower rising in their midst. It seemed odd to George, finding a village isolated like that, just dumped in the dusty plain without orchards or gardens or hedges or fields. There were no leafy lanes about it, nor even a street worth the name, save one wide, barren thoroughfare of tawny earth with a footpath on either side that ran straight from the church to a solid two-storeyed building, more pretentious than the rest, with a flagstaff from whose peak there fluttered a Union Jack.

The sight of the flag of freedom under which he had fought for his country did not cheer George Dicketts. It filled him not with pride, but with disquietude, as being the only flag on earth under which his freedom was in danger. As they rode towards it down a wide track scored in the veld by the wheels of wagons, he had a feeling that he was putting his head in the lion's mouth. If he had known where he was or how to get back to his friend, he would have turned his horse's head and bolted, hell for leather; but even such a retreat might prove dangerous, if only by calling attention to himself. Acutely conscious of his tell-tale grey uniform, he insinuated himself and his mount into the middle of the bunch of horsemen in the hope that he might not be noticed.

There was less fear of this, in fact, than he might have expected. At that hour of the afternoon the whole village of Grahamstown lay sunk in a hot siesta. A few oxen, outspanned from wagons that lay like stranded ships, had wandered off in search of such shade as they could find and lay chewing the cud under a solitary tree that stood in the middle of the road in front of the church. If there were sentries posted at the Drostdy, where the flag flew, they probably slept too, in the certainty of not being disturbed. George felt as nervous of that flag as a horse that shies at a fluttering paper. It seemed as if they were going straight up to it, till, of a sudden, old Adrian and Sarel Prinsloo and Jan Bothma detached themselves from the rest and rode on ahead and came back, at the end of another half-hour, with a sleepy ill-tempered officer and a couple of soldiers who led the way to the back of the barracks where, in two walled enclosures, dense masses of patient cattle stood wedged shoulder to shoulder.

When he looked over the wall of the kraal, Jan Bothma gave a great shout of triumph. "Ha! Blauwberg!" he cried, and all the others smiled. Adrian Prinsloo addressed the officer in halting English. He nodded his head and answered. The young man had a pleasant, cultured voice, but spoke so fast that old Prinsloo knitted his brows in the effort to understand him, though George Dicketts, still hidden in the midst of the group, could hear every word.

"It was a bit of sheer luck," he was saying. "A patrol of the Seventy-Second coming in from the fort at Trompetter's Drift bumped into the devils just after dawn not far from the river. The Kaffirs must have got the surprise of their lives: they just lost their heads and bolted, and our fellows collected the cattle and drove them in here. They're yours, aren't they?"

Adrian Prinsloo nodded. "Mine and Jan Bothma's."

"Well, they're safe enough now, anyway."

"We can drive them home?"

"Drive them home? I should damned well think not. They're Government property."

"But I tell you they're mine and my nephew's.

There are neighbours here riding with me who can recognize the marks and swear to them."

"I don't doubt your word or theirs," the officer said. "But even supposing that they swear these cattle are yours, I can't let you take them. I have to fulfil my instructions, the same as anyone else. It's no use blaming me, Mynheer Prinsloo."

"Then what can I do, Lieutenant?"

"For the moment, nothing. I don't want to make any unpleasantness, but the position is perfectly clear. The Attorney-General in Capetown gave his ruling last year, and we can't go beyond it. After all, we can't waste our time sorting people's cattle for nothing. We have plenty of work on our hands, protecting the frontier. What happens is this: when the kraals are full, as they are now, the magistrate arranges an auction. It is open to you to buy back what you want at the sale."

"To buy my own cattle, Lieutenant?"

"I admit it sounds a bit hard; but there it is. After all, your Kaffir war cost the Government a mint of money, and someone has got to pay for it. We're still patrolling the frontier, remember."

Old Prinsloo's eyes flashed. "Well enough to get hold of my cattle," he said, "but not well enough to prevent the Kaffirs from lifting them."

The officer laughed pleasantly. "Yes, I see the point of that."

"I have heard of this rule before," the old man said,

"but I did not believe it, no, I did not believe it. I have always stood for the Government when others complained; but this is not right."

Jan Bothma lurched over towards him. "I have counted my two new spans, Uncle Adrian," he said. "Not one of them missing. You and Sarel had better pick out your beasts. If we stand here talking we shall never get home by dark."

Sarel Prinsloo answered him. While his father and the officer had been speaking he had not uttered a word. Though his sanguine, handsome face grew dark as he listened, he had controlled, as was his habit, the fury that boiled in his heart.

"We are going home now, Jan," he said. "The game is finished. This time, I think it is finished for good, God be thanked."

"We are going home now?" the big man blustered. "What is the meaning of that? You may do as you will with your own cattle, Sarel; but I shall not go back to Welgelegen without my two new spans—and Hendrik's pet, the little black Zuurveld, too. Let me tell you that!"

"Very well," Sarel answered sardonically. "You had better make your arrangements to stay till the Landdrost orders the auction. It may take a week, as the Englishman says."

"I don't understand what the Englishman says and don't want to. What auction is this? All I want is my two new spans."

"Then you'll have to buy them."

"What madness is this? I bought them in Swellendam only two months ago. I bought them and paid for them: sixty-six dollars apiece!"

"You may get them cheaper next time."

"Next time? I want them now. I recognize every one of them, and none can dispute it. They are my property, no?"

"They were up till last night. Now it seems they belong to the Government."

"The Government? What is the Government?"

"Ask this Englishman here. He has forbidden us to move them."

"And who is he to forbid us?" Jan's voice rose threateningly. He clenched his fists and towered over the officer, waving his hands and letting forth a flood of excited speech. The young Englishman held his ground. On his faintly smiling lips there was the calmness of a man aware of his own authority, the politely repressed but none the less obvious contempt of a civilized gentleman for a blustering yokel who had not even the wits or the grace to learn an intelligible language. He let the hot spate of Jan Bothma's splutterings sweep over his head, then raised his eyebrows and quietly turned away. But Jan Bothma had not done with him. The very quietness of the officer's demeanour infuriated him the more. Whether this damned redcoat understood what he said or no, he was determined to make him listen till he had finished. As the officer turned Jan shot out an enormous hand which caught him by the epaulette and swung him round.

"Damn you, sir! Keep your hands off me!" the officer cried.

The two stolid soldiers, who had watched the whole scene with sleepy incomprehension, awoke and jumped forward to lay hands on Bothma. Barend Prinsloo, already spoiling for a fight, rushed in to his cousin's aid. The two Nels and the younger Oosthuizen leapt from their saddles and advanced with guns in their hands. ("Now which bloody side do I come in on?" George Dicketts thought. "That's a poser, that is.") There seemed, suddenly, to be all the ingredients for a pretty flare-up when Sarel Prinsloo threw himself into the midst of them. He caught Barend's arm and pulled him back and stepped in between Jan and the officer.

"You great thickhead," he said, "would you make things worse than they are? Do you want to fight the whole garrison single-handed, and get a pistol-shot through your silly skull for your pains? Go back to your horse, and leave this matter to me." He bowed to the dishevelled lieutenant. "I apologize, sir, for my cousin," he said in his stilted English. "He lost his temper. He was angry at what we all of us think an injustice; but that does not excuse him."

"I've a damned good mind to put him under arrest whatever he thought," said the officer hotly. "There's a sight too much of this sort of stuff on the frontier just now, and it 'ld serve him right if I clapped him into the *tronk* for a couple of days to cool him. However, since you've apologized and no harm's been done, I'll let it pass this time. As for your cattle, you know what to do: you put in your claim at the Landdrost's office. It's his business, not mine. As a matter of fact, between you and me and the gatepost, I agree with you it's a damned scurvy deal. Good day to you, sir."

He turned back to the barracks, the soldiers following him, while Sarel, remounting his horse, set the party in motion. George Dicketts was unfeignedly thankful to move out of range of the law. It had been, as he told himself, a beggar of a situation. "For if it had come to a fight and I'd stuck to these foreign chaps," he reflected, "I should have finished up with a firing-squad, and if I'd gone in with the soldiers, the same as I ought, they'd have wanted to know who I was, and I should have found myself back in leg-irons in no time. That's what comes," he thought, "when you meddle and mak in other folks' business. Thank God I'm well out of it!"

The ride home was a solemn affair. They rode as fast as the tired horses could move over a recognizable track, with a red sun rapidly sinking on their left hand. Old Prinsloo and Sarel led the procession in silence; and though Barend, still hot with indignation, talked excitedly to Jan Bothma, the giant sulked like a surly child and would not answer him. The sun went down. They rode on through an eerie stillness, with no sound save the rhythmical thudding of unshod hooves on the dusty track. They had covered, by George's reckoning, at least forty miles since dawn, and might still be, for all he knew, another twenty from home. He had well-nigh fallen asleep in the saddle, so easy were his horse's paces, when a sharp exclamation from his shaggy blond-bearded neighbour aroused him. He looked up and saw, far ahead, a pale glimmer of light, and at the same moment the whole weary cavalcade swerved right-handed and cantered towards it, coming to rest, at last, on the wide expanse of bare earth in front of the house where Jan Bothma's wagons still stood.

CHAPTER EIGHT

MANIFESTO

THEY trooped clumsily, those ten weary men, into the candle-lit *voorhuis*, their eyes dazzled even by that mild light, their limbs stiffened and cumbrous after fourteen hours in the saddle. George Dicketts, limping in the rear, looked round anxiously to see whether John were still there, but saw only the three women whom he had noticed the night before, the little boy, and a tall, black-coated stranger with a rugged, clean-shaven face. The eldest woman still sat where he had last seen her, slumped down massively on the backless rest-bench at the head of the table. Her eyes were anxious as they entered, checking their number. When she saw that none was missing, she sighed with relief and smiled; yet all were silent until Adrian Prinsloo suddenly spoke, as though emerging from a dream.

"A *soopie*, wife," he said. "It has been a long day."

Anna hurried round with a black earthenware jar and a cup into which she poured a dollop of peach-brandy. The tired men gulped it down, one by one, and smacked their lips. The fiery stuff made George Dicketts choke, but it put new life into him. The silence became unbearable. Jacoba spoke:

"Well . . . what happened?" she said.

"What happened, aunt?" Jan Bothma burst in before Adrian could answer. "You shall hear what happened!"

Sarel interrupted him: "Much more would have happened, Jan, if you and Barend had had your way. If you'd had your way, we might all of us be in the *tronk*. Even now you can't hold your tongue. Let the old *baas* speak."

"There is not much to tell, wife," Adrian said. "We spoored them for more than six hours, and lost them. We came back to the fort to complain. The cattle were there in the Government kraal. They are still there."

"Still there?"

"We are not allowed to take our own cattle away. This is the new regulation. The Landdrost will sign a paper and put them up for auction. Any man who comes to the sale can bid and buy them. The Government takes the money or keeps the cattle. It comes to the same."

"But that is a monstrous thing: that is what I call robbery. We call the Kaffirs thieves, but the English are no better."

"Have the soldiers got Slingveld, my little black bull?" the small boy cried. "Did you see my little black bull in the kraal, cousin Jan? You did? Then you ought to have shot them. That's what I should have done."

"Quiet, quiet, child!" Jacoba tried to suppress him. "You don't know what you're saying."

"The child knows better than we do," Jan Bothma declared. "*Out of the mouths of babes and sucklings.* Isn't that the word, predikant? He says nothing but what hundreds and hundreds of men are thinking. We keep our mouths shut, but he has the courage of the innocent and speaks. If the men of the frontier got together and took their guns and raised a commando, they could drive these damned redcoats into the sea and have done with them. If we had the spunk to take our lives in our hands . . ."

"You would lose them for certain," Sarel answered contemptuously. "You'ld be hanged within a month, like your cousin Stephanus."

"Well, what matter? A man can only die once. And to die for freedom . . ."

Sarel laughed at his bombast. "The taste for martyrdom runs in your family, Jan. You are like an angry rhinoceros: you charge with blind eyes. If I have to do anything for freedom, I'd rather live than die for it."

"Yet we cannot live as we are, Sarel." It was the younger Oosthuizen, the blond-bearded man with the hot blue eyes, who spoke; and the *brandewyn* had made his eyes bluer and hotter. "Jan Bothma is right. It is time we acted together. I'm with him for one."

"And I for another," said Barend.

Old Adrian glared at him angrily. "Be done with this childish talk. I'll have no sedition under this roof as long as I'm master. There are better ways of righting injustice than shedding blood. I learnt that lesson from Slachter's Nek before you were born, Barend. I say there are other ways."

"There is one other way, father."

"Yes, yes, I know your way, Sarel. It is a natural way for the young who can never set eyes on a mountain without being certain that paradise lies just beyond it. Young colts in a paddock, my son, always think the veld outside the fence is sweeter. When you come to my age you will have learnt that grass is grass, the sour and the sweet mixed together, wherever you go. And you'll have learnt yet another thing: that the young will never believe what you tell them—and a third: that the young always have their own way in the end."

Sarel smiled. "That may be true, father. But remember this: it is not only the colts that want to jump the fence and break out of this paddock. Old and young, we have fed on sour grass for long enough and gone thin on it. If we thought of none but ourselves we might say with Jan Bothma: 'A man can only die once.' But we have to think of others, of our women and those who come after us—our children, our grandchildren. And we cannot stand alone, father: we are members all of one family. We have a duty to our kin."

Adrian Prinsloo shook his head. "I know the way of your thought, Sarel. You make up your mind and seek out your reasons afterwards."

"And what does that matter, provided the reasons

are good enough? I will tell you the truth. Until yesterday I had not fully made up my mind. I am a young man, but not hot-headed. I think, in fact, I am more cautious than most men of my age. But if I like to think for myself and go my own way, my mind is not shut up; it is ready to take some count of the reasoning of others; and since I left Welgelegen the other day I have come on reasons that set my own thoughts in order and made clear what I think. Piet Retief . . .”

“Piet Retief! I thought we had heard the last of that meddlesome fellow.”

“He has gone to the north; but I do not think we have heard the last of him. Before he trekked he published a manifesto in the *Grahamstown Journal* last month.”

“That is just like that mountebank! The man has a passion for seeing his name in newspapers. Who cares what he has to say?”

“That is what I myself would have said before I read his letter. Now I think differently, father. It is a voice that speaks for me and hundreds of others who have only thought and muttered but never spoken before. I have the paper here. Will you read it for yourself?”

“I have no glasses to read with,” Adrian answered petulantly. “Besides, it is written in English, no doubt, and I can guess, without reading, what rubbish the fellow has written. I know Piet Retief.”

"May I read it aloud in Dutch, father?" Sarel persisted.

Adrian grunted. "You may do what you will."

"I will read it, then. Lisbet, bring me the candle. The light is dim. That is better . . . yes. It is dated the second of February. This is how it begins." Bending over the crumpled paper, Sarel read in a level voice:

" 'Numerous reports have been circulated throughout the Colony, evidently with the intention of exciting in the minds of our countrymen a feeling of prejudice against those who have resolved to emigrate from a Colony where they have experienced for so many years past a series of the most vexatious and severe losses; and as we desire to stand high in the estimation of our brethren, and are anxious that they and the world at large should believe us incapable of severing that sacred tie which binds a Christian to his native soil, without the most sufficient reasons, we are induced to record the following summary of our motives for taking so important a step; and also our intentions respecting our proceedings towards the native tribes we may meet with beyond the boundary.' "

Adrian laughed. "That is one for the missionaries anyway. I hope they will read it."

"There is more of that later. I will go on: '(1) We despair of saving the Colony from those evils which threaten it by the turbulent and dishonest conduct of vagrants who are allowed to infest the country in every part; nor do we see any prospect of peace or happiness for our children in a country thus distracted by internal commotions.' "

"That is right, that is right," the blond Oosthuizen muttered, as Sarel went on: " '(2) We complain of the severe losses we have been forced to sustain by the emancipation of our slaves . . .' "

"Two million pounds out of the three that were due to us! What did I tell you last night?" Jan Bothma said bitterly.

" '. . . and the vexatious laws which have been enacted respecting them.' Next: '(3) We complain of the continual system of plunder which we have endured from the Kaffirs and other coloured classes, and particularly by the last invasion of the Colony, which has desolated the frontier districts, and ruined most of the inhabitants.' Then: '(4) We complain of the unjustifiable odium which has been cast on us by interested and dishonest persons, under the cloak of religion, whose testimony is believed in England to the exclusion of all evidence in our favour; and we can foresee, as the result of this prejudice, nothing but the total ruin of the country.' "

Sarel paused in his reading. "Is not that just, father? Even now the missionaries are saying that the men who have trekked have only done so to keep their slaves and their compensation. But listen to this: '(5) We are resolved, wherever we go, that we will uphold the just principles of Liberty; but whilst we will take

care that no man shall be held in a state of slavery, it
is our determination to maintain such regulations as
may suppress crime and preserve proper relations
between master and servant.' "

Adrian nodded. "Good, good. He could not have
put it better. That is the right answer to give them.
Go on, Sarel."

Sarel went on: " '(6) We solemnly declare that we
quit this Colony with a desire to lead a more quiet life
than we have heretofore done. We will not molest
any people, nor deprive them of the smallest property:
but, if attacked, we shall consider ourselves fully
justified in defending our persons and effects, to the
utmost of our ability, against every enemy.' There are
four more paragraphs, father . . ."

"Read on, read on."

" '(7) We make known, that when we shall have
framed a code of laws for our future guidance, copies
shall be forwarded to the Colony . . .' " ("But
why?" Gert Oosthuizen broke in. "What business
is it of theirs? That is weaker than need be.")
" '. . . shall be forwarded to the Colony for general
information; but we take this opportunity of stating
that it is our firm resolve to make provision for the
summary punishment of any traitors who may be found
among us.' "

"That seems to me strange," Adrian said. "I would
have thought one might take it for granted that a
traitor would be shot."

"But supposing the traitor were English," Sarel explained, "the Government might find in his punishment an excuse for making war on us. It is as well to make such matters clear, father."

"Yes, yes. That is wise. The fellow is slim. He has thought of everything. What next?"

" '(8) We propose, in the course of our journey, and on arriving at the country in which we shall permanently reside, to make known to the native tribes our intentions and our desire to live in peace and friendly intercourse with them.' "

Adrian chuckled. "Ha . . . that reads very well in print. He has caught the missionary style thoroughly with his 'friendly intercourse.' They will like that phrase in London. One hears rumours that they have already had some 'friendly intercourse' with the Matabele, when five thousand Kaffirs butchered the wretched Liebenberg and Long Hans van Rensburg! However, it will pass, since only fools read newspapers. What comes after this 'friendly intercourse'?"

"The last paragraph but one. '(9) We quit this Colony under the full assurance that the English Government has nothing more to require of us, and will allow us to govern ourselves without its interference in the future.' "

"I should like to know who has assured them. Now for the last."

" '(10) We are now quitting the fruitful land of our birth, in which we have suffered enormous losses and continual vexation, and are entering a wild and dangerous territory; but we go with a firm reliance on an all-seeing, just, and merciful Being, whom it will be our endeavour to fear and humbly to obey.' Then it is signed—'By the authority of the farmers who have quitted the Colony, P. RETIEF.'"

Sarel folded the paper gravely. He gazed at his father with a steady challenge in his eyes.

"I have thought on these matters for many months, father," he said. "I have doubted and wavered and hoped and sometimes feared; but now I have made up my mind. What happened to-day at the fort made me know I was right. It is useless to go on hoping. Things go from bad to worse. Whatever you may decide, I know what I must do. I think we have found a leader. I shall follow Pieter Retief."

For a moment the old man returned his son's serious gaze without flinching. His face was aged and lined in the candlelight. He bowed his head in thought, his hand slowly stroking his beard. Then, at last, he looked up with a smile and laid his hand on Jacoba's.

"Wife," he said, "our son is right perhaps after all. We will trek."

"God be thanked for that!" Barend cried. "At last . . . at last!" His face as he rose was radiant; his eyes shone; his dark cheeks were flushed. "Anna, give us another sup. Let us drink to our *trekkie!* At last life begins."

Old Adrian held up his hand. "Take no heed of

him, daughter. And you, Barend, be still. You should know it is no time for drinking or merrymaking. This is the moment for prayer. The predikant is here. Say, do you trek with us, predikant?"

"I trek with you, Uncle Adrian, if so God wills; and I think He calls me."

"Then choose us a portion and read it. Here is the Book."

Andrew Blair stepped forward into the candlelight and unclasped the great brass-bound Bible. As he turned its pages, his hands trembled; the sharp shadow thrown by the flame showed the pulse in his temple throbbing with an excitement his stern, lined features did not betray.

"I choose the Epistle to the Hebrews," he said, "and the Eleventh Chapter, for it seems to me what we need at this hour is faith."

He began to read in his heavy, rasping tones, the broad Hollands vowels and gutturals giving the rhythmical words a solemn roll, as though, indeed, portentous things were spoken.

"*Now Faith is the substance of things hoped for, the evidence of things not seen. For by it the elders obtained a good report. Through Faith we understand that the worlds were framed by the word of God, so that things which are seen were not made of things which do appear. By faith Abel offered unto God a more excellent sacrifice than Cain . . .*"

(But the words blurred under his eyes. He saw

them no more, but knowing them, spoke on in a dream. "What are Cain and Abel to me?" he thought. "This is not the end after all," his exultant heart told him. "I shall still see her; I shall be nearer to her than ever before.")

"By faith Abraham, when he was called to go out into a place which he should after receive for an inheritance, obeyed; and he went out, not knowing whither he went. By faith he sojourned in the land of promise as in a strange country, dwelling in tabernacles with Isaac and Jacob, the heirs with him of the same promise. For he looked for a city which hath foundations . . ."

("An old man," Adrian Prinsloo thought, "an aged man more than ninety years old, with two sons, like myself. He obeyed and went out, not knowing whither he went. But we do not go alone!")

"These all died in faith, not having received the promises, but having seen them afar off, and were persuaded of them, and embraced them, and confessed that they were strangers and pilgrims on the earth. For they that say such things declare plainly that they seek a country. And truly, if they had been mindful of that country from which they came out, they might have had opportunity to have returned. But now they desire a better country. . . ."

("A better country," Sarel thought. With closed eyes he saw the vast rolling grasslands of which report had spoken: a great sheep and cattle country, green and

L*

well-watered, where flocks and herds could find easier
living than in the karoo-bush, where a man could keep
his eye on them however far they strayed. And Piet
Uys, they said, spying out the land beyond the Berg
with his *commissie-trek*, had come upon valleys even
richer and greener, the country the Portuguese had
called Natal: a new Eden—*Alle wereld!*)

"*By faith Moses, when he was born,*" Mr. Blair
read on, "*was hid three months of his parents, because
they saw he was a proper child; and they were not
afraid of the king's commandment . . .*"

("Must I keep him hidden so long as that?" Lisbet
thought. "But now that the rest of them have been
drowned and buried, the soldiers may not be looking
for him; and when once we have trekked beyond the
Great River this brutal English law will not be able to
touch him. He will be one of ourselves, for if we trek
men will be needed, and they will be glad to take him.
He will be a stranger within our gates whom we must
protect as Jacob was protected in the tents of Laban.
But Rachel was the younger daughter!" she remembered, her thoughts running on, "and I am the
elder . . .")

"*And others had trial of cruel mockings and scourg-
ings,*"—Mr. Blair's voice sank lower—"*they were
stoned, they were sawn asunder, were tempted, were
slain with the sword: they wandered about in sheep-
skins and goatskins, being destitute, afflicted, tormented: they wandered in deserts and in mountains*

and in caves and dens of the earth. And these all, having obtained a good report through faith, received not the promise: God having provided some better things for us, that they without us should not be made perfect. Wherefore,"—and now Mr. Blair's voice rose triumphantly—*"seeing we also are compassed about with so great a cloud of witnesses, let us lay aside every weight, and the sin which doth so easily beset us, and let us run with patience the race that is set before us."*

Mr. Blair closed the great clasped Bible. A deep silence possessed the *voorhuis*. Outside, in the dark, an owl called and the little jackals whimpered.

"And now, my brethren," he said, "we will sing one psalm together. The hundred and twenty-first: *I will lift my eyes unto the hills, from whence cometh my help.*"

He began to sing in his harsh and tuneless voice. All the others joined in with him, save only Jan Bothma, who, being a member of the Calvinist sect of the Doppers, considered music in worship a regrettable levity. They sang slowly, drawling the lovely words after the fashion of their Church, so that this song of faith and of consolation was made to resemble a lament; yet the voices of the three women rose true and sweet, if somewhat pitiful, to lose themselves in the sombre enveloping silence of the African night, lying black over virgin bush and veld and forest from the Antarctic swell to the verges of the Sahara.

John Oakley, lying awake in Jan Bothma's wagon,

heard the sound of singing and wondered what it meant. Neither the words nor the tune were known to him; yet he propped himself on his elbow and listened eagerly, for among the three women's voices he thought he recognized Lisbet Prinsloo's.

BOOK THREE

EXODUS

CHAPTER ONE

PREPARATIONS

To the household at Welgelegen, as to many others,
the persuasion of Retief's manifesto had come as a
welcome relief. There was nothing in the document's
firm and temperate phrasing that could offend the
most law-abiding nature, while its reasoned, dispassionate enumeration of common grievances was sufficient to crystallize the vague resentments (which, in
minds such as Adrian Prinsloo's, had been overbalanced
by the natural caution of age and a reluctance to
exchange a settled life for one of uncertainty) into a
fixed determination to have done with doubt and to
trek.

The spirit of such conversions is contagious; their
effect was cumulative. Not only at Welgelegen but in
dozens of other farms the Grahamstown manifesto
confirmed wavering resolutions. The itch for migration which, up till then, had been sporadic, became
pandemic, and swept the whole Eastern frontier from
the berg to the sea. To these scattered communities,
with their minds so profoundly steeped in Biblical
memories that even the events of everyday life were
interpreted in terms of Scripture, it seemed as though

the children of the captivity had been granted their Moses, and that the summons to deliverance and exodus had at last gone forth.

For many of them the process of dislocation was simple and painless. They had not been settled long enough on the frontier to make roots in its soil or to establish bonds of local affection. Their houses were makeshift, with no more pretension to permanence than a nomad's bivouac. Their only possessions were flocks and herds, happily mobile and capable of transporting themselves on their own hooves. Their lives were self-sufficient and self-contained; they needed no better home than their tilted wagons. They were herdsmen and flock-masters, impatient of tillage, demanding no more of the soil than a catch-crop of corn or pumpkins that grew of themselves, folk whose staple food consisted of their flocks' natural increase and the milk of their cattle and the abundant game that fell to their unerring guns. When the head of the family, the *groet heer*, made up his mind and said: *"Myne vrouw, wy moen trek,"* it was a simple matter to bundle their household goods into a couple of hooded wagons, to round up the cattle and sheep from the veld, to inspan the teams of wide-horned Afrikanders, to crack their whips and move on their way. For they knew that wherever they went the eye of God watched them from the skies, that the Lord was their shepherd and that they would never want.

The uprooting of the Prinsloo family was a more

complicated affair. They had been settled at Welge-legen for more than a quarter of a century. Their house was their home; their life was of settled habit. They were people of substance, encumbered or blessed with material possessions, and used to a standard of comfort from which the elders at least had no wish to depart: though they had lived on the frontier for years they had not been born there. Their wealth in livestock alone was considerable. In spite of the depre-dations and losses of the last Kaffir war, it comprised no less than a thousand horned cattle and ten thousand sheep. The mere collection and herding of such a vast number of animals was no small matter, and the pros-pect of finding pasture for them on trek seemed equally difficult, since earlier migrants would surely have skimmed the cream of the feed from the veld, while their presence, in any case, would act as a brake on the speed of the *trekkie's* progress—for though loaded wagons could move as much as twenty miles in a day, driven sheep, which grazed as they went, could not cover more than four. It would be wiser, perhaps, Adrian thought, to halve their number by keeping only the pick of the livestock and selling the rest. But he was not the only man of that way of thinking. The market was glutted with surplus cattle and sheep, stock-prices had dropped catastrophically; and Adrian Prinsloo, that hard-headed man, disliked losing good money—though of what use money would be to him in the wilderness, God only knew.

Then the question of wheeled transport became urgent. At the moment the Welgelegen sheds held only four wagons, survivors of the five in which the family had originally trekked from the Cape. Since those days they had scarcely been used; their canvas tilts had rotted; the very wood of which they were built was not above suspicion. Jan Bothma had two of his own; but that only made six, while Sarel and his father between them calculated that at least a dozen would be needed. New wagons, then, must be bought —and not only wagons but tackle and harness and *trektows* and well-broken spans of oxen fit to master the mountain passes; and the price of wagons had risen more than the price of stock had fallen. No wonder Gert Maritz, the wagon-maker, had scooped up a fortune!

Yet needs must when God calls or the devil drives. There were not merely masses of household furniture to be transported—Jacoba, whose will was of iron, refused to part with the great beds and the glossy, solid stink-wood furniture she had brought all the way from French Hoek, to say nothing of the small ancestral possessions that she prized—but also the yield of the last summer's harvest (which might be needed, Heaven knew!) and young fruit-trees, carefully lifted and packed; and ploughs and farming implements which, sold in Grahamstown, would fetch next to nothing, but out in the wilds would be priceless if not unobtainable; and stores of necessary luxuries, such as tea and coffee and spices, and, even more necessary, barrels of powder and lead for bullets.

In the case of the season's grain-harvest there was much leeway to be made up, for the bulk of the corn had not yet been threshed. The first job to which John and Dicketts put their hands was that of pitching the sheaves into a circular railed enclosure, where twenty horses trampled them out on a surface made smooth, like the floor of the house, with a varnish of cow-dung, while Hottentots, skilled in the task, lifted the straw with forked sticks of mimosa and wafted the chaff away with fans made of rushes.

They were both of them happy in this work. It "came natural" to Dicketts, a labourer born on the land, whose military adventures had been no more than a stirring interlude. He would have been happier still if they had allowed him to thresh with a flail, for he found the Boer method of treading-out the grain with horses wasteful and primitive; while the corn itself, for that matter, seemed to him poor, "daddaky" stuff compared with the product of his own mid-Worcestershire loams. Yet he worked with a will, always cheery and pert as a sparrow, and the sly jokes he cracked at the Prinsloos' expense with John Oakley were not understood. He had slipped into his place as a useful member of the community and a valuable addition to the party available for the trek without any difficulty; for he had been used all his life to roughing it, his soldiering had made him adaptable, his sinewy body was toughened by all sorts of hardship, and his agility, in spite of the missing leg, was remarkable.

Nor did he seem in the least out of place. There were many men of his kind, old soldiers, English and German, attached to the households of frontier Boers in those days. For the most part they acted as "*meesters*," being allotted the task of instructing the children of the family in reading and writing and ciphering and other such refinements of civilization. The fact that George Dicketts could neither read nor write nor understand a word of the Cape Dutch dialect disqualified him for this calling; but his general usefulness and his unfailing good humour atoned for these defects; he was too handy a man to be lost, and indeed, when Jan Bothma had contemptuously furnished him with an outfit of cast-off cut-down leathers and mole-skins, he appeared, apart from his stature, a not incongruous member of the household at Welgelegen.

The adjustment of John Oakley to his physical surroundings was a matter more difficult. The hasty changes which Lisbet had made in his attire served to emphasize rather than to conceal his difference of type. Among that company of hard-bitten, well-fed, sun-weathered men, his spare figure, thinned by prison fare, and his face, its natural pallor further bleached by confinement, made him appear not merely oddly frail and refined but essentially alien: a creature of another race—one would almost have said of another species.

John's difference cut both ways. If, on the one hand, it excited the scorn and spite of Jan Bothma (and of Barend and Anna, who aped him) for a *verdomde* Englishman, on the other hand it had won for him Lisbet's romantic interest, confirmed and made mystical by their first dark encounter, and the protective compassion of Jacoba, whose large heart instinctively embraced him as a boy in need of mothering. It was lucky for him, indeed, that Jacoba was on his side; for in this remote, patriarchal society, the dislike or approval of the mother of the family were matters of the first importance, and her preferences could not easily be disputed by her own children—much less by a mere dependant such as Jan Bothma.

The attitude of the rest of the household towards him showed no partiality. Old Adrian's mind was too deeply preoccupied in the organization of this momentous adventure for him to bother himself with his children's personal likes or dislikes. He regarded John and George Dicketts merely as strangers whom the Providence in which he trusted had brought to his door at a time when men who could use their hands were most needed. Like any other unbidden guests they must pay for their footing with willing labour, and provided they did so, they were welcome to partake of a traditional hospitality as long as they liked to stay. Sarel's attitude towards them was similar, but less

detached. If Sarel deferred to his father and mother
in everything, he was, none the less, the mainspring of
the house's mechanism, and carried the whole material
weight of the trek on his sturdy shoulders. He rarely
smiled—yet when he did his lips had a serious sweetness. He rarely spoke, but his words were always to
the point, and though hardly an hour would pass
without some minor obstacle or frustration, Sarel
seemed to take all of them easily in his measured
stride. He had been born, it seemed, to be a leader of
men. His calm, which had in it something of his
mother's patient inertia combined with his father's
strength, was a perfect corrective to the more hasty
natures of Jan Bothma and Barend, who, vigorous as
they were, had little continuity of purpose save in
their prejudices. John Oakley, watching him as he
moved about his business observing everything with his
steady but rather distant blue eyes, was not long in
coming to realize this grave young man's distinction—
a certain nobility in the cast of body and mind which,
without any conscious effort, asserted itself and made
the rest of them—not only the members of his own
family but also the various Nels and Oosthuizens who
had attached themselves to the Welgelegen *trekkie*—
seem, somehow, fashioned on a less generous scale than
himself. And since John's nature too was generous,
and also, because of his youth, prone to hero-worship,
he conceived not merely a liking for Sarel Prinsloo
but a quick, unquestioning devotion which, he was

proud to believe, Sarel recognized and accepted with pleasure.

There were other reasons why their undefined friendship was not wholly one-sided; for John Oakley, when once he had recovered from his collapse, soon proved himself (as surely as Dicketts, though in different ways) a useful addition to the party, being quicker-minded and, because of his training, more deft-fingered than the rest. He found plenty of scope, indeed, as Jacoba had cunningly foreseen, for the exercise of his trade. In the life of Welgelegen leather was the most abundant and important of all raw materials, for iron and fibre were scarce. The sheds on the farm were crammed with hides of cattle and game, scraped and dried or rudely tanned with acacia-bark. Chairs were seated and beds were sprung with leather strips; men warmed themselves with karosses of skins, clothed themselves in leather garments and took shelter in leather tents. Every function for which in Europe chains of metal or ropes were in use was performed at Welgelegen by reims of cut hide made supple by greasing and stretched and thinned and knotted together. All the gear of the wagons, the sleeping-stretchers and the harness for five spans of oxen, were cut from the same material. Even the massive *trek-tow*—the main trace that took the full strain of the load—must be built up of thongs strained and twisted on wooden winches. There was no lack of employment for hands that could use a knife cun-

ningly and shape leather and sew the skins together
with sinews; and though Oakley's were accustomed to
the shoemaker's more delicate craft, they needed no
teaching, and his work had a finish that Sarel was
forced to admire even if he were sparing of praise.

In the stress of this emergency there were no set
hours of labour. John woke in the golden hour of
dawn and worked until sunset. Yet, though he was
grateful when the sudden falling of darkness released
him from toil, he was never fatigued. He worked all
day, for the first time in his life, in the open air, and in
an air so dry and brilliant that even in the heat of
noon every breath of it seemed to infuse his body
with new vigour and strength. The mere fact
of using his hands and the familiar tools of his trade
was a stimulation and a relief after the endless, melancholy boredom of the convict-ship's 'tween-decks. And
with that renewal of vigour and pride in living came a
spontaneous renewal of hope.

There was a spirit of confidence and of adventurous
anticipation in the very air of Welgelegen in those
days. These kindly folk into whose company he had
stumbled so blindly were, strangely enough, in much
the same case as himself. They had all of them, like
himself (though for different reasons), been forced to
make a clean cut with the past, and were preparing,
with the same hopes as he, to leave all established
things behind and launch forth into a new land, a new
life, in the great plains beyond the mountains, beyond

the law. The spirit of the time was cumulative and infectious. The mere anticipation of such an adventurous freedom was of itself enchanting, exhilarating; yet it would have been less enchanting and less exhilarating, perhaps, if John had not known that his new path, wherever it led, would also be Lisbet Prinsloo's —if he had not been eighteen years old and, for the first time, in love.

It was this last miraculous circumstance, more intoxicating to the spirit than his late hairbreadth escapes from death (or from a life worse than death), more exciting to every sense than the brilliant African air with its burden of unfamiliar sights and smells and sounds, more enthralling to the imagination of youth than the challenge of heroic and hazardous adventure in unknown lands, that transported John Oakley and gave his life a new impetus: a consciousness of strange freedom, a sense of confident power, of bodily and spiritual expansion, resembling the sudden growth which takes place in a living cell newly fertilized.

Up till now, for all the vicissitudes of his chequered life, he had been no more than a boy, his mind full of vaguely romantic ideals and aspirations, somewhat bruised, bewildered and embittered by the first impacts of rude reality and inclined to accept defeat. Now, suddenly (and perhaps unreasonably—for his case was little bettered: being still, in fact, that of a fugitive from justice with liberty at stake), he believed himself to be master of the world that had used him so vilely and able to face the still doubtful future with a courage more than his own. As a boy he had felt himself aged and disillusioned. In the confidence of this new manhood he was even more conscious of his youth, and of the buoyant strength of youth serene in its disregard and contempt for the worst that the grudging fates could muster against him. For whatever might happen now the world was full of wonder.

This ecstatic state of mind, which not merely made the dawn of each day a challenge to splendid living but actually tautened his body and made his eyes shine with a light that was new to them, investing the very drudgery of labour with an inexplicable enchantment, was wholly irrational.

Apart from his persuasive memories of that unique encounter which sheer physical exhaustion had endowed with an air of exalted unreality, he had no reason to suppose that Lisbet Prinsloo had ever been moved by any emotion towards him more tender or intimate than that of a woman's natural compassion. On the contrary, in those rare moments when reason returned to him, when at night, with muscles that ached with tiredness, he lay on the wagon-bed alongside George Dicketts and saw through the torn tilt of Jan Bothma's wagon the diamond-dust of the southern galaxies, he was compelled to confess that, since those dear dark hours of enchantment, Lisbet had scarcely spoken a word to him and had even seemed to avoid him.

A man more experienced in love than he might well have been puzzled and daunted by this deliberate withdrawal, and have tormented himself with asking whether it meant that Lisbet felt she had acted too impulsively, or even have wondered whether, on second thoughts, his confession had shocked and scared her. But John Oakley knew no such doubts. Whatever Lisbet might do, however she might use him, he felt confident of her absolute wisdom and rightness. His passion was of that rarefied kind which only the youngest and least experienced of lovers know: strangely innocent, and so sufficient in itself that the idea of possession hardly entered into it. He asked nothing of Lisbet beyond what her beauty gave. In this state of selfless adoration it was enough for him to know that she existed. The mere fact that the hostile and desolate world contained such a wonder as she, filled his life with a new, an almost intolerable sweetness, a heady exaltation capable not only of lifting him high above such vulgar emotions as jealousy—of Jan Bothma, so obviously hungry for Lisbet's favours, or of the predikant, with whom she shared such an affectionate intimacy—but also of disarming him and of allowing him to forget the precariousness of this paradise.

It was only in moments of sudden, disquieting illumination, as when George Dicketts, in his drowsy nocturnal discourse, mentioned the *Minerva's* name, that John realized the shakiness of the foundations on which his happiness rested, that he saw himself and his comrade as what they actually were: a couple of fugitive convicts wanted by the powers of the law, whose life and liberty—so much more precious now than ever before—lay still at the mercy of their first chance encounter with any of the law's servants.

When he thought of this he went cold and panic gripped him. He was seized with an overwhelming desire to escape. Even the flimsy wagon-tilt seemed a bar to freedom. He had visions of being recaptured while he slept. There was no safety for either of them, he felt, except in perpetual movement, no sure hiding-place save far from the habitations of men. At such moments it seemed to him there was only one reasonable thing to be done: to slip away quietly in the night and press on northwards—always northwards—until, at last, the boundary of the Colony lay behind them. Yet even when panic drove him towards that project, he shrank from it. He realized now that in their first blind dash from the coast they had been lucky to escape with their lives, and in the wild country to northward the prospects of danger and hardship were even greater.

Though he could not as yet understand all the talk that he heard, he had been able to grasp the drift of the stories that were told round the fire at night—tales of vast barren mountain ranges where men had been frozen to death as they slept; of bushmen with poisoned arrows and bands of marauding Griquas

whose hand was against every man; of the roving
cannibal hosts of the Mantatees, led by a woman whose
name was Mantata, of fabulous cruelty; of sly tigers
and hungry lions that could leap a cattle-fence with a
man in their teeth; of the great thirst-land, whose very
name was a terror. How should two lonely, unarmed
men, with three legs between them, confront such
perils, day after day, for months on end? Better
accept the chance of recapture and stay where they
were, reason told him, than risk their lives against such
desperate odds. But persuasions stronger than reason
constrained him. If he yielded to these promptings of
panic he knew he must lose the one thing on earth that
made life most worth living. If he left Welgelegen he
might never see Lisbet Prinsloo again, and he would
sooner risk losing his life than losing her.

Indeed, when the nightmare panic passed, he con-
soled himself with the reasonable hope that he might
not be forced to lose either. The colonial authorities,
from what he had heard, paid scant attention to far-
lying farms at the best of times, and were concentrating
their energies at the moment on closing the frontier to
the export of powder and lead, providing thereby a
grand new grievance (and one that was just enough)
for Bothma and his friends, who found in it another,
and a typical, example of English hypocrisy and
enlarged on it passionately. It was like the English,
he said, to announce that they had no legal objections
against armed emigrants crossing the border and to

demand, in the same breath, their only means of defending themselves against savages and of filling their larders.

The soldiers, in fact, were so busy in the north rummaging innocent trekkers' wagons for contraband ammunition that the policing of the eastern districts had gone by the board, leaving the frontier open to Kaffir raiders and completing the vicious circle by compelling more farmers to trek. This was all to the good, as far as John Oakley was concerned; what was even better was the fact that, so far as he knew, there was only one living soul—and that one, Lisbet Prinsloo, incapable of treachery—who shared his dangerous secret. These simple Dutch folk apparently took him for granted. Since he had answered Jacoba's embarrassing domestic questions he had not been asked to account for himself.

There was only, as far as he could see, one source of potential danger: the continued presence at Welgelegen of his compatriot Mr. Blair, a man of intelligence who, with a few shrewd and obvious questions, could easily catch him out, compelling him to give himself away. During the first few days he had gone in terror of the predikant's forbidding face and dreaded the moment when he would be forced to blurt out the truth and throw himself on his mercy. But Mr. Blair persistently (and unnaturally, as it seemed) paid no heed to him: a circumstance which, in itself, seemed a little sinister, suggesting that, having divined the truth, he might be biding his time and waiting for the proper moment in which to proclaim it, unless—and here a glimmer of hope appeared—unless Lisbet, realizing the menace of Mr. Blair's presence, had taken the even graver risk of letting him into their secret, in which case, no doubt, Mr. Blair felt himself awkwardly placed between his duty to the State on the one hand, and the respect for a woman's confidence on the other. That he knew, or had guessed, far more than he chose to say, John felt certain; but the predikant's solemn face, his continued reticence, and the unnatural stiffness of his manner made it impossible to judge whether his attitude was benevolent or hostile. A full week had passed before Mr. Blair showed the faintest sign of interest in him. Then, one evening, as they sat side by side in the candle-lit *voorhuis*, he had turned to him and opened fire of a sudden:

"I understand that you and your friend have come from the coast, Mr. Grafton?"

The bad moment had come. John's heart went cold; his skin tingled. The question was simple enough and could be answered truthfully; yet the truth, in this case, seemed itself a damning admission. He said: "Yes, sir . . ." and stopped. He was thankful that this dangerous conversation had begun in English and that nobody, therefore, took any notice of it, except Jan Bothma, who, at the first sound of the hated tongue, had scowled and glared and irritably moved away from them.

"I think you did well to move farther inland," the pastor continued in his low, grating voice. "Those low-lying regions are none too healthy. The air suits some people, but they say the high-veld beyond the colonial boundary is more salubrious still."

("He is playing with me," John thought. "Why doesn't he say what he knows and have done with it?" On the other side of the room, through the haze of tobacco-smoke, he saw Lisbet's face, sweet and pallid. She was watching them both intently and wondering, no doubt, what they said; yet it seemed to him she smiled faintly, and he took heart from that smile.)

"Ay, yon's a tragic, dangerous coast," Mr. Blair droned on reflectively, "and many lives have been lost on it. There was the *Grosvenor*, a braw East Indiaman, long before my time, with a million pounds of specie aboard her and all hands lost, and many another good ship that has never been heard of. When the south-easter blows that's a bad lee shore to lie on, as you'll know for yourself having seen it, with the Indian Ocean pounding in on the sand. But maybe there were no ships wrecked when you were there, Mr. Grafton?"

"There were none that I ever heard on, sir."

"I fear many are never heard of; yet only a week ago—just after you came here, maybe—I was called to Meerlust to give Christian burial to eight poor fellows whose bodies were washed up on the shore. Two soldiers there were, and half a dozen more, but no signs of wreckage except a few odd spars. From what I saw of their clothes—and there wasn't much left—I suspect the others were convicts drowned on the voyage to Botany Bay."

"Then perhaps God was merciful, sir. I am told that is a terrible place."

"God is always merciful, Mr. Grafton. He moves in mysterious ways and it is not for us to question them."

"But men are less merciful, sir. I have heard that in these days many simple, innocent folk are transported from England for trivial offences, or even for no crime at all."

"That may well be true. It is one of the greatest mysteries that the innocent so often suffer along with the guilty. Yet surely the knowledge of guilt is its own retribution, and the consciousness of innocence is surely its own reward. A man who thoroughly repents of his sins, Mr. Grafton, is certain, as we believe, of God's forgiveness."

"And what of one who is at peace with his conscience, sir?"

The words were so tensely spoken that Mr. Blair was startled. He turned slowly to meet Oakley's eager gaze, and as their eyes met, his own softened, his grim lips grew kind.

"Why, then I should say such a man has the right to face the world as you face me now." He laid his big hand on John's arm and grasped it reassuringly. "I am glad you and I have had this candid talk," he

M

said. "I expect you'll have been wondering why I refrained from speaking to you before. Well, perhaps you can guess the reason now. I admit that I shrank from it. When I came here a week ago and found you here and heard what some other people—and one person in particular—had to say of you, I must confess I was troubled. Putting two and two together I had formed certain suspicions, and could not convince myself just where my duty lay. Even now I don't know the whole of your story. I don't want to know it. Some day, later, if you want to tell me, you shall. In the meantime I think we understand one another, and that is as it should be: after all, we are fellow-countrymen, strangers in a strange land, and our ways lie together. I should like you to think of me as a human being as well as a pastor. You are a boy, of course, and I am an ageing man with some hard experience of life; but if we are always as candid with one another as we have been this evening, we should be friends. I am not a demonstrative man—perhaps you have gathered that —and I don't make friends easily; but I want you to know that you can rely on me, and I should like you to feel you trust me, as I have trusted you."

Andrew Blair's hard mouth trembled as he spoke. Without waiting for John to master that infectious emotion and reply, he went on rapidly:

"Before we have done with this subject there is just one thing more. Your companion—Dicketts, I think the name is . . ."

John Oakley smiled. "Poor George! If you only knew how simple and brave and good he is!"

"Then we'll say no more about it. I take your word for him. I am a happier man to-night, my boy, than I was this morning. It will be a happier day still for you, I may tell you, that sees us all over the border."

A distant day, too, it began to seem. Another week passed, and then yet another. In that serene autumn weather, now that the last rain had fallen and each halcyon day resembled the next in everything but the gradual shrinkage of light and the increasing chill that succeeded each cloudless sunset, it was difficult to keep count of time in days that were crowded with hours of unremitting toil. Yet Sarel, who had the whole business in hand, seemed pleased with this almost invisible progress, and so satisfied that all went well that he left them now for days at a time, riding off to Bathurst and Uitenhage and Grahamstown in a last attempt to find a buyer for Welgelegen.

Old Adrian willingly left the selling to Sarel. He himself had been known as a man who could drive a hard bargain over the sale of produce or livestock; but over Welgelegen he could not haggle; to him it represented not merely so many acres of land taken up from the Government and paid for with hard-earned money, but a personal creation, the product of thirty long years of labour and love, the altar of all his manhood's devotion, the birthplace and

grave of half a lifetime's hopes. The worth of these
things was not to be measured in money. The silver
that came from them would surely carry a curse with
it like the thirty pieces that paid for the potter's field.
He would have no truck with the deal, though Sarel
might do as he liked.

But Sarel could not do as he liked. The dusty out-
spans on the verge of the villages were thronged with
intending emigrants who had come there on the same
errand as himself. Though Welgelegen was worth
many thousands of dollars and known as a farm on
which money and skill and labour had been spent without stint, no buyers would bid for it. What was the
use, folk asked, of land, however valuable, on an un-
protected frontier? Who would look at a farm that
had been burnt and pillaged twice within living
memory? As for that, what man in his senses would
squander good money on buying a farm at all—at a
time when dozens had been deserted and could be
picked up with improvements and *opstal* for nothing?
Places bigger than Welgelegen and just as well kept,
with title-deeds all in order, had lately changed hands
"for an apple and an egg" (as the saying went).
Surplus cattle, farm-gear, wagons . . . these were
another matter; they were movable, negotiable
property and could always fetch a good price. But
lands and even houses, alas, could not be moved. They
must stay where they were. And the Kaffirs, by every
sign, had not learnt their lesson yet. Young Prinsloo's

only chance of a sale, by the look of things, was to light on some hare-brained English settler with a liking for hazards and rather more money than sense. But even the English, in these days, were short of cash and not such fools as they used to be.

Sarel was luckier than he had any right to expect in coming to terms at last with a trader named Mulder, a fellow of rather a chancy reputation with whom, in the ordinary way, he would not have moved three paces to shake hands, who, banking on better times, had plunged into land speculation—so deeply, in fact, that his money and credit were both exhausted. He knew Welgelegen well, and had always coveted it, and professed himself, in a moment of alcoholic exuberance, ready to barter the farm for three thousand head of sheep.

Sarel clinched the bargain. At that moment he was so discouraged that he would have grasped at less. The sheep were a sad-looking lot, lately come in payment for a debt, so Mulder said, from the north where four years of drought in succession had driven many of the Tarka farmers to drink and ruin. It pricked Sarel's conscience a little to think that, if Mulder's story were true, he was profiting by some other poor devil's misfortune; yet it seemed even more probable —for even in liquor Mulder was likely to lie—that the sheep had been smuggled out of Kaffirland in payment for the gas-pipe muskets in which Mulder was suspected of doing an illicit trade—which troubled his conscience even more. Sarel didn't want more sheep in any case. Welgelegen already carried one of the largest flocks in the district, of a quality that would not gain by mixing with these bedraggled creatures, and it might be difficult to find keep on trek for half as many again.

He was just on the point of driving the sorry flock home, resigned, reluctantly, to the bad bargain, when his luck took a turn for the better: he fell in, by chance, with an Englishman from the Zuurberg who had made up his mind to join in the trek some months previously and then, changing it, had found himself left with a couple of spare wagons on his hands. Now that he had decided to stay on his farm he had no more use for the wagons and had brought them in to sell.

The mere sight of these wagons ravished Sarel Prinsloo. They had come, brand-new, from Gert Maritz's workshop in Graaf Reinet and were the latest thing in comfort and elegance. Their gleaming sail-cloth tilts were lined with green baize; their sturdy, graceful wheels painted red, their bodies sky-blue, with fanciful decorations of hair-line tracery, and each was drawn by a well-matched span of sixteen short-horned oxen. The two wagons, the farmer said, had cost him a hundred and fifty English pounds in Graaf Reinet. He had been lucky to buy them so cheaply, for prices were rising, but he expected to have no difficulty in getting his money back. As for the spans—anybody could see the value of them. They were none of your Afrikander stuff, but Fatherland cross-breeds, matched for height and pace and as well-trained as they were strong. Such spans, he reckoned, were worth sixty pounds apiece to any man who had an eye for a trek-ox. He was prepared to accept two hundred and fifty pounds for the lot as they stood, and if that wasn't a thundering good bargain he'ld eat his hat.

"What's more, I'll throw in the drivers, April and Cobus," he said. "They're good boys, and know their places. There's no damned missionary nonsense about either of 'em, thank God, and they know their oxen as well as the oxen know them. Look here, to settle the matter I'll make it two hundred and forty."

Sarel made a swift calculation, translating the foreign currency into Cape rix-dollars. Two hundred and forty pounds meant four thousand eight hundred of these. Mulder's sheep should be worth a couple of dollars a head—say, six thousand in all. That left him a margin of twelve hundred for bargaining. He offered two thousand sheep in exchange. The Englishman laughed at him.

"What! two thousand of that Kaffir rubbish? You've come to the wrong shop, young man! The brutes are half-starved; they've been living on the fat in their tails. And you've the brass to ask me more than two dollars—four shilling apiece!"

They were all of them yearlings, Sarel explained.

They had just been driven down from the dried-up north, and a month or two on good veld would certainly fatten them. Well-fed yearling wethers in Grahamstown were fetching two and a half. "But to satisfy you," he said, "I'll make it two thousand three hundred."

Still the Englishman shook his head.

"Well, two hundred more. Two thousand five hundred."

"How many are there in all?"

"Three thousand."

"They're so thin, they look more like two. I'll have the lot or nothing."

"Very well. Shake hands on it, then."

"Hey, hey, not so fast, young fellow!" His face grew suspicious. If a Boer came to the point with so little haggling there must be something wrong. These fellows, for all their seeming stupidity, were as slim as the devil. Good bargains—and this was a thundering good one—were apt to shrink on the way home. "I reckon we'll count them," he said, "before we shake hands on it."

Sarel sat on his horse like a statue, patiently waiting, while the Hottentot nicked off the numbered sheep on his tally-stick. They were six short of three thousand, the Englishman discovered triumphantly. "If you like I'll take your horse, and we'll call it quits," he said, cunningly.

"I will give you twelve dollars," Sarel said.

"Twelve? I like that! Why, you told me yourself that yearling wethers were selling in Grahamstown for two and a half. That makes fifteen, not twelve, if you please."

"I will give you fifteen. You are a good business man, mynheer."

"You bet I am!" laughed the Englishman, vastly flattered.

Sarel drove on his way through the dusk to Welgelegen. His horse was tired, so he handed it over to one of the Hottentots to lead, while he himself rode on the wagon-seat. He knew he had been worsted in his bargain, and that by an Englishman. But he did not care. That was the way life went in these days. "They have taken our country from us," he thought, "they have taken our slaves, they have made us buy our own cattle. But when we are gone and the Kaffirs come over again they will miss our muskets and be sorry they drove us away."

Sarel's thoughts were sombre enough, and yet without rancour. He had none of his cousin Jan Bothma's turbulence in his composition. He was by nature moderate, devoid of bitterness, and believed, as he had been taught, that vengeance was the affair of God, not of man. There was natural violence enough in that country, he thought, without men adding to it or embittering their souls with ancestral grievances. All he demanded of life was a reasonable tranquillity and leave to live as his fathers had

M*

lived before him; but there would be no peace in South Africa, he knew, so long as a government of foreigners that took its orders from an office more than six thousand miles away and changed its head every few years, imposed an alien manner of life and behaviour on a long-settled majority who had already, through six generations, evolved and established their own. He did not even hate the colonial government; he was ready to believe it inspired by a misguided and un-balanced benevolence rather than by ill-will. He only knew that he had reached a point when he could no longer live under it. All he asked of it now was to be permitted to go in peace.

That evening, jolting home through the darkening bush with his pipe in his mouth, on the driving-seat of Gert Maritz's sky-blue wagon, he had a feeling that these slow miles were, in fact, the first of their exodus, that, in spirit at least, the trek had already begun. God in heaven only knew when and where it would end; but the mere fact that these wagons would never turn back relieved and inspired him. In the whole of that journey only one pang assailed him, in the moment when, through the trellis of thinning bush, the windows in the *voorhuis* at Welgelegen flashed forth their greeting.

He had known that bright welcome ever since he was a boy. These steadfast lights, so lively, and some-how so pitiful in the surrounding vastness, had been the symbol for him of all settled, familiar things, the fixed centre round which his life had revolved, and to which it had always returned. As he gazed at them now there came to his mind not a vision of what Welgelegen was now, but rather memories of small and quite unimportant things that rose unbidden out of the garners of childhood—above all, smells: the perfume of lemon-blossom wafted along the path, the tang of sun-caked earth when the rains had broken; the scent of the first December peaches plucked from his private tree; the sappy savour of millet-grain pounded by Hottentot poles in a quern; the reek of smouldering dung in old cattle-kraals; and, more provocative than any of these, that composite odour—of wood-smoke and tan and tallow, of fresh-roasted coffee and fleeces and reedy thatch and black tobacco and charcoal-fume and stinkwood furniture—which, although something like it could surely be sniffed in every old farm on the frontier, was so characteristic of Welgelegen that he was ready to swear he could recognize it blindfold.

That subtle essence of all things familiar and shabby and friendly was, it seemed to him, what he would miss more than anything else in his wanderings. When he tried to recapture it, wistfully, his eyes filled with tears, and the *voorhuis* window-lights swam and dissolved before him. This softness was unbecoming. He rubbed the weak tears from his eyes and drew a deep breath. His nostrils inhaled the smell of the newly-painted wagon, the smell of his brand-new home, uncomplicated by any suggestions of memory. Its simplicity, if hardly savoury, was symbolical of the new life. As the slow spans dragged to a halt and he leapt down from the wagon, he knew the weak moment had passed. He had no regrets.

CHAPTER TWO

EVE OF THE TREK

WITH the arrival of Sarel's new wagons the work of preparation at Welgelegen took on a spurt. It was no longer confused and uncertain, but moved swiftly and smoothly, like water running to the lip of a weir. Now, too, the results of the labour during the previous three weeks began to be seen. The harvest was threshed and sacked; the livestock, collected and driven in from the outer veld, filled the air, day and night, with sounds of uneasy lamentation; the old wagons had been overhauled, their torn tilts patched, their axles dismantled and greased with mutton-fat, their doubtful joints braced with angle-blocks and leather reims; every fragment of portable junk that might some day prove useful had been sorted and piled into separate heaps—here old barrels and troughs and iron, there rusty ploughshares and harrows and packs of raw hides and tangled reims and whipstocks—until the circle of barren, tawny earth surrounding the farm resembled nothing so much as the yard of a scrap-merchant.

There was reason for hurrying now; for Sarel had heard in Grahamstown, whither all news and rumour of the migration filtered down from the

351

north, that Retief, with his trek of a hundred wagons and six score men, had already lumbered down to the drifts of the Orange, where Maritz, lately returned from his punitive pursuit of the Matabele, was moving to join him. There was no time to be lost, Sarel felt. He had set his heart from the first on attaching his party to Retief, not only because he believed in Retief as a leader, but also because, in the perilous north, there was safety in numbers, and a solitary *trekkie* ran risks for the womenfolk that he had no right to take. When it came to the point, the whole weight of the undertaking lay on his shoulders; for old Adrian, though recognized as the titular head of the party, was too bewildered and hurt by the vast uprooting to lead, while Jan Bothma, skilled and capable as he was in his own leisurely routine, had no head for organization in an emergency and was infected, too, with the racial inertia summed up in the comfortable proverb: "To-morrow is also a day." Yet to-morrow, in their case, might well be a day too late, Sarel felt; and in spite of Jan's grumbling he drove him unmercifully, knowing well that in the final scramble of loading and starting more time would be lost than anyone counted on.

He had all his plans made in advance. Everything had its appointed place. The old wagons that had come from the Cape thirty years before, with their patched tilts and bodies warped and fissured by long exposure, had been fitted with new iron-wood *disselbooms* and would carry such heavy stuff as ploughs and farm-implements, reserve stores of grain and lead and powder and primitive firearms, kegs of tallow and candles and soap, tubs of salted butter, wrapped mummy-like bundles of young fruit-trees, sacks of seeds, and the more massive pieces of furniture which need not be unpacked until some place of permanent habitation was reached.

Jan Bothma's two would be loaded with articles required for more immediate use, such as spare wagon-gear for making good breakdowns on the road, spades and picks, iron cooking-pots and brass-banded churns, stout yellow-wood wagon-chests crammed with old clothes and blankets and linen and other perishable materials, doubly precious because none of them could be replaced in the wilds, together with bales of tenting canvas and sail-cloth which, slung between wagons, might give shelter from sun and rain at an outspan.

The new elegant wagons from Graaf Reinet had a finer function. In the first on the wagon-beds, slung from the rails, the three women would sleep securely, while the menfolk dossed down on the ground in the lee of the tilts or took shelter in the five-foot track beneath the bodies. In the second were stores for the journey: flour, coffee and tea and sugar and salt and spices and jars of preserves and ropes of tobacco, glass, china and old Dutch silver and precious heir-looms such as the gilt-framed mirrors, the pastel-portraits of delicate frivolous ladies at the court of

Louis the Fourteenth, which had wandered from France to French Hoek and remained, for sentiment's sake, the most precious of Jacoba's possessions. Here, too, in painted kists with faded, fanciful decorations, lay, carefully folded, old Adrian's best clothes, his Nagmaal suit of smooth-faced broadcloth and striped cashmere trousers, the girls' sprigged summery prints and figured Lyons satins, Jacoba's lace-fichued green silk wedding-dress with its strips and flounces (too slimly-cut now, alas, for anyone but Lisbet to wear), and bunches of ribbons and filmy fragments of Mechlin and lace-fringed cambric *kappjes*, one cashmere shawl which, long ago, an old flame of Jacoba's had brought her from India, and two coy parasols with adjustable jointed sticks.

All the most fragile and perishable things were stored under the new tilts which were sure not to leak, packed snugly away in the soft folds of the spare feather-beds; yet hardly an hour would pass without Jacoba discovering in a panic some new small treasure which she could not bring herself to leave behind; for Welgelegen was as full of such hoarded trifles as a jackdaw's nest. She would waddle out to the stoep and call to little Hendrik, who was never tired of watching what went into the wagons; and Hendrik would reluctantly drop the long whip with which he was practising, teasing the long-suffering Hottentots and the three house-dogs, Bles, Flam, and Wolf, who lay sweltering in the dust with their tongues out, too hot to move, and run back to the wagon with some small thing of no value the keeping of which had become, at that moment, the dearest wish of his mother's heart.

These were great days for little Hendrik, more exciting by far than any he had ever known; exciting, also, for the girls, who were young and hopeful, too young to have formed as yet intense local affections. They came out from time to time in their white wide-flapped sun-bonnets to watch the progress of the loading. They thought Sarel's new wagons, with their great splashes of sky-blue and vermilion and green-lined tilts, the most elegant that had ever been seen. The prospect of travelling and sleeping in such gay and gallant vehicles gave the trek a picnic air. They were both of them shocked when they found George Dicketts at work blotting out the brightness of the wheels and painting the under-carriages with tar; but Sarel, who ordered this, knew that the trek would be no picnic. And though the sisters talked and joked with Dicketts as he stood with sweat dripping from his face into the tar-pot, neither Lisbet nor Anna was really interested in his explanations. Anna's eyes were proudly watching Jan Bothma's titanic shoulders as he swung up a sixty-pound powder-keg that two Hottentots had carried between them.

"See how strong Jan is, Lisbet," she said. "Do you blame the poor fellow for boasting sometimes of his strength?"

And Lisbet said "yes" when, of course, she should have said "no," for she, too, was distracted watching John Oakley as he came swinging towards them with his check shirt wide open at the neck, his throat tanned brown as an egg, and a confident smile on his lips that she knew was meant for herself.

"How strong and happy and well he looks now!" she was thinking. She was glad he was well and happy; yet somehow this spectacle of lithe and radiant health destroyed a personal vision that often came to her secretly, of a waxen face, faintly flushed, yet more delicately featured, of a red wound streaking the death-pale temple, and closed, long-lashed eyes. There had been none of this buoyant strength in the anxious hand that had feebly sought hers and clutched it. Perhaps the emotion she missed as she looked at him now was the luxury of pity, and what hurt her—if "hurt" were the word for this vague disappointment—was the evident fact that he no longer had need of her, or, at least, of her care and compassion. Her protection he still might need. Though he smiled so bravely and looked so happy, she knew that he would not be safe until they had passed the frontier. And as yet they had not even started to trek. Would they ever start?

By the following evening, indeed, all the long preparations were over. The Nel and the Oosthuizen *trekkie* had rolled up and outspanned at Welgelegen, ready for the start. Thirteen wagons in all stood waiting with their *trek-tows* and yokes stretched out on the ground in front; thirteen spans lay down beside them. The kraals could not hold the mass of gathered cattle; so the boys, to keep off lions, had lit brushwood fires that encircled the house with a broken girdle of lights which, from time to time, as dry thorns lugged from the abandoned kraals were thrown on to them, broke into fierce crackles and flared and suddenly spurted, to spray the cold vault with meteor-swarms of sparks; and when these tongues of flame leapt skyward, the empty darkness was peopled with figures of small dark-skinned men who leapt too and clapped their hands; for all the native servants and freed slaves of the three households had fore-gathered and were celebrating the event in their own mysterious ways, with dancing and drinking of beer and smoking of *dakka*. Sarel listened to their revels anxiously, and wondered how many would be too drunk or dazed next morning to take the road.

They would none of them sleep that night. Indeed, it was doubtful if anyone at Welgelegen would sleep. Two hours later than usual they dragged in (all save Sarel, for whom the cares of this day would last twenty-four hours) dead-tired and dusty, greedy for their evening meal. There was no foot-washing that evening. The hungry men bolted what food they could snatch as they stood or gratefully squatted on the floor, for there was no seat of any kind left in the *voorhuis* but Jacoba's rest-bench, on which she still sat calmly, with the comforter under her feet, as she had sat for most of the time when she was not sleeping for the last ten years, marooned in the midst of the wreckage and desolation of the house she loved, yet always smiling her patient benignant smile, always watching to see that every man had his fill.

One would have thought that on such an occasion the ritual of evening prayers might have been neglected, for Mr. Blair, who had worked hard all day with the others, was still in his shirt-sleeves, his arms and face caked with red dust; but no sooner had he swallowed his last mouthful than Jacoba called him and handed him the great Bible that still lay on the table before her.

"You shall read us a portion, predikant," she said, "and offer a prayer, and then we will sing the psalm the old *baas* has chosen."

Mr. Blair pulled on his black coat and read a few verses and prayed. All those who were sitting rose to their feet. Mr. Blair read the verses and prayed; then all raised their voices:

"When Israel went out of Egypt," they sang,
"The house of Jacob from a people of strange language,
Judah was his sanctuary,
And Israel his dominion . . ."

There was a rapt passion in their singing, for each

man interpreted the words as an exposition of his own case and as an assurance of divine protection, though the droning tune to which they were sung was not inspiriting. When they had ended, and stood for a moment in silence, Jan Bothma spoke:

"This is the last time, uncle," he said, "that we shall eat and pray in this house. It has been a godly house; but now that we have prayed and the Almighty has had His due, let us drink a last *soopie* together to sleep on and wish ourselves luck and give ourselves heart for to-morrow. That is the right thing for men to do . . . no?"

"But, Jan, there is nothing but tea to drink your toast in," Jacoba protested, uncertain, in any case, whether Adrian would approve.

The big man laughed. "Ha, there you are wrong, aunt." Like a mischievous boy, he produced from his bulging pocket a black bottle of peach-wine brandy. He tilted the bottle at his mouth and gulped a stiff dollop.

"Health, uncle!" he said. "Health to you and to all of us! And here's another toast too. The trek! I give you The Trek!" He waved the black bottle high and drank again, then smacked his lips and passed it on to his neighbour, who followed his example.

"The trek. . . . The trek. . . . The trek. . . ." the men cried one by one as the bottle went round, their voices roughened by the bite of the fiery spirit. Old Adrian watched them impassively. When the bottle of *brandewyn* reached him he pushed it aside. But

Barend, whose turn came last, drank deeper than any.

"The trek!" he cried, with flushed cheeks and eyes shining. "Health to all—and may the devil take all the damned English!"

Jan Bothma laughed loud and slapped his huge thigh; Jacoba looked up sharply. "Be silent, Barend!" she said—and now the calm voice was commanding. "You talk like a drunken Kaffir. We have guests in the house, and your words are unforgivable." She turned towards Mr. Blair. "I ask pardon, M'nheer," she said gently. "My son is more than seventeen years old, but alas, his manners are no better than a baboon's. Never till this night has a stranger been insulted at Welgelegen. This is a bad farewell; but it will not happen again," she sighed, "no . . . it will not happen again."

Barend tossed the empty bottle into a corner. He turned and went, humiliated, with a face of thunder, and stalked out on to the stoep. The other men followed him clumsily one by one. In the awkward silence the old slave Ayah crept round, collecting the broken victuals and watching her mistress's stony face anxiously with her cunning black eyes. The two girls slipped away—they were to sleep in the new wagon that night. Mr. Blair pressed Jacoba's plump hand, murmuring words his emotion made almost inaudible, though she heard them, and gently smiled, and shook her head as he went. There was nobody left in the *voorhuis* now but the two old people, sitting side by side in its emptiness. For a while they were silent. No sound was heard in the room but the scratching rustle of insects in wall and thatch. Outside, cattle sighed and moaned and a single lamb bleated. From afar came the muted metallic tinkle of a Hottentot guitar. There was no squealing of jackals, for the watch-fires kept them away. Suddenly old Adrian emerged from the stupor of resignation in which all that evening he appeared to have been sunk.

"That was a bad thought of Barend's to speak as he did before guests, ma," he said. "If Sarel had been here there would have been a fine to-do. I am too old and weary to deal with him."

"He got more from me than he would have got from Sarel," Jacoba answered grimly; "for Sarel might have been violent, and that would have pleased the Bezuidenhout blood in him by making him feel himself important. Barend's weak spot is his pride. I made him look small. He will not forgive me."

"It is a good thing for him we are trekking, I think," the old man said, "before he takes a jump down at the end of a rope, like Stephanus Bothma. He was born hot-blooded and a rebel, that fellow. Over the berg, with no English to fight against, he may change."

Jacoba shook her head. "He will always be a rebel, and never change. Wherever he goes I think trouble will follow him—and his cousin Jan, too. Jan finds trouble because he is stupid and does not think. Barend finds it because he thinks and feels too much. But the end is the same."

Old Adrian rose. "It is time you went to the wagon and slept, ma," he said; "it is late and we start at dawn. Come, give me your arm."

"So late that it is hardly worth while moving now. I shall stay here till it is light and I hear them stirring. But you should go. I shall get all the sleep I need. To-night I would rather be alone in the house."

"You shall do as you like, then," the old man said tenderly. He bent over and kissed her. She smiled and pressed his thin hand.

When she had watched him go and sat on alone, her arms folded as usual upon the table before her, in the midst of which a single candle burned. She listened while the sound of his slow steps faded away, and a little longer. Then, clutching the table to give herself support, she rose, breathing heavily. She took the candle and set it in the bed of molten tallow at the bottom of a lantern and made her way slowly to the stoep. Descending the shallow steps sideways, she threaded her way through the masses of prostrate cattle that lay chewing the cud or sighing heavily in their sleep. Past the Oosthuizen wagons she went, walking always slowly and sometimes pausing for breath; past the last of the bivouac fires, where a strange Hottentot, aroused from his dog-sleep, jumped up aghast at the sight of this apparition advancing out of the night in its pale print dress.

Jacoba went on without heeding him. Her eyes, out of habit, were fixed on the ground, amber-pale in the candlelight; for though it was autumn the days were still hot, and night-adders or even puff-adders might well be abroad in search of the rats that haunted the cattle-kraals. Beyond the range of firelight, eyes of small furtive creatures glared green in her lantern-beam, reminding her that quite possibly she might meet a lion, attracted by the scent of the herds and prowling hungrily outside the circle of light; but she did not think there were lions about, the dogs kept so quiet, and even if she had heard one she would not have turned back, for the secret mission on which she went could not be evaded or even postponed.

She went on and on with her lantern held before her to guide her steps, yet hardly needed it; the air was so thin and pure, the stars seemed so near the earth, their fierce pulsations shedding a radiance sharper than that of moonlight, which made the candle-flame look common and pale; and at last she slowed the pace, which had made her heart flutter, for she saw before her the plumes of pepper-trees, like puffs of still silvery smoke, surmounting a whitewashed wall.

She had never before approached the family burial-ground in starlight, for, like most women of her race in those days, she was more frightened of ghosts than of death itself; but the ghosts of this place, if ghosts there were, belonged to her and could not wish her harm. There was a wooden gate in the wall; it creaked when she opened it, and the sound distressed her, irreverently breaking the silvery silence. She moved cautiously into the little enclosure, like a mother who enters the room where her children are asleep and goes on tiptoe, step by step, for fear of waking them, though the children in this small room slept too sound for waking. There was no bench or stone on which she could sit, though the length of the walk had tried her. She stood in the midst of the graveyard, gradually recovering her breath. She blew out the candle and snuffed it and laid the lantern on the earth. In this still and sacred hour mere starlight seemed kinder and more in tune with the quietude of her dead.

As she stood there, a bunched, ungainly figure in her faded print dress with the black quilted kappie shading her face like a cowl, she closed her eyes and thought of them one by one. And the visions on which her memory dwelt were not those her eyes had last seen—Hans and Pieter bled white by assegai-wounds, Gerrit's dark head battered in by the knobkerries, or Katjie as she had carried the limp little body back from the dam. She saw them all not as grown men nor even as children, but as the babies she had taken to her breast and suckled as soon as they were born, each so different from all the others; and, as she thought of them thus, her pale face beneath the black kappie became transfigured by a surpassing content and tenderness which gave back to her shapeless features the beauty they had long since lost.

Jacoba stood there motionless for longer than she knew—the trees and the little crosses that marked the graves, the very dead themselves, were hardly stiller than she—until, the day's last heat exhausted, a colder breath suspired from the cooling earth, chilled her skin beneath its many layers of petticoat, making her shiver and bringing her back to the reality of her loneliness, and of herself standing there so small and helpless under the remote, dispassionate stars. So she left the burial-plot for the last time, carefully closing the gate behind her—not that it gave the abandoned graves any protection, but because, till the timber rotted, it would give the little enclosure an air of seclusion. She walked back towards the house, more slowly than she had come (and the way seemed much farther), no longer watching the ground nor caring what snakes she trod on, triumphant and thankful, in spite of her tiredness, in the knowledge that she had performed a necessary rite, the neglect of which, if she had failed in her purpose, would have haunted her all her days. This was to her the saddest and hardest of all her sad farewells.

When she reached the fire she had passed she found it abandoned and falling to ashes. Her apparition had been too much for the solitary Hottentot's nerves. Methodically, she pulled more branches on to the embers and waited until they caught, for she knew it would be tempting Providence to leave a gap in the fiery circle. By the time she reached the stoep her strength was almost spent. The interior of the empty *voorhuis* loomed black, reminding her that she had left her lantern behind; but no power on earth could have compelled her to retrace her steps and recover it. It was a pity, she thought, for it was a favourite lantern which she had used for thirty years, and now it would lie there rusting until some curious native found it. With the support of the table she guided herself to the rest-bench and sank, with a sigh of relief, on to her accustomed seat. Then she folded her massive arms on the brass-clasped Bible in front of her. Her shoulders slumped; her head nodded and drooped; she slept. The grey eastern sky was banded with blood-red streamers when Sarel found her sleeping and touched her shoulder and woke her.

"It is time to go, ma," he said. "The oxen are all inspanned and the wagons are waiting. Take my arm. You need not hurry."

She took his arm. He bent and kissed her gently. Yes, Sarel was the best of them all: as strong as a tower, she thought, with all the grave Huguenot virtues her own blood had given him. She descended the steps of the stoep. She must not look back, she told herself, lest the sight of the empty house, the grave of so many joys and hopes and sufferings, should move her beyond endurance. She must be worthy of the strength of this man to whom she had given his strength. Sarel helped her up the rough ladder and into the foremost wagon. The eager faces of Lisbet and

Anna welcomed her with smiles, and she forced herself to smile back at them.

"Not an ordinary wagon. More like a queen's boudoir, or the fairy coach of Cinderella, no? We shall sleep here like royal folk."

The long whip-lashes cracked like pistols. To an accompaniment of harsh cries the great wagon gave a lurch forward and rolled on its way. From the distance behind them they heard a succession of loud reports. The young men were discharging their muskets in a ragged, wild *feu de joie*. What bold, high spirits they had! "That is youth," Jacoba thought. She sank down on the stretcher-bed that swayed with the roll of the wagon. The sky was lightening now, but she did not look back.

CHAPTER THREE

THE OUT TRAIL

THIRTEEN wagons left Welgelegen that May morning. Each seventeen-foot wagon, with its full span of sixteen oxen, covered twenty-five yards of track. They moved forward at intervals of another fifty because of the dust, which only the first wagon escaped, dislodged by the oxens' padding feet and churned up in tawny clouds by the following wheels. When the wagons kept the stations in which they started—and this was not often, for the lean cattle of the Nels and the Oosthuizens were no match in speed for Sarel's new Fatherland spans, and their party usually straggled and lagged behind—the whole *trekkie* extended over the better part of a mile. And this was not all, for after the hindmost wagons came the three families' separate flocks and herds, which moved slowly, reluctantly, straying and grazing whenever they could escape the attentions of the Oosthuizen children and the Hottentot herds: a dense concourse of fifteen hundred horned cattle and sixteen thousand sheep. It was well that the trek had started so early in the autumn, before the last summer moisture had drained out of the soil and made its soaked crust friable. As it was, there rose from that following host of seventy thousand hooves a vast cloud of particles which, towering above them, still hung and floated on the air when their bodies had passed, and trailed behind, marking their passage, for mile after mile.

It was well, too, that the trek had started so late. The first stages of its course ran parallel with the upper waters of the Great Fish River, a region of dense bush traversed by innumerable twisting spruits and deep dongas that when the rains hung on late (and this year they had only just ceased) might be transformed at any moment into fierce, impassable torrents, and lie sodden for a week, when the flood had passed, axle-deep in muddy quicksand. It was for fear of these rain-scored waterways, running into the river from the south and each crossing the line of march, that Sarel had allotted the care of a wagon to each of the white men available; for his Hottentot drivers, unused to long treks, had little more intelligence than their oxen, and unlike the oxen, which plodded on automatically at their unvarying pace of three miles an hour until they could go no farther or were called to a halt, were capable of falling asleep with the whips in their hands (particularly after such a debauch as they had enjoyed on the night of the start) and letting their wagons plunge over the lip of a donga with unlocked wheels or tilt suddenly sideways among the water-worn boulders that strewed the spruits, and capsize.

Old Adrian led the procession on the seat of the women's wagon, sitting alone with his thin shanks wide apart, the pipe, which never left his mouth, in his teeth and a loaded gun on his knees. The events of the past month had stunned him, and aged him sorely. As he had told Sarel often enough, he was too old a tree to transplant. Like an aged or lightning-blasted tree he seemed, so shrunken and sere, his fine features grizzled and sharpened, his beard ragged as a lichen-tuft. The arteries stood in relief on his sunken temples like stems of dead ivy; his steel-blue eyes were sunken too and dim. He looked like a man who knew little where he was going and cared less.

Sarel rode with the second wagon, but rarely stayed beside it. The whole trek was his care, and as often as not he was to be seen cantering back in wide circles to round up the laggard livestock. In spite of the strain he had borne and the weight of responsibility he still carried, his face was composed and good-humoured—one had almost said gay. As he rode down the dusty file he had a smile or a friendly word of encouragement for everybody, even halting to talk for a moment in his stiff sing-song English with John Oakley who, following Barend, Jan Bothma and Dicketts, brought up the rear.

John was pleased and felt honoured when Sarel pulled up and spoke to him. He admired the sinewy strength of Sarel's erect, well-knit figure, the grace that distinguished it from Jan Bothma's, the superb balance and ease with which he sat his horse as though he were part of it. He liked Sarel's kind, grave mouth in its frame of crisp beard and moustache, and the frank, fearless gaze of the hazel eyes which put him in mind of Lisbet's. That treasured resemblance, alas, seemed to be all he was likely to get of her so long as they were on the move. The leading wagon was half a mile ahead of him, and the road through the bush took so many twists and turns (being, in fact, no road at all, but merely the track of least resistance) that it was only occasionally that he caught sight, through the drifting dust, of the gleaming tilt lifting as her wagon breasted a rise.

Yet, for all his disappointment at being so far removed from the sight of her, John Oakley was strangely happy that morning, his imagination strung to a high pitch of vitality not merely by the odd exaltation that follows a sleepless night (who could possibly have slept in an air so tense with excitement?) but by the sheer feeling of movement, the sense of having finally broken loose from a static condition never devoid of danger, and by the prospect of active adventure, gallant and hazardous, in an unknown country where even the stars were strange. That morning so many exciting thoughts kept him company that he did not even feel lonely. He was glad, none the less, when, at the first of the four-hourly halts, Mr. Blair trippled back on his cream-coloured nag and squatted down beside him to share his breakfast.

"This is a grand adventure for a lad like you, John," he said. "I could find it in me to envy you. Well I

N

mind the day when I landed at Algoa Bay—ay, that'll
be seventeen years ago—with a young man's eye keen
to pounce like a hawk on all it sees, and so full of spirit
that everything seemed a joke and nothing any trouble.
Those times seem a long way off to me now and life
a deal more difficult. Thank God for your youth and
be glad of it as long as you can."

John smiled to himself. Mr. Blair's ruminations
were apt to be sententious and sombre and to include a
dose of self-pity. It was a harmless foible of his, it
seemed, to speak of himself as a finished man and enjoy
it. Yet John liked his companionship. Since the grounds
of doubt between them had been cleared, they had seen
a good deal of each other. Though he had thrown in
his lot with foreigners, it still pleased Mr. Blair to speak
his own tongue and indulge his sentimental regrets for
his vanished youth in the company of a fellow-countryman so blissfully young and so fresh-minded. In his
odd, repressed way, he was capable of affection and
timidly eager to show it, losing his wonted stiffness, inviting John's confidences and receiving them—in all
matters but one.

"Yes, it's a great adventure for me, sir," John said,
"and a strange one too. What makes it all the stranger
is that I hardly know where I am or where we are
going. Before I came here I had never set foot out of
Worcestershire except once when I walked up to
London. I know this is Africa: and that's about all. I
reckon I never had any schooling to speak of, and a chap

like me gets no chance of coming by books, however much he wants to."

Mr. Blair wagged his head. "That's the difference," he said, "between England and Scotland, where any crofter's lad like myself has the chance of bettering his mind if he puts himself to it. There'll be few books for any of us to read, I'm thinking, in the parts where we're going now. Still, there's no time like the present, they say, John, so here we go. First of all, d'you ken the shape of Africa? Can you read a map?"

Without waiting for a reply he pulled open his clasp-knife and scored on the ground between them an in-verted pear-shaped outline; then, scraping the loose sand together, he moulded it into three lines of hum-mocks and ridges, with deep valley-troughs and wide shallow plains between. John watched the contours grow with fascinated eyes. The man chuckled to him-self as he worked, as entranced with it as a child build-ing castles of sand.

"Now here's your Dark Continent, as they call it," he said, "and as good a map as the prince of cartographers, Mr. Bartholomew of Edinb'ro' himself, could have made for ye! Four great terraces rising in three steps from the sea with a lip to each of them. Yon's the Cape of Good Hope, or the Cape of Storms as some call it, and the coastal plain, not much above sea-level, running east and away round the rim of Africa. And here,"—he pointed with the blade of his knife to his first ridge of sand—"comes the first of

the coastal ranges, rising well-nigh sheer from the sea
to a level of more than two thousand feet, a tidy height
for a mountain in lowland countries like England. Now,
behind that range you'll see a narrowish strath—a
valley you'ld call it. But the northern dip of the mountains is smaller and the slope less steep than the one
that faces the sea. When you reach the foot of them,
you'll still be no less than fifteen hundred feet up. And
that valley, because it's no more than thirty miles wide,
which counts for next to nothing in a country the like
of this, is called the Little Karroo. That's more or less
the level we stand at now, though this country we're
in is not Karroo, which signifies "dry" in the Hottentot
tongue, and at this particular point the land is more or
less confused and broken by rivers. But see, on the other
side of the valley the mountains leap up again in the
ridge of the Groot Zwartbergen or Great Black
Mountains which are five thousand feet above sea-level
and higher than the Grampians or Ben Nevis—to say
naught of that wee hillock named Scafell which you
southrons boast of. And when we've topped these, we
drop down the same as we did before to a great strath
a hundred and fifty miles wide which is less of a valley
than a huge, dry mountain-girt tableland called the
Great Karroo. Graaf Reinet, the first place of any size
we shall pass (and the last, forbye), lies tucked at the
northern verge of it in a crook of the Sunday's River
at a level of two thousand-odd feet. But though you
might think we'd had enough climbing by then, we've

not done with mountains yet; for here, in our path, lie the Snowy Mountains, the mighty Sneeuwbergen soaring up to a height of six thousand eight hundred feet and covered in snow. That is a bitter country, by all accounts, and wild tribes live there: the Bushmen, who, folk say, were the first men in Africa, and the Bastard Hottentots, who call themselves Griquas and are none the better, to my way of thinking, for their dash of white blood. That is a thing our race will have to answer for some day, John, you take my word for it."

"And the cannibal Mantatees," John asked, "with their queen, the witch Mantata?"

Mr. Blair laughed dryly. "I can see you've picked up enough Dutch to listen to Jan Bothma's stories. I don't know who the Mantatees are, and no more does he. But I think the odds are they'll be nothing more than weak Kaffir tribes driven out of their land by the Zulus, like those we have suffered from in the south. Mind, I will not deny that they're cannibals. That tale may be true. If the Zulus have got their cattle they may have been forced to it. They are spreading east, I am told, like a locust swarm. Before long they will reach the land of Moselikatze who murdered the Liebenbergs' trek. When they meet him and his Matabele, then God help them!" He was silent and shook his head solemnly.

"And after the Snowy Mountains?" John enquired.

"To be sure. I am forgetting your lesson. Why, then we drop down again to the great plains they call

the high veld through which flows the Orange River.
That is the border of the English Colony and the end"
(he smiled rather wryly) "of the English Law. That
will be the end of one trek and, I suppose, the beginning of another. Where that takes us we shall not
know till Retief decides."

"Where do you think we shall go?"

"That is hard to say. All Africa lies before us. We
can choose as we will. Beyond the mountains again to
the east lies Natal, which the *commissie* treks, who went
before like Joshua's spies, call an earthly paradise; but
I think there are serpents in that Eden as in the first.
That is the Zulus' land, and we have seen enough of
their work to be chary of them. He who sups with
Dingaan will be needing a mighty long spune. Or perhaps we might push on north after Louis Trigardt to
the Salt Pan Mountains. They say there are endless
plains of green grass, a great cattle country, going on
and on for a thousand miles and more; but nobody has
reached those parts but a handful of missionaries, better
men than myself, Scotsmen too, I've the pride to say,
like Robert Moffat, who must be a man of my age and
came out here some years before I did. And nobody
knows for certain what lies beyond, though I have my
own fancies, John, and like to play with them. But,
maybe, there's nothing in them," he added, shyly.

"What fancies, sir?"

"You'll have heard of Milton, the poet?" John
shook his head. "A grand poet and a grand Puritan.

He wrote a poem called *Paradise Lost,* and two lines of that poem have stuck in my mind from the time I read them first in a great east wind on the links of St. Andrews:

> "*Mombaza, and Quiloa, and Melind,*
> *And Sofala, thought Ophir . . .*"

"But Ophir . . . That's in the Bible!"

"So it is, lad. And there was another great old-fashioned book that I read before I came out here: Ogilby's folio of African Geography. Ay, Ogilby, and going by that name he must have hailed from Angus. There was a passage in that which stuck in my fancy too; but it was too long to commit to memory, so I copied it out, and it's lain in my pouch ever since." He took out a wallet of folded leather and unfolded a sheet of paper closely written over in faded ink.

"Your eyes are better than mine, John," he said. "Read it out for yourself."

John Oakley read:

> "*Yet divers make Ophir the same with Sofala, because it has much gold and ivory, and if all the main land included between the river Magnice and Quama and submitting unto Monomotapa . . . .*"

"Monomotapa, ay, that is the word," Mr. Blair interrupted dreamily. "Monomotapa . . . though whether that be the name of a place or of the great chief who rules it, the Emperor of the Sacred Mountain called Fura, opinions differ. A great black empire, lost in the wilds since the time of Solomon's glory. Only think of it! But go on, lad . . ."

". . . *be all, as Barros calls it, Sofala, as well as the rest of the sea-coast, it can with great reason be judged that this country be none but the Golden Ophir of Solomon, partly because of the houses there to be found near the gold mines, not built after the manner of the country, but seem the work of foreigners, and partly because of the inscriptions being strange and unknown. Moreover, T. Lopez, in his voyage to the Indies, affirms that among the inhabitants of this country there remain books which shew that Solomon every three years had his gold thence . . ."*

"I would gladly set eyes on those books, lad!"

"Besides," John went on, *"the Septuagint Interpreters have translated the word Ophir into the Greek word Sophira, which agrees very well with Sofala, and Josephus, the Jewish historian, calleth it Indian Ophir, adding, moreover, it was called the Gold Country. Besides gold and ivory this country produced apes in myriads; and if, for peacocks, we read ostrich feathers, and for almug trees we substitute ebony or stinkwood, it leaves nothing to be denied.* That is all, sir."

"Yes, that is all. *It leaves nothing to be denied*. And who knows but that we may see it? Who knows but that these simple people of ours, moving out of the south with the faith that brought Israel out of Egypt, may not be led by Providence towards riches surpassing all dreams—to Solomon's Ophir? *They looked for a city that hath Foundations*. And, in another place: *The City was pure gold*."

"Then some day we may all be rich, sir?"

"Ay, if this is true, some day we may all be rich. But we may not be any more happy for that, John. Gold is a metal I fear. Ordeal by Gold is a sterner test than Ordeal by Fire or Ordeal by Battle, and we may have a share of all three before we have finished. Yet one likes to meditate, lad. Ay, one likes to meditate. . . ."

Sarel Prinsloo rode past with a wave of the hand and a smile: he was setting the trek in motion again. Mr. Blair rose to his feet and stared down sombrely at the African map in the sand.

"Well, the geography lesson is finished," he said, "and now you know just as much as any of us, about where we are going and what we are likely to find there."

He clumsily mounted the cream-coloured mare and moved on sedately, and John Oakley's eyes followed him jealously, for he knew that, in half a mile Mr. Blair would escape the dust and catch up with the leading wagon, and talk, as he rode, with Lisbet and look in her hazel eyes. But there was no time for reflection on this, nor even on the mysterious wonders with which Mr. Blair had thrilled and beclouded his mind. The wagon in front was already under way. His Hottentot's long lash swirled in the air and cracked; the small child who led the oxen twisted the reims round his forearm and tugged at the leaders' great horns. The wagon floundered forward.

They rolled on and on, climbing always by slow degrees. The character of the grey-green bush through which they passed varied little. The low thorn-trees looked wiry and dry, their leaves already sickened by the touch of autumn were tinged with pale gold. At intervals congregations of fleshy *spek-boom* stood clothed in round succulent leaves; thickets of aloe thrust upward their clustered sword-blades and spires of vermilion bloom; here and there a gaunt candelabra-tree lifted its suppliant arms, its warty, hide-like bark so ashen-hued that it was hard to tell if the creature were dead or living: it appeared less a tree than the skeleton of a tree. The growths on the ground were wiry and sapless too, and some, like the trees of the bush, armed with secret spikes and claws: a hostile, grim vegetation it seemed, and jealous of man's intrusion, throwing out on the dusty air, as the wagon-wheels crushed it, gusts of hot aromatic odours resembling those which the glands of some animals secrete and discharge for spite and protection.

When the hot sky paled at noon the bush grew deader than ever. It lay flattened and shadowless, silent and deathly still. No bird uttered a call or a twitter save melancholy doves whose crooning, lost in the dry recesses, seemed heat itself transformed into sound. No life stirred in the mortal waste, save now and then a startled *rheebok* plunging away through the undergrowth, or guinea-fowl whirring across the track and rocketing like high pheasants. No other game met their eyes. The herds that pastured this wilderness had scattered fanwise from the head of the advancing trek which, like some mile-long dragon breathing out smoke of dust, or gigantic millipede, crawled slowly forward, driving all before it.

So slow, so somnolent, its progress seemed. Yet the man on the driving-seat could not afford to drowse when the wheels might strike an overgrown tree-trunk or an ant-heap that looked soft as a mole-hill but was set hard as stone and made the whole wagon shudder and creak; when the solid-seeming track might subside without warning, and the front wheels sink in to their axles pitching him forward; when the leaders might suddenly flounder into chasms four foot deep where the banks of a spruit, undercut by flood water, had fallen in, and the wagon itself, slumped down over the drop, seemed hopelessly wedged fore and aft in the spruit's narrow channel; when the willing oxen staggered and strained and slipped and collapsed in their tracks though the whirling lash still stung them onward and wild curses and cries filled the air. Then out came picks and spades and a five-foot track was dug for the wheels; and the whip cracked again and blows of the *sjambok* fell dully on quivering flanks and quarters; and *"Trek maar!"* the men cried: "All together now . . . *Amper gewin!"*—and up the great wagon shot like a surf-boat taking the crest of a comber and then sliding on for a while.

It was a kind of travelling that made the mired winter roads about Grafton Lovett seem by comparison smooth as a turnpike. There was hardly a moment but called for a wary mind and well-skinned eyes. Indeed, it was far less tiring, as John soon discovered, to walk than to ride, and even so, by the end of the day, he was exhausted. They encamped that night, and for many nights after, in trampled clearings where other wagons had halted before them, and always within reach of water. The "boys" made their own fires and bivouacs, but the white men gathered about the two leading wagons, and sang their psalm and heard their portion and ate their dinner.

This was the only hour, during those long, long days of trekking, when John Oakley set eyes on Lisbet. He looked forward impatiently to these moments, brief as they were. He was still in a state of ecstatic humility in which he found it hard to believe that such perfection existed, and was grateful for the smallest of mercies: the sight of her face flushed or shadowed by flickering firelight; the sound of her voice; above all, her quiet laughter. It did not trouble him that she rarely looked his way and hardly ever spoke to him, for he guessed he was not alone in his adoration—every evening he saw Jan Bothma's hot, hungry eyes devouring her as she sat and following her as she moved, while Anna's gaze followed Jan's. He knew that these two were no friends of his, for Jan Bothma did not disguise his contempt for him as a man and his dislike of him as an Englishman, and Jan could neither do nor think wrong in Anna's eyes. He knew too that if Lisbet were even polite to him in their presence there was bound to be trouble, and approved of the tact with which she devoted herself to Mr. Blair, with whom it seemed natural that she should speak English; and sometimes, with a glow of secret triumph, he perceived that the words she spoke to Mr. Blair were intended for himself.

They did not sit long by the fire. Everyone was dog-tired, and to spare the oxen from trekking in the heat of noon they were always inspanned and set on their way before dawn. As soon as the men had eaten they went back to their wagons and wrapped themselves in their karosses and slept with their saddles behind their shoulders.

George Dicketts always kept John company at night. They lay on their backs side by side, gazing up at the stars. The sup of peach-brandy had usually made

George Dicketts talkative and, if he had managed to drink more than one, a trifle maudlin. His insular soul refused to immerse itself in this new, adventurous life. He took it for granted and was not even impressed by its strangeness. In those starlit vigils his mind returned obstinately to Grafton Lovett.

"I reckon the country ought to be looking a treat by now, John," he said, "with the plum-blow coming out in the archards and the hedges a-turning green, and the rabbits beginning to kindle and all the lambs skipping about. Did you ever see such rum sheep as they have in these parts—with hair like a goat and them whopping great tails? If they put me to shearing them beggars I shouldna know where to begin. Ay, there ought to be a rare show of plums round about Grafton this year. Last spring, if you take your mind back, the blow was kind enough, but the late frostses nipped it just when the buds comed to bossen, about cuckoo-time. That's a queer thing too, when you come to think of it: Here we be, at the end of April or the beginning of May—I'll be damned if I know which it be—and ne'er a one have I heard. Summat must have gone wrong with the seasons for certain, and the same with the blackbirds and throstles too. These birds you get here, John, I don't call them birds rightly speaking, all fancified up like bloody parrots, and not a song, to say song, among the lot of them! Why, when I was a lad in Grafton and went to work in the morning about this time of year, you could barely hear yourself speak for the row they made nesting. And the primmyroses and cowslips too. Do you mind that piece of Tom Collins's as they call Long Dragon? I've seen cowslips so thick at the top of that meadow you'ld have thought there wasn't a blade of grass to it. But rare pasture it was, all the same, except for them ma'shy bits down by the brook, which was all rushes and king-cups and such-like. I've told farmer Collins time and again as that meadow would pay for draining, but I couldn't insense him: you know what Tom Collins is, John: a stiff-necked one-sided beggar if ever there was one. . . ."

So George Dicketts' slow rustic voice droned on and on, his sleepy mind endlessly, tenderly brooding over the beloved fields which had been all his world like an earth-bound ghost; and John Oakley, listening to his ruminations and seeing in the dark the scenes his love remembered, was surprised to find himself oddly unmoved and unhurt by any vague nostalgic pang. After all, though the years he had spent in Grafton Lovett had been relatively happy, his roots had been no deeper sunk in those red marls than in the wind-swept cindery slopes of Dulston. So far in his life he had found no spot on earth of which he could feel, as George Dicketts felt of Grafton, that he belonged to it. It was not of Grafton or Dulston that he thought as he fell asleep, nor even of the strange and darkling waste that surrounded him. His spirit's home, the fixed point to which, wherever they wandered momentarily, his thoughts always returned and came to rest, was the tilted wagon in which Lisbet Prinsloo slept. It was all the joy he asked of life to know that she would still be there when he woke next morning, and that when the wagon moved on he would follow it and still be near her.

For ten days the trek plodded on beside the Great Fish River through almost level lands. Due west they trekked, with the rising sun behind and the sinking sun in their faces, till they came to another stream, the Small Fish River, running in from the north; and here they turned northward too, through a narrower kloof (or glen, as Mr. Blair called it) with mountains on either hand, passing here and there deserted cattle-farms, rude boxes of daub and wattle planked down on the veld without gardens or tilth or any sign of activity but vast kraals of tangled mimosa whose emptiness heightened their air of desolation. Yet this bush itself seemed more lively for man's desertion; and the game were less shy. The course of the falling stream was clogged with a green growth of impenetrable thorn; but in the open stretches beyond, across which the wagons cut to avoid the river's meanderings, over rough ground scattered with huge ant-hills and undermined by treacherous porcupine-burrows and ant-eater-holes, small herds of dancing springbok and troops of jackals and here and there a floundering ostrich were seen.

Barend killed a couple of springbok for the pot: delicate-footed things with snow-white bellies and lyrate horns, and brought back the limp fawn bodies slung over his saddle-bow. John thought he had never seen such innocent graceful creatures; and George reckoned that the larger would keep a labouring chap's home in good meat for a week, though if you touched one of the like of them there deer in England, let alone two, you'ld have the keepers after you quick and soon find yourself in the dock and half-way to the gallows. Mr. Blair shook his head. Ay, the beasties were pretty enough to look at and no' bad to eat, and a pleasant sight to see in a small herd like that; but when tens became hundreds and hundreds thousands and the *trek-bokken*, as they were called, spread over the land in countless hordes, nibbling every green thing they met to the ground, the pretty things were as great a pest as any of the ten plagues of Egypt, including the locusts, which behaved in much the same way. But the venison was excellent, he admitted, and a welcome change from greasy mutton stews and grilled guinea-fowl. And the air of these uplands, at two thousand three hundred feet, gave a man an appetite.

On the fifteenth day they came to the village of Somerset. Mr. Blair had spoken of it as one of their first objectives, and John had looked forward to seeing it as the first South African village on which he would have set eyes; but it turned out to be no more than a mean hamlet of two dozen mud-built hovels set in a swampy hollow, with the Small Fish River encompassing it on three sides. Sarel passed it by without halting, for they had reached it soon after dawn, and there was no time to waste: the mountainous spurs of Bruintjes Hooghte rose behind it, and the back of the bleak ascent should be broken before the light failed.

"But I doubt if thirteen heavily-loaded wagons will get over the heights this day," Mr. Blair told John mournfully. "By to-night you'll have learned, maybe, what a wagon-trek means."

He was to learn pretty soon what it meant. The road over the heights was no more than a series of narrow precipitous ledges strewn with massive boulders, some bedded deep in the living rock, others lately fallen. They had not climbed far before the leading wagons were in trouble and Jan Bothma came riding back to collect an extra span. Sarel's Fatherland oxen, unused to the mountain passes, had refused to take the slope, and swerved outward so near to the precipice that the near leader had actually lost his footing and, pulling his yoke-mate with him, hung strangled by the *trek-tow*, over the edge. It had been touch and go with the rest of the span and with the wagon itself. Sarel, taking no risks, had lightened the wagon and made the women dismount.

Jan Bothma was in no humour for trouble that day. They had passed not far from the home of that Hendrik Prinsloo who had been hanged with his cousin Stephanus after Slachter's Nek. Jan's mind was already black with the memory of that old grudge, and his face like thunder. At such a time the mere sight of an Englishman was enough to infuriate him, and he let himself go on George Dicketts, who, he said, made a clumsy job of unyoking his team. Even when they had been unyoked, it was no easy matter to drag them forward through the narrow space left by the wagons in front. The sun had reached the mid-northern sky before they had cut the *trek-tow* and let the bodies of the two leaders go crashing down into the abyss, and inspanned the second team of long-horned Afrikanders, and, with coaxing and violence, forced them over the brow.

But that, Mr. Blair—who was always inclined to be gloomy—suggested, would not be the end of the trouble. If wagons so lightly loaded as Sarel's new ones had needed a double span to pull them over, what would happen to the more heavily burdened wagons behind? As he sat talking to John he recalled the most hair-raising stories of trekkers who, in a like case, had been forced to dump their loads and dismantle their wagons and carry them over in pieces.

"You may take my word," he said, "we'll be sticking here for three days."

He seemed almost disappointed, indeed, when at last they moved on. It was only the Englishman's raw oxen, it seemed, that had been at fault—as an Englishman's oxen would be, Jan Bothma said; and the rest of the wagons topped that pitch without mishap. Yet the dizzy descents in that series of precipitous switchbacks were even more perilous than the climbs. Before they dared to start moving downward both hind-wheels must be locked, and the wagon skidded and bumped from boulder to boulder and ledge to ledge with impacts so violent that it seemed a miracle its suffering timber stood the strain. John himself took over the leaders from the little *voorlooper's* hands and steered them, himself moving backward step by step, while Dicketts and Mr. Blair threw their weight on the stay-ropes to check the sway and strain the top-heavy wagons away from the edges.

So they painfully rose and descended even more slowly, hugging the inner edge of the narrow track that skirted the mountain's contours: above their heads towered vast columnar buttresses of stone; at their feet the cliff fell away into chasms whose depth could not be gauged because of the thorns that choked them. Up and down they toiled and twisted, always rising by degrees; but by sunset, when Sarel called a halt, the foremost wagons had not yet reached the summit. Nor did they know (for the road was strange to them all) how far they might be from it. Streaks of mist, condensed by the cool evening air, appeared beneath them, spanning the sunken kloofs with festoons of suspended gossamer. Looking back, below and beyond these gauzy filaments, they saw, for one moment, the valley of the Small Fish River and the wooded spurs of the Boschberg that sheltered Somerset incredibly near and clear and soaked in the blood-red hues of sunset. Then, almost as though the very air were curdled by some chemical change, the transfigured landscape vanished utterly. They were enveloped in a white milkiness so dense that neither the rising scarps nor the brink of the precipice could be seen. It was a good thing that Sarel had bidden them halt; for the first step of a man or an ox might well be his last. They could only stay where they were and watch the white blanket darken.

There was no question, that night, of the usual routine of communal prayers and food. John and Dicketts kindled a fire at the tail of John's wagon. They sat shivering near it and chewing biltong, which was all the food they could get. The oxen lowed piti-fully, lying down in their yokes. They had toiled patiently all day and needed water; but though sounds of falling water could be heard far below in the pit of the abyss, there was no possibility of reaching it, and the poor beasts went thirsty. Within an hour of sunset the mist had grown so dense that the light of the fire could not penetrate it, but threw the shadows of themselves and of the wagon on what looked like a solid white wall. The appearance of Sarel, suddenly looming out of it, startled them. He was threading his way back on foot to see how the cattle were faring in the rear.

"You had better look to your dogs to-night, fellows," he said. "These kloofs are full of tigers, and if a tiger smells a dog he'll snatch it from under your nose.

Keep your guns beside you loaded, and see that the mist doesn't damp the priming or you'll have a misfire."

It was a wretched night. No amount of huddling in sheepskin karosses could keep out the insidious cold. Dicketts swore it was freezing. But heat and cold are relative sensations, and their thinned blood could not adapt itself to a drop of more than forty degrees from the morning's temperature. It seemed no warmer when, in the middle of the night, the mist turned to a mizzle of fine rain.

Yet day broke clear and brilliant with an unclouded sky. A shrewd wind whipping down the gully from the north had driven the mist before it and piled it in billows of foamy cumulus over the lost plains. There was a sting in the high, bright air that put new heart into them; and their oxen too, though still thirsty, had recovered their strength and pulled with a will. Under that brilliant sky, the track itself seemed to lose the terrors that had increased and gathered round it as the light of the last day faded; and they were not, as it turned out, so far from the summit of the heights as they had imagined, for by midday they had reached the head of the kloof and emerged on to a high smooth shoulder, wide enough for the wagons to stand outspanned and the oxen to graze, while the men talked and smoked and laughed over their difficulties and escapes. An air of quiet exhilaration permeated the whole camp that morning. All felt that the struggles of the day before had been well worth while and that it was good to be alive.

In this happy morning mood, John left the wagons and wandered over the watershed with Mr. Blair. The plains they had left behind still lay hidden by heaped banks of cloud, dazzlingly white; but before them, at the foot of a slope that declined more gradually, stretched an endless plain whose surface glowed beneath the high sun with a radiance almost as rich as that with which sunset had drenched the landscape the evening before. At first sight, indeed, this vast expanse looked less like land than a sea-firth, or the estuary of some great river issuing from the heart of the mountain mass on whose foot-hills they stood to widen and lose itself in the level immensity of a western horizon that seemed to join with the sky in a mingling of filmy blues. Observed from that height, the plain showed no variation of height or texture, and little of colour save where, here and there, its surface lay dappled by huge patches of shadow that moved like those cast by clouds drifting so slowly as to seem motionless. Shadows they must be, John thought, till he looked up to the sky and saw it was cloudless. Then he heard Mr. Blair, who had long been silent, speaking:

"What a sight!" he said. "Do you see the game moving there? You'ld be wondering where such great herds could find food or drink in such a wilderness, but there they are. We're going up in the world, John, bit by bit; and this is the third of the steps I made on your map. Yon's the Great Karroo. It'll take us some days to cross it, but there'll be no more hills, as you see, till we get to the Sneeuwberg, if that's any comfort. Ay, the Great Karroo, and great and dry it is."

In the evening light they dropped down from the foot-hills through green thickets of *spek-boom* and turned due north with a red sun plunging down on their left. These bare open plains were a blessed relief after so many days of anxious progress through twisting bush-paths, against the grain of a broken country scoured by torrents. The mood of exultation which had quickened his blood so joyously that morning showed no signs of fading. On this tableland the air tasted even sweeter and drier: every breath seemed charged with new life; and with it there entered into him an odd sense of physical freedom which the pressure of the silent dust-choked bush and the mountain *kloofs* had denied: a feeling that bade the spirit as well as the body expand and take wings like a bird in the joy of illimitable air.

There is some magic of that sort in all deserts; yet most deserts have aspects of terror, and the Karroo looked kind. Nor, indeed, was it wholly desert, as, from afar, it had seemed. The whole waste was peppered with a heathlike vegetation low-growing in tufts like the wool on a Hottentot's head. Thick-stemmed and twisted the dwarf brushwood grew, as though wind and drought had hard-pruned it, and

starred with humble flowers that were like the centre
of a daisy whose petals had been stripped; but its
leaves, by some miracle, had moisture in them yet;
they gave out a crisp, crackling sound underfoot, and
when the sheep reached them they fell on them with a
voracity that excited George Dicketts' scorn.

"Just look at the poor fools a-nibbling," he said.
"Them there rubbidgy weeds can't do them no good,
though I suppose they be used to it and knows no better.
If you was to take one of them there sheep, John, and
set him down in the cowslip field I was talking about
the other night, Tom Collins's Long Dragon, I reckon
the poor beggar would blow his belly out."

Yet the sheep knew better than he. It was strange
to see how their trailing column suddenly dissolved and
spread into a crescent, with two eager horns advancing
on either side. Nor was the great waste as waterless
as it looked. Through its shallow dongas, only made
visible by borders of scrubby mimosa with sickle-
shaped pods and silvery spines, slow water ebbed rather
than flowed over sandy bottoms to join the Melks
River. It was only in the crossing of these sands that
the wagons found any difficulty. Elsewhere the plain's
surface lay paved, as it were, with a mosaic of ruddy
sandstone and glistening quartz, so close-set and
cemented by recent rain that no dust-clouds rose from
it, and so level that a man could sit on his driving-seat
and dream or even go to sleep, rolling on and on over
the rosy earth and through the serene golden air with-

out fear of any mishap, leaving the oxen to follow the spoor of the wagon in front.

It was the quality of this vital elixir, which even in the blaze of noon did not lose its exhilarating virtue, that (more than the sense of relief and boundless freedom) made John Oakley's heart sing as he rode or walked on his way. When sunset had drenched the plain once more with its incredible rosy splendour, the air grew icy, indeed, but was still so dry as not to seem cold. Even the flames that rose from their crackling fire of sere thorn appeared to exult and aspire; even the stars exulted; they hung low in the vault of indigo and blazed like single sapphires or slashed it with cold blue rays that were like swords of steel, giving night a glory more spacious than that of day. Even Jan Bothma under its influence grew less surly. He rode wide afield with Barend in search of game, bringing home buck for the family and quagga-meat for the natives. And Hendrik shot his first springbok.

John wished the Karroo might never end, though end it must. Every day the blue mountain barrier that closed the road to the north and which had borne the likeness, when first they viewed it, of low banks of cloud, towered higher and grew nearer and more substantial —most of all at evening when cloudbanks gathered above it and the difference between rock and vapour became more clear. To Mr. Blair the increasing imminence of the Sneeuwbergen was more welcome. He was highland-born and found all plains wearisome, and the sheer magnitude of this mighty chain made him glow with enthusiasm.

"I've never set eyes on a mountain yet, John," he said, "but I wanted to get atop of it and look beyond it; and that range, as you'll mind from the map I made you, is by all accounts the greatest in Africa. The Quathlamba, the natives call it; but the Dutch name rings finer to my mind. The Drakensberg. The man who gave it that name was a poet—though whether there be dragons in it (or anywhere else, for that matter, since the one Bel had to deal with in the Apocrypha—and that, mind, is no Scripture!) is more than I'ld care to vouch for. Do you mark yon black cloud that goes scudding across the top of them? Many's the time I've seen the like of that moving over the head of Glen Clova, and wakened next morning to see the whole forest of Atholl glittering white. Ay, man, I should like to feel my fingers stinging with snow again. That's a thing I haven't done these thirty years."

So they came, after three weeks' trekking, to Graaf Reinet, and halted there for two days on the outspan in front of the church, an arid flat of red Karroo soil worn bare by those who had lodged there before them, strewn with blackened embers of camp-fires and the stubs of gnawed corn-cobs.

Even George Dicketts, loth to confess that anything African was worth looking at, found the change from the wild to Graaf Reinet to his liking. It was a gay, orderly little place, laid out in a quadrangular plan of clean, whitewashed houses and wide avenues bordered by lemon and orange trees. Steep, conical hills, their slopes green with *spek-boom*, hid the menacing scarp of the Sneeuwbergen, and a loop of the Sunday's River, fringed with weeping willows and feathery-leaved mimosa, drew a green belt about it and fed furrows that watered orchards and gardens where birds sang such as even George Dicketts could not complain of: yellow weaver-birds twittering round their hanging nests, and the gay green shrike that is called, from its blithe fluting, the *bok-makirri*. All the birds of the bush and the last of the departing migrants seemed to come to those sandy-bottomed furrows to sip.

John Oakley, with more imagination than George, felt less sure of himself. This was the first time since his landing that he had set foot in a place within the reach of the law. Yet he need not have feared: Graaf Reinet, more than any other town in the Colony, was a Dutch reserve and contemptuous of authority. It was, moreover, the recognized starting-point of the trekking movement, from which not merely the wealthy wheelwrights and wagon-makers such as Gert Maritz had profited, but the most humble trader who kept a *winkel* for the supply of stores; it was also the clearing-house for all news and rumour connected with the trek.

On that evening, indeed, it resembled nothing so much as a busy base in the rear of an invading army.

The Prinsloo party was not the only one encamped on the outspan. One was dumped there already when they arrived, and two others, from the western Karroo, arrived before nightfall. There were transport wagons, too, off-loading merchandise brought by sea from Capetown and landed at Algoa Bay.

At that moment there appeared to be no inhabitant of Graaf Reinet who was not anxious to sell something. They clustered about the outspanned wagons like bees, proposing their wares and proclaiming their cheapness; there was nothing a man on trek could possibly want that they were not able and ready to supply at the shortest notice, and this was the last chance. There were packmen too and pedlars or *smouses* who had descended on Graaf Reinet from every corner of the Colony like vultures scenting a kill, selling French ribbons and shoe-latchets and tortoise-shell combs and Redditch needles and many small fripperies calculated to catch the eyes of women from back-veld farms who rarely see such things; and among the rest there wandered by a solemn, melancholy German with a pack of books, guaranteed to have been printed in Holland and mainly devotional, and a couple of English maps of Africa of the sort that missionaries used to demonstrate the continent's vastness and its need for conversion.

John saw Lisbet eagerly examining the books one by one, yet none of them pleased her. He himself would gladly have bought a map, but remembered suddenly that he had no money, and, indeed, had had none since the day he returned from London with his uncle's guineas tied up in a handkerchief; while Mr. Blair, the only person from whom he could conceivably have borrowed any, had put on a black coat and departed to pay a formal visit to his colleague and fellow-countryman, Mr. Murray, the resident minister of the Dutch Reformed Church.

As soon as darkness fell, each party lit its own fires on the outspan. The wagon tilts shone white in the flickering flames and caught fantastic shadows; but all over the square the buzzing activity showed no signs of ceasing, and grew noisier as the brandy bottles went round. It was natural enough for men who had seen no stranger's face (and particularly no woman's) since their last Communion, to mix with their fellows and listen greedily to the news of the great world. Among them, the party who had travelled east from the Groot Zwartbergen lurched over to pay their respects to old Adrian and stare at the girls in the firelight. They were men of enormous stature, of a family named Botha, who made even Jan Bothma look small. Their talk was all of the trek, and they were anxious to know how things went on the eastern frontier. In their mountain fastnesses the wildest of rumours found credence.

"Is it true," they asked, "that the Hottentot Corps has mutinied and joined with the Kaffirs? Is it true that the Government has made a pact with the Pope of Rome to change our religion and take over the churches? Is it true that every man who can carry a gun is to be conscripted and put into British uniform?"

None of these things were true, Adrian told them, as far as he knew, nor could he believe them; but the eldest and hugest of the Bothas shook his head. As to the Hottentot mutiny and the Pope of Rome he was glad to be reassured.

"But the other business," he said, "I think more likely. It is a slim trick, that. As soon as a man's in uniform, he's under martial law, no? And a man whom the Government dislikes can be easily shot under martial law without any trial. I am certain that this must be true," he said, "for a cousin of mine was in Capetown six months ago and saw them unloading uniforms at the Castle, thousands and thousands of uniforms, so many that he couldn't count them; and they can't put as many soldiers as that into uniform because, don't you see, there aren't enough of them. So they must be for us, uncle. I say it stands to reason they must be for us. There's one good thing about it, anyway," he went on with a laugh: "if they want to fit me and my brothers here they'll have to find something bigger than any damned Englishman I've ever seen can wear."

They were full of wild rumours, too, from the north. They had heard of five wagons loaded with women being lost on the Orange ponts and eaten by crocodiles. They had heard that Retief was dead: a school Kaffir, paid by the missionaries, had assegaied him as he slept, though another tale said he had been mauled to death by a lion. And, if he wasn't dead, he had certainly quarrelled with Maritz, just as Maritz had quarrelled with Potgieter—because one was a Dopper and the other a member of the Reformed Church—though some folk were sure that Potgieter and Maritz, the two of them, were long past quarrelling, having been taken prisoners by an English force sent over to the Orange by the new Lieutenant-Governor Stockenstrom to collect all the Boers' arms and ammunition by force, and had been brought back secretly to the Cape in chains. And now a new ordinance had been written, if not signed by Queen Victoria, making it illegal for any British subject to cross the border. What could a fellow believe?

"It is better far to believe nothing," old Adrian said. "Soon, God willing, we shall see for ourselves what is true and what lies."

"Well, one thing is true for certain—and that is that the soldiers are off-loading every wagon that passes in search of ammunition. So, before we trekked, my brother Theunis and I made false bottoms in two of our wagons and stowed away all the lead and powder in them. They'll be safe enough there, I should say; for no Englishman knows what a wagon ought to look like."

As they rose to go, the three Bothas shook hands punctiliously with the men and kissed the women. That was the old country custom which of late years had been abandoned; but changes of fashion did not reach the recesses of the Zwartbergen. John went hot with fury to see the three men kissing Lisbet, one after another; but Jan Bothma appeared to accept the procedure as natural, and Lisbet only smiled. The memory of that gross sacrilege and of her accepting it agonized him all night. He felt he could never forget it. It kept him awake until, long after midnight, George Dicketts, somewhat unsteadily, stumped back to the wagon.

"John," he said confidentially, "I've drunk more than a drop in my time. I've drunk army rum, I've drunk Hollands, I've drunk gin, I've drunk bottles and bottles and bottles of the stuff the French soldiers call 'vin'; but never have I drunk aught so almighty fierce to the guts as the brandy-wine or whatever it is that these here chaps swill like water. I know when I've had enough, lad, and always did, and I've had enough this evening—but, by God, what wouldn't I give for a quart of good English beer!"

The morrow was Sunday. In accordance with the inflexible rule, this was a day appointed for rest, and no new start could be made: no ordinary Sunday either, for they were within reach of a church, and Mr. Blair had accepted his colleague's invitation to occupy the pulpit, and would probably do so for two hours at the very least. The arrival of a visiting pastor made a great day in Graaf Reinet. It was certain that every notable would leap at the opportunity of such edification—including the new Lieutenant-Governor, the trekkers' natural enemy, Andries Stockenstrom.

This was a great day for Anna and Lisbet. It was many months since they had had the chance of wearing their Sunday clothes. All their most elegant finery was stowed away in the chests of the baggage-wagon, yet both the girls had kept enough by them to make a fair show with clean summery prints, lace mittens, and, instead of the white linen sun-bonnets they usually wore, coquettish silk kappies tucked and embroidered. Anna had done up her hair at the front in elaborate plaits; but Lisbet's, as usual, was parted in the middle and smoothed over her head. Excitement made them both gay and talkative. John could hear their light voices laughing and whispering together inside the wagon; and when Lisbet appeared at last he thought he had never seen any creature more delicately lovely, nor, alas, more unapproachable. He could not help wishing he had better clothes of his own, for, that morning, even the giants from the Zwartbergen had turned out in blue nankeen coats striped with red, and green velvet trousers, and high bell-shaped hats which must surely have belonged to their grandfathers. He felt himself dreadfully drab and undistinguished; he envied these cumbrous dandies, who so clearly fancied themselves and wanted to make an impression on Anna and Lisbet; and yet, on the whole, it was better perhaps that he should not be conspicuous: at that moment, certainly, nobody would have taken him for an Englishman in his check shirt, his flapped leathern *klapbroek* trousers and thong-sewn *veld-schoens* and the wide-brimmed straw hat that Sarel had given him. He looked better thus, if he had only known it, than the Zwartbergen beaux. He was very different now from the pallid, half-starved lad who had collapsed on the *voorhuis* floor at Welgelegen. His shoulders had broadened, his body filled out; there was a glow of rich health beneath the tanned skin of his shaven cheeks; his lax muscles had hardened; his brown body was lithe and strong.

So Lisbet thought, approvingly, when, emerging from the wagon that morning, she saw him standing there envious and disconsolate. It was cruel, she knew, to point the contrast between them, yet she was so entranced by her own elegance that she could not resist the exquisite temptation of flaunting it for a moment before him (it was he, more than anyone else, she wanted to please) with the pride of a newly-hatched butterfly spreading its wings. She moved slowly towards him, with the dignified steps of a great lady entering a ballroom, allowing him time to feast his eyes on her. She saw how shattered he was, and was thrilled by her conquest, yet saw, too, how conscious he was of his shabbiness, and felt a quick pity for him that softened her shining eyes and compelled her to be kind and show him that such things made no difference. A swift glance assured her that nobody was looking. She smiled and dropped him a curtsy, then whispered:

"How do you like my Sunday best, John?"

He blushed and said quickly: "I think you are more beautiful than anyone I have ever seen."

His own daring staggered him. He felt as though he had been guilty of an enormity. But Lisbet, although her smiling eyes dropped for a moment, did not appear in the least discomposed.

"Hush, hush," she said, with a teasing affectation of modesty. "Where have you learnt this bold gallantry, John? One would guess you have been reading romances . . . unless you have picked it up in the Great Karroo. But I am glad you like my dress," she added demurely. "As a matter of fact I find Anna's much more becoming. And so does she; so, thank Heaven, everyone's satisfied."

They had no more speech together that day. At that moment Anna, impatient and flustered, appeared, and Jacoba, in a voluminous flounced dress of black silk, came painfully after her. Anna showed no signs of recognizing John's presence save one quick, suspicious glance which appraised and dismissed him; but Jacoba smiled when she saw him and wished him good day, and her heavy-lidded eyes dwelt on him for a moment almost wistfully. It pleased her to see how the new life was making a man of him. Whenever she looked at him now he reminded her more and more of her Pieter, the boy she had lost in the Kaffir War, and the finding of anyone on whom, even unconsciously, she could lavish that flow of affection which death had so rudely checked, gave her happiness. Though she rarely spoke to John, she had found satisfaction and pride in his swift recovery, and her benevolent eyes often rested on him, watching his progress, adopting him, without question, as one of her own. She was a woman whose heart found its only pleasure in giving.

Lisbet saw the kind glance her mother gave John and was touched by it. She hoped Anna had seen it too. It would serve her right if she had. She took Jacoba's arm gently.

"Come along, ma," he said, "or we shan't get to the church before Mr. Blair has come to 'Thirteenthly . . .'"

Sarel had given orders for the wagons to be inspanned at dawn; but with dawn came only confusion. Half the Hottentot boys were missing, and half the remainder still stupid with drink or *dakka*. That was always the danger of halting near towns, where unprincipled traders were ready to sell natives liquor on the sly. Jan Bothma and he took the ones who appeared most sensible to rout out the rest from the reed-huts of the stinking Hottentot village where they had spent the Sunday in drinking and lechery. Such as were able to stagger to the outspan were driven back with threats of the *sjambok* or made to carry others who could not walk and would have to be stowed in the wagons until they recovered their senses. Thus two hours were wasted, and even so the drivers of the two new wagons could not be found. This was a great score for Jan Bothma.

"Ha, you see what we come to!" he said. "Your cursed Englishman's Hottentots. That might only have been expected. 'Good boys. . . no damned missionary nonsense about them!' Was that what you told me he said? And of course you believed him and had the worst of the bargain. All those boys of his wanted and got was a free ride to Graaf Reinet. I tell you, Sarel, from the moment I saw their sly yellow faces I knew what they were. Missionary boys perhaps, but *tronk-volk*, jail-birds for certain. If you want to find them now, you go round to the prison and knock up the jailer; but if you'll take my advice you'll leave them where they belong and do without them. Now *my* boys, though they may take a drop, have been brought up in the good old way with a *sjambok* over their backs and know their places. They'll hear about this to-morrow and be all the better for it."

By the time they had collected the cattle and got under way, it was broad daylight. Clouds burdened black with snow still obscured the crests of the Sneeuw-bergen, increasing their height and menace. The track followed the swift Sunday's River through green foothills dense with *spek-boom*. The risen sun only made the great crags and the clouds above them seem blacker and more threatening. The stream, swirling sullenly over the rocks, showed the greenish opacity of new-melted snow. There was a touch of cold in the air:

not that exhilarating cold of the clear Karroo nights which made the skin glow and tingle, but a darkness that, as soon as the sun clouded over, chilled to the bone.

Soon the *spek-boom* bush thinned; the slopes on either side of the track became barren or scattered with wiry brushwood. Drooping veils of mist or drizzle swept down between them, and once, like a flight of butterflies, a brisk flurry of huge snow-flakes passed to melt as they fell. The white vapours hung too low for the mountain-summits to be seen; only the vast columnar bastions of basalt supporting them rose grimly on either hand and towered out of sight. Yet the imminence of those tremendous invisible heights could be felt, almost as though their impending masses compressed the air; and their shadow, if not their substance, asserted itself—for by mid-afternoon, when the sky should still have been bright, the hanging mist overhead turned grey as though darkness were near.

More light snow fell that night. The flakes spat in the bivouac fires of wiry rhinoceros-bush that Sarel had prudently gathered as they went, having been warned beforehand that little wood fit to burn could be found on the upper slopes. It was a night not merely of penetrating cold but of some anxiety. All the Hottentots who had recovered from their drinking-bout were armed with muskets to defend themselves and their cattle, and a strict watch was kept. These cavernous *kloofs* of the Sneeuwbergen were still infested with creatures more dangerous than tigers: bands of runaway slaves, some armed with stolen firearms, and hordes of wild Bushmen, whose hand was against every man.

Round the fires that night many stories were told of the Bushmen's cunning; the skill with which a dozen could creep naked into a kraal and steal a man's cattle without his knowing it till he saw, next morning, within a few yards of his camp, his beasts' pitiful carcasses from which the flesh had been torn in strips while they still lived. And if they were caught in the act, the Oosthuizens said, the devils were apt to turn nasty. Each carried as many as seventy arrows in his quiver, tipped with ostrich-bone and barbed with a thin triangle of iron dipped in poison. Some used euphorbia-sap and some tobacco-juice, and others, folk said, a black substance that sweated from the roofs of their caves. The elder Oosthuizen could remember the good old days when an uncle of his who lived in the Tarka always shot a Bushman on sight, as he would have shot a cobra—one morning he had shot six. But Jan Bothma could cap that story. His cousin Hans Bezuidenhout in the Bamboesberg knew a better trick than that. When he and his friends heard Bushmen were about they rode out and rounded them up, keeping well out of range of their arrows and killing the males, but keeping the females as slaves to pay for lost time and ammunition. The Council in Capetown had passed a law rooking him ten rix-dollars for every slave sold; but the Governor had turned that down. And his cousin's best bag, Jan Bothma said, was a dozen. Lisbet did not smile.

A Bushman's life in the Bamboesberg, it seemed to John Oakley, could not be much fun. Yet the idea of their poisoned arrows was not inviting. He slept with his musket by his side (it was good to know that George Dicketts knew how to kill Frenchmen) and was glad when dawn broke.

No wonder they had been cold. The ground lay an inch deep in powdery snow; the valleys were furred with it. On every side peaks that the snow-clouds had veiled stood glittering white from their jagged peaks to the brink of black bastions of rock so sheer that not a flake could lodge on them. They had come, without knowing, it seemed, to the stony heart of this high desolation. Not a tree, not a bush, not a living thing could be seen. They moved on through a deathly silence so intense that the feeblest sound came clear and magnified; through a whiteness that, if it enhanced their beauty, robbed the mountains of some of their grandeur and brought their summits so near that they seemed almost friendly. Yet there was one peak that not even the snow could dwarf: the vast crag of the Spitzkop (or Compassberg, as some called it), the greatest known mountain of all the Quathlamba, Mr. Blair said, which, rising sheer in the midst, dominated the whole range with an overwhelming majesty.

The sky was now clear; no more snow fell that day. Under the heat of the sun the night's fall quickly

o*

melted. Though the track was rough and precipitous, the wagons, moving carefully, suffered no mishap. By noon all the snow had vanished from the lower slopes, and the land over which they trekked revealed itself as turfy plateau flawed with rushy patches, which enchanted Mr. Blair even more than the snow.

"But for the lack of heather beneath," he said, "and something a wee bit wrong with the smell of it, I could fancy myself on the tops of Dalnaspiedal of a September morning, with the stags grazing down in the corries and ptarmigan rising from under my feet. This takes me back forty year, John, to the time when I went on the hill with my Uncle Jock. An old man was my Uncle Jock and a rare stalker, and I can mind his telling me how his father, my grandfather, was one of the men the Duke took with him when he cornered Rob Roy Macgregor."

So they crossed the ridge of Sneeuwbergen and slowly descended. This was the beginning of the true High Veld. Before their eyes the great plains billowed away to the Orange, the Vaal, the Limpopo—some believed to the Nile itself—perhaps, John thought, to the great black Empire of Monomotapa and the City of Gold. Every morning the veld lay glistening with rime that vanished when the sun rose. It was a great game-country. Uncountable myriads of springbok whitened the plains. Vast herds of blue wildebeeste snorted and stamped and swished their tails as they stood in defiance or plunged away in a cloud of dust, with ferocious heads lowered and hooves scattering clods. There were lions, too, that drowsed in the dongas by day and shook the air by night with their deep-throated purring. It was, in its way, a populous country. Many Boers had settled there on farms of ten thousand acres and more; for the mixture of grass-veld and karroo-bush (which still, north of the mountains, persisted in patches) was equally good for cattle and sheep. Every ten miles or so they came in sight of lonely mud-built farmhouses, and, even before the houses, of the vast mounds of kraal-dung that overshadowed them and provided the only fuel known in this treeless land.

At each farm, as a matter of courtesy, the *trekkie* halted, and one or two of the men rode over to pay their respects and drink a cup of tea-water or a *brande-wyn soopie*. But most of these farms were empty— some deserted by men who had joined in the trek, and others left temporarily by farmers who had no liking for cold and had already driven their stock to the Orange flats for winter grazing. By one farm the great mound of dung had been fired and still smouldered. Its heat was so fierce that the horses dared not approach it. Sarel reckoned it must have been burning for more than six months. A waste of good fuel. There were many nights on which they would have been glad of it.

A small river, whose first trickles they had traced from the foot of the Sneeuwbergen, bore westward, threatening to head them away from their course. It was well that they took the chance of crossing the first fordable drift, for no sooner were they on the other side than the stream deepened rapidly into long sluggish pools. It was called the Zeekoe River, because of the hippopotamus that frequented it, and these sullen stretches, or *zeekoe-gats* as Jan called them, were the monsters' home. What mattered far more was the fact that this stream was the only available watering-place for miles. Herds of game wandered down to it every evening to drink, and the lions that lay in wait for them had more fancy, it seemed, for cattle than for their natural prey.

In that treeless plain it was impossible to protect the sleeping herds with a ring of fires. Every night was a sleepless vigil broken by alarms. The dogs barked incessantly; the cattle themselves were restless, stamping and moaning and bellowing as they sniffed the wind of the prowling beasts; the sheep filled the night with their ceaseless pitiful bleating, and the horses would not be still.

By the time the party had lost twelve head of cattle and three nights of sleep, the strain of constant vigilance became unbearable. Sarel organized a lion-hunt to deal with this nuisance. He and Barend, three Nels and two Oosthuizens, rode out with the dogs to search the reed-beds in which the lions hid in the daytime and bring them to bay. Little Hendrik cried bitterly because Sarel would not let him go with them, and Dicketts, although he had proved himself as a marksman, was left behind too; for this was a highly technical business: dismounting and backing the haltered horses before them and firing a concentrated volley as the lion crouched and measured his distance, and sprang. It was a touchy method, and one well spiced with danger. But though, in two days, the men managed to shoot six lions—and lost, in the process, a roan gelding on which Jan set much store—there were plenty of lions left. The Zeekoe flats swarmed with them. The cattle still spent the night in terror, and six more were taken. It seemed hardly worth while tempting Providence further in this unequal struggle, so old Adrian decreed, next day, that they must trek farther east.

The week that followed was a torment of drought and heat. At a little distance from the river the ground was utterly barren. Not a living stream flowed to join the Zeekoe River: the spruits they crossed were all dry. Not a tree, not a bush broke this brown veld's arid monotony. The breeze which had stirred the reed-beds that fringed the river seemed to falter and fade of very exhaustion the moment it moved away from them. The motionless air had neither moisture nor life: it was as though the virtue had been burnt out of it by the salamander glare of white-hot sky from above and the grilling heat of baked clay beneath. For grilling it was. The hooves of the cattle and horses cracked, the dogs' feet were blistered—they limped up and held up their paws to be dressed with tar from the buckets that swung under the wagons. The fierce heat burned through to the soles of John's feet through the hide of his *veld-schoens;* it scorched the bottom-boards of the wagons. The wood of the new wagons from Graaf Reinet, where the women stifled, suffered most, for it warped and cracked and gaped at every joint. The iron tyres expanded; the wooden fellies shrank. They had to drive wedges between them to keep them from parting. There was even danger of the spokes slipping out of the fellies and the whole wheel collapsing, till they sluiced them (and the linch-pins too) with water to make them expand.

Water. . . . That was another anxiety. It seemed wicked to use it for this. John felt a pang as he saw the precious drops that fell sucked in by the greedy soil. There was enough in the tubs they carried to satisfy human throats if it were used with economy; but the draught-oxen suffered thirst with a heart-breaking dumbness. There was not enough water left in their tissues to allow them to sweat. Their bodies shrank visibly day by day like drying fruit. Of the sufferings of the livestock that followed John was glad he saw nothing. The sheep, it seemed, fared best; they could pick up small succulent growths wherever they went; but the case of the cattle was desperate: the most fortunate beasts were those the lions had taken.

No water on earth, no promise of rain in the sky: yet always, magnificent on the southern horizon, the Sneeuwbergen's snowy ghost with its torturing memories of moist green turf and rush-plats and falling streams. They passed on through a landscape that would have seemed lunar had it not been so red—rather, perhaps, the outer crust of a cooling planet. Sometimes the surface was clayey, like brick from a kiln; sometimes it stretched grey and brittle with mica-flakes, sometimes frosted with nitre, yet always hot and bone-dry—as dry as the myriads of bleached skeletons of game with which it was strewn.

From the hot air that quivered above it there was born a new, exquisite torture. A hundred times a day they would see the horizon swimming with streaks and lagoons of opalescent mirage that seemed to their eyes more liquid than any water. The oxen, too, saw these cruel phantoms and lifted their heads, and strained at the yokes as they plodded towards them until they vanished.

And at last there came the vision of a great lake more permanent than any mirage, which did not dissolve into air and cheat them as they advanced. Even old Adrian, shading his eyes as he sat on the foremost wagon-seat, pronounced it no cheat, though he could scarce believe what he saw. An hour passed, and still it remained there, beckoning, inviting. As they drew nearer, the thirsty bullocks could no longer contain themselves. The poor beasts, who for three whole days had hardly found strength to drag one foot after another, burst suddenly into a run which became a stampede, jolting the wagons mercilessly behind them over the ant-hummocks as though, in this last mad explosion of energy, they must reach it or die. They raced to the brink and stopped dead. It was a gigantic salt-pan fringed with bitter brushwood. There was a mute and moving misery in their dull eyes. One by one they sunk under their yokes and lay down on the frore margin. The crust crackled under their weight like rimed grass. That day they could stir no farther.

As they advanced on the next, a saffron dawn outlined a new horizon that seemed an unbroken escarpment, but resolved itself into a congregation of detached hillocks, of uniform height and as flat-topped as though all their summits had been sliced off with a knife. At one moment they seemed many miles away; at the next quite near. The arid air played many such tricks of refraction (as Dicketts had found when he guessed his range and fired high), and these *kopjes*, in fact, were nearer than anyone reckoned. The least variation in that monotonous landscape seemed a relief, and the rising land, barren though it looked, suggested the possibility of finding water.

During the morning a head wind had arisen—not the refreshing breeze every man and beast would have welcomed, but one that blew over the plain like the draught of a white-hot lime-kiln. When it reached the scattered *kopjes* it became subject to an odd turbulence. It whipped their bases, sucking up stones and pebbles and whirling them into the sky in furious spirals that broke, at last, into expanded heads shaped like monstrous arums, blotting out the sun. In the spaces between these spinning devils the air was still. Then one of them, in its haphazard course, caught the column of wagons in the midst and struck it a glancing blow. The impact could not have lasted more than two seconds, but less would have been enough. At one moment John Oakley was staring up at the lurid sky. In the next he found himself swept from the driving-seat and struggling to save himself from a welter of plunging oxen. He saw the tilt that had sheltered him stripped and carried away like a scrap of waste-paper; he saw the wagon itself as it staggered and heeled and lifted and collapsed on its side dragging the after-oxen along with it. He saw, through a shrapnel-blast of pebbles and sand that half-blinded him, the three following wagons behave in the self-same manner: their teams plucked up and blown bodily sideways, their white tilts stripped, their great laden bodies lifted clear from the ground and dropped in a series of sickening crashes. Two seconds . . . and then the vortex spun off to the left like a top that has bumped a kerbstone. The wagons lay smashed on their sides, their off-wheels in the air like the legs of cast sheep; the entangled oxen still roared and bellowed and struggled; Jan Bothma, who lay face downward, twenty feet away from the horse he had been riding, slowly raised himself to his knees, then lifted himself, and stumbled and fell again.

John, falling amid the oxen, had come off more

lightly. He was bruised and shaken, but no more. His dazed mind had room for only one emotion: a bewildered thankfulness that the whirlwind had struck the middle of the column and not the women's wagon at its head. His next thought was for his friend. His wagon, following next behind John's, had been overturned, but George Dicketts was nowhere to be seen. It was quite probable that he had been crushed to death beneath it. John freed himself from the legs of the oxen and staggered back to look for him. He found Dicketts lying pinioned on his back surrounded by splintered wreckage, his body mercifully clear of the capsized wagon. His face was composed, but red and resentful. He had the aggrieved look of a man on whom someone had played a practical joke.

"This here is a pretty business," he said. "Come on, give us a hand. A moment ago I was setting smokin' my pipe, and the next, here I be with my bloody leg broke and two tons on the top of it. When I heard the crack, I says to myself, 'That's done it!'"

What a man, John thought, admiringly, who could lie with a limb crushed to pulp and speak of it as though it were nothing! Such were the heroes of Waterloo.

"Let me know if I hurt you too much, George."

"Go on, lad, there bain't no hurt to it. But it's no good you heaving and pulling about that road," Dicketts told him impatiently. "I reckon 'tis all chawed up along with the spokes of the wheel. Better get an axe to it, John, if so be as you can lay your hand on one, and chop him off where he's broke. Here, lad, wait now while I gets the other one clear."

With a mighty wrench he pulled out his foot, stripling off the *veld-schoen*. It was a foot of flesh and blood. He looked at the scraped ankle ruefully, then turned round, with hurt surprise. "What's the matter with you, then?" he asked.

John shook his head helplessly. His strung nerves had found an almost hysterical relief from the shock of the catastrophe in uncontrollable laughter at the thought of how his feelings had been harrowed and his sympathy wasted over Dicketts' wooden leg. But George Dicketts did not find the situation amusing.

"You may laugh," he said, "but that there old peg of mine was the best friend a man ever had for twenty year. I'll ne'er get a leg as good as him if I live to be ninety. Oak he were, and I reckon you'll never find no wood in these parts to touch British oak. When I heard him crack, it was like a gun going off."

Jan Bothma, pale and still half-stunned, had picked himself up again and reeled towards them, leading a lamed horse. Sarel galloped back in a cloud of dust and shouted for help. White men and natives between them outspanned the oxen, cutting the reims to disentangle those that were sound from three wretched brutes that lay with legs broken. (Sarel put them out of their misery with bullets through the brain. In all, twelve draught-oxen were maimed and shot that evening.) Then, all together, they drove up the fallen wagon, while John hauled Dicketts out head-foremost. His precious leg was intact after all; the seasoned oak had stood the strain. But the wheel that lay on it had splintered to matchwood. So, too, had the wagon-sides and the upper and lower rails. However comical George's adventure might be, the damage to the three wagons was no joking matter. The repairs they made kept the whole *trekkie* at a standstill for three burning days, during which two other wagons, off-loaded, trailed back to the Zeekoe River to fetch tubs of water; for though the undamaged wagons and the livestock might more easily have moved on in search of it and of grazing, Sarel refused to take the risk of splitting so small a party in a country where Bushmen—and quite possibly Griqua bands—were about.

On the third evening, when the rough repairs were completed, a column of dust appeared in the eastern sky. The men loaded their guns and looked to the priming and waited with horses saddled to see what it signified. They need not have been alarmed: the doubtful dust arose from a couple of transport wagons returning empty to Graaf Reinet from the Orange.

Their owner, a man named Vanderwalt, outspanned for the night beside the Prinsloo party. He was engaged in a profitable trade, making monthly journeys to and fro, undertaking commissions of every kind and forming a link between the Colony and the emigrants over the border. This was not, he told them, his usual route. He had taken that line in the hope of joining a brother-in-law from the Sneeuwberg who always spent the winter months by the Zeekoe River. If the Prinsloos had set their course a day's journey farther to the east they would have struck the usual trek-path, clearly scored already by the wheels of hundreds of wagons, and found springs with water of sorts all the way. As it was, they need not be discouraged. By noon next day they would find themselves on the edge of a good grass country, and need fear no more trouble until they reached the Great River. Trouble from lack of water or grazing, that was—other trouble they might find in plenty: the Government patrols were perpetually scouring the southern bank and stopping every wagon they met to search it for ammunition.

"What is the best thing to do?" Sarel asked.

Vanderwalt shook his head. The soldiers were not such fools now as they had been a few months ago, and had tumbled to most of the more obvious smuggling tricks—double bottoms in the wagons and so forth.

"The best thing you can do," he said, "is to keep your powder handy, so that it can easily be moved, and well to the rear. Let one or two men ride on well in front of the *trekkie* but just in sight, and keep their eyes skinned for the first sign of any patrol. They ride in twos and threes, so it's easy to tell their dust. When the soldiers are sighted, the riders in front give a signal. You off-load the powder and lead from the wagons and bury it and mark the place in some way by which you can recognize it, and move on till the cattle have reached the spot and covered it. Then you halt—you can always find some good reason for halting—and wait for the patrol to ride up. During the night, of course, you send back to collect the stuff you've buried. When they've been through your wagons once, the soldiers won't worry you again.

"But mind," Vanderwalt went on, "it's the greatest of all mistakes to bury everything. If you say you've no powder at all, that makes them suspicious. They'll stick to you, like a dog hanging on to a buffalo's nose, till they've caught you out. How much ammunition have you, uncle?"

"Seven sixty-pound casks in all, besides the loose powder."

"Almighty! Four hundred and twenty pounds? Anyone would think you were going to war."

"One never knows," Adrian said darkly.

"That'll take some hiding! The great thing is to talk and joke with them. These English, though nobody would guess it, are men like ourselves. They like a *soopie* and the sight of a pretty girl, and they hate the sound of Dutch, because they don't understand it and think you're making fun of them. If any of you can speak English . . ."

The transport-rider left them next morning, wishing them luck. By noon they had reached the grass-land of which he had spoken and a muddy fountain by which they camped for three days to patch up the splintered wagons more thoroughly and rest themselves and their cattle. But old Adrian could not settle his mind: he was still troubled by Vanderwalt's stories of the frontier patrols. The prospect of meeting them—his first contact with hostile authority—distressed him far more than all the other dangers of the trek.

"I am a law-abiding man," he said. "I have always rendered unto Cæsar the things that are Cæsar's, and it is not my custom to lie. But we cannot trek north without ammunition. That would be suicide."

Lisbet, too, was uneasy. Though she told herself that all the odds were against John's being questioned or recognized, though she felt it was even doubtful if anyone in the Colony but herself knew who he was or cared where he came from, she had moments of panic in which she feared nothing less than the worst. That would be utterly cruel, she thought, now that he was so well and so happy and things had gone so smoothly. Every night she prayed for his safety, yet had little faith in her prayers.

Jan Bothma and Sarel were all for following Vanderwalt's plan, which seemed to them right and reasonable; but old Adrian's scruples would not let them accept it. There must be some better way. And then, by God's will, as he thought, when he read his portion of Scripture on the night before they broke camp, the better way was made plain. It was the thirty-first chapter of Genesis that he read; the story of

Jacob's flight from the tents of Laban, and Rachel's theft of her father's images. He read of Laban's pursuit and of how he searched for them.

And Laban went into Jacob's tent, he read, *and into Leah's tent and into the two maidservants' tents; but he found them not. Then he went out of Leah's tent and entered into Rachel's tent. Now Rachel had taken the images and put them in the camels' furniture, and sat upon them. And Laban searched all the tent but found them not. And she said to her father, Let it not displease my Lord that I cannot rise up before thee; for the custom of women is upon me. And he searched, and found not the images.* . . . His eyes brightened as he read on to the end of the chapter: *And early in the morning Laban rose up and kissed his sons and his daughters and blessed them: and Laban departed and returned unto his place.*

Adrian Prinsloo closed the book. "The Lord has spoken," he said, "through the mouth of his servant Moses. When the time of trial comes we shall do as Rachel did. It is a pity, though, that we have no camels," he added reflectively.

That night, preparing for the morrow's start, they transferred all the powder-kegs on which they could easily lay hand from the rear to the leading wagons. Some they bundled in as they were and others they emptied into the bags of spare saddles, and one they left open for any eye to see. During the next day they struck the trek-path. It seemed strange that they should ever have missed it. It lay like a gigantic firebreak, half a mile wide, running straight as a sword-cut behind and before them, a streak of red earth worn bare by the wheels of a thousand wagons and hooves innumerable.

Now the real danger began, but the plan of campaign was all settled: Jan Bothma with Sarel, who spoke some English, rode on well ahead yet never so far as to lose sight of the leading wagons or pass beyond signalling distance. It was easy trekking, for the oxen knew how to follow the spoor ahead. Now that she was free from the scrutiny of Jan's jealous eyes, Lisbet relaxed a little of her caution. In the cool of early morning she would leave the other women to find company in Mr. Blair, dropping back, as it seemed by accident, to the level of John's wagon, and there John would join them.

They walked, and talked together in English, occasionally of serious things, but more often of the little daily adventures and humours of the trek; and, whether it were only the exquisite thin brightness of that morning air or the golden light in Lisbet's hazel eyes that entranced him, John Oakley found those moments rapturous. Lisbet was always at her best, it seemed to him, in the early morning—much more awake, indeed, than poor Mr. Blair, a slow starter (though sure, mind!) in most things nowadays, although, as he assured them both, in his student years, he would be up and at his books with the laverock, ay, even when he had only snuffed his candle a few hours before: "What a thing it is to be young!" he said, with a sigh—knowing full well, of course, that Lisbet would reassure him (as he longed to be reassured) that he was still at his best. For a wonder, John was not jealous of Mr. Blair when she took his arm, being even more conscious of Mr. Blair's antiquity than the predikant himself. One could afford to be magnanimous when one walked in heaven.

One evening towards sunset as these three walked in company, they heard two reports close together.

"Sarel has shot at a koraan and missed it," Lisbet said. But old Adrian thought differently. This was the signal of alarm on which he and Sarel had agreed. He pulled up and passed back the word to out-span immediately. Even though this were a false alarm he was taking no risks. In the distance he could see that Sarel and Jan Bothma had stopped and were standing in their stirrups, gazing ahead. They had seen dust on the skyline that was not the dust of wagons.

Methodically the two leading wagons were drawn up alongside one another and a sailcloth spread to convert the space between into a tent in the midst of which they piled the saddle-bags full of powder and pigs of lead and covered them with karosses. Jacoba climbed down from her wagon and sat, as she had sat from morning till night at Welgelegen, with her great arms crossed in front of her on a table and the open Bible before her. If she were given out to be an ill woman she might easily be taken for one; for the trek—and above all the heat of the waterless flats—had tried her more than her courage allowed her to confess. At some distance behind—they dared not take risks for fear of the powder—the Hottentots kindled a fire, and old Ayah set pots to boil for the evening meal.

Old Adrian came round, extinguishing his pipe, and sat by her.

"There are three men," he said laconically. "You had better lie down, wife."

"I am better as I am," Jacoba said, "with the book before me. You shall not say I am ill, Adrian. That would not be true."

"You are right. Yes, yes, you are right," the old man admitted. "But I wish it were over."

"Then pray that we may be delivered," Jacoba said.

They waited in nervous silence. The wood-fire crackled. Sparks blew towards them from it, sucked in by the funnel of the tent.

"Hold a kaross in front of the fire, the wind blows this way, my daughters," Jacoba said calmly. "No, no. . . . It is now too late."

They heard the sound of horses approaching, and voices. Sarel was talking to the soldiers in his halting, sing-song English. There were three of them, two young privates and a grizzled sergeant. They looked weary and bored, as though this work were not to their liking.

"This is my father," Sarel said, "and that is my mother."

The sergeant saluted jauntily. "I've told your son we have orders to search for powder and ammunition, mynheer. Exportation forbidden beyond the Colonial Border. You understand?"

Adrian bowed to him gravely. "Tell the man he must do his duty, my son," he said in Dutch. "The wagons are all outspanned. He may look where he pleases."

Sarel translated. The sergeant nodded. It was pleasant for once to escape violent protestations. But these Dutchmen were wily. A fine-looking old boy, he thought, but not long for this world, I reckon. As brittle as a pipe-stem. Some difference from the old woman! And the daughters were both of them pretty pieces, though the fair one was likely to run to fat like her mother.

"Ask m'nheer what he will make use of, Lisbet," Jacoba said.

"My mother asks if you would like anything to drink. The tea is not ready because we have only just outspanned; but there is peach-brandy if you would like some."

The sergeant winked. "The custom of the country, eh, miss? And a damned good custom, I say. What's more, I don't mind sitting down to it, if the lady has no objection. We've been in the saddle all day."

Jacoba listened. Though she did not understand his words she was quick to grasp their significance. She smiled, nodded and moved sideways to make room for him on the mound of saddle-bags. The painfulness of her effort could almost be felt: it put the sergeant to shame.

"Don't trouble yourself, ma'am," he said gallantly. "The ground's what I'm used to these days. Thank you kindly, miss." He took the *soopie* from Lisbet and swigged it. "That warms the cockles no end," he said, smacking his lips. Then, suddenly, his mind returned to his duty. He glared at the soldiers. "What do you chaps reckon you're doing? Get to it! I'll take care of the first two wagons myself while you go through the rest of them. And look sharp, mind: the light's none too good, and you'd best not be poking around with candles if there's powder about or you'll be pushing up daisies before your time and never see England again, the pair of you."

The two men moved off sullenly, and Sarel went with them, while the sergeant, willingly accepting another *soopie*, made himself at home. He was delighted, it seemed, to find that Lisbet spoke English, and, under the influence of the *brandewyn*, became sentimental. He belonged to the Seventy-second regiment of Infantry and had been more than sixteen years on foreign service. South Africa, in his opinion, was no sort of country. He was only waiting for the day when he would get his discharge and go home; for he was a family man by rights, with a wife and two children, one of whom he had never seen.

"She's a girl," he said, "and she must be about your age, miss, by now. If her looks are anything like her mother she won't stay single long either. A fine, bouncing piece my wife was at the time when I married her; but that's twenty-two years agone, and God knows what she looks like now. If she's took after her family, she'll have put on more than a bit of flesh like your mother here; but I'ld rather a woman was comfortable, mind, than a parcel of skin and bones. 'Tis a burden for them to carry, no doubt, but it keeps them quiet— and that's what a man wants most when he gets to my time of life."

The two soldiers came back with Sarel, and the sergeant again became businesslike. "Well, what have you got?" he asked sharply. "One full sixty-pound keg? I wager I'ld have found more than that if I'd been on the job! Still, it's better than nothing." He turned to Lisbet. "If you've got another drop of that brandy-pawnee to spare, miss, I doubt if my chaps would say no to it; and while they're putting it down I'll have a look through these two wagons. Have you got any powder or shot in there, gaffer?" he shouted at Adrian.

The old man looked to Sarel to answer.

"There is powder in all the horns," Sarel said, "and a few bags of shot, as well as one open keg. You can see for yourself."

"Bring it here, and let's have a look at it."

Sarel brought out the keg, the leather bullet-bags and the powder-horns. The sergeant measured their contents with judicial eyes.

"Forty-five pounds I'ld call it, as near as makes no matter. Well, you can't do much harm with that, and there's a lot of rum characters knocking about between here and the river, what with Bushmen and Griquas and stray niggers of one kind and another. I shall have to take charge of the stuff my men found behind there as a matter of duty, but I'll leave you the rest in case you run up against trouble, and I'll give you a *chitty* to say you've been examined, so that if you're held up by another patrol they won't stop to bother you."

Sarel thanked him.

"There's no call for that," the sergeant declared. "As I say, duty's duty, and there's no getting beyond it. To tell you the truth, it's a treat for us, dealing with decentish folk like you. Some of them Boers, you know, they kicks up such a breeze and gabbles that much Double Dutch, it's enough to turn anyone wicked."

"It is late," Sarel said. "Will not m'nheer off-saddle for the night?"

"No, we'll ride on a bit," the sergeant said regretfully. "The moon's coming up. I've another patrol on this job keeping watch to the westward, and we reckon to join up at sunset. Here's your *chitty*. Don't lose it, now. Good night, ladies. Good night, gaffer."

The three mounted and rode away, one of them

nursing the keg of powder. The others stood in silence till the faint thudding of hooves died away. Then old Adrian took the Bible from the table and opened it.

"The Lord has been mindful of us," he said, "and delivered us out of their hands. Let us praise Him and magnify Him."

For three days they followed the wide swath of the trek-path through an open grass-country scattered with clumps of camel-thorn whose feathery parasols gave grateful shade in the swelter of noon. A great shadow had been lifted from the minds of the Prinsloos (and one even greater from John Oakley's) now that the frontier guards had been passed. There was no further obstacle between them and complete freedom but the Orange, or, as most folk called it, the Great River— the colony's boundary. It was a good thing the sergeant had given them his *chitty*, for twice, after that, they were held up by British patrols, detachments of the Seventy-second, who seemed only too happy to pass them through. They were generally friendly enough and glad of a drink, but even more glad of a talk; for this civil police-work was hardly a soldier's job, they were bored and sick of solitude.

On the morning of the fourth day the veld began to shelve gradually to a shallow valley through which the river wound. It was scattered with driftwood left high and dry by the December floods, and patches of sand or baked mud lay in every depression. As they grew nearer, wide belts of incredibly vivid green appeared. Both banks were fringed with Babylonian willows which, even when the river ran low, trailed their weeping fronds in the current and in time of flood must have been almost submerged. Here, a hundred yards from the bank, the trek-path widened into an enormous, trampled outspan, where, from time to time, many wagons must have waited for the water to fall before they could cross, one by one, on the willow-wood pont.

Sarel and Bothma rode on to reconnoitre, while the long trail of wagons lumbered up to the halt, and came back well pleased: the stream ran neither too high nor too low, and the approach to the pont would not be dangerous, for the approaches were dry. And the land beyond the river, they declared with delight, was the veld of which they had heard, a rolling plain of tall grass where the cattle that had suffered so many privations would soon grow fat again. It would be better to get them across the river first, Sarel thought. Jan had waded in up to his waist to test the depth of it. Though they would have to swim and take the chance of crocodiles or floundering hippopotamus, the current was not over-strong. There was a half-breed down at the pont who spoke passable Dutch and kept a black he-goat there to act as a pilot for the sheep.

"If we get them and the cattle over to-day," Sarel said, "we shall have done well enough. Outspan the teams, but let the boys see that they don't stray, and bring up the wagons as near as you can to the slope, for to-morrow we shall have to pull them on to the pont ourselves."

They arranged the wagons in three rows of four with one over; outspanned the oxen and drove them away to graze. It would be an hour or two before the beasts came up from the rear; so, when that work was done, Mr. Blair and John walked down to the river. At this point it ran sluggishly in the trough it had sunk for itself: a great stream of yellowish water, three hundred yards wide, with thickets of huge trailing willows on either side. Except where the shelving ramp which had been cut to the pont divided them, the banks were clean-cut and precipitous, showing a section of clay and mica coated with slime that had dried to a varnish resembling the dull glaze of Samian ware. Though the current was moderate and the stream here of no great depth, this vast expanse of smooth, opaque water sullenly flowing out of the unknown between its green willow-fringes, with its dazzling reflections of fierce sunlight, gave an impression of sinister power and secrecy. Here and there, where the current encountered a sunken snag or boulder, its surface was flawed by whorls and eddies. Sometimes the trunk of a huge uprooted tree came slowly drifting down, changing course as it went, as though, guided by some profound and monstrous in-telligence, it knew where it was going. Sometimes detached islands of matted reeds and earth floated by; and once, from the polished brass of the flats upstream, the black head of some huge amphibian rose slowly

and floundered and sank. As John held his breath at
the spectacle, Mr. Blair caught his arm.

"Behold now, Behemoth," he quoted, *"he eateth
grass like an ox. Lo, now, his strength is in his loins
and his force is in the navel of his belly. He moveth
his tail like a cedar: the sinews of his thighs are knit
together. His bones are as tubes of brass; his limbs are
like bars of iron. He is the chief of the ways of God:
He only that made him can make his sword to approach
unto him. He lieth under the lotus trees, in the covert
of the reed and the fen. The lotus-trees cover him with
their shadow; the willows of the brook compass him
about.* (Mark well, John, the Word says 'willows!')
*Behold, if a river overflow, he trembleth not: he is con-
fident, though Jordan swell even to his mouth. Shall
any take him when he is on the watch, or pierce through
his mouth with a snare? Canst thou draw Leviathan
out with a fish-hook, or press down his tongue with a
cord?"*

He rolled the tremendous words off his tongue with
gusto. "That's one of the greatest poems that ever was
written or ever will be, my lad. That's the Book of
Job. *Behold, now, Behemoth,* he says: and between you
and me I'ld sooner behold yon brute at this safe distance
than have the pleasure of his nearer acquaintance—
though, from all they tell me, the poor beast eats no
flesh and is mild enough when fools will leave him alone.

Though Jordan swell even to his mouth, he went on:
I've been thinking on that, John. This is Jordan indeed
for these poor people we trek with, and even more
Jordan for you. Over there lies the Land of Promise—
that's another great phrase, mind! The Land of
Promise. . . . But from what the Scriptures tell us,
the Land of Promise brought none too easy living, and
more trials than triumphs. Still, here is your River
Jordan, John. When you step out on the farther side
you'll be able to count yourself a free man and a new
life will begin for you. Heaven grant it may be a
godly and righteous life, for you and for every one
of us."

"A new life. . . . That is true, I know," John
Oakley said. "But before we cross there is one thing I
should like to do. You have taken me on trust too long,
Mr. Blair, and I would rather you knew the truth about
me before we go further. May I tell you?"

"Ay, of course you may tell me if you wish it."

As they sat there together on the shingly verge of
that sullen river, John poured out the story of his life
from his cindery childhood in Dulston until the day
when he ran before the blast of the south-easter into
the bush. Mr. Blair listened to him in silence, occasionally nodding his head in understanding or grunting
approval, his hands toying abstractedly all the time
with the many hued variolite stones that lay at his feet
—hyaline opal, carnelian, striped agate, chalcedony—
which the grinding of the Orange's pebbly bed had

rounded and smoothed through secret centuries. When the long tale was finished, the predikant tossed the last pebble into the stream and laid his hand on John's arm.

"I am glad you have told me all this, lad," he said, "for it has helped me to understand you the better, and I want to do that. It is a bitter story, but I doubt you are any the worse for it. It is said we are taught by suffering, and that I believe. We are both of us strangers and sojourners in a distant land, and it is something for a man to know that he has a friend he can count on. During this strange exodus I have taken a liking to you, and I wish you well."

They walked back to the wagons in silence.

Next day, after all but three of the cattle had swum through safely, and the sheep, which obstinately refused to follow the Griqua's black goat, had been ferried across, they lowered the first of the sky-blue wagons down the incline, and tied it with reims to the pont, and poled it over. Jan Bothma attempted to ride by the side of it; but the bottom, half-way across, was of yielding pebbles, and the stream always deepening. When the water reached his thighs he was glad to slip from his horse and let it swim on without him while he waded back again. As soon as the first wagon was safely landed they hauled it up the steep bank with two spans of trained oxen, and returned with the pont for the second, in which the women would cross.

By this time it was evening. A low sun deepened the green of the Babylon willows. Under their shadows the water shone like polished ebony. In the open its gleaming flats were flushed with a delicate iris of lime-yellow and silvery blue and amethyst; beyond, the far mountains from which it came rose stark and red as blood. In that hour the river had lost its sullenness. It smiled, and its silence was that of a trance or dream.

Jacoba dreaded the crossing. This was the first time in her life she had ever trusted herself to water; the pont seemed so frail and the wagon dangerously top-heavy, and her heart was no longer adventurous. But the girls were gay and excited. They laughed as they helped her down the steep ramp and on to the rocking pont, and Jacoba, although her heart sank, knew better than to let them see how much she was frightened. When the men had pushed off she opened her psalm-book and bade them sing the psalm they had sung on the night they left Welgelegen:

When Israel went out of Egypt,
The house of Jacob from a people of strange
    language. . . .

The water rippled against the sides of the pont as the men plunged in their poles. The sound of it made a serene accompaniment to the women's clear voices as the raft took the current and solemnly drifted across, the wagon's tilt rosy in the sunset like the breast of a floating flamingo.

John stood at the foot of the ramp and watched them crossing until the voices of the singers grew faint and died away, and the wagon itself looked no bigger than a child's toy floating on the water. As the sun sank, the surface of the river lost its delicate hues. Reflecting the crimson splendours of the day it glowed darkly, like the water of the rivers of Egypt which God turned into blood. By the time the pont touched the farther side there was no light left in it and the figures that climbed the bank were almost indistinguishable. John turned back to the outspan to help his own wagon down the incline, for it was his turn to cross next.

"Mr. Blair was right," he thought, "when he said that this was my Jordan. Who knows if, when once I have crossed it, I shall ever return?"

But this solemn reflection did not in the least perturb him. He was young enough not to shrink from starting life over again—even eager to do so, seeing all that made life most precious for him was already on the other side.

CHAPTER FOUR

UNITED LAAGERS

At Winburg, the Town of Victory, which Hendrik Potgieter had founded and named thus to celebrate his punitive victory over the Matabele, many hundreds of wagons and more than two thousand emigrants were encamped on the open plain within reach of the Vet River's water.

By the time the party from Welgelegen reached it, after a month of leisurely trekking through the long grass, the camp of the United Laagers (as it was called) had attained a certain degree of order and shape. The haphazard groups of wagons had been sorted and straightened into lines with wide spaces between. Each party had been allotted its own station, and the boundaries within which it might range its wagons and pitch its tents and spread its awnings of sailcloth. As the Prinsloos approached it, crawling over the veld, the distant sight of this vast spread of canvas —white tilt, tent and awning—with small human shapes moving hither and thither in the alleys between, and smoke rising into the still evening air from half a hundred fires, was impressive, surprising, inspiriting, and even beautiful. Folk had fretted and grumbled individually in market-places and on the stoeps of their farms and made up their minds to trek and stolen away by themselves without realizing the material magnitude the movement of which they were part would achieve when its scattered units gathered and coalesced. Here, in the camp of the United Laagers, their numbers and strength were made clear, and the sight put new heart into them.

"Almighty!" Jan Bothma exclaimed. "Who could ever have guessed that our folk were such a multitude? Who need fear the Kaffirs now—or the English for that matter? I tell you, Sarel, if we raised a commando here, every man with a couple of guns, we could ride back over the rivers and drive the damned government into the sea inside of two months!"

Sarel laughed. "Must you always be thinking of fighting, Jan? I've had all the fighting I want in this life by now. I have trekked over six hundred miles to seek peace, not trouble; though no doubt you'll find some for yourself before you've finished."

Even so, when at last they had come to their place and outspanned and set their wagons in orderly rows and settled down for the night with a sense of freedom and security such as they had hardly known in their lives, Sarel was proud to feel himself one among so many; if there were offensive power in numbers, there was also safety. Yet even numbers were of little avail without unity; and the Laagers, "United" in name, as

P*

he learnt to his sorrow next morning, were as little united in fact as they well could be.

From the moment when the first parties had crossed the Orange, the trekker community had shown a disposition to disintegrate. Hence the early disasters that had overwhelmed the Van Rensburgs, the Liebenbergs and Louis Trigardt. Potgieter and Maritz had joined hands for a while in the task of vengeance, with Maritz as the civil and Potgieter as the military leader; but no sooner had they routed the Matabele together than they had fallen to quarrelling. How could it be otherwise, folk asked (and Sarel agreed with them), with two men as unlike and as little capable of mixing as oil and water?

Sarel knew both of them slightly, but well enough to appreciate their incompatibility. Maritz, the oil of the imperfect mixture, though he lived in Graaf Reinet, had been a familiar figure in Grahamstown where he sold his wagons: a dynamic man not yet middle-aged, and young for his years, with a handsome, sanguine face, a mouth ready for laughter and a liking for elegance that showed itself not only in his gay, sky-blue wagons but also in a certain dandiacal elaborateness of dress—in his well-cut coat with its swinging skirts, his long, townish trousers, and the buff beaver hat he wore tilted rakishly on his well-shorn head or swept off with a gallant gesture when he bowed to a lady—women, old and young, were attracted by him wherever he went. A man, moreover, with a restless and eager mind, sharp in matters of business, self-willed, self-reliant, self-opinionated—and why not, after all, since he had made a success of his life and become a man of substance by the time he was thirty? A humorous man, with a twinkle in his eye, who enjoyed a joke that need not always be delicate, and was equally ready to laugh with people or at them . . . particularly at pious Doppers who took life (and themselves) with exaggerated seriousness.

That was part of the trouble—perhaps the greater part. Potgieter—the water of the mixture—was the strictest of Calvinists: a Dopper from the straggling dark hair beneath his green-lined straw hat to his sagging trousers. There was no elegance or lightness of touch about him: he would have regarded either as out of place in a God-fearing man. Yet though he had none of his partner's fluency of tongue and masterful swiftness (which some called rashness) of decision, this ungainly, dour, taciturn man, standing six-foot-one in his *veld-schoens*, long-armed, and lumbering in gait, possessed powers of leadership which made Maritz appear somewhat flimsy. His face, with its bright blue eyes, heavily-furrowed forehead, blunt, pugnacious nose, large, firm mouth and scrubby chin, had a massive quality, resembling that of mountains, illuminated, at rare moments, by the peculiar tenderness which distant crags and peaks, transfigured by certain lights, can reveal. For this surprising gentleness no less than for his candour and simplicity, "Blauwberg" Potgieter

—the general acceptance of a nickname was significant —commanded a deeper devotion than Gert Maritz, for all his gay brilliance and flashing humour, could ever achieve. Men (and children too) loved him, perhaps even more than they trusted him. And many of them did not trust Maritz at all. The two men's personalities were so distinct that there could never have been much hope of their travelling in double harness; and even if they had refused to quarrel themselves, their friends would have quarrelled for them.

There was little else to do at Winburg in those days. While the trek was in progress, while the Matabele were being pursued and broken, there had been plenty to occupy men's minds. In the static existence of this canvas city, where they found themselves herded together like townsmen, elbow to elbow, undecided whither to go next, with endless time on their hands and no outlet for their energies but gossip, love-making, religion and politics, they were glad of any excuse for excitement, and found one in backing their fancies in the Potgieter–Maritz dog-fight.

The Prinsloos had not been in camp for twenty-four hours before partisans of both sides were trying to enlist their sympathies. They had no lack of friends and acquaintances or even of relations: in this isolated, inbred Afrikander community it was hard for one man to meet another whom he could not rightly call "cousin." They dropped in, one by one or in groups, to the Prinsloos' laager, ostensibly to enquire for the latest news from the south or to give a friendly welcome, but actually to make good their cases. The bucksail-roofed space between the two wagons, which had been turned into a living-room and furnished with the tables and rest-benches and wagon-chests from Welgelegen, became noisy from morning till night with fierce discussions.

"Maritz wanted his own way in everything," Potgieter's supporters declared, "and Blauwberg was always too easy with him; but when he tried to plant his own brother-in-law on us as a paid predikant—that fat old squinting Hollander Smit who married his sister Susanna—it was asking a bit too much."

"What's wrong with old Father Smit? Isn't he a righteous and godly man? Why should anyone object to him just because he happened to marry Susanna Maritz?"

"Because that shows it was a put-up job between him and Maritz. But that isn't the only objection. Old Father Smit began life as a teacher in the London Missionary Society. That speaks for itself. The London Missionaries have always been our worst enemies. But for those devils, I tell you, we should never have been robbed of our slaves. Who told the whole world we were savage tigers who maltreated the Hottentots? Who worked with the English to set the Kaffirs on us? The London Missionaries! You people have short memories. I'ld sooner give up religion for good and all than sit under Smit."

"Well, what about Archibald or Archbell or whatever he calls himself, this fellow Blauwberg Potgieter brought back from the Matabele and thinks such a lot of? Isn't *he* a missionary?"

"Not a *London* Missionary. Mr. Archbell's a Wesleyan and an American."

"Father Smit says he's an Arminian. I heard him with my own ears."

"I tell you he's an American, not an Armenian. All three of those missionaries were."

"Well, isn't American the same as English? He speaks Dutch like an Englishman, anyway."

"The same as English! That's the kind of ignorant talk we have to put up with. Don't you know that the Americans did what we ought to have done long ago? The Americans turned on the English and drove them into the sea. The Wesleyans are good people."

"I know nothing about these Wesleyans. I'm a Dopper, like Hendrik Potgieter. I was born and bred a Dopper, and I don't like these new religions whatever they're called. If they can't get a Dutchman . . ."

"Erasmus Smit is a Dutchman!"

"I've finished with him. As I say: if you can't get a Dutchman, the next best thing is a Scotsman. The Scotch understand our ways."

"Now it's you who are showing your ignorance. Don't you know for a fact that all the Scotch predikants in the Colony have been getting up in their pulpits with long faces and denouncing the trek?"

So it went on, hour after hour and day after day. The two factions were irreconcilable. It was impossible, it seemed, for anyone in the United Laagers to live peaceably, without taking sides. The elder Prinsloos were bewildered and sickened by this ferment. Old Adrian, on whose ageing mind the wrench of leaving Welgelegen and the ardours and anxieties of the trek had left their mark, wanted nothing but quiet in which to end his days; while Sarel, who saw these petty differences with the eyes of a newcomer, found the furies of either side not merely out of proportion but a threat to the national unity he so passionately desired.

Jacoba was only anxious for her husband's quietude. Though she was thankful to have finished with travelling in the wagon, which had jolted her helpless body and bruised it unmercifully, she knew the Winburg laagers were only a halting-place. Her thoughts went back more and more (for she was growing older) from this bivouac on the treeless, dusty veld to the solidity and security and comfort of her childhood's home at French Hoek, the stately white farm with its graceful rounded gables, the camphor-trees (the memory of their scent became sharpened with age) that shadowed the stoep, the green vineyards, the orange-groves. She could not be happy again—if she were ever destined to be happy—until this nomadic life was ended, until she could sit all day and sleep all night under a roof and within four walls, and see, round her, the little material treasures which, almost as much as her

children, had become part of her life. It troubled her
to think of these inaccessibly packed away in the wagons
month after month: the brass tarnished, the copper
streaked with verdigris, the furniture possibly splintered and ravaged by ants, the fine fabrics fretted with
moth. All these fierce religious and personal differences seemed to her childish.

But Jan Bothma, to whom contention was as the
breath of life, threw himself into them as though
nothing else were of any importance. He was a Potgieter man—and this not only because Potgieter was a
Dopper like himself and the chance of having a fling
at the degenerate Dutch Reformed Church was too
good to be missed, but also (and ever more) because
poor Father Smit, in his distant and worthy past, had
actually served the London Missionary Society. There
was not going to be anyone or anything even remotely
connected with England north of the Orange if Jan
could help it!

He stood with Potgieter, too, because he was a
man of his own kidney: hard as nails, rough and
ready, caring nothing for appearances. In the early
days Jan had been glad to quote Maritz as an
example; he had respected him as one of the prime
movers of the trek; but the Maritz he met for the
first time in the laagers at Winburg, with his gay
manners, his swinging coat-tails, his buff beaver hat,
was (quite apart from his doubtful doctrine) not at all
Jan's idea of a leader. Who could trust a fellow who

did not always speak seriously, and whose jokes—if indeed they were jokes—a plain man could not understand?

"Wherever he treks," Jan declared, "I follow Potgieter."

And Barend stood by him, partly, perhaps, out of loyalty to his cousin, but even more because his hot blood must always force him to extremes, and because it pleased him to show his father and Sarel that he was no longer a child to be humoured and patronized, but a man with a will of his own. Through the long months on trek the gulf between him and Sarel had been widening. He was jealous of Sarel's influence over his father; he despised his forbearance and unadventurous caution; he had been born a rebel, and kicked against Sarel's authority on principle, as he would have kicked against any other. Beyond the Great River all men who could handle a gun were equal. And he was a man.

Sarel listened to Barend's extravagances patiently. He knew both Potgieter and Maritz, and liked and respected each for different reasons. They had played the part for which they were destined by avenging the Matabele massacres; yet, as each was as powerful and obstinate as the other, it seemed clear to him that neither could lead in the end. Gert Maritz, at least, was wiser than his partisans, and realized this. Only a month before the Prinsloos arrived at Winburg, he had smoothed over his difficulties with his rival and ridden down to the drifts of the Orange to meet Piet Retief, inviting him, on behalf of the United Laagers, to become Governor and Chief Commandant of the whole Company. The generous move was good sense. It was also good policy. For Retief brought with him a hundred more wagons, and a hundred and twenty men every one of whom carried a gun and, more than a gun, a vote.

Retief was the man. From the first Sarel had declared it. Though his father could never quite forget Retief's failure in Grahamstown—a man, as he still maintained, should pay his debts—it was, after all, the dignified strength and sobriety of Retief's Manifesto that had finally persuaded him to trek. Jacoba, too, though she spoke little, was a more powerful influence in the family's affairs than anyone would have suspected. She stood for Retief because, like herself, he came from the Western Province, of a solid, well-balanced stock with French blood in their veins. Since the financial disaster in Grahamstown, of which Adrian made so much, he had spent ten years in the solitude of the Winterberg in which to think things over and find himself. He was twelve years older than Potgieter and old enough to be Maritz's father: in short, old enough to stand no nonsense from either of them or from anyone else. Jacoba distrusted young men.

And the folk, as a whole, were with her; for when, a few weeks later, the first General Assembly was held and votes were counted, Piet Retief was elected

Governor and Commandant-General with Maritz as President of the Volksraad and old Father Smit, come into his own at last, as the Head of the Church—and Blauwberg Potgieter, strong man as he was, in no position whatever!

Then the trouble began all over again. There was hardly a party in Winburg not rent by dissension. Jan Bothma came back to the Welgelegen laager in a towering fury.

"This is Gert Maritz's dirty work," he said; "he has engineered the whole business and got Piet Retief in his pocket."

"He will need a pretty big pocket to hold Retief," Sarel said. "What is more, I do not believe it. The folk have chosen. You will have to leave it at that."

"And sit under Erasmus Smit? I'll see him damned first! Maritz has feathered a pretty nest for his sister's husband for the rest of his life."

"You know that is not true, Jan. There must be a head in religion as in everything else. For the sake of peace they have started a fund to get up a minister, properly ordained, from the Colony. Smit only holds the position until he arrives."

"If ever he does arrive! And if he comes, do you think old Smit will make way for him? Trust Maritz to look after his brother-in-law!"

"Maritz will submit to the will of the people expressed through the Volksraad. If he doesn't, he'll have to resign his Presidency. If you don't like what the

Volksraad decrees, you can show your disapproval at the next General Assembly. Your vote counts as much as mine . . . or Gert Maritz's."

"Volksraad, Presidency, General Assembly, Votes!" Jan Bothma groaned. "All these offices and titles! I came north to be free; but at this rate we might just as well have stayed in the colony. At Welgelegen, thank God, the Government, bad though it was, was in Capetown, four hundred miles away. Now we're going to have one sitting right on top of us by the look of it. Retief will be making new laws to suit himself next, and collecting taxes to buy Maritz a gold chain and a hat with feathers in it!"

He was already making laws. There was far more need for them among these idle folk gathered together in the almost urban conditions of the United Laagers than among a pastoral community sparsely scattered over the veld. The fierce schisms he found when he arrived were warning enough. Without law, this people, already split in two, would fly into fragments innumerable. First, a basic code of nine articles was promulgated, establishing the authority of the judges and other elected officers over the whole community, with what looked like a sop to the opposition in the shape of a decision that nobody was to have anything more to do with the London Missionary Society.

"That's cooked old Father Smit's goose!" Jan Bothma cried triumphantly.

It had cooked Archbell's, Potgieter's fancy, even more thoroughly. For Archbell was still paid from London, while old Smit owed allegiance to nobody.

"The fellow is slimmer than I thought," Bothma said reluctantly.

And then came a series of by-laws, infractions of which the Field Commandants could punish by thumping fines. No grass must be burnt: men had always burnt grass to encourage new growth; it was a time-honoured custom. No game must be killed without permits. Yet the grass-land was swarming with game. Was the game Retief's private property? ("Must I pay a fine of a hundred and fifty rix-dollars," Jan fumed, "if I shoot a duiker? What next, in Heaven's name?") Next, reasonably enough, every burgher must take his turn on protective patrol; but the burghers on patrol must never molest a native. ("It was true, then, that story the lads from the Zwartbergen told us," Jan Bothma said bitterly. "Conscription's the word. But the new uniforms they saw at the Castle must have been ordered not by the English but by Retief.")

With every week of inaction the laagers became more turbulent. Rumour fanned the smouldering uneasiness: the English were at it again. They had sent messages (through missionaries, of course) to the Griqua captains, encouraging them to raid the cattle of the emigrants, who now were outside the law; and the Griquas were far more formidable than any Kaffirs, being mounted and armed as well as the Boers themselves. The tale was so circumstantial that even Retief believed it. There was talk of raising a force to make the first move and deal with the Griqua peril before it materialized. This was not bad politics either, Sarel thought shrewdly, to divert internal dissensions and grievances by uniting the folk against an external enemy.

But the diversion came from within. Piet Uys, who for several months had been lying apart and watching and waiting his opportunity, three days' journey away on the banks of the Caledon, rode up to the dis-United Laagers looking for trouble, and found it: a short, thick-set, shaggy young man with a liking for violence as strong as his hatred for Maritz. He was a man with some reputation already, having ridden with the exploring trek to Natal; and the fact that he had taken no part in the recent quarrels made him welcome as a powerful outsider, still unprejudiced and well worth a hearing. Uys looked at the situation and saw that, from his point of view, it was as good as it could be. The forces of the two factions were so nicely balanced that the weight of a single strong man could easily tip the beam. He leapt, like a stalwart young bull, on his kinsman Potgieter's side.

What was the meaning of all this high-handed new legislation? Who was Retief (above all, who was Maritz?) to set himself up as a tyrant over a free community? What right had these fellows to forbid men

as good as themselves to burn off their veld or shoot
game which was the gift of God to all sons of Adam?
What was the worth of this Constitution, this Code of
Laws, on which his father Jacobus Uys, the oldest and
godliest man in the trek, had not been consulted? He
and his friends could soon deal with that: they would
simply refuse to acknowledge it or its maker either!
And what was this newfangled nonsense of making
treaties—treaties, forsooth!—by word of mouth with
Griqua captains and native chiefs, when everyone in
Africa but the English knew that a Kaffir's promises
were only made to be broken? Away with these childish
formulas! The emigrant farmers' claim to their
Promised Land rested on something more substantial
than treaties: on their strong right arms and their
horses, on shot and powder, on the word of the Lord
that had given the heathen into their hands!

The Potgieter faction took heart again. The old
struggle over the fat body of poor Father Smit blazed
up. Retief, wise and level-headed as he was, felt
rattled. There was even a quarrel between him and
Maritz: their first and last. Appalled by a feeling of
isolation and insecurity, he went about by himself,
moving from wagon to wagon, canvassing friends and
enemies. He knew that a petition against him, launched
by Piet Uys and his father, was being passed round for
signature and that many were signing it.

John Oakley saw him for the first time when he came
to the Prinsloos' tent: a heavily-built man of no more

than middle height, with piercing dark eyes, brown hair silvered at the temples, a dark beard, streaked with iron-grey, and a firm mouth full of kindliness.

"He has something of Sarel about him," John thought. "If these people had any sense, they would follow him anywhere."

Old Adrian listened to all he said with attention, often nodding his head in approval. Retief had no gift of words. He spoke clumsily, marking his points with a short blunt forefinger; but when he spoke, his dark, wide-set eyes flashed in the firelight; the heat of a concentrated purpose quickened his speech and made his face glow with a sombre inward light.

"We are a simple folk," he said, "and the more easily led astray for that reason. We pride ourselves, each of us, on going our own way, not realizing that as soon as we separate we lose such strength as we possess. We must have law, uncle. I say it again: we must have order. Without these we are lost. Have they brought round this paper of Uys's for you to sign?"

"I have seen this paper and Sarel read it to me. We did not sign."

"And you, nephew?" The dark eyes challenged Jan Bothma, who had sat glowering outside the circle of firelight with a contemptuous smile on his lips.

"I signed Piet Uys's paper, Commandant, and I stand by what I signed. I voted against you and Maritz in the Assembly, and I'ld do so again. I've trekked these five hundred miles over the berg to be free—not to be fined a hundred and fifty rix-dollars for killing a buck! Why, not even the English . . ."

Retief smiled like a man who humours a petulant child: "You shall have a permit for shooting to-morrow, my friend," he said, "though already too much shooting has frightened the koedoe and wilde-beeste away."

"You can keep your permits," Bothma answered scornfully. "We do not acknowledge your power to grant or withhold them, or your right to make laws for us. We recognize only one law in this land: the law of God. I am a Dopper and know that the Lord will guide us. His Word is enough."

Retief turned to Barend; he smiled: "And you, nephew?"

"I signed the letter too, Commandant. My thoughts are my cousin's. I follow Uys and Potgieter."

"So . . . Two against two. It is a pity you are not with your father, young man. That is one of God's laws. *A house divided against itself shall not stand.* Yes, so it is written."

"It is you who divide us, M'nheer Retief," Bothma said.

Retief slowly shook his head, then wished them good night and departed. Jan Bothma laughed as he went. Old Adrian brought down his fist on the table with a thud that made the great Bible jump.

"This is no laughing matter," he said. "This man

has spoken the truth. Our house is divided, and only evil can come of it."

Neither Bothma nor Barend answered him. They rose and went out together. Bothma hurried away to tell Piet Uys what had happened—how Retief had bribed him by offering him a shooting-permit—and to boast how he had refused. But Barend, parting from him, went to the other end of the camp, where the wagons of the Potgieters were laagered. Since childhood his mind had taken its colour from Jan Bothma's lurid political prejudices; but during the last few weeks an influence even more powerful had bound him to the Potgieter faction. Barend Prinsloo had fallen in love.

This was not surprising. He was a sanguine and virile young man of a passionate disposition. During the years of his adolescence at Welgelegen he had thought little of women and set eyes on none but his sisters save when the wagons drove in to Grahamstown for the quarterly communion, and even then he had thought it unmanly to be concerned with them. But the trek had made a man of him, and in the camp at Winburg he began to look upon women with a man's eyes.

Even if he had not come to this naturally, it would not have been easy to remain insensible to the erotic heat generated by this prolonged congregation of lusty young men and women unused to propinquity and left together with time on their hands. There was nothing for a young man to do when he came off patrol. The bigger game, as Retief told Jan Bothma, had silently drifted away out of range through the long grass, and the smaller buck were so reduced by the concentrated battery of five hundred flintlock guns all shooting for the pot, that, but for the system of permits, they would have been exterminated. If men could not spend their energy in hunting or fighting, what outlets were left for them but politics, religion or love? And to the young of both sexes the most attractive of these pursuits was making love—the more so because, in the exceptional conditions of camp-life with its general air of make-shift and holiday, the strict conditions of Boer court-ship were relaxed. There was no longer the traditional routine of formal visits and nocturnal upsittings, the prologue to an unemotional marriage of convenience. The young men from the farms had never before had so many girls to choose from; they had plenty of time to look round and to pick their fancy, the adventure sharpened by a spice of competition, unfamiliar and stimulating.

Barend had fallen in love with Hendrik Potgieter's niece Alie, from the moment he set eyes on her, and Alie had leapt at the chance of securing such a hand-some, dashing young man. Her family, too, had favoured Barend's attentions, for Alie was an orphan without any fortune—and certainly none in her person, which Lisbet, naturally critical of her brother's choice, found distressingly plain: a pasty face, a rather sullen mouth, with front teeth widely separated, lank brown hair, with no life in it, and a sturdy, shapeless figure not improved by the dowdiness of her clothes.

"You could guess that girl came of a Dopper family a mile away," Lisbet said; "though I suppose that anyone quite so unattractive as that must be a good housewife and know the whole Bible by heart."

From Alie's relatives' point of view the match appeared extremely desirable; for Adrian Prinsloo was old and a man of substance, while Jacoba, too, had possessions; and, since there were only two girls and three boys to divide their fortune, Barend's share of it would soon be ample to support a wife and children without making any demands on his wife's relations, and in these days a strong young man was an asset to any family. So Barend, approved and accepted, spent most of his time courting Alie in the Potgieters' laager; and John Oakley, for one, was not sorry. From the first there had been between him and Barend an instinctive, mutual antipathy.

What troubled him now was the number of young men whom Lisbet and Anna attracted to the Prinsloos' tents. None of these were more persistent than the Bothas from the Groot Zwartbergen, who had gaped at the girls on the outspan at Graaf Reinet. There was no getting rid of this incubus. Every evening, when the fire was lighted, the three giants appeared and solemnly sat down, filling the tented space with their titanic bodies. From the beginning to the end of these visits they rarely uttered a word. They sat silently gloating on Lisbet and Anna with hot, hungry eyes. It was an odd form of courtship, and made no impression on either of the girls. Lisbet took it humorously and laughed at them when they were gone, declaring that it must be Anna whom they were after, and teasing her for her cruel lack of response; but Anna denied this indignantly, fearing that what Lisbet said might prejudice her in Jan Bothma's eyes. Jan was taking no risks with Lisbet. Whenever the Bothas arrived he appeared and, silent as they, sat eyeing them and Lisbet, ready to spring like a jealous dog watching a bone. And for once, John, equally jealous, was glad of his presence.

In his own relations with Lisbet there had been no change. He was more deeply in love than ever, but her attitude of frank and kindly friendliness gave him no help or encouragement. He had less speech with her now than in the days when they had been on trek; for Mr. Blair, who had provided an excuse for their walking together, was too busily engaged in his roving ministry, reconciling religious divergencies and tending the sick, to spend many hours in the Prinsloos' quarters.

There were times, indeed—particularly when Bothma was present—when her manner seemed to John deliberately distant. If she spoke to him then it was always in Dutch, not in English; and this calculated remoteness filled him with anxiety lest the words he had blurted out at Graaf Reinet had seemed to her overbold. He was infinitely humble and overwhelmed by his own idea of her delicacy; so thankful for the least demonstration of feeling on her part that when she smiled at his stumbling Dutch he became transported with joy.

The need of a confidant pressed on him so heavily that one night, as they lay side by side, he opened his heart to George Dicketts.

"I can't think about nothing but her, George," he said, "but I know it's no good: she'll never look at a chap like me."

"Never look at you, lad? What's put that there maggot in your head? If you'd half an eye and the courage to use it, you'ld know, as I do, that her's always a-looking at you! I've finished with women, thank God, these many years; but when I was a gay young cock with all my limbs, I knew as much about them as I wanted—ay, *and* a bit more. And one thing I'll tell you for gospel: there's no woman living this day, nor never will be, what a man can't get round if so be as he sticks to it. And another thing I'll tell you, John: there be no woman born what's worth losing half an hour's sleep for, as you've made me do this night. Leave her be and stand by, and some day, when you'm least expecting it, the wench will drop into your mouth, as they say, like any ripe cherry!"

"Ah, no. Lisbet's not that kind, George. I know better than that. She's different."

"Well, have it your own way, lad. They'm all of them different. Just so different as peasen in the same pod. Now let's have some sleep."

A month passed. Pieter Uys had ridden back to the Caledon; but the ferment he left behind him still worked: the laagers were still divided. It was now midwinter. Though the veld lay golden all day in unbroken sunshine whose very brazen monotony wearied the eyes, the nights grew colder and colder. The mountains to westward and southward shone white with snow, and the air that seeped from their icy summits to spread over the plain (the bald-veld, they called it) crept so deeply into men's bones as they slept that no sun could thaw it. Ice coated the water-tubs every morning, a quarter-inch thick. Hail drummed on the taut wagon-tilts and swept the veld with such a fierce shrapnel that lambs and small buck were killed. The folk who came from the ranges, the Sneeuwbergen, the Winterberg, were used to such bitter violence; but those who had lived in the tepid plains of the south and the coastal zones were too thin of blood to resist it.

The great camp, too long inhabited, became foul. The icy winds that stripped through it were laden with a poisonous dust of ordure and refuse. Through neglect of sanitation fever broke out: enteric, the scourge of all stationary hosts. Men and women sickened and children died. Such visitations, folk said, were never natural or undeserved. The anger of God was kindled against His people, and not without reason. There was sin in the camp—but what sin and whose? The deadly sin of pride, the Potgieters answered: the stiff-necked pride of false prophets: Gert Maritz and Piet Retief!

Retief had played his hand with wisdom and patience; he had smoothed out his difference with Maritz (both men were generous) and patched up Maritz's differences with nearly everyone else; but feelings were still not far from the surface and tempers shortened by sickness and cold. There was only one way he could see to keep the laagers together: and that was to give their hands work to do, their minds something to think of.

"We are all ready to trek," he told them. "I shall go north, and then over the Berg and then down into the warmth of Natal."

This was stealing Piet Uys's thunder. He had already been to Natal himself and was inclined to consider it as a family preserve; and wherever Retief had proposed to go, the Potgieter faction would certainly have discovered some reason against it.

"If you follow this madman," Jan Bothma declared, "you will go to perdition. Natal's a fine country, no doubt, with good grass and water and timber. But there's country as good and better than that, and warmer too—country fit for corn and tobacco—on the other side of the Vaal where Blauwberg Potgieter has got a grant of land from the Kaffirs they call the Makwana."

"What? You believe in treaties with Kaffirs?" Sarel rallied him.

Jan brushed his banter aside. "The Makwana are nothing. But the Zulus with whom you will clash in Natal are a different pair of sleeves. They'll eat up the lot of you."

"My father decides where we go," Sarel said. "He is the head of this party."

"We go to Natal with Retief. Enough of this talk," Adrian growled.

"Then we part, uncle," Jan Bothma said. "Retief I can stand, though I do not like him. But Maritz, never. It's a pity."

He looked pleadingly towards Lisbet, but her face was like stone.

"I go, too, my father," said Barend. "I am a man. It's time I was married and Alie is ready for me. It's much better that I should go. I've seen, for a long time, that Sarel and I can never agree, and the Scripture says that a man must forsake his father and mother and cleave to his wife. Give me one of the oldest wagons with its span and a few sheep, to start my own life with. I will never ask you for more."

"You shall have the half of your rightful portion, my son," Adrian said. "That will be enough for you now, and you may not have to wait long for the rest. We will settle these things to-morrow. Then go, if you must, with my blessing."

Jacoba sat listening to their words without a sound, her arm round the slender body of Hendrik who stood beside her, tall, slim and eager. During the last three months the child had shot up like a corn-lily. She had known, for long enough, that the time of cleavage would come. Though it hurt her to lose Barend, she was reconciled to his going before his smouldering impatience with Sarel broke into a flame that would scorch them all: it was more than she could have hoped that the parting should be so friendly.

From the material point of view the loss of Jan Bothma was graver. In spite of the odd, rebellious kink in his mind, there was no harm in him. The *trekkie* would miss his untiring strength, his resourcefulness, his native skill in veld-craft, his surprising faculty for rising to an emergency. It was a pity, she thought, that Lisbet refused to look at him, or, alternatively, that he could see nothing in Anna. When these two men had gone they would have nobody left to defend them but Sarel and the two in-blown Englishmen. It seemed now as if Providence must have had a hand in sending them to her door. Sarel turned away. She was thankful for his forbearance. Since Barend and Jan were going, she wished they would go quickly. The silence was tense and ominous. If the wrong word were spoken, an explosion might come even now. It was little Hendrik who spoke in his eager, childish voice:

"Barend, Barend," he said, "if you're really going away, will you leave me your little gun? You need only lend it me. When they give me one of my own you shall have it back again."

Jan Bothma's great laugh rang out. Old Adrian smiled; Sarel and Barend were laughing. Jacoba blessed the child for having given them an excuse for laughter.

"Yes, I'll lend you the little gun, Hendrik," Barend said. "When you've learnt to shoot straight and killed a Kaffir I'll make you a present of it."

Anna Prinsloo did not laugh. Her face, in the shadow, was flushed deep red. Her fingers were clenched in her lap, her eyes hurt and savage and full of tears. Lisbet, sitting beside her, knew she was on the edge of one of the tempests of which she was capable; and no sooner were they alone that night than Anna turned on her.

"It's you, you hateful devil," she said; "it's you who have driven him away!"

Lisbet sighed. "If I took him and he came with us, would you like me any better?"

"I don't know. I have never liked you. I have always hated you. You've ruined our lives, Jan's and mine. Some day his eyes will be opened, and then he'll hate you as I do. But he's blind . . . he's blind!"

Next morning, as they had appointed, Barend chose his wagon and span of oxen. Sarel wisely left the choice of the stock to Jan Bothma. He was prepared to lose by it rather than run the risk of a flare-up. In the afternoon, when Jan and Barend moved off with their three wagons to the Potgieters' laager, he kept out of sight.

It was oddly quiet in the Prinsloos' diminished encampment that day. Anna, savagely mute and inconsolable, sulked in the wagon and did not appear. She had cried all night and was ashamed of her swollen eyes. Lisbet, too, was unhappy and listless. She felt vaguely guilty, and lonely as well, although she knew the sense of guilt was unreasonable. She felt an urgent need to explain and defend herself, though neither was necessary, and there was nobody, nobody in the world in whom she could confide—save, perhaps, Mr. Blair, whom she seldom saw nowadays, he was so busy treating the fever that ravaged the camp. Or, possibly, John Oakley? No, no, that would never do. At the mere thought of making John her confidant she found herself blushing as fiercely with shyness as Anna had blushed with fury when Jan Bothma went.

"Yet I must tell somebody," she thought. So she made an excuse to stay by the fire for a little while after the others had gone to their beds, in the hope of catching the predikant when he returned.

It was a still night, but bitterly cold. The vast camp slept. There was no sound but the distant barking of dogs that bayed the jackals. The tilts of a thousand wagons and more shone soft in the steely starlight like a flock of gigantic sheep. There were no clouds to reflect the glow of the dying camp-fires. Lisbet Prinsloo crouched close to the embers, her chin in her hands, gazing into their incandescent caverns and wondering why the thought of confiding in John Oakley had fluttered her. She heard slow steps approaching, and was glad to think Mr. Blair had returned before she was frozen. She looked up with a smile to greet him, and saw Jan Bothma towering above her.

"Do not stir, cousin," he said. "There is nobody awake to see us, and I want to talk with you."

"What are you doing here, Jan?"

"I was behind the wagon, watching you. Why am I here? I couldn't sleep over there. I felt like a dog that has been taken away in a basket. I got up and smelt my way home. I share the Potgieters' thoughts on many things, but they are not my people. For the last time, I want you to listen to me."

She shook her head. "Jan, Jan . . . I know what you will say."

"That is so," he said solemnly; "but I must say it again. To-night I have thought more than usual. I have been thinking of all of you, the old ones as well as Anna and yourself. You have only one grown man who is not a stranger left with you, and that is not enough. The English are all very well; but one is a boy and the other a cripple, and neither of them knows how to manage natives. No, I say it is not enough."

"Then why do you leave us, Jan?"

"You should not ask that question. You know the answer already. I am against Retief, and I have no faith in Maritz. That is one thing. But there is another. I cannot be near you all the time without aching for you. I have wanted you and waited three years. I have been away to the Cape and seen other women, but it makes no difference. My thoughts about you do not change. There are limits to what a fellow can bear, and I can bear this no longer."

Lisbet sighed and was silent.

"Now listen, I have a plan," he said. "I know you laugh at me; I know you think I am ugly and clumsy like a rhinoceros; but with you I can only be gentle and kind, you know that too, cousin, and if you will marry me—no, don't speak yet . . . you must hear me out—if you'll marry me, Lisbet, I'll bring back my wagons and join up with the *trekkie* again. I'll do more than that, little one: if you'll only marry me, I'll have done with Potgieter and Uys and I'll follow Retief—ay, and Maritz too, though I hate the sight of the fellow—and I'll stick to them both to the end! Shall we make a plan, Lisbet . . . for your father's sake and your mother's as well as our own? Don't answer yet. Think, and then tell me."

"I can answer you now, Jan," she said. "If I waited and thought for a year, the answer would be the same as the one I've given you before. You mustn't think ill of me, Jan. I don't hurt you because I want to. I know you are kind, I know you are gentle, I know you love me—ah, don't I know you all through? But I know something else, dear cousin, and I've always known it. I know I could never marry you, Jan, never, never . . ."

"What's wrong with me?" he demanded.

Lisbet smiled. "No, there's nothing wrong with you. It's probably something wrong with *me*. I don't know."

"Some other man, then? I've seen those three from the Zwartbergen hanging about."

"No other man has asked me."

He rose heavily to his feet.

"Then you drive me away. I go back to the Potgieters' laager. This is the end."

He threw up his arms in a gesture of angry despair and went.

Lisbet did not move. The fire was nearly spent, with no more than a sullen glow beneath branches that still kept their shape though consumed to powder. No sooner had his ponderous steps died away than her conscience smote her. It was true enough, as he had implied, that she had driven him away and bartered the family's safety for a personal caprice. There came a moment of panic in which a sense of their helplessness overwhelmed her. Had she used Jan too roughly? Wasn't there, perhaps, some way in which she might have humoured him and done her duty to the family without being wholly dishonest? If she had begged him to stay with them, pleaded even, he might have consented and nothing would have been lost. There might be time for that now. She jumped up to follow him. She would have called after him if the starry silence had not intimidated her. As she stood, in two minds, she heard steps. Was he coming back? They grew near. "Is that you, Jan?" she said.

The gaunt figure of Mr. Blair appeared, his face haggard in starlight. Since the outbreak of fever he had worked day and night without respite, for he was the only man in the camp with a smattering of medical science. The strain—not so much of work as of his impotence—had told on him. (Again and again during the last two weeks, the grimness of his face had brought back to John's mind the memory of his uncle Jabez's at the time of the cholera epidemic in Dulston.) When he reached the wagons that night he was so deeply sunk in thought that he did not hear Lisbet's question, and the sight of her eager, ghostly figure startled him.

"You, Lisbet?" he said. "What are you doing abroad at this time of night? Nothing is wrong, I hope?" In these sombre days he was always prepared for the worst.

"No, no, Mr. Blair," she said. "I was by the fire, and I thought I heard somebody coming."

"And somebody came, though more dead than alive. I have had a sore day, Lisbet."

"More fever?"

"Another death. Poor old Smit's son, Salomon. He is brave, that old man, and good, and so is his wife Susanna; but this boy was the light of their eyes. The elder one would not trek. My heart still bleeds for them. But what are you doing here, Lisbet? You have not answered my question, and you look like a wee ghostie yourself."

"My troubles are small ones, Predikant," she said.

"Your troubles are mine. Let me share them."

"You have always been good to me."

Standing there, by the warmth that rose from the mounded ashes, she poured out her heart to him, beginning with the story of Jan Bothma's and Barend's departure and ending with that of Jan's secret return.

"I told him I could not marry him. He says I drove him away. I could never marry him, Mr. Blair. Yet when he was gone, I wondered if I had done rightly. You must tell me. I cannot think or judge. Perhaps I was wrong. If I was wrong I will do what you tell me," she said submissively.

Mr. Blair remained silent for so long that Lisbet, waiting on his words, felt sure he was condemning her but trying, out of the kindness of his heart, to soften his verdict. His solemn face showed little of the conflict by which his mind was torn. But when he spoke his formal voice could not conceal a tremor of mingled elation and timidity. He had never felt so conscious of his age or resented it so bitterly.

"You were right, my child," he told her. "You need have no doubts about that: for to marry for any other reason than love is a wanton desecration of that which is holy. Yes, yes, you were right, and yet . . ." he hesitated, ". . . yet, Lisbet, my dearest child, you should not shrink from marriage. I want to tell you

Q*

something that has been in my heart since first I saw you. The words have often come to my lips, but I have felt too humble to speak them. Even now my courage fails me: and love cannot cast out fear. I am not a young man, Lisbet; I feel the weight of years, and you, my darling, are no more than a child—that is the bitter part of it. But if utter devotion, if a love that is sure of its own strength and has never wavered, if the desire to protect and cherish you as long as God grants me life can persuade you to think of me as something more than your friend . . ."

He stopped suddenly. Her face told him already that he had failed. It was full of kindness and pity and sweetness, but the verdict was clear.

"Oh, why do you ask me this, Mr. Blair?" she said gently. "Why do you force me to wound you—the very last person in the world I want to wound?"

She held out her hand to him. He took it in both of his. It was icy cold, and she shivered.

"I understand," he said slowly. "I understand. I think I know what this means. I am sorry if I have distressed you. I didn't mean to. I should have guessed it before, I suppose. Only remember that your happiness is more precious to me than anything else in my life, and forgive me."

She shook her head, for she could not speak, and left him. His eyes did not follow her. When she was gone like a ghost, he looked up from the spent fire to the shivering stars. He raised his gaunt hands slowly to the sky. His lips moved in silence.

CHAPTER FIVE

ONWARD . . .

STILL the laagers lay in Winburg, and still the folk quarrelled.

One morning, early in August, Retief gave the word to advance. This move was an acid test of loyalty: the only means by which he could tell how many would follow him; for in those days allegiances strengthened and weakened and shifted with every breath of rumour and gust of passion, and no leader knew from one day to the next who were his friends and who his enemies.

From the first Retief's chief determination had never wavered. He was going to cross the Drakensberg into Natal, and make the best terms he could with the Zulus beyond the Tugela. Though his folk were farmers, this man was a trader at heart. Others might be content to live on the land with no fixed abode, striking camp and moving their wagons as soon as the pastures in which they had settled failed them, trekking on and on, with no other ambition, until they died. But Retief, and Maritz too, had wider desires. They wanted to trade. For trade they needed access to the sea; and they knew that the English at Port Natal felt friendly towards them and had as little liking for the Capetown government as themselves.

477

So Retief broke camp and moved north-west to the Sand River, and many who were sick of inaction trailed after him out of sheer boredom, until soon the grass-lands between the Vet and the Vaal were scattered with units of the United Laagers, united in little now save their common restlessness. Even the Potgieters, with Jan Bothma and Barend among them, found them-selves caught in the general drift and sullenly followed, saving their faces by the reservation that even if they seceded and settled, as they intended, on the High Veld ridges, they must first cross the head-waters of the Vaal. If they could not divert Retief and his folk from entering Natal, they could still be a thorn in his side and make trouble for him whenever they had the chance.

The diminished Prinsloo *trekkie* moved forward. It was smaller than ever now. Mr. Blair no longer went with them; for old Father Smit had got over his tiff and returned to Retief, and there was no need for two predikants in the same party. The Prinsloos followed close on the heels of Retief. They were hardly strong enough now to stand by themselves. There was another cause for this association. During the touchy days at Winburg, Retief had discovered in Sarel a man of his own type, grave, steadfast and bold, of whom he knew he could make use; and Jacoba, shy after many years of loneliness, had made a new friend in Retief's wife, Lenie, and was glad of it. When they halted, the Prinsloos' wagons were outspanned and drawn up beside the Retiefs', giving shelter with them from the icy August winds.

They moved slowly in these days, for now the first fierce impetus of the trek was spent. The winter veld stretched away on every side, a pale sea of unending grass with ripe tassels of purple, amid whose whispering waves the cattle fed and grew fat, and widow-finches, trailing their black weeds, fluttered heavily.

It was the time of late lambing too. The still air was full of faint bleatings; the veld scattered with tiny white bodies, newly born. In the gold of evening, they staggered and frisked and leapt sideways, as much hampered by the weight of their tails as the fluttering widow-birds. George Dicketts, who reckoned he knew all about lambs, said their tails should be cut and doctored with tar; but Sarel only laughed at him, for the wealth of the flocks consisted in the fat of their tails which, when the time came, would make soap and grease and candles. He was glad, none the less, to have with him a conscientious man accustomed to awkward yeanings. For this alone George Dicketts was worth his keep. If he lost one lamb—and, perforce they lost hundreds, while many ewes, frightened by jackal-yelpings, slipped them—George could not be reconciled. The Worcestershire shepherds, he said, could teach these yellow-faced beggars a thing or two—and their master, for that matter. How could a ewe be expected to carry her lambs and yean proper with naught but stuff as stiff and dry as a bezom to feed off?

If one of them ewes set eyes on the grass in Long Dragon, let alone Tom Collins's field of Swedish turnips, her'ld go off her head for certain.

It was not only the yeaning itself that delayed them. Until they had found their legs, the lambs could not move far in a day. The long grass, growing thick, must have seemed to them like a dense, mysterious forest. It held other dangers than hungry wild-dogs and jackals; for once, as the great flocks slowly crawled on their way with a following wind, a grass-fire broke out behind them. What started it, none could say: perhaps the firestick of a Bushman or a Hottentot lighting his pipe of *dakka*; perhaps the sun's rays concentrated on a tindery filament by some curved crystal of quartz. Whatever the cause may have been, the first that the sleepy herdsmen knew of it was the drift of smuts settling from the sky; and then the smell of the fire on the wind, and then the heat of it; and then finally, advancing faster than a man could walk, the mile-long wall of fire shooting tongues of flame into the crackling curtain of smoke and rolling down on them with a hoarse purring sound like the thunder in a lion's throat, and small game, made bold by terror, stampeding before it; and, high above, where the black smoke curdled to a fulvous haze, myriads of birds that recklessly fluttered and darted and hovered on air that must surely have singed their wings, as they glutted themselves on the scorched insects sucked up by the draught. Then the tired flocks must be harried out of the path of the flame while men armed with whatever branches they could find beat down grass in a vain attempt to lay a fire-break. But such demons, when once they had taken hold of the winter grass, could not be thwarted by powers so feeble as man's. They leapt crackling over the beaters' heads and went roaring on and on till water lay in their path, or the wind that winged them failed, and then sank, as suddenly as they had flared, to a sulky smoulder and flickered and went out.

It was no wonder, John thought, that Retief had forbidden grass-burning at Winburg. Thrice, during the new trek north, they fell in with fire. Once they saw the smoke coming to meet them and swerved in time. Once the wind that carried it changed and swept it away from them. And once, when they seemed at its mercy, a thunder-storm broke in flickers of ghastly lilac, and a barrage of hailstones as big as eggs damped the fiery fury and thrashed it out, and the doomed flocks were saved—but for a few luckless lambs that were struck by lightning, and some which were caught before they could shelter under their mothers' bellies, and beaten to pulp by the hail.

The bursting of that great storm, which lasted three days, keeping pace with them as they trekked and terrorizing them when they halted with claps and reverberations of thunder that seemed to shake heaven and earth, marked a change in the seasons, shooting back the bolts that held the hot sky's sluice-gates, releasing a deluge of rain that darkened the sky for a week and turned every spruit to a torrent. The livestock rejoiced in it; but the standing laagers were flooded. Water poured through the wagon-tilts and the tentings, and extinguished the fires. There was no escaping it. Yet, when the sky cleared again, the far peaks of the flanking Drakensbergen had lost some of their snow. There was a softness of spring in the air, sweet-scented and languorous; and behold, of a sudden, a miracle: beneath the matted grasses the rain had lodged, and in every fire-blackened patch, tender green was already springing!

It was as well for the trekkers that these symbols of hope and new life appeared, to encourage them; for the veld they traversed now was scattered far and wide with grim emblems of mortality: not only with vulture-picked skeletons of game killed by lions which, when the grass grew high, had been hidden from their eyes, but also with pitiful human debris—great thighbones cracked for their marrow by the teeth of hyenas, and skulls battered in by knobkerries. This Golgotha marked the westward track of the Matabele horde, flung off some years before from the fierce core of Zululand and ploughing its way, like the fragment of a burst planet, through the flesh and blood of the peaceful tribes who lay in its path. The bones of the victims lay bleaching there in hecatombs, and beside them the snapped shafts of stabbing assegais.

It was a sombre spectacle, and one that carried a

warning of Zulu ruthlessness. For these Matabele were part of the host which under Chaka, the Battleaxe, had spread bloody terror through all black Africa—though Dingaan, that monster's brother and murderer, Retief said, was less formidable.

"The English at Port Natal are on good terms with the Zulus," he said, "and a missionary, a Mr. Owen, lives close to Dingaan's Great Place, and is much in his confidence."

"Some of our folk would not find that a point in Dingaan's favour," Sarel said dryly.

"That is true enough, more's the pity; yet I, for my part, have never known anything but kindness from the English settlers. I made many good friends among them in Grahamstown. I had bad luck with my building contracts, yes; but I cannot say that they did not treat me fairly. And after all, there cannot be so much difference between us. They say the English first went to England from Holland. We both come of the same stock, nephew, and I see no reason why we should not be one people, forgetting England and Holland, which are no more than names to us, and thinking only of Africa, which is our land. Still, it's early days to be dreaming of that," he said bitterly, "when it seems we can't even agree amongst ourselves."

That was true enough. When he heard that Retief was making for Natal, the land he had earmarked for himself, Piet Uys came skimming back over the sea of grass like a stormy petrel. The petition he had sent round the laagers at Winburg had fallen flat and finished with less than two hundred signatures. But Uys would not accept defeat: the northward trek had now reached the cross-roads at which those who were bound for Natal and those who favoured the lands beyond the Vaal must separate. If Retief's power were ever to be broken, now was the time. Once more he launched a defiant manifesto. He and his friends would settle in Natal, as they had always intended, but on their own conditions and under their own form of government.

Retief took up the challenge. He could do nothing else. Though he chose to speak of the Zulu power as a trifling obstacle, he was well aware that every available man would be needed to face it. He could not do without Uys's help, and he knew it. Nor could he afford to slacken the reins of authority. He summoned another General Assembly to meet at his camp under the mountain called Tafelkop and waited there to receive his friends and opponents.

From all the scattered laagers between Vet and Vaal they swooped down like *aasvogels* hungry for carrion, six hundred shaggy horsemen with guns slung on their backs and bags of meal and biltong and tobacco enough to last them a week. They knee-haltered their horses and slept on the veld with their saddles behind them.

John Oakley had never seen such a desperate-looking set of men. All day they kept riding in, some singly and some in groups that galloped up and fired salvos to announce their arrival. With so much inflammable stuff about, there had been from the first a danger of conflagration; for passions ran high and all were armed, and whichever way Uys and his men might jump, Retief and the Potgieters were clearly irreconcilable. Every man had the right to speak; most were anxious to use it, and few kept to the point. There were long disquisitions larded with Scripture on both sides; fierce harangues, threats, insults. By the end of the first night's debate, the Assembly had shouted themselves dumb and decided nothing. It was a matter of luck— sheer good luck—that no shot had been fired.

Both Jan Bothma and Barend took part in that riotous meeting. The hostility between the two factions was so acute that they did not come over to the Prinsloos' encampment when it was over. Jan Bothma had bitter reasons of his own for keeping away from them, but it cut Jacoba to the heart when she heard that Barend was in camp and had not troubled to come and see her.

"Is he no longer my son, then?" she said.

Sarel, seeing how deeply she was hurt, slipped away in silence to the lions' den of the Potgieters' bivouac and brought Barend back with him, sullen and sheepish. He looked years older already for his two months of married life.

"You need not have sent Sarel to fetch me, ma," he said. "I should have come here in any case as soon as the Assembly was over; from the way things are going it looks as if it may be years before I see any of you again."

Jacoba enquired after his wife.

"Alie is well enough," he told her. "She is going to have a child. That is one of the reasons why I was coming to see you. Alie is not a strong woman; they say she has always been frail; she has no sister of her own to be with her now that she needs one. So I have been thinking: 'Why should not Anna come along with us?' She and I have always been friends, and Alie is a quiet woman, not difficult to live with. You are a small party now, and I think, for myself, you could spare Anna easily; but that is for you to decide."

"It is for Anna herself to decide," Jacoba said coldly. "When I was a girl every family was united; but nowadays all that is changed: we are divided already. That sort of loyalty, it seems, has gone out of fashion. The young folk come and go as their fancy takes them; the old ones look on and wonder who will go next. If Anna wants to leave us, let her go. I have nothing to say."

Barend turned to Anna: "And you, sister?"

Anna Prinsloo blushed hotly. "I will go with you, Barend," she said.

"Perhaps she will get her Jan after all," Lisbet thought.

Next morning the Assembly was at it again, and no cooler for the discussions that had flared on through the night. The tempest raged all day, Retief riding its fury close-hauled, as near the wind as he dared. He held on his course till the storm, from sheer violence, had blown itself out. A lesser man had gone under long before that. Piet Uys knew he had had enough. He turned and stalked out of the meeting and jumped on his horse. His followers crowded round him.

"Where are we going?" they asked.

"Each goes his own way," he said: "one straight forward, another to the side, but none following either."

One by one, with surly, bewildered faces, the others saddled their horses and rode away. The silence, after such turmoil, was almost frightening. Round the headquarters-tent the exhausted remnant gathered for evening prayer. There was no thought of thanksgiving or supplication that evening, men's minds were too hot and too sore. Their mood was that of the psalm they sang; though nobody knew who had chosen it, it spoke their minds and gave vent to their bitter anger. It was the Hundred and Ninth, that fierce Hymn of Hate in which David wished ill on his adversaries:

"Hold not thy peace, O God of my praise," they sang; *"for the mouth of the wicked and the mouth of the deceitful are opened against me; they have spoken against me with a lying tongue; they compassed me about with words of hatred and fought against me without a cause; and they have rewarded me evil for good and hatred for my love. Set thou a wicked man*

*over my adversary, and let Satan stand at his right
hand. When he shall be judged let him be condemned,
and let his prayer become sin.*

"Let his days be few, and let another take his office!

"Let his children be fatherless and his wife a widow!

*"Let his children be continually vagabonds and beg,
let them seek their bread also out of their desolate
places!*

*"Let the extortioner catch all that he hath, and let
the strangers spoil his labour!*

*"Let his posterity be cut off, and in the generation
following let their name be blotted out!*

*"Let this be the reward of mine adversaries from
the Lord, and of them that speak evil against my soul!"*

After this, the righteous felt better; but it took them
another day to get over their indignation. Then, with
no more hesitation, Retief set his face to the Berg. He
had finished with prayers and persuasions and arguments. He would waste no more time in trying to
convert the faithless. This was the second month of
spring; soon the rains would break and make trekking
with wagons impossible. His attitude of unending
patience was changed to a brisk impetuosity. Let those
who would, follow him. He was moving on. When
the leaders in the scattered laagers heard the news of
his starting, they began to move too. Some crawled on
slowly, still hoping that some miraculous change of
heart would bring the factions together. Many, less

hopeful, turned west to the Vaal; others, and fewer, east on the road to Natal. But there was less heart than there had been before in either adventure. The Trek was the Great Trek no longer. It had been broken now once for all and could never be mended.

Retief's column advanced, always dwindling by degrees—for even now there were folk who could not make up their minds—over the grassland that swept gradually upwards to the foot of the Berg. Life seemed to John almost unnaturally smooth and peaceful in those days, without Barend's fretting and Jan Bothma's rages to keep them all on tenterhooks, without the perpetual scrutiny of Anna's jealous eyes. It was an easy, homely life of quiet friendliness. By this time he had come to feel himself one of the family. Though Lisbet still smiled at his Dutch and teased him over it, he had now no difficulty in understanding all that was said; and this acquisition of the new language brought him closer to Jacoba, whose motherly heart, deprived of Barend, adopted him as one of her own, admitting him to the place left vacant by her dead boy Pieter, whom she had always thought he resembled. The only thing in this charming relationship over which John's conscience still troubled him was the fact that when first Jacoba and he spoke together he had lied to her. There seemed no reason, now that they were so far beyond the reach of the law, why he should not resume the name that belonged to him. He confided this trouble to Lisbet.

"Whenever your mother and Sarel call me 'Grafton,'" he said, "I feel guilty of false pretences. I am like a thief, using something that isn't my own."

Lisbet laughed at his scruples, although, in secret, they pleased her: it was like him, she thought, to be so honest, and a little pathetic, too.

"Why worry about such a trifle?" she said. "I like the name 'Grafton.' You have worn it so long that it fits you now. I think it fits you even better than 'Oakley.'"

John gasped with surprise. "How do you know my name is Oakley? I never told you."

"No, of course you never told me, poor innocent; but I have known it for months. Your friend George is no better than you at keeping a secret. You were neither of you meant to be criminals, I'm afraid. And what does it matter, anyway? Among us you are neither 'Grafton' nor 'Oakley,' but 'John.' And 'John' suits you best of all."

It gave him exquisite pleasure to hear Lisbet speak his name, though she found it difficult to call him anything but "Yohn"; and her name, too, when he spoke it, had a peculiar sweetness on his lips, having ceased to be mere syllables and become, instead, the symbol of all her perfections. In those days they were never long divided, for the stages were short and the trekking easy, with leisurely halts between. In John's present state of ecstasy any season would have pleased him; but this was spring—the short-lived Bloemtyd of the African high-veld, more fiercely rapturous than any known on earth. There, spring is not a process of drowsy awakening, foretokened by delicate stirrings of life so subdued that eye and ear must be strained to discern them. The rains fall, and earth wakes with a sudden gigantic zest. Trees break into leaf and blossom; the veld quickens in a night; league on league, it lies starred with flowery miracles that droop almost as soon as born and wither unnoticed: yet so profligate in its wealth of bloom is this passionate soil that neither mind nor eye can keep count of its flowering and fading—for that which enraptured one day, on the next is gone and hardly regretted, so bewildering is the torrent of transient beauty.

In the eyes of the old, perhaps, fate seemed to brood over that quickening loveliness, investing it with the pitifulness of things foredoomed, the intensity of brief and tragic loves. But John and Lisbet were blind to such admonitions. They were young, and walked in Eden. There was spring in their blood no less than before their eyes; and if the earth rejoiced with them, scattering beauty at their feet, this seemed to them theirs by right of their own sublime exaltation, and less to be marvelled at than that which was their own secret possession. They were so intent on the many discoveries to be made—in themselves even more than in each other—that much of the beauty (and all the poignance) escaped them; yet even their eyes' rapt self-sufficiency was pierced by the unimaginable colour that glowed on those high lawns. The grasslands lay below and behind them now; the turf was smooth and springy, and every emerald island between the scattered boulders and falling streams was decked with clumps of moraeas, babianas, gladioli, ixias, tulips and lilies innumerable, or sheeted with vermilion drifts of a long-stemmed daisy as brilliant as that anemone of Lebanon which, for its beauty, the Syrians still call the Blood of Adonis. Lisbet picked the red flowers in armfuls and carried them back to the wagon to show Jacoba; and Jacoba took them and smelt them (although they were scentless) and smiled the benignant, slow smile of a carven Demeter, with love and sorrow for Proserpine in her heavy-lidded eyes.

The trek had come, in fact, rising so gradually that they would never have known it but for the air's pure, cool sweetness, to the knees of the Drakensbergen. Before them, a wall of rock, rose the range's unbroken bastions; above them its tables and pinnacles pierced the sky's burning blue. One evening when the shadows of the tired oxen lengthened in front of them and those of the great tilts loomed monstrous behind, the land suddenly fell away at their feet, plunging sheer for a hundred fathoms into the abyss of shadow cast by the mountain itself. For the width of a mile and more that shadow blotted the land; but beyond its advancing edge, in an infinite, soft greenness, passing belief, stretched the tumbled expanse of domed hills and wooded valleys that was their Promised Land.

At the first sight of this Pisgah-vision they gasped and stood in awed silence. Their eyes could not measure, their minds could not compass, the amplitude of this inheritance: this lush country of rolling green hills that distantly faded to blue and then, grey as smoke and as unsubstantial, were lost in a shimmer of white that, for all they knew, might be sea. When they spoke at last, their talk was high-pitched and excited. Was there ever a land such as this? they asked one another. No wonder Piet Uys had wanted to keep it for himself! They gazed on it possessively; their eyes refused to leave it, until the mountain's creeping shadow thinned and advanced no farther; the whole scene grew dim, and night fell. Among all of them old Adrian was the only one whose imagination appeared to have been untouched by the spectacle. While the others stood fascinated, gazing down on it, he moved away silently and lay down in the wagon-bed. "Alas for the land," he muttered, "that has shadows on its borders!" The altitude, which excited the rest of them, embarrassed him and made him so short of breath that his nostrils twitched as he breathed. He was glad of a *soopie* of brandy to whip up his flagging heart.

That night, before he lay down wrapped in his kaross, John walked out with Sarel to the escarpment's edge. The vast void at their feet lay black as the vault above. It was hard to say where sky ended and land began, for, with sunset, the mountain-summits had gathered cloud about them and no stars could be seen. It seemed, indeed, as if the land were more starred than the sky, its darkness being pricked here and there by red pinpoints of light that momently glowed and vanished. They might be the fires, Sarel guessed, of the party Retief had sent on in advance to survey the pass for the wagons' descent. Yet that explanation could hardly account for so many.

"It may mean," he said, "that the Zulus have heard of our coming and are waiting to meet us. In that case we had better stay here for a while till others come and we feel ourselves stronger. Uncle Piet declares that the natives here are friendly. That is the man. His nature is generous and unsuspicious; his heart so open and good that it is difficult to convince him that other folk are less to be trusted than he. If I had my way, I would rather make sure of Maritz's reinforcements before we go down."

Retief, too, it appeared, was a little worried by Maritz's delay; but now that he had looked down on Natal, he was on fire and nothing could hold him. Two days of waiting were as much as his fretful impatience could stand. On the third, he decided to wait no longer. Though Maritz had not yet appeared, fifty wagons had reached the pass: a force large enough to be left to look after itself. There was urgent work to be done. First of all he must ride through the land to the coast and see for himself where the best of it lay, and, while he was there, establish relations with new English neighbours who he hoped would be friendlier than the old. And then he must visit Dingaan—not only to obtain a concession of grazing and hunting rights for his folk, but also (the old fear haunted him still!) to forestall the malignant machinations of the Colonial Government, whom rumour had surely told which way he went, and who would do their best to prejudice Dingaan against the trekkers. He took Sarel Prinsloo with him.

Four wagons and fifteen men began the descent at dawn. It was the first time wheeled vehicles had ever crawled down the face of the mountain. There was no visible track, though a sure-footed horse might pick its way through the debris of fallen boulders. Yet down they blundered, light-laden, with only one pair of after-oxen inspanned to drag the skidded wheels forward a yard at a time, while men strained at the reims attached to the bodies to keep them even-keeled, or lifted the wagons bodily when wheels became blocked or impacted. Yard by yard they went down, sometimes poised on shelving ledges where another degree of tilting would have sent them crashing down a sheer three hundred feet, sometimes wedged with their floors awash in muddy torrents whose force was enough of itself to sweep them away. By sunset that evening, after twelve hours of mighty labour, they were no more than three miles from the brow from which they had started, and less than half-way down the face of the Berg. John and Lisbet, standing upon the escarpment together, could see the four white tilts huddled like sea-birds' eggs on a ledge at the verge of the precipice—so far beneath that the figures of men were too small to be seen; so near that it seemed a pebble idly tossed outward would surely fall on them. If this pass were indeed the best to be found, the prospect was gloomy. Yet by next evening the four white tilts were no more to be seen: only vast ribs of rock reaching into the plain like bare roots of a tree and between them a growth of dark moss, which, in fact, was the serried tops of tall forest-trees.

At the headquarters-camp in the first valley beneath the Berg's escarpment, which had been chosen for shelter from the winds that swirled round the crest and blew tents and tilts away, there was nothing to do but wait. It soon proved itself no place for long sojourning, for by now the summer rains had broken in earnest. New-born torrents, suddenly leaping into fierce life, came foaming down from the scarp and carried cattle away with them. Cloud mantled the mountain-tops, and above it, day after day and night after night, thunder crashed and rolled echoing from crag to crag as though there were war in heaven. Soon the valley in which they sheltered lay knee-deep in water; so they dragged their wagons back to high ground again. There were lions that preyed on the cattle too, and these less easily dealt with on those rock-strewn slopes and in the deep gullies than in the open plains.

For weeks no news came of Retief. Jacoba grew anxious for Sarel. From time to time rumours were born, insidious as the fever which had swept the camp at Winburg. None knew whence they came, none asked and none reasoned: yet all of them were believed and all told of disaster: Retief and his party had been massacred at the coast; the English had landed there in force and were marching to turn them back; the English had bribed the Zulu king to attack them and eat them up. Yet the strength of the laagers stranded on the heights increased. Day by day new parties rolled up to the crest and stared down in wonder at Natal. Gert Maritz arrived, in his skirted coat and his buff beaver hat, as sanguine, as gay and as debonair as ever. He rode down the pass that Retief had conquered and came back less cheerful. This was no sort of going for his elegant sky-blue wagons. Other possible tracks must be searched for farther to the north where the fall was less precipitous. In the meantime, everything possible must be done to make the best of this terrifying job. Gangs of volunteers went ahead to pick the best way and clear the track of every movable boulder. As soon as men found work for their muscles once more the hatching of rumours ceased.

And then—it was mid-November now—a small party came back from the coast with news of Retief. All was well and would soon be better. Like Joshua's spies they came laden with strange new fruits from the Promised Land. There never was such a country, they said, as that they had traversed, with its rolling grassy uplands and sheep-runs, its multitudinous streams, its valleys of deep black cotton-soil and slopes of red marl waiting for the plough. As for the natives: in all their trek they had hardly seen a black face. This Eden was empty. All the Zulu villages lay far away beyond the Tugela. Retief, even now, was riding in from the coast to make a treaty with Dingaan. In another month the best of Natal would be theirs, and the Englishmen down at the port would be only too glad to have them as allies.

By next evening hundreds of wagons were on the move. There was no longer any need to hang back; the land lay open. The wagons of Retief's head-quarters-camp went down first, eighteen in all. Old Adrian walked all the way—though his legs would hardly carry him, every downward step gave relief to his labouring heart—but Jacoba stayed in the wagon, jolted to and fro, with closed eyes; for she had a horror of precipices, and would rather go to her death blindfolded than dazed with terror.

So the wagons dropped down, in half the time that Retief's had taken, without mishap, and out-spanned, the adventure ended, in a green valley watered by a stream with a bottom of golden sand. Three days they rested there, and then trekked on slowly, in the company of many others, to the Blauwkrans River, there to wait for Sarel's return.

It was here, one evening, as they sat round the fire

after nightfall, that a ghost appeared to them. It came slouching out of the dark, the figure of a bearded man supernaturally tall, heavy-limbed and slow-footed. Some newcomer, Jacoba thought, must have lost his way; but, as he approached, the dogs, Bles and Flam, ran out to meet him and leapt up at him, yelping with pleasure. He stalked straight into the circle of fire-light and up to Jacoba. He bent over and kissed her cheek.

"Why, Jan," she said quietly. "I thought you had gone over the Vaal."

"I have been there and back again," Jan Bothma said. "But this is my place. I felt it was time to come home."

"And Barend . . . and Anna?" Jacoba asked eagerly.

"They are still with the Potgieters. Perhaps they may follow later. Who knows? I am hungry, aunt. I have trekked sixteen hours this day."

He sank down on the ground and warmed his hands at the fire. He sat patiently, like a well-mannered dog that waits to be fed. But his eyes were always on Lisbet, and on John Oakley sitting beside her.

CHAPTER SIX

THE FOOTHILLS

WEEK after week, in an endless trail, the trekkers' wagons came lumbering down from the Drakensberg. By the end of November more than a thousand had made the descent. They were no longer concentrated, as in the old days at Winburg, but spread out in small groups along the banks of the streams that fed the head-waters of the Tugela River from the south. They lay waiting there impatiently, each party a law unto itself, until the pressure of others, moving up from behind, driving multitudes of hungry live-stock in front of them, pushed them forward by slow degrees and thrust many over the line which Retief, before his departure, had fixed as the Eastern limit of the Boers' present advance.

Hunting-parties pressed even deeper into the Tugela valley. The game laws promulgated at Winburg no longer ran; and why should folk slaughter their precious cattle for food when there were herds of fat eland only waiting to be shot? The farther the hunters wandered afield, the more ridiculous did Retief's shadow-line of restriction appear. The country lay empty of natives, the rich veld ungrazed;

and, in any case, there was no authority to restrain
them.

This easy state of anarchy suited Jan Bothma. Old
Adrian was too feeble by now to trouble himself over
the complications of a life on which his own hold was
so precarious. Jan stepped straight into Sarel's shoes
as leader of the Prinsloo party. This was natural
enough—there could be no doubt as to his qualifications—yet his brief authority did not improve his
manners. Since his rebuff at Winburg he had evidently
been thinking the matter over, and decided that
Lisbet's rejection of his advances was no more than a
transient feminine caprice. He returned to the charge
with overweening confidence, determined to make
short work of her coquetry and have his own way
with her.

Up till now, Lisbet had found it fairly easy to keep
him at arm's length, relying on Anna's jealousy as a
barrier between them. But now Anna was gone (how
gladly would she have returned!) and, in Sarel's
absence, there was none other behind whom she could
shelter. Jan knew this and rejoiced in it. He took
courage and changed his tactics. His blundering
advances turned to a bold pursuit; his attentions became persecutions. However carefully Lisbet avoided
being alone with him, she could not always escape
him. He no longer wasted time in entreaties, but took
it for granted that in the end she would have to submit
to his physical preponderance. He lay in wait for her,

like a hunter stalking his quarry. There was no moment in which she could feel herself safe from his bearish embraces, and the fact that she struggled and tried to escape from them added zest to his sport and excited him to a frenzy that filled her with terror.

"It's no use your fighting now," he told her triumphantly. "You may do what you like, but you'll have to give way in the end. I'm a man who's always got what he wanted—remember that! I've wanted you these five years, and I'm going to have you. Didn't you tell me at Winburg that you had nothing against me?"

She had more than enough against him now. She began to dread the sound of his voice, to shrink when she heard his footsteps. She dared not move from the camp, but clung to her mother's skirts like a frightened child. There was no peace in her mind nor sense of security save on the days when he rode out to hunt in the Tugela valley.

Jan's mind, slow in most things, was shrewd enough to grasp this. He was a hunter born, and studied her movements and reactions with the skill and pertinacity he had often devoted to the pursuit of shy game. One morning, when she had watched him ride away with provisions for two days' hunting, he dismounted, knee-haltered his horse behind the nearest ridge, and lay watching the camp. He lay there in wait till the sun declined. In such matters there was no end to Jan Bothma's patience: it was no unusual thing for him to

lie thus for hours on end with lazy eyes watchfully
fixed on a water-hole waiting for the moment when
the game he was after would come down to drink. He
lay there so still that more than once during the day a
grazing buck wandered within range, and his hands,
automatically, went to his gun. But, though sorely
tempted, he did not load it; for he knew that the
sound of a shot so near the camp would betray him.

The day passed; but the fading of light gave no
relief from its heat. There was thunder about. Tattered
cloud pressed low on the Berg and engulfed the sun.
The scattered thorn-trees stood motionless, islanded
blue-black in the sea of grass. He watched the great
herds moving slowly in to their kraals and grazing as
they went. It seemed to him that his day-long vigil
had been wasted. Under that threatening sky it was
unlikely that anyone would venture far from the
camp. He had almost made up his mind to abandon
his watch and return—the imminence of those solemn
masses of cloud would have been a sufficiently plausible
excuse—when suddenly, in the distance, the gleam of
a white kappie caught his eye.

Lisbet had left the bivouac and was walking rapidly
over the veld on the side that was farthest away from
him. Jan's moment had come. He rose heavily, recaptured his horse, and cast a wide circuit, riding round
under the cover of the ridge to cut her off. There was
no fear of his losing sight of her: the white kappie
made her as conspicuous as a springbok's snowy flash.

He cantered along with a smile on his lips, his heart beating fast in hungry anticipation. So, hugging the shoulder of the ridge, and peering cautiously above it from time to time to check the white kappie's advance, he reached a point within a hundred yards of her and dismounted again. If she held on her course it would bring her straight to his arms. He stood motionless, waiting behind a conical ant-heap, and watched.

Then, suddenly, anger seized him. As the kappie came into sight through a gap in the bush, he saw, to his consternation, that Lisbet was not alone. A man walked beside her. Though he was too far away to distinguish his features, he knew who it was: the younger of the two Englishmen. His hands jumped to his gun, as they had jumped when he saw the buck. The weapon came up to his shoulder. Indeed, he would have fired at sight—for his mind was in a ruthless blaze that knew no reason—had he not suddenly, thankfully, remembered that it was not loaded.

The shock of realizing how near he had been to murder shook him. It pulled his senses together and sobered him, but did not check his rage. In that moment his anger against Lisbet surpassed his desire for her. She had not merely thwarted him but cheated him, lied to him. She had told him at Winburg that no other man concerned her, and he, in his foolish, infatuated simplicity, had believed her. As if any man could believe what a woman said! Well, now that he had discovered her lies, he would know how to deal with them. He would know how to deal with her, and her Englishman, too.

But not yet. . . . Since the double treachery—to himself and his race—was out, he found an exquisite pleasure in whetting his anger and torturing himself by holding his hand and watching them and awaiting the worst affront his wounded pride could sustain, his last justification for the vengeance the chance of the unloaded gun had frustrated. Now his anger was steely cold, his purpose determined. With hands that did not tremble he poured powder down the gun's barrel and rammed the charge home. He looked to the flint and saw that the priming was ready. His cold blue eyes, fixed on the couple, calculated the shortening range and the space between them. At the first sign of love-making he was prepared to shoot Oakley like a dog. If the shot were to kill Lisbet too, he would not care. There was no law to be feared in this land, and he had no doubt but that many men who thought like himself would approve of such righteous vengeance.

He sat, with his gun on his knees, in the ant-hill's cover. As the couple drew nearer their steps verged towards him. They were steering straight for his ant-hill now. In a moment, it seemed, they must pass within an arm's length of him. His hands gripped the gun more tightly. They were talking light-heartedly, easily. Jan could hear every word they said in that breathless air, yet understand none, because they were speaking English; and the sound of that tongue which he hated for itself, and hated the more because it concealed their thoughts from him even when he heard it, infuriated him.

From the tone of their voices he judged that they were speaking of common things. But who could tell? Lisbet stooped to pick a flower. John Oakley stood clear of her, waiting, the perfect target. But now she had reached his side again. She held the long-stalked flower to his face, inviting him to smell it, and laughed as he shook his head. That light laughter of hers was harder for Jan to bear than her secret speech. He knew Lisbet's laugh so well; the sound of it had always thrilled him; but this laugh was different in quality from those she gave him; there was no mockery in it. He remembered suddenly—and smarted, remembering—the evening when he had last returned from the Cape to Welgelegen and her laugh had cut short his boasting.

They were abreast of him now. He knew that if he was to keep them within sight without their knowing, he would have to leave his cover and cut into the bush. Their attention was so deeply engrossed and he himself so skilful a stalker that this should not be difficult —unless his untethered horse chose to follow him and gave him away. But keep watch he must; for this was the critical distance at which, thanks to the contour of the land, they would drop out of sight of the camp. If these two were lovers—and he could not believe they were not—they would surely betray their secret as soon as they thought no human eye could see them.

They were so near him now that he could hear the dry swish of Lisbet's skirt as it swept the grasses. They passed. Before they were twenty yards beyond him he was on the move, creeping forward on hands and knees towards a clump of thick thorn which he had selected as his next point of cover. He reached it in safety, and then stole on, cautiously shadowing them. They halted, and Jan stopped, too. The moment for which he was waiting had surely come. He knelt, with the gun at his shoulder covering Oakley.

Then Lisbet turned, looking full in his direction. Her glance, it seemed to him, ran straight to his aiming eye along the barrel of his gun, yet, though his finger trembled on the trigger, his crouching figure was so still that she did not see him. For one endless moment she gazed at him, past him, unseeing, then slowly raised her eyes to the inky sky. She turned again, speaking to John Oakley; but this time Jan neither saw her face nor heard what she said, for, even as she spoke, lightning blinded the air between them, the charged vault split with a crack like a bowl of metal hammered and fractured from rim to rim, and down came a deluge. The next moment his dazzled eyes saw her running back to the camp with John pounding after her, the two dwindling figures dimmed by the veil of descending water and the mist of broken drops that danced back from the earth waist-high.

Again lightning fizzed in his ears. The tall mimosa under which the pair had been standing was riven and fell to pieces before his eyes. Jan lay flat on the ground and threw his gun away from him. He was frightened of lightning. Such was the fire and brimstone that the Lord once rained out of heaven on the cities of the Plain. This clanging fury in the sky was the voice of God speaking—though whether His anger were kindled against Lisbet for her falseness or himself, who had lately cherished thoughts of murder in his heart, he could not decide.

He lay there for an hour while the thunder pealed and clattered with gigantic echoes rolling back from the Berg. When the storm retreated westward there was no more than a lurid gleam of light left in the sky. His body was soaked to the skin through his leathern clothing, and the hollow in which he had lain was brimfull of water. He picked up his gun and went in search of his horse. It lay dead, its legs bent and its lip twitched back by the final spasm, its teeth so firmly clenched that he could not withdraw the bit. So he cut loose the bridle-leathers and left it, making note of the spot where the poor beast lay (for he was thrifty by nature) in order that he might recover the bit when the vultures had finished with the carcass, and walked back, with the saddle on his shoulder, over the darkening veld. In this case the intentions of the Almighty did not appear to be very clear—unless he were intended to take the destruction of a well-trained horse as a broad hint or a warning against harbouring unjust suspicions.

Yet, just or unjust, the suspicions remained. It usually took Jan a long time to get things into his head, but when once they were there, there was no getting rid of them. Though he still had no proof that there was anything more than a common friendliness between John and Lisbet, his attitude towards them became wary. He was so anxious not to lose sight of them that he abandoned his habit of riding away to hunt towards the Tugela valley. Every night he watched them. During the day he planned that John Oakley's work should take him away from the camp, and missed no opportunity of making that work unpleasant. He had never liked John or George Dicketts. The mere fact that they were English had been enough to set him against them. Now he did his utmost to prejudice their position in old Adrian's eyes.

"These damned Englishmen," he complained, "they're no more use to us than a couple of mission-Hottentots. The one-legged fellow is not so bad—he's a man at any rate; but the young one's a shirker, as slim as he is idle. Unless you kept your eye on him all the time, you'ld never know what tricks he was up to."

"Sarel found them both useful enough, Jan," Jacoba told him.

"Sarel's no judge of men. He's used them too

softly; he's spoilt them. If I'd had the ordering of the scoundrels from the beginning, they might have been worth their keep. When I'm not there, they're useless. The natives do what they like with them, that's the trouble. As everyone knows, it takes a Dutchman to manage natives."

"Sarel says . . ."

Bothma would not wait to hear what Sarel had said. The longer Sarel remained away with Retief in the Zulu country, the better he would be pleased. But Jacoba was growing anxious. There had been no news of the embassy to Dingaan since the messengers had come back from the Port: and that was a month ago. It was a sad time for her, sitting there on the Blauwkrans River, watching her husband's life ebbing away from him, never knowing, from one moment to the next, that she would not be told that the favourite son on whom she counted was dead.

They heard no more news of Sarel, in fact, until, of a sudden, one evening he rode up to the camp. His face was graver than ever, and older. It was only when he saw Jan Bothma that it broke into one of those rare, quick smiles that made it so pleasing.

"What, Jan?" he said. "Have you fallen out with the Potgieters?"

"I came back because I thought men were needed," Jan said.

"And Barend?" He looked round anxiously.

"Barend has stayed with his wife."

Sarel did not say he was glad; but his face showed relief.

When they had eaten, they all sat and listened to him as he told them of his wanderings.

"First we rode to the Port," he said. "The land drops in terraces. The coast is more swampy than ours used to be—and steaming hot: I thought we should all have died of it. We talked with the Englishmen there. They are like ourselves, split in two parties. There are only forty or fifty of them in all, and not a white woman among them. Both parties seemed friendly to us."

"They are English," Jan Bothma growled.

"They are English, that's true; but they are the first in-dwellers in Natal; and the best of them, a Scotsman called Biggar, and a big fellow called Cane, are doing their best to keep out the Government's influence and want us as neighbours. When we'd seen how the land lay there we went off, with this Cane and another called Halstead, to talk with Dingaan."

"You took an Englishman with you?" Jan Bothma scoffed. "That was not very clever."

"Retief needed interpreters, and Halstead speaks Zulu."

"How could you know that he interpreted rightly?"

"We couldn't, Jan; but in this life, alas, one has to trust somebody sometimes."

"When I have to trust anyone but myself," Bothma said, "I won't choose an Englishman!"

Sarel laughed. "There was no choice in this case. These fellows knew the way to Dingaan's Great Place, which is more than we did, and were good friends of the only man whom Dingaan listens to—a missionary called Owen."

"What . . . another of that breed? Have the damned missionaries poked their noses in there already?"

"Mr. Owen seemed to me a man one could trust."

"Trust . . . trust. . . . There is too much of this trusting about you. You've caught that from Retief."

"Retief knows what he wants, and is ready to take risks to get it. Let me tell you what happened. It will make you open your eyes. That Zulu country looks about the best cattle-land I've ever seen, and the Zulu cattle are better than any native herds I've seen either, just as the Zulus themselves are a better people. It's no wonder they drove the other Kaffirs before them. They're a fine, proud race, well-ordered and disciplined, and, to tell you the truth, I'ld sooner be friendly with them than have them against me. There's nothing haphazard about their methods of warfare. The whole tribe is organized for war into regiments, a thousand strong, each regiment with its own uniform, head-dress and shield. Dingaan says he can put fifty regiments into the field in a night. Fifty thousand trained men! That is not a force to be sneezed at. One thing is certain. If we are going to settle in Natal, Dingaan will have to be dealt with."

"And have you dealt with him?"

"I think we are on the way to it. Retief sent a message to him from the Port that he was coming to see him, and a reply came back from Owen, his missionary: a friendly reply, in which he said he was sorry for what the Matabele had done to the Liebenburgs. He even offered to send us back the skins of some of our cattle which his men had captured from Moselikatze. When we reached the Tugela drift, which is a good twenty-four hours' ride from Dingaan's Great Place, we left the wagons behind and rode on— just half a dozen of us: Retief and myself and the Englishmen Halstead and Cane and two other fellows."

"That was taking a great risk," Adrian said.

"It was a risk, yes. But Retief thought the risk worth taking: and, to show he was right, here I am!"

"God be thanked!" Jacoba murmured.

"It took us more than two days of hard riding," Sarel went on, "to reach Ungungundhlovu—that's the name of the place as well as I can remember it. Halstead told me the meaning of the word, but I've forgotten it. I shall never forget the first sight of it, it was so different from any of the villages I've seen in Kaffirland. We came to a *koppie*, with a small stream running at the foot of it. There were women bathing in the stream; they ran away like springboks, and there, on the slope beyond, we saw this great oval kraal: a thorn fence outside hundreds of beehive huts set in rows six deep, and an open space of two or three acres in the middle. At the top of the oval, looking down on the open space, you could see Dingaan's private quarters and the huts where he keeps his women. It was a bigger house than the rest, with a black floor polished like ebony, and pillars covered with beadwork. When we rode into the kraal at the lower end and up to that house, I can tell you it gave one a funny feeling. There must have been two thousand armed men standing there naked and staring at us. If Dingaan had wanted to finish us off, he had only to give the word. But he didn't."

"What did he look like?" Jan Bothma asked.

"A tall fellow, near as big as you, Jan, but gone to seed. He sat on a wooden chair, with his great paunch sagging on his knees, and a mangy dog he calls Makwilana lying at his feet. Many of these Zulus are not black for Kaffirs—no darker than some of our Hottentots: but Dingaan's as black as jet—polished jet, you'ld say, for his skin is shiny with grease. From his face you wouldn't imagine him to be the monster they say he is. It's a humorous, good-natured face, one would say at first sight; though I don't like his eyes: they're too small and they're crafty, and even when he smiles they don't change. If he has any humour, I'ld sooner laugh with him than at him."

"Still, he seemed to be friendly."

"As friendly as possible. 'You do not know me, nor I you,' he told Retief, 'and so we must become better acquainted.' The trouble with him, like the trouble with every Kaffir, was that you couldn't bring him to the point. Time means nothing to them, and Retief, of course, was in a hurry. Dingaan kept us there hanging about for three days."

"You slept in the kraal?"

"No, we camped on the slope outside, between it and the stream. It was none too pleasant. Hot days and hot nights, and the stink of the village blowing our way all the time. Yes, we had three days of it before we could get Dingaan to talk. I think what he wanted to do was to impress us with his power. We had two days of dancing, sham-fights and the like. Two regiments danced and fought on the first day and two on the second, and their oxen danced with them."

"Their oxen danced with them?"

"Yes, they've trained them to drill, like soldiers. They have strips of calfskin hanging from their foreheads and shoulders and from under the throat. Each regiment has its own oxen, all of one colour and hornless. The sham-fights were terrific. Never in all my life have I seen a finer body of men than the older warriors—the Umpakati, they call them. Their shields are longer than any I've seen before. A tall man need hardly stoop to take shelter behind them, and every regiment has a colour of its own: white spotted with black for the veterans, and black for the young men. Then their assegais: you can see they're not meant for throwing. They carry five or six, all short-hafted, broad-bladed, and stab rather than throw. That is why they prefer to fight in open country."

"In open country a man on a horse can make rings round them and pick them off as he pleases," Jan Bothma said.

"That is true, and some day they will learn the truth of it. At present they think that they're invincible. While they danced they sang, praising Dingaan. The Englishman, Halstead, told me the meaning of the words. They were something like this: "Arise, vulture! Thou art the bird that eateth other birds! Thou art the great elephant! Thou art high as the heavens! Where is the strength of the forest before the great elephant? His trunk is breaking the branches of the forest. What is this thunder? It is the sound of the shields of the sons of Markobane! He breathes upon their faces: it is the fire among dry grass. We are hard as stones——" That's what they sang—"and nothing can hurt us. Who can fight with thee? No other king can fight with thee. They that carry fire cannot fight with thee!"

"That remains to be seen," Jan Bothma growled. "But what happened next?"

"On the third day, when he was satisfied that he had impressed us sufficiently, Dingaan consented to talk business. Retief spoke with him through Halstead. 'What are you wanting here?' Dingaan said. We were glad he had come to the point at last; we were tired of waiting. 'What we want,' Retief said, 'is to purchase land from you. We come from afar; our country is small and we are becoming too many for it. We see you have a large country which lies waste and unoccupied between the mountains and the sea. That is what we want to buy from you.'

" 'How can you ask such a thing,' Dingaan said, 'when you know you have lately shot my people and taken their cattle?'

"That was the last question we expected. Retief said we had done nothing of the sort. Dingaan wouldn't have it. There was no doubt about it, he said. Only a couple of months ago men dressed and armed like ourselves and riding oxen without horns (that's what they call horses) had raided one of his kraals and lifted three hundred cattle.

" 'That must have been Sikonyela,' Retief told him. 'He is the only Kaffir who has horses, and some of his people are clothed as we are.'

" 'Well, if it was Sikonyela and you are innocent,' Dingaan said, 'you had better prove it. I will make the owners of the cattle go with you, and one of my generals. Go back to your people,' he said, 'and give mine the opportunity of seeing your cattle to find if theirs are among them; and, if not, go and show my people where their cattle are. After that we will talk about land.' "

"And that was the end of it?"

"Yes, that was the end. Or rather, it is the beginning. To-morrow we shall ride into Sikonyela's country and find out the truth. You had better come with us, Jan. This is a job to your liking."

Jan Bothma shook his head. "If you are away, I shall stay here, Sarel," he said. His sullen eyes searched the faces of John Oakley and Lisbet to see how his words affected them. But John Oakley was staring at the fire; and Lisbet only smiled.

Sarel rode off with Retief again next morning over the Drakensbergen. The New Year had come in before they returned; but the commando had made no mistake about Sikonyela: they brought him with them in handcuffs along with his guns and his horses, the three hundred stolen cattle the Zulu indunas had picked from his herds, and four hundred more as a guarantee for his future behaviour.

Retief came back to Blauwkrans in buoyant spirits. It seemed to him that the heaviest part of his task was over: there was nothing left but to ride back to Dingaan and claim the land he had promised. He could leave the folk with an easier conscience and less anxiety now: for Gert Maritz had crossed the Berg while he was away; the sky-blue wagons, way-worn and red with dust, were laagered beside his own, and the truant himself, as dashing and gay as ever, was ready to take his part.

Yet new worries, of the same old order, awaited Retief and had to be dealt with. Father Smit was in trouble again, in a mighty huff because Sarel Cilliers, a mere layman, had been preaching sermons without his permission: when Retief's back was turned, no power on earth could keep Cilliers out of the pulpit. Besides this, another awkward party had arrived: a man with pretensions to leadership and a popular following—Andries Pretorius, and, as bad luck would have it, that stormy petrel Piet Uys, full of new confidence, flushed with the final defeat of the Matabele, and determined to assert his old claims to the possession of Natal. The scene was set for another stormy Assembly. It took all Retief's tact and patience and Maritz's generous good nature to straighten things out. And another cause for uneasiness haunted the back of his mind: the fact that the folk had strayed past the line he had fixed, and lay scattered, beyond recovery now, in a hundred bivouacs, detached and vulnerable. More than ever it seemed to him that there was no time to be lost.

Retief lost no time. By the end of a week of impassioned debate he had achieved what he wanted: Father Smit and Cilliers were reconciled; Gert Maritz and Uys shook hands and Uys pledged his allegiance to the United Laagers.

Now for Dingaan! This was a matter that would not wait; for already rumours—and rumours with some apparent foundation—were flying. A trader, arriving from the Port, had heard native talk. Dingaan meant not business but mischief. The story of the defeat of the Matabele, with which Retief had hoped to impress him, had made him uneasy: if this were a sample of Boer native policy they might prove to be uncomfortable neighbours. Another warning filtered through the uncertain channel of the half-caste interpreter, Biggar: Dingaan was summoning his scattered regiments of warriors to his Great Place. There had been war-dances, beer-drinkings. The young men were on fire, and eager to give their assegais a new blood-bath.

In the council held at Retief's headquarters all these rumours were known and discussed. Both Maritz and Cilliers were doubtful.

"If you must go to Dingaan," they said, "get the folk together and call out a strong commando. Let us take the cannon with us and wagons to form a laager. These Zulus are not ordinary Kaffirs: they are strong, and they know it."

Retief shook his head:

"I have promised Dingaan to bring back his stolen cattle myself," he told them. "I believe he trusts me. If I came with a great force of men, he would trust me no longer. We have got to live with the Zulus as neighbours in any case. It is better we should begin as friends."

"If you go with a few, you will be tempting him," Maritz said, "and not only him, but all the young warriors he has gathered together. Even if Dingaan be trustworthy, how do you know that he can control them?"

"They fear him, as they feared Chaka, his brother.

They dare not move a finger without his leave."

"I do not like it," Maritz persisted. "I do not like it. You have brought us so far without any mishap. You are the only man in this company whose authority everyone is prepared to respect and acknowledge; and we cannot afford to lose you. The risk is too great, Uncle Piet: you are putting your head in the lion's mouth. If we decide to send a small force to bargain with Dingaan—and perhaps you are right about that— let me go instead. I am younger than you, and my life is of less value than yours."

Reticf smiled. "That is bravely spoken, Gert Maritz, but I cannot accept what you offer. I have told you, I think, that Dingaan trusts me. We must not change spans in the middle of the drift. I have begun this business, and I think I should finish it. The folk have chosen me as their leader, and I am going to lead. We will go without wagons or cannon. I shall take Sarel Prinsloo with me as I did before. For the rest, I will give no orders: all I need is fifty or sixty volunteers. Who rides with me, then?"

In an instant seventy stepped forward. Sarel Prinsloo's eye swiftly appraised them. They were the pick of the gathering; he could not have wished for a bolder body of men. Yet one who he had thought would surely be among the first was missing. Jan Bothma sat motionless, sullenly staring before him. Sarel stepped over and spoke to him.

"Are you not with us, cousin?"

"I will go in your place if you ask me," Jan Bothma said; "but, if you go, I stay with our people. There is no other man. And a man may be needed yet. For once I agree with Maritz. I do not like this. No . . . I do not like it."

CHAPTER SEVEN

THE CATTLE-KRAAL

SAREL PRINSLOO rode down with Retief to the Tugela River. Sixty-six armed white men were there, with thirty Hottentot *achter-ryders* leading the spare horses, and the ten Zulus driving home the stolen cattle.

Retief was still in high spirits, and so were the rest of the company. After months of monotonous trekking they were on the brink of adventure. Many stories had been told of the barbaric splendours of Dingaan's Great Place: of the huge oval kraal, the king's hut with its beaded pillars, the blood-soaked execution-hill, with its piles of human skeletons, over which Dingaan's hungry "children," the vultures, perpetually wheeled in slow circles, waiting for their father to feed them.

They were wheeling high in the upper air, so loftily that they looked no bigger than flies, when the dust of Retief's cavalcade of two hundred horses curled up from the plain. Sarel saw them there and remembered a tale that Halstead had told him: of how Dingaan, on the rare days when no crime had been punished by death, would upbraid his servants for starving his "children" and order them to knock some old man or woman on the head and throw out their aged bodies for the obscene creatures to tear with their bloody beaks and talons. Such was the monster, he told himself, with whom they were going to deal. Perhaps, as Maritz had said, Retief was too trustful. Perhaps, after all, it would have been wiser to ride up in stronger force and to camp within an impregnable wagon-laager with Maritz's cannon trained on the entrance-gap in the thorn palisade. Perhaps . . . But there was no time now for regrets or reflections. Retief had given the order for the column to form and to load their guns with blank charges. In a thunder of galloping hooves and a fusillade of musket-shots they swept over the brow and through the stream, to come to a halt in front of the kraal's main entrance, while out of the huddled huts there poured to meet them a host of black figures running this way and that and swarming about them like ants from a broken ant-heap.

"There are more warriors about than when we were here last," Sarel said. "That rumour, at least, was true, and these Kaffirs are wearing their war-plumes."

Retief smiled: "Yes, that is so. Dingaan wants to impress us. That was what Maritz wished me to do. Black or white, our thoughts are the same."

"We should find out from Owen the missionary," Sarel persisted, "what has been happening since we were here."

"There is no harm in doing that. We will see what he has to say."

They rode back, still surrounded by the curious multitude, to the brow of the hill where the missionary had built his two huts. Mr. Owen had only just finished his morning prayers, which the sound of the Boers' fusillade had interrupted. He had plenty to tell, both of hearsay and observation. Dingaan had given orders, he said, for them to be attacked when last they departed. A party of six hundred warriors had actually been sent in pursuit of them to cut them off at the Tugela drifts; but the plan had somehow miscarried, and, in punishment for their failure, most of the six hundred had been killed.

"We are stronger now," Retief told him. "This time you need not fear for us."

"Ay, but Dingaan is stronger too," the missionary warned him. "There must be three thousand fighting men in the kraal at this moment, and another regiment of black-shields came in yesterday. They were dancing and shouting and drumming on their shields with their knobkerries all night."

"Three thousand? But we are sixty. That is only fifty to one. With the Matabele the odds were heavier, yet the Matabele were beaten. If trouble comes, we can certainly hold our own. But I do not think trouble will come," Retief added serenely. "Dingaan trusts me; and I shall trust him."

Mr. Owen shook his head and sighed: "I am afraid,

Mynheer, I know Dingaan's nature better than you."

Retief laughed. "So you think, my friend. But I tell you it takes a Dutchman to understand Kaffirs."

"Dingaan has been worrying the life out of me to get him firearms and teach him the use of them. He has even sent men to ransack my wagon, pretending to look for cloth. But it was guns he was after. He talks of nothing else since I read him your letter about the defeat of the Matabele. You see, that frightened him. And it's when they are frightened that wild animals are most dangerous. That is why you must be careful. At least, I beg you, keep an eye on your arms."

There was more dancing in the great kraal that day to celebrate the recovery of the cattle from Sikonyela. Sarel had seen such displays before, and once was enough; but to most of his comrades the spectacle was a novelty; they were glad to see the incredible dancing oxen of which they had been told, and amused by the savage exultation of the dancers who leapt and stamped and howled and whistled and hissed as they charged, while the women chanted and clapped their hands. As Sarel had noticed already, the warriors of every regiment were wearing their war-dress; tossing head-plumes of crane-feathers and widow-bird tails, fringes of cow-tails swishing from shoulder and waist and ankle. But there was something else that impressed him even more deeply than the numbers of the warriors and their dress: a new air of nervous excitement and tension which could only be felt. Since his last visit the atmosphere of Umgungundhlovu had changed.

It was not enough, that day, that the Zulus should dance. Dingaan would not be satisfied until the Boers had danced too. So Retief gave orders for them to stage a sham-fight of their own, forming themselves into two bodies and charging to meet at a gallop and firing their muskets from the saddle as they charged. This exhibition of power and swiftness would do no harm, Retief thought; but he smiled and shook his head when Dingaan demanded that every man should fire a hundred rounds. Powder was not so plentiful that he could afford to waste it. It was evident that the king's fear and lust for firearms still dominated his mind. When the dancing was over, and Retief had retired to rest and taken shelter from the heat under the shade of a huge wild fig-tree whose green-black foliage stood out dark against the sere grass of the hillside, an *induna* came with a message for him from Dingaan——a happy afterthought: Retief had brought back the cattle Sikonyela had stolen. Well and good. It was a pity he had not brought Sikonyela too. But what about Sikonyela's guns and horses? Unless and until those were handed over as well, the king would not feel disposed to talk about making a grant of land.

Halstead translated the message. "Is that what he says?" Retief asked. He pointed to his iron-grey temples. The hair of his head had whitened during the last three months. "Let him tell Dingaan," he said, "that he is not dealing with a child."

Sarel slept uneasily that evening. The air was stifling hot and intensely heavy. The great kraal, on the opposite bank of the stream, buzzed angrily all night through like an angry beehive, and the smell of it—that odd dusty pungency of the African village— wafted over the narrow valley and tainted his throat and nostrils. He had spoken a few hours since with a boy from the mission—the son of Wood, Mr. Owen's interpreter—who understood Zulu speech and had heard some young men talking. There was mischief brooding beyond the stream, the child said. But when Sarel told Retief what he had heard, the Commandant only smiled.

"If we listened to every rumour of that kind," he said, "life would not be worth living. I think I am not a bad judge of men, nephew. Dingaan's no fool. He knows we have the whip hand of him. His heart may be as black as his skin; but his intentions are good. By to-morrow night the whole affair will be settled."

The next day was Sunday. Mr. Owen was too busy with his Sabbath devotions to be of much help; but Retief and Sarel and Halstead spent most of the afternoon in interminable talk with Dingaan, while the rest of the party lounged on the hillside, their guns on their knees. Once more Dingaan persisted in his demands for Sikonyela's horses and firearms. Once more Retief refused. There was no keeping the king to the point. He was eager to talk about everything but the one they wanted. By the end of the day they were no nearer a settlement than at the beginning.

"We must be patient," Retief told Sarel. "This is only the Kaffir way."

On Monday morning early another regiment marched in. They were young warriors, Halstead said, with spears yet unblooded. They wore otter-skin casques with bunches of widow-bird plumes on their shaven heads, and kilts of wild cat-skin. Their shields were all of black ox-hide; they beat them with kerries as they ran with a swift prancing gait. When they came to the entrance of the kraal, the women ran out with shrill screams and their comrades' roar of welcome greeted them. They swept on through the press to Dingaan's bead-pillared house and raised their spears and their shields as they hailed him. *Bayete, Bayete, Bayete!* they cried and hissed: and the sound of their hoarse acclamation echoed back from the rising ground where the Boers were sitting and the scarps of the execution-hill over which the high vultures wheeled.

The regiment danced before Dingaan so long that there was no chance for further negotiation that morning; but later in the day Retief entered the kraal again with Sarel and Halstead, taking with him, for Dingaan to sign, the written form of concession he had

made out the day before. Halstead stumblingly translated the words into the Zulu tongue:

KNOW ALL MEN BY THIS [it ran]: *That
whereas Pieter Retief, Gouvernor of the Dutch
emigrant South Afrikans, has retaken my Cattle, which
Sinkonyella had stolen; which Cattle he, the said
Retief, now deliver unto me: I, DINGAAN, King of
the Zoolas, do hereby certify and declare that I
thought fit to resign unto him, Retief, and his countrymen (on reward of the case hereabove mentioned) the
Place called "Port Natal," together with the land
annexed, that is to say, from Dogela to the Omsoboebo
River westward; and from the sea to the North, as far
as the land may be useful and in my possession. Which
I did by this, and give unto them for their everlasting
property.*

Dingaan listened, or seemed to listen, and yawned.
He had thrown off his red-and-black robe because of
the heat, and sat there, an ebony Hercules shining with
grease and sweat—a Hercules gone to seed, with his
vast paunch sagging. He had danced with the young
men himself, and was drowsy with beer and fatigue.
When Halstead had finished speaking he scowled at
Retief. "Tell the Boers," he said, "they may come
to-morrow and bring this paper. We will dance again
and eat and drink beer, and then I will sign it and say
farewell and let them be gone in peace. To-morrow,
early."

He rose and rolled heavily into his hut.

"Will he sign the concession to-morrow, Commandant?" Sarel asked.

"To-morrow perhaps. Perhaps the next day. Perhaps the day after that. He is a Kaffir. But what does it matter when, so long as he signs it?"

The great kraal was more quiet that evening.

At sunset, Jane Williams, who lived with the Owens, chaffed William Wood's boy:

"You said Dingaan was going to hurt the Boers," she said; "and look, Mynheer Retief has been there again and again, but nothing has happened!"

"You will see: they will kill the Boers to-morrow," the lad said sullenly. "*They* know it as well as I. . . ." And he pointed upwards to the winged specks that floated like circling flies in the thin blue above the hill of execution.

"This time we will go all together," Retief said next morning, "and we will take our guns with us, and loaded."

Sarel thanked Heaven for that. He loaded his *snaphaan* with slugs, and saw that the flint was clean and the priming in order. When they reached the gate in the palisade, a press of armed warriors surged into the gap and blocked it, brandishing their spears. An old man, a grizzled *induna*, stepped forward and spoke to Halstead.

"The king says," he interpreted, "that it is against

the custom of his people for strangers to enter the Great Place carrying arms. With your guns, he says, they will not allow you to come in. You are to take them back to the fig-tree where the horses are tethered, and then all will be well."

For one moment Retief hesitated. Many men in the ranks were murmuring; some would have drawn back.

"I think that is right," he said at last. "The old man says such is their custom. After all, the king has told me he is ready to sign the concession. Three times Sarel Prinsloo and Halstead and I have been to his hut and talked with him unarmed. If Dingaan had meant any mischief he could have killed us easily. So far he has given us every reason to trust him. If we draw back now, he will have a grievance. What's more, he will think we are afraid of him. And that, with a Kaffir, will never do."

"Let us leave an armed party outside, Commandant," Sarel suggested.

"No, no. That would make him more certain than ever that we fear him. We will leave our arms with the horses, as the old man says. We have trekked a thousand miles under God's protection. It would show little faith if now, at the last moment, we ceased to trust Him."

They entered the great kraal unarmed. The warriors made way for them in silence; the women shrilled round them. They came to the cattle-kraal beyond Dingaan's house. He was dressed in the ceremonial robe of red plush he had stripped from his murdered brother Chaka. He shook hands with Retief and nodded and smiled. All round the walls of the cattle-kraal warriors squatted, twenty deep, in the dry dung and dust, a circle of living ebony broken only in the narrow gateway through which Retief had entered; and when the last Boer had passed in, that gap, too, was closed. The faces that stared at the visitors out of this wall of black flesh were sullen, incurious. Sarel noticed with satisfaction that these men appeared to be unarmed.

Retief produced his treaty, and Dingaan, always smiling, put his mark to it. Three *indunas* witnessed it, and three *burghers*, a Greyling, a Liebenburg and an Oosthuizen. Retief folded the precious paper and put it away in a leather wallet slung over his shoulder. His face glowed with satisfaction. He had come, at last, to the end of his appointed task: all Natal from the coast to the Drakensbergen was now his by right of cession. Women came with earthenware pots of seethed beef that smelt and tasted, like all Kaffir food, of wood-smoke. Some ate a little out of politeness, but many refused with wry faces. Other women carried in gourds of millet-beer. It was right, Dingaan urged, that a friendly bargain such as. this should be wetted with liquor; but Retief refused the beer, so they brought him milk instead.

And now, Dingaan said, his warriors must dance

again: one last dance to speed his friends while they drank their stirrup-cup. Retief had seen all the dancing he wanted to see and more during the last three days; but now that the treaty was signed he could hardly do less than humour his host. He assented, and Dingaan commanded his warriors to dance, while the women who had carried in the meat and the beer swayed their bodies and clapped their hands.

The men rose at his bidding. Sarel Prinsloo saw that they were not unarmed after all: their knob-kerries and assegais had been hidden in the dust at their feet.

It was a slow ceremonial measure they danced. They were packed so densely that there was no room for frenzied capers. They went round in a circle, lifting and lowering their arms like men pulling bell-ropes, and stamping heavily so that the air was full of noisome dust. And as they danced and sang in a deep-throated howling monotone, the huge circle gradually contracted. By slow degrees it closed in on the Boers standing in the midst with their stirrup-cups in their hands, closed in till the reek of black flesh was in their nostrils and the dust of the stamping enveloped them. Then, all of a sudden, Dingaan roared like a wounded bull:

"*Bulala amatagati!* Kill the wizards!"

"What is this? What is this? Let me speak to the king!" Halstead cried.

But his voice was choked with blood as an assegai pierced his throat.

Mr. Owen, the missionary, sitting in the shade of his wagon and reading, heard the slow chant swelling on the air and wondered uneasily what it portended. He was a brave man; but many months of living on Dingaan's doorstep had frayed his nerves. He could not keep his mind on the text. As he turned the page of his Bible, a breathless Zulu rushed up to him.

"A message from Dingaan: he says you must not be frightened," he said. "He is going to kill the Boers, but you and your people are safe, he says, for you are King George's children."

Mr. Owen jumped up in alarm. The moment of dread had come. "I must warn them," he thought; but, even as he started to run, a maidservant shouted: "Look! They are killing the Boers now!"

It was too late. The measured chanting had swelled to fierce howls and agonized shrieks. Looking down on the cattle-kraal, he could see a black mass swaying this way and that. Ant-like figures swarmed through the gate in the palisade, women screaming, men leaping in frenzy. In the midst, like ants tugging at small particles of carrion with locked jaws, small clusters of Zulus, each attached to its victim, dragged the sixty-six bodies, dead or alive, out of the village and up the bare trodden path to the hill of execution. They howled as they went, and others leapt and whistled and howled about them. On they surged, up the dusty slope, till they reached the crown of the blood-soaked hill; and there, on the top, they cracked the skulls and beat out the brains with their kerries, and left the remnants amid the piles of bleached skeletons, and came down again, shouting and singing the praise of Dingaan.

Mr. Owen, haggard and impotent among his sobbing womenfolk, watched them go and return from the hill. But before the last of them had left that scene of carnage, the high specks that had hovered in the sky like circling flies had grown larger, drifting earthward. From invisible depths of the sky the vultures swooped down in hundreds to gorge themselves on the carrion Dingaan their father had given them.

Such was the end of Sarel Prinsloo and Piet Retief.

CHAPTER EIGHT

WEEPING

In the little camps along the Tugela's tributaries, the
Blauwkrans, the Bushman's and the Mooi rivers, the
folk waited, full of hope yet impatiently, for Retief's
return. They lay widely scattered now over a forty-
mile front in open bivouacs; their wagons stood ready
for the next forward move that should bring them at
last to a settled life and the end of their year-long
wanderings.

Ten days passed, and still Retief did not come.
Gert Maritz, now in command and encamped on the
Bushman's River, was besieged with questioners, but
refused to admit anxiety. Retief's force, after all, was
sufficiently powerful, he said, to face any mischief the
Zulu king might have planned. They must remember
too, he told them, what a laborious business it was to
deal with the shifts and quibbles of a cornered Kaffir;
while, apart from all this, the Tugela might be in flood
and the drifts impassable—on the Berg it had rained
for a week, and all the great river's tributaries were
muddy torrents. Yet, for all his persuasions, the folk
would not be satisfied; and at the end of a fortnight
he gave orders for a small party to move out and

reconnoitre, under the pretext of a buffalo-drive beyond the Tugela.

Jan Bothma brought back the news of this plan to the Prinsloos' camp. He was glad of any excuse for movement and action. He had reproached himself many times for his refusal of Sarel's invitation to volunteer. Nothing less powerful than his obstinate suspicions of John Oakley and Lisbet could have forced him to forgo an adventure so much to his taste. Yet this sacrifice to a consuming jealousy now seemed to have been wasted; for, craftily as he watched them, neither Lisbet nor the young Englishman had given him any excuse for the outburst to which he had keyed himself. The only revenge his blunt mind could devise for the imagined wrong was to make John Oakley's life as little worth living as possible; and this he did to some purpose, always hoping (yet dreading) that the intensity of his persecutions would sting Lisbet into some protest that might provide an occasion for the violence which was his only means of giving vent to his jealousy. But Lisbet, although she burned with indignation and suffered, had held her tongue, in the knowledge that when Sarel returned, this tyranny would cease. Had Jan Bothma realized how the excesses to which he was driven increased her dislike of him, he might have thought twice; but logical thought was no part of his natural equipment, and if he made John and Lisbet suffer, he suffered equally.

She was thankful, indeed, when Jan brought back

from Maritz's headquarters the news of the projected buffalo-hunt, if only because it was likely to give John a brief respite from this harsh persecution, and save herself from the strain of witnessing it in silence. Bothma saw the relief in her face when he made his announcement, and was quick to dispel it.

"I shall take young Grafton with me," he said, his eyes watching her narrowly. "Though he's no more use with a gun than most Englishmen, he can lead the spare horses and help to load in case of trouble."

"The other one is a better shot," Lisbet gently suggested.

"That is true enough; and that's why I shall leave him behind. What's more, he's less likely to get into mischief," he added darkly.

Lisbet said no more. Before dawn next morning, Jan and Oakley rode off with four horses to meet Maritz's hunting-party. Jan carried his long-barrelled *roer*, an elephant-gun that fired a four-ounce bullet of lead and tin. He had thrust a flint-lock pistol into his belt as well, and a sheath-knife with an eighteen-inch blade of the sort they called *Herneuters*. It looked an odd kit for buffalo-hunting, old Adrian said; but Jan only laughed.

"We may meet more buffaloes than we think when we reach the Zulu country, uncle," he said.

Lisbet knew what he meant. She knew also, now, why he had planned to take John with him. It was not after buffalo that they were riding beyond the

Tugela. Her heart grew sick with anxiety. She did not trust Bothma. She remembered King David, who had put Uriah the Hittite in the forefront of the battle; and the searching glance Jan had given her when he said he would take John with him troubled her.

The party rode down the left bank of the Blauwkrans and forded the Little Tugela. At its confluence with the greater river they crossed a drift. The water, though muddy with rain, ran no more than thigh-deep: one reason at least that Maritz had advanced to explain Retief's delay was not valid. They rode on into Dingaan's territory. The smiling land was empty of game no less than of men. At the end of the afternoon, in broken country, with the wooded kloofs of the Biggarsberg on their left, an old man with a walking-spear in his hand ran out from the bush excitedly and asked their business. They were after buffalo, they told him. That was a waste of time, he assured them: there were no buffalo in those parts. Farther down the river they would find herds in plenty.

"This old devil is trying to turn us back," they told one another.

"Yet what he has said is true. There are no buffalo hereabouts. And there seem to be no Kaffirs either. That is what Maritz wanted to make sure of, and now we know it. If we refuse to listen to this fellow he will guess that our story of searching for buffalo was only an excuse. We had better make believe to take his advice and go on down the river."

"Better still, go back. Wherever the Kaffirs may be, they are certainly not here. For all we know at this moment they may have got in behind us, and we are not strong enough to take such risks. Let us go home to Maritz and tell him what we have seen. That is all he wants. He will be glad to hear that the country is empty."

They rode back to the drift and encamped, with a loop of the river protecting them on one side and pickets set on the other.

There was no sound through that watchful night but the rushing of the Tugela, the chorus of frog-castanets, and, now and then, the whinny of a hunt-ing owl which some, who were skilled in such signs, said might well have been mimicked by Zulu scouts signalling to one another. And next day, without having fired a shot or seen any native but that one over-anxious old man, they rode back, well satisfied, through the green, sun-drenched land, to Maritz's laager. They were prepared to find that during their absence Retief had returned. His continued delay was mysterious.

During all this expedition, Jan Bothma had been in good spirits. While John Oakley led the spare horses close behind him and miles away from Lisbet he had nothing on his mind. But no sooner were they in sight of camp than the old jealous glooms returned. When Adrian asked him about the trip he answered him gruffly.

"There's no sign or news of Retief," he said. "The one thing we know for certain is that there are no Zulus in any numbers within ten miles of the river. That means there is nothing to fear. All last night we were on the watch; but to-night I mean to get the sleep I deserve."

He slouched away sullenly to bed. Since Sarel's departure, he had hauled one of his wagons into line with those in which the Prinsloos slept, so that the five which were set together formed an open crescent with its concavity facing the falling plains and the stream. Next to Jan's stood the wagon occupied by the old people; next to theirs, but separated from it by a space roofed with bucksail, the one in which Lisbet and Anna had travelled, and, after that, Sarel's. George Dicketts and John still slept, when it rained, in Bothma's old wagon which had first sheltered them at Welgelegen ten months before.

John was as ready for sleep as Jan Bothma that night. In the last thirty-six hours he had ridden eighty miles, with no respite save one broken night between. He would have dropped off at once if it had not been for George Dicketts, who chose this inappropriate hour for a rambling recital of grievances.

"That big beggar Bothma," he said, "he've got a reg'lar down on you and me, John. He's been at this game, on and off, ever since the young master—Sarel, or whatever you call him—went away. I've kept my mouth shut tight all these weeks, but one day soon I shall let the beggar have it. I'ld a'done it afore if I'd got the hang of his bloody lingo. Why does he want to go taking *you* along of him hunting, when he knows I'm as good a musket-shot as himself, for all his boasting? Contrariness, that's what it is, just contrariness! Why does he leave me behind with a lot of jabbering niggers that can't take in a word I say no matter how loud I holler, when you, being quicker-like at them sort of things, can say what you want and tell them to go to the devil? I'll tell you why, straight: 'tis because the beggar reckons they be likely to land me in trouble of one sort or another and give him a chance of miscalling me, the great scowling son of a bitch! When the young gaffer comes back, I be going to have it out with him, damn a horse if I don't! I know why he's hot on you, John: that's plain enough—'tis on account of the wench, who likes his looks, by all appearance, no better nor I do. That's nature, that is. But what have *I* done agen' him that he should use me the way he do? I tell you straight, lad, I've had more than a bellyful on him."

"It'll be all right, George," John told him sleepily, "when Sarel comes home."

"That may be or no. 'Tis all accarding," George said. "But who knows what lies that beggar Bothma may tell on me? You know, John, there be times when I start up, like, and ask myself what the hell we be doing in this rum country, you and me. Here we be, with Christmas just past, and the sweat pouring off of us, and the lambing finished these three months. 'Tis untimely, I say. And I'll tell thee another on-natural thing, John Oakley: this here moon be the wrong way about."

"The moon?"

"Ay, the moon. 'Twas a week agone I noticed summat amiss with her. You know as well as I do, or ought to, that when the moon's on the wax her turns her face to the left, like; and when she do wane 'tis just the other way round. But last time this beggar was waning, I caught her a'looking to the left. Now that's agen' Nature, I say; and mark my word, when the moon starts cutting such capers, it signifies summat, and no good will come on it. I don't say but what her'll come to herself next month, mind. It'll be another week afore her pops up again. 'Tis the dark of the moon just now."

It was indeed the dark of the moon that night. The stars were shrouded, too, in a sultry sky. John turned over with his face in his arms and one leg drawn up in the fashion months of sleeping on the veld had taught him. But he could not sleep—George's chatter had broken the chain of drowsiness—and this he did not resent, for all his fatigue, because darkness and silence helped him to think of Lisbet as he had seen her that evening, and to imagine her as she lay calmly sleeping, within a few yards of him, in the wagon opposite. Had she missed him? he wondered; had she been anxious for him? There was no way of telling.

Her face was purposely secret, and she had taken care not to let him see her eyes.

The more weary he became, the less he felt like sleeping. An hour or two after midnight—he guessed it might be two o'clock—the dogs, Bles and Flam, woke suddenly and began to bark. Most likely, he thought, they had got the wind of a leopard or lion; perhaps their quick ears caught sounds of distant hoof-beats; perhaps, at last, Sarel had come home. John crawled to the tail of the wagon. He stared into the dark and listened. Now he too heard steps, the steps of a heavy man running fast and bare-foot. A white figure came plunging out of the darkness into the crescent formed by the wagons: the figure of a bearded man, clad only in shirt and drawers. He staggered forward and swayed and fell on one knee. John slipped down from the wagon and ran to him. He was a man he knew already by sight, named Daniel Bezuidenhout, so blown with running that he could hardly speak.

"The Kaffirs . . ." he gasped. "They're on us. They've got the Liebenbergs."

John saw that his shirt was slashed from shoulder to breast and black with blood. The man held his left thigh with both hands, and blood oozed between them. John shouted for Bothma, who came lumbering up in his shirt, rubbing eyes still dazed with sleep. Bezuiden-hout poured out his story in gasps:

"They fell on the Liebenbergs first—farther down

the river than us. I woke and heard the dogs barking. I thought it must be a tiger and ran out, just as I am, to urge the dogs on. Then I heard an assegai whirr past my head. I shouted to my father: 'There are Kaffirs here, and they're stabbing the dogs.' I ran back to the wagons to get my gun. There were Kaffirs three deep around them. My father cried out: 'O God!' His voice was choked with blood. Roelof Botha had fired three shots. Three Kaffirs lay dead. Then I heard him too cry 'O Lord!'—and I knew they had got him. I fought my way through them. One assegai caught me here, look, in my thigh-bone. I found myself in among the cattle and stood a moment listening. Not another voice! They were tearing the tents to shreds and breaking the wagons. They had killed every one of us but me—my mother, my wife, my four sisters, my brothers, my little Anna. . . . There was nothing to be done. I ran on up the river to Sybrandt van Dyk's to warn them. The devils were on my heels. I could hear them howling when I left the van Dyks'. And now I must go on again up the river to Hans Roet's and Piet Retief's."

"Let my aunt bind up your wound, or you'll faint," Bothma said. "You're drenched with blood."

"I must go on . . . I must go on," Bezuidenhout answered wildly. "And you, cousin, set your wagons in laager and load all your guns before it is too late. Quick—quick: I think I hear them."

He staggered once more to his feet and plunged off

again into the dark, tears streaming from his eyes.

Now Jan Bothma was wide awake. He was roaring out orders. Old Adrian appeared, a bewildered wraith. Scared Hottentots, running in from the cattle-kraal, fluttered hither and thither like a covey of guinea-fowl. Jan Bothma swore at them: "Bring in the horses!" he shouted. He himself led in the two tired beasts that had carried him and John the day before. The Hottentots scattered into the darkness. There was a scurry of hooves. They had mounted the horses and ridden away. There was none on whom he could rely but John and George Dicketts.

"Come along, you damned Englishmen," he shouted. "Lend a hand with this wagon. Uncle, look to the guns and have them ready loaded. Get these women out of the way. Come on, now!"

He put his vast shoulder to the wheel of a wagon. As he rolled it, the felloe sank in the rain-soaked soil. Though John and George Dicketts pushed with all their might, they could not budge it. Jan Bothma laughed mightily. This was a proper ploy for his strength. With his great hands clasped round the disselboom he lifted the front of the wagon with its three-ton load high and clear of the mud and pulled it bodily sideways into the gap. John heard his great shoulder-muscles crack as he heaved. He felt like a pygmy before this titanic strength. Then a second wagon was rolled and heaved into place. Apart from one narrow port between them the laager was closed.

None too soon. As Jan Bothma straightened his back, an assegai, hurled at long range, whistled past his ear and buried itself in the fire, scattering sparks and ashes. He darted back to where Adrian stood fumbling with the guns, and snatched up the mighty *roer* he had loaded with slugs.

"Spread yourselves round the laager," he shouted. "Each man with a gun and powder and shot to hand. But don't waste your fire. Hold it, until the devils are in range. Hendrik, what are you doing here? Get back into shelter, you little fool, or I'll shoot you."

"There's nowhere to shelter," the child said calmly, "and I've got Barend's little gun."

"Then keep behind me," Bothma laughed, "and don't shoot till I tell you. They're coming! All steady now!"

John Oakley heard a strange sound: a high and not unmelodious ululation like the lowing of cattle: after that a shrill whistling and a hissing like that of some monstrous snake. A flight of thrown assegais whirred through the air and fell in the laager. John Oakley heard a groan and saw old Adrian pitch to the ground, his hands tugging at his throat.

"Fire!" Jan Bothma shouted.

His elephant-gun spoke first. The charge spurted from its muzzle with the flash of a cannon. Four other shots followed; then, quickly, two more: Jan Bothma and Dicketts each had a second gun. From the darkness outside came a shriek of pain. Then silence. As he reloaded, John heard old Adrian choking and spitting. A faint lantern-gleam showed the slave Ayah kneeling on the ground beside him, and in the black cave of the wagon-tilt two white faces, Jacoba's and Lisbet's. Jacoba was trying to get down from the wagon. Jan Bothma, too, saw her.

"Stay where you are, aunt!" he shouted. "Lie down flat on the wagon floor and the assegais will pass over you."

As he spoke he was pouring more powder down the muzzle of the *roer* and pounding the stock on the earth to ram the charge home. He was loading with slugs that would scatter. Jacoba neither answered him nor heeded his warning. She lowered her enormous bulk over the tail-board and crept on hands and knees to where Adrian lay. He was coughing no more: only a sound of rasping breath could be heard. Jacoba thrust Ayah aside and spoke to him, but his whispered reply was inaudible.

"It's too dark to aim rightly," Jan Bothma muttered. "Don't waste your fire, fellows. Wait till I tell you, and then let them have it. Look out! They're coming again."

Another flight of assegais ripped through the air. The Zulus were pitching them high, so that they fell almost vertically. One plunged and pinned John's leather trouser-leg to the ground. He turned hurriedly to snatch it away, and his arm struck something soft. Lisbet was kneeling behind him.

"Go back to the wagon, for God's sake!" he said. "Didn't you hear what Jan said?"

"I would rather be by you, John. Here is a spare gun I have loaded. That will save time. As soon as you have fired pass the others back to me and I'll load again."

"I wish you would go to the wagon and take your mother with you."

"I couldn't move her. I think my father is killed; she will never leave him. Listen!"

As she spoke, Bothma fired. John, too, fired twice at the flash of a white shield which swayed sideways and vanished. Lisbet thrust the third gun into his hand and he fired again. In the dark, invisible Zulus were rattling their assegais on their shields in a dry tattoo, yet only for that one moment was any target to be seen. Lisbet loaded swiftly. The first gun came back in his hands for him to see that, within an arm's length, a black shape had swarmed through the space between the wagon-wheels. He fired point-blank. The man rolled over without a gasp. Behind him John heard a sound of ripping canvas. The Zulus had climbed up and were slashing the tilt of the women's wagon with their assegais. He thanked God that Lisbet was there beside him after all. He turned and raked the tilt with a cross-fire, and heard a scream and a thud which gave him a fierce satisfaction.

Jan Bothma was cursing. "If I could only see

the devils! We have to fire blind. Hold your fire till you hear them. Ah, would you?"

Another wounded Kaffir had crawled through and thrust at him. Jan threw himself forward on him. As they rolled over together he drove the eighteen-inch blade of the Herneuter between the savage's ribs. "That's one less," he laughed; but the last thrust of the assegai had sliced through the ankle tendons, and one of his feet hung useless. Old Ayah crawled towards him and bound up the welling wound as he lay loading again.

"I think Barend's gun is mine now," little Hendrik whispered proudly. "I'm sure I've killed one."

"Load up again quickly, then," Bothma gasped. "Don't fire till I do. Rest the barrel on the spoke of the wheel to steady your aim. Ha, they're quieter now: we've given them something to think about."

It was mortally quiet. From far away on their right farther up the river came a rattle of musket-fire.

"That must be Hans Roet's," Bothma said. "It sounds as if Daniel Bezuidenhout got there in time to warn them. I shall not forget Daniel Bezuidenhout. We owe him our lives. If we can only hang on till daylight! It is the darkness that baffles me. They're too silent for my liking too. How goes it, Tante Jacoba?"

"It is finished. Your uncle is dead. The assegai ripped his throat."

"Then go back to the wagon. You can do no good here."

"I shall stay by him," Jacoba said. "One place is the same to me as another now. Let me have my way, Jan."

"And where's Lisbet?"

"I'm here, Jan," Lisbet's calm voice replied. "I'm loading the guns for John Grafton."

"Then lie flat on the ground when they charge again—if they do. Can you hear me? They may feel they have had enough—but I doubt it. Where's the other Englishman?"

"All right, George?" John asked.

"Right enough. I don't reckon I've wasted a shot as yet. 'Tis the same as old Quarter Brass, if you could only see them. But you can't till they're on you, and one of the beggars got through and ripped my best shirt down the shoulder."

"Are you wounded, then?"

"Naught but a scratch. More mess than damage."

So they talked, in hurried whispers. Far away to the north, the hot fusillade from the van Dyks' camp broke out once again; but the nearer darkness betrayed neither sound nor movement. They waited there, in that deathly silence, each man's gun in his hands and two more ready loaded within reach. Waited endlessly. . . . It began to seem as if Bothma's hopes were justified. Perhaps, as he said, the Kaffirs had had enough and had streamed on northwards, leaving this prickly prey in search of one less wary. So they hoped, though none dared speak of such hopes; for perhaps they still lay about them, waiting for the light to prove the little laager's strength or its weakness. The moonless sky had begun to clear. The veld showed itself pale in starlight, and against its pallor they saw prostrate black bodies, one straight swath marking the line swept by the slugs from Jan Bothma's *roer* which had mowed them down like the swing of a scythe. One had fallen almost at little Hendrik's feet.

"That's the one I killed," he claimed proudly. "Will you tell Barend when he comes home, Cousin Jan, or ought I to shoot him again to make sure?"

"Let him be. The little gun is yours, lad. You've blooded it finely."

Jan Bothma spoke without looking. His eyes were strained intently examining the dim middle distance of starlit veld.

"Now I see them," he whispered. "It's as I thought. They're still there, squatting down in a ring about us and waiting for daylight. My eyes are keen. A man who was not a good hunter would never have seen them. But one dipped his shield, and that was enough to give me the line. They are white shields dappled with black: that means they are veterans. And the shields of the fallen are black and white too. Let them wait: the longer they wait, the better for us, for then we can pick them off before they get within assegai-range. This is playing our game." He spoke to John. "Are there any on your side?"

"I can see none. The trees give them cover," John answered.

Bothma laughed scornfully. "If there were no trees, *you* wouldn't see them."

John knelt, staring outward between the spokes of the wagon-wheels. On his side the land sloped gently upwards to a thicket of thorn-trees, a black fringe against the faintly starlit sky. Between the wagon and these, the grass, beaten down in patches, grew waist-high. It was not surprising that his unpractised eye could see nothing more. With such perfect cover a hundred Kaffirs could easily have hidden themselves. Though he had lost all sense of time, two hours or more must have passed since Bezuidenhout staggered in to give the alarm. The sky behind the fringe of thorn-trees was gradually lightening. Already the earliest waking birds, the bush-francolins, called, and a fiskal scolded.

This half-light, in which only vague forms could be seen, played tricks with the fancy: it brought back George Dicketts' mind of a sudden to Grafton Lovett. Even so, in a summer dawn, he had seen the coarse grass of the common stretching away towards Pritchett's Wood, on whose verges, even as these mimosas, English hawthorns stood solitary or straggled above the hedge. Yet though the same strange resemblance touched John Oakley's mind, it did not hold it. If he felt the landscape's reminiscent loveliness, he was even more deeply moved by the fact that in this moment of extreme peril, wherein beauty and awe were mingled, Lisbet Prinsloo had chosen and dared to come to his side. They were nearer each other now, not only in body but in spirit, than ever before. Their time might be short, not a word of tenderness might be spoken before their lips were silenced for ever. But there was no need for speech. He knew, without words, that she loved him. And even though death overwhelmed them together, as well it might, this proud moment, he told himself, was one for which it was worth having lived.

No other sound than those faint notes of earliest bird-song broke the dawn's peace. There was no more gun-fire now to be heard from the neighbouring camps; about these too, perhaps, the Kaffirs were waiting for light; yet from time to time Bothma's keen eyes discerned slight movements; and twice, as he fired, the long-barrelled *roer* spurted flame. With each passing moment the strain of anticipation grew more intense and less tolerable. John found himself wishing that they would launch their attack and end it.

"I see something moving," Lisbet whispered at last. "I think they are coming nearer. Look!" She laid her hand on John Oakley's; the touch of her fingers ravished him. It was the first time their hands had met since the night of that dark encounter at Welgelegen. "Look!" she said, and immediately, the deep stretch of grass that had seemed so dreamily peaceful leapt into life. In a moment hundreds of assegais whirred through the air like angry hornets: some pierced the wagon-tilts; some whizzed overhead; some hung for an instant and swooped with a dropping trajectory, burying their blades in the ground; some, aimed more cunningly, stripped through the spaces between the wheels; some, deflected by spokes, ricochetted and flew off sideways. And before they had found their mark or fallen, those who had thrown them plunged forward, wave on wave, their dappled shields held before them, their stabbing assegais brandished above. John heard again that fierce and sinister sound of men hissing through their teeth. His first fear was for Lisbet kneeling beside him. With reckless violence he pulled her down.

"Lie flat!" he said. "For God's sake keep your head low."

He was firing now faster than she could load. There was no time for aiming, and no need—for the ranks were closed, the tossing head-plumes sharp against the grey sky as they leapt through the grass. It was clear by now that the whole attack was concentrated on their side. The Zulus had crept round and massed themselves in the cover of the thorns, and were charging downhill. Jan Bothma was quick to notice the change of direction. Through the storm of flying assegais he limped over. A ricochet ripped his sleeve as he crouched between John and Lisbet, resting the barrel of the elephant-gun on a wheel-spoke to steady his aim. There was a risk in leaving the other side of the laager open, and he knew it. He yelled to Hendrik:

"Keep on firing as fast as you can. Don't trouble to aim. It's only to let them know there's a gun on that side."

Jacoba had left her husband's body. She was loading for Dicketts, who kept up a methodical fire, his eight-pounder crammed with slugs. There was no question now, as Bothma had said, of selective aiming. He fired where the Zulus were thickest, raking their front. Lisbet was loading for Bothma now as well as for John. The barrels of the smaller guns were so hot that they burnt her fingers; but she could not stop to think of the pain: no sooner was a gun discharged than it came back to her hands for reloading. And the three men had fired to some purpose. At a distance of twenty yards from the wagons, dead and wounded lay like a fringe of driftwood washed up by waves, with here and there some desperate warrior who had crawled forward in spite of his wounds to be finished off by a shot from Jan Bothma's pistol, and lay clutching the wagon-wheels in death like a swimmer pulling himself ashore.

How long that fierce fusillade lasted, John could not tell. Time had ceased to have any significance. He only knew that as soon as a weapon reached his hands he must fire. His gun-shoulder was bruised to a pulp, his burnt fingers smarted; his eyes were bleared, his throat choked by the nitrous fumes of powder. And then, suddenly, it appeared that there was nothing left to fire at. The last wave had broken and spent itself. Beyond the ring of heaped dead, the trampled grass lay as quiet as though the storm that had lodged it had passed.

Jan Bothma heaved a deep breath and laid down his gun.

"They've had enough for the moment," he said; "but that doesn't mean they have finished with us. There must be a whole regiment. If they had attacked on all sides at once, I don't know where we should have been. We must now make a plan while we have a moment to think in. Are the horses unwounded? Go and look to them, you, John Grafton. They've cut the strings of my ankles; I cannot walk."

John rose to his feet. Lisbet turned towards him and smiled. Her hands and her cheeks were smudged with powder, her face deathly pale and small beneath her dark braided hair; but her eyes had the courage to meet John Oakley's now in spite of Jan's presence, and they told him all he wished. He walked over unsteadily to the two horses. The firing had pulped his brain as well as his shoulder. He felt giddy, and strangely elated. The horses, it seemed, were none the worse for the tumult: they had been trained to the shock of shots fired from the saddle as they stood, and had not moved. One was cropping a tuft of grass at his feet flecked with blood that had dripped from a slash in his shoulder. The other, unwounded, looked at John with mild, enigmatic eyes. The air of the little laager was filmed and acrid with powder-smoke; the ground within it littered with debris of the assault. The wan light showed it strewn with hundreds of assegais lying like a spilt box of matches. The Zulu whom Jan had spitted with his Herneuter lay where he had fallen. Over Adrian's body Jacoba had thrown a sheepskin kaross. Old Ayah squatted beside this shrouded figure like a watchful dog, her wizened face wet with tears.

"The two horses seem right enough," John said, "though your grey is wounded."

Jan Bothma nodded. "That is good," he said. "I have now made my plan. We have beat them off twice," he said, "but next time it may not be so easy. They are stronger than I thought; I was wrong when I said that daylight would help us. Next time they attack they will be able to see for themselves that there are only three of us against them—three men and a child. That will put new heart into them, and it will shame them to think that so few of us have been able to drive them back. They will know also that if they persist they can overwhelm us. Perhaps, if we held on long enough, we could hope that Maritz might send a strong party to help us. But we cannot count on that: I have heard no shots from the north for a long time now, and that seems to me bad. Therefore, what I say is this: I am the strongest of us all and the best shot too, but my ankle is finished. On foot I cannot fight with them. So, when they come on again, I shall mount and ride out to meet them. When they see me, the devils will say: 'This is the big man, the one we want, and he thinks he can get away.' They will fall on me, mark my words, like a pack of wild dogs, and if my horse isn't dragged down I may even get through them. Then you, aunt, as soon as the dogs start worrying me, will ride out of the laager on the other horse, making straight for the Berg. I know you are heavy, but the beast is a strong one and has rested all night: he can carry you easily, while Hendrik and Lisbet and the two men run beside you. The Kaffirs may turn from me and try to catch you, but if they do, I can ride round and harass them from the flank. This is not a good plan, perhaps, but it is the best I can think of. If we stay in the laager and fight it out, I know for certain what the end will be, and so do you, aunt. What do you say, then?"

Jacoba, who had scarcely seemed to be listening, shook her head.

"Your plan is a good plan, nephew," she said, "but it is not for me. We have trekked a long way, Jan, and this is the end of my wandering. I have come far enough. I would sooner stay here and lie by my husband's side, as we have lain for forty years, than be buried away from him. And even if this were not so," she went on pitifully, "I don't think I could get on the horse. No, no . . . I am too old and too fat to ride, too old and too tired. Think no more of me, children. I shall stay here with Adrian and be well content. But for Lisbet and Hendrik and the others, your plan is a good one. Let them do as you say, Jan."

"And leave you behind? I will never do that, mamma!" Lisbet cried.

Jacoba smiled wearily. "My child, you do not understand. You cannot judge for me. Every heart must speak for itself, and mine is dead and cold. Do you think it matters to me what the Kaffirs do to my body? The poor thing has lived its life and played its part. But for you it is different. All your life lies in front of you. So do not argue with me, Lisbet: be ready to mount the horse and do what Jan tells you. He is the leader here now that the old one is dead, and you must obey him."

"If you will come with us . . ." Lisbet began.

Jan Bothma broke in on her: "Your mother is right," he said. "Of her other thoughts I cannot judge, and no more can you; but it is certainly true that she is heavy and not used to riding. The horse is strong, but he could only move slowly with her on his back, and speed is what matters. There is no saying that any one of us is certain to escape; but what she says is true: without her, you others will have a better chance of living. I will speak the truth: it is Lisbet I want to save."

"And what of you?" Lisbet answered passionately. "Why should you throw your life away? Is mine worth more than yours?"

"It is worth more to me," Jan Bothma said. "And your mother is right: we have no time for argument. The plan is made. Let us keep to it. She will stay behind, as she says, and you will ride with the Englishmen."

Dicketts caught the last word. "What's all this about us, John? No good, I'll be bound."

John explained Bothma's plan of campaign. Dicketts' face went red.

"Well, if that isn't like his brass!" he exclaimed indignantly. "You can tell that great hulking beggar from me, John Oakley, that if so be as the old lady stays, I stays along of her, see? Does the beggar think that a chap who's stood up to old Boney at Quarter Brass is a'going to run from a parcel of bloody black niggers with feathers on their heads, or take orders from a Dutchman either, for that matter? And if 'run' 's the word—why, any damned fool with two eyes ought to know as a chap with one leg bain't cut out for running. I can fight as well and shoot as straight as him; but I be going to fight and shoot my own way. You tell him that straight!"

John translated the outburst: "Dicketts says he can't run with one leg. He can be of more use, he thinks, if he stays in the laager."

Jan Bothma laughed. "Maybe he's right and I was wrong. Let him stay if he wishes. A man can only die once. Tell him to see that the guns are all loaded while I look to the horses. You and Hendrik will keep a sharp watch, one on either side, and give warning at once if anything stirs. But don't fire: when they start we shall have no time to waste in reloading."

John moved to his post. Passing close to Lisbet, he looked full in her eyes, but it seemed that she did not see him. She stood alone, with clenched hands, looking straight before her in an almost unhuman stillness. Jacoba, who saw her thus, approached her and put her arms round her.

"You mustn't rebel, my little one," she whispered. "You must do as Jan tells you. He is wise in such things; Sarel always trusted his judgment in matters of this kind, and his plan is the best for all of us. Jan knows his own mind, and nothing on earth will stop him. As for me, you need not trouble. I am well content to stay here till the end. When it comes, I am ready. When you see our Sarel, tell him you left me happy to be with your father. You must promise to tell him that. And now there is one thing more. This English boy, Lisbet. . . . I have watched him for many months and I know he is good. I love him as if he were my own, and he loves you, Lisbet. That my eyes have discovered, although he may not have told you. You can trust him: remember that. If God grants you your lives, be kind to him. He is lonely, Lisbet, and you will be lonely, too. I am glad he is going with you, for I know you will be happy together. Now let me see you smile. There must be no tears, or your father would be ashamed of us. If the Kaffirs kill us, it is the will of God. That is what he would say . . . yes, that is what he would say. Now kiss me, my child."

Lisbet kissed her, and gave her, wanly, the smile she had asked for.

"That is brave, that is good," Jacoba said.

T

Jan Bothma stalked over. "I have shortened the stirrups," he said. "When you have set your course—see, the Berg is clearing already—give the horse his rein. He's a stout-hearted beast and sure-footed. Do not think of the others and do not look back. Keep your eyes on the mountains and ride towards them till he drops. If you get a fair start, the Kaffirs will never catch you, and from what I saw, I think they have moved from that side and the way will be open. I shall keep them busy, wherever they come from. Have no fear of that."

Lisbet held out her hand to him. Jan Bothma took it and smiled.

"This may not be farewell after all," he said. "And even if it is . . ."

He stopped with a laugh. Lisbet looked at him piteously. Her lips trembled so that she could not speak, but her eyes were tearless.

"They are coming, Jan; they are coming!" Hendrik cried.

"God in heaven be thanked!" Jan Bothma roared. "They come from the east!"

They were coming more cautiously this time, but in greater force, creeping stealthily through the grass and trailing their shields. Before this, they had pranced and shouted and drummed on their shields with their assegais as they advanced; but now they were silent. They came in the Zulu order of battle with which Chaka, Dingaan's brother, had shaken black Africa: in a dense central phalanx, ready at a word to expand into wide encircling horns like the claws of a scorpion.

"Come quickly: now you must mount," Bothma said. He picked Lisbet up in his great arms and kissed her mouth as he swung her into the saddle. "Why, you're half a man's weight," he said; "the horse can take Hendrik as well. Come, Hendrik!"

The child scrambled up in front of her. "Oh, but give me my gun, Jan," he said. Jan picked it up, laughing—it looked like a toy in his hands—and gave it him. Then he himself mounted.

"See, now, what I shall do," he said rapidly. "I shall ride out crossways before them—a tempting bait, no?— but always just out of range of their assegais. I shall not hurry: I shall give them time to look at me and to wonder what I am about. That will draw their eyes. Their minds only take in one thing at a time. I shall hold on slowly until they begin to think I'm escaping, but always so near that they will count me an easy prey. When I see that every eye is on me, then I shall fire. And that is your signal. Out you go, the three of you! Make straight for the bush and the Berg —and do not look back. Do you hear me, Lisbet? I say you mustn't look back. Now I go."

He pressed in his knees, and the horse moved forward, lightly clearing the brushwood that had been hurriedly thrust into the gap in the laagered wagons. He rode out superbly. The huge man looked bigger than his horse. His feet, long-stirruped, swung within twenty-four inches of the ground; the barrel of the elephant-gun peaked above his shoulder. He rode easily, with a proud nonchalance, towards the head of the bristling phalanx. The Zulus, seeing this portent, checked their advance and stared, incredulous. There was something beyond belief, and therefore not to be trusted, in this mad daring. Jan Bothma walked his horse on and on till he came within forty yards of the Zulu front and stopped dead. ("My God, that's a man!" Dicketts muttered. "I give him best.") But not a sound came from the black ranks; not a spear was thrown. Then he turned his horse's head southward and moved left-handed into a light tripple. All along their front he rode, a fair target, just out of range. As he neared the end of it, he kicked in his heels. The horse slipped into a canter. At last something happened. The massed Zulu front, that had crouched as still as a group of carved ebony, leapt into life. The set front dissolved and exploded in hurtling fragments. The whole host streamed after him as he swerved to the right, breaking into a gallop, already outflanking their line. He was riding now in the rear of the first great wave. It curled round to meet him. He had drawn the rest now. The body that lay in reserve leapt forward with tossing plumes to join with the first, while Jan thundered down between them, his head low on his horse's neck. ("The beggars will have him," George Dicketts gasped. "He'll never get through!") They were hurling their assegais now at the galloping figure. Another fifty yards and he would be through. Then the signal-shot rang out. "Come along," John Oakley said.

Dicketts was clearing the brushwood away from the gap in the laager. John took Lisbet's horse's bridle and dragged the beast through. He pounded along beside them through the long grass towards the belt of thorn-bush. He could not keep up with them. They were drawing away from him. Yet still he must run: if his heart burst, still he must run. He saw Lisbet lower her head as the horse crashed through the cover and out of sight. Twenty yards. . . . Were they after him? Would the grass ever end? He had reached the trees. An ant-heap tripped him and threw him headlong among fallen thorn-spikes.

As he picked himself up he glanced hurriedly backward. The space between the bush and the laager lay empty: there was no pursuit yet, thank God! Over the falling ground he saw the white-tilted laager. The doomed wagons looked homely and peaceful, as quiet, almost, as if they had been deserted. But on the open veld beyond them all hell was loose. John could see the black figures clustering thick as a swarm of bees round their queen, and, in the midst, towering above them, Jan Bothma, still horsed, and still ploughing his way through the press like some noble buffalo with a pack of wild dogs about him, pulling him down. One moment he saw the Herneuter flash red in the rising sun: the next the tall head was down—neither horse nor man could be seen. And with that fall there rose from the multitude a sound that was not like the separate voices of men but the bellow of one great animal. It rose high on the air, drowning the clatter of musket-shots that George Dicketts, cool as his comrades at Quatre-Bras, fired into the mass that surrounded Jan Bothma's body. Many Zulus fell under his fire, but none heeded him. The monster had got its teeth in its chief enemy and howled as it tore him to pieces. No wonder Jan Bothma had told Lisbet not to look back. . . .

John brushed the horror from his mind. He ran on through the bush in the same direction as before. It seemed, by some miracle, he had got his second wind. His heart no longer laboured to bursting. He had only one thought: to catch up with Lisbet. At the end of a glade of purple-headed grasses he caught sight of her, less than a hundred yards ahead. She had halted the horse and stood waiting for him. He waved her on excitedly—he dared not shout for fear that some stragglers of the Zulu host on that side might hear him —but she misunderstood his signals or disregarded them, and still held her ground.

He came up with her, panting. "Ride on, ride on!" he entreated. "It is madness to stop."

"I heard a terrible sound," she said. "I thought they had caught you. What was it?"

He shook his head.

"Take hold of the stirrup-leather and run beside us,"

she said. "We must keep together now. The bush grows so tall that I cannot see the Berg any longer."

"No matter," John gasped. "The sun is rising behind us. We go north-west."

They went on without further words. Now the bush grew thinner. The monster had ceased its howling; not even a shot could be heard—nothing now, indeed, but the padding of the horse's hooves, and in the bush about them the low crooning of doves and the whistle of guinea-fowl. The horse went at an easy tripple. Though he hardly seemed to move, it was all that John could do to keep pace with him. They crossed three muddy rivulets flowing to join the Blauwkrans. The beast put down his head to drink, but John pulled him on.

A bare shoulder of down lay before them. Open ground spelt danger, so John swerved to the south along the stream for a while, keeping under the ridge and anxiously looking for bush to cover them; and soon, to his joy, they came to a cleft in the downs, thick with aloes and tufted fern-fronds and clumps of palmetto, through which the tiny stream ran; a silent and ghostly gully with steep crags on either hand. John looked at the sun lifting over the rocks to northward. He judged that they must have been on their way for three hours and travelled, perhaps, fifteen miles; but the danger of the open hillside had beaten them off their course, and they were possibly nearer the Blauwkranz line than they reckoned, so he dared not halt yet.

The kloof ran on into the mass of the hills. It appeared to widen in front of them as they plodded upward, at a walking pace now. The stream had shrunk to a trickle. Before it vanished it would be well to let the horse drink and to slake their parched throats as well. Lisbet suddenly spoke:

"John. . . . There's something the matter with Hendrik. When I speak, he doesn't answer. His head hangs down. He lies limp in my arms."

"The child's fainted, perhaps. We will stop for a moment. Let me lift him down, and we'll see."

He took little Hendrik from Lisbet's arms. The child's trousers were stuck to the saddle-bow with a glaze like dark varnish, and Lisbet's dress, too, was sodden and stiffened where he had pressed against her.

"He must have been wounded and never told us," John said.

"Oh, John. . . . Why didn't he speak? Not a word did he say. The horse's shoulders are sticky too. He has fainted from loss of blood."

John Oakley laid the child tenderly on the ground. His face, in its bloodless pallor, showed the refinement of feature Jacoba had given to Lisbet and Barend; it was smooth and miraculously delicate, a mask moulded in wax. John stripped the blood-stiffened leather from the small, perfect body. An assegai-wound in the groin had severed the veins, but the wound no longer bled. John put his ear to the child's chest and listened intently. The small heart gave no flutter; the skin was blanched and cold. This was no faint. He knew it now. He looked up at Lisbet, speechless.

"What is it?" she cried. She slipped down from the horse and joined him. "I see . . ." she said. "He is dead." She was pale as death herself. "He was trying to be brave, that was it, and never told me. But what can we do? Oh, John, tell me: what can we do?"

His heart yearned for her in her distress, yet he knew this was no time for tenderness.

"We cannot take him with us," he said. "We are not out of danger. You are living, and you come first."

"But we cannot leave him here, John."

"We must leave him here. The ground is hard, but I will do what I can with my knife."

"I have a knife too," she said.

She knelt down beside him. Between them, with knives and fingers, they scooped and scrabbled a hole in the ground by the stream where the soil was softest. The grave they dug was shallow, but deep enough to hold that small body.

"I think that will do," John Oakley said at last.

"Yes, that will do. Lay him gently in it and cover him, John. I will not look. I don't want to see any more."

She turned aside with her hands to her eyes. "She is praying," John thought; "I ought to pray too, but can there be a God in this cruel world?" He gazed at Lisbet's small desolate figure in its blood-sodden skirt. His heart was full of pity and sorrow, but fuller of

T*

love. Tears came to his eyes. But when Lisbet dropped her torn hands from hers there were no tears in them. They met his with sorrowful courage. He held out his arms to her; but she only shook her head.

"We must go, my love, my sweet, brave love," he said in a broken voice. "Let me help you to mount."

She put her foot in his hand and lifted herself by the blood-stained saddle-bow.

"Which way?" she asked.

The sun was now almost overhead. He had difficulty, for a moment, in finding his bearings.

"At the top of this kloof," he said, "we may catch sight of the Berg and see where we ought to go."

She sighed heavily. "Does it matter where we go, John? This day is so full of fire and blood that I feel as if nothing mattered any more."

"Yet you and I are living," he said. "And we are together."

"Yes . . . we are together, John. That is something."

"To me it is everything in this life," he said quickly.

She did not reply. But he did not care now whether she answered him or no. In that moment of utter bitterness and distress, while the wings of death still shadowed them, he had spoken, at last, the words that, unspoken, had burdened his heart overbearingly for seven months. As he walked beside her now he was no longer in his own eyes a footsore bedraggled fugitive, but a hero superbly exultant and magnified in a pride of spirit transcending the mere accidents of life or of death. Though they were alone in the world, and that world full of horror and desolation, this proud moment was his—inalienably his and eternal. The world was his; and Lisbet, that uncomely, pitiful figure astride of the sweating horse, with her small, pale, suffering face, was to him the mystical chalice of all beauty, of all desire, of all hope, of all aspiration.

In this tumultuous silence they reached the head of the kloof. Over fold beyond fold of rolling land, the peaks of the Drakensbergen rose magnificently into a sky that ached with heat. The sun was now slanting rapidly westward, but the face of the Berg with its grilled scarps of bare rock and flutings of timbered chasms stood up sheer as a wall, impassable as it seemed.

Yet now their direction was sure. John knew that through three or four invisible gaps in the blank escarpment the trek-paths the wagons had followed crawled down to the foothills. If they kept the Berg on their right hand, he told himself, and moved parallel with it, they were certain, sooner or later, to strike one of these. And then? . . . It was hard to say what came next. He had no means of telling how deeply or how disastrously the Zulu wave of destruction had penetrated. For all he knew, Maritz's laager and Retief's headquarters at Dorenkop might have been swept away or engulfed like their own little camp. There was still danger behind them to threaten what to him was dearer than life. The nearer the Berg the safer, he thought.

Yet the main plan held good; for even if all the folk were driven to retreat, they must surely still use the trek-paths by which they had come. In all that desolation he knew of no other promise of safety.

They toiled on till the hot sun dipped to the crest of the Berg; its shadow crept over the rolling land towards them. John remembered the prophetic word old Adrian had spoken when first he saw that encroaching darkness below him: "Woe to the land," he had said as he turned away, "that has shadows on its borders!"—and surely the shadow of woe had fallen on them. The sun sank; for a moment the mountain's crenellations were rimmed with white fire. Then a warm dusk fell on the foothills. Neither he nor Lisbet had spoken a word since the tragic, triumphant moment of their avowal. Though his heart bled for her in her silence, he had not dared to break it. It was she who spoke first.

"I am thirsty," she said.

"We will go on till we reach a stream. There is plenty of water in these hills, so we ought to come on one presently."

"I hope it will not be long," she said. "The horse must be thirsty too. He has stumbled twice. That means he is tired. And it will soon be dark."

"No wonder he's tired: I rode sixty miles on him yesterday."

"Yesterday," she repeated. "Was it only yesterday?"

They dropped from the shoulder of downland into a

shallower valley. A slow rivulet, fringed with tall reeds, twisted through the sodden bottom, reflecting a steely light. Night was falling rapidly now. He was glad they had come on water so soon; for it was still the dark of the moon, and night would be black and trackless. When they reached the stream Lisbet checked her horse, and he held out his arms to help her dismount. She put her hands on his shoulders and slid from the saddle into his arms. It was the first time in his life they had known that precious burden; he had never dreamed it could be so light and her body so fragile. But now, as he held her, the hands that clutched his shoulders relaxed. Her body lay limp in his arms as the body of little Hendrik. Panic terror seized him. He was not wise in such matters, and for a moment he feared she was dead. As he laid her down on the ground her white face lolled over helplessly. He ran to the stream, floundering knee-deep in spongy mosses; he brought back water in his hat and sluiced her face. That instant of doubt and fear was the most agonized through which he would ever live. He bent over her, calling her name and kissing the small, pale face dabbled with water until, at last, she opened her eyes. They surveyed him solemnly, huge and black in the dusk.

"What happened?" she whispered. She put her hands to her head. "Did I fall? My hair is wet. Is it blood?"

"You fainted, I think—and no wonder!"

"Was that it?" she said mildly. "How strange! I remember nothing. When I woke I didn't even know where I was. Now it all comes back." She shivered. "My mouth is so dry."

He returned to the stream for another hatful of water. He raised her head and helped her to drink, clumsily spilling it over her.

"That's enough," she said. "It chokes me. I'll have some more later."

He took off his coat and stuffed it under her head. She lay gazing at him, mutely, solemnly, with a mild and puzzled air as though she were a sleepy child and he some kind stranger. There was no movement in her body but that of the quick, shallow breathing that stirred her breast; but there was more colour now, he thought, in her pure, pale face. Its suffering beauty wrung his heart, yet its remoteness disarmed him: there was nothing more, it seemed, for him to do or say. She raised her hand feebly, groping for his. It was torn and muddy and caked with blood and mortally cold. He took it and kissed it.

"I am better now," she said faintly, "but my head still swims. I don't think I could go any farther just yet—unless you say that we must," she added submissively.

"It's too dark to go on, my love," he said. "But even if it were light, I couldn't let you. We will stay here till dawn. Lie quiet while I make a bed for you."

He pulled armfuls of grass and strewed them thick on the slope above the stream, where the ground was drier. The horse stood knee-deep in water, cooling his legs as he drank. John envied the beast. He would gladly have followed his example. Now that he had stopped running and walking, he was aware of a mortal fatigue: his legs seemed no more to belong to him. When he had made a soft, sweet-smelling bed of grass for Lisbet he staggered back to her.

"All is ready," he said. "Put your arms round my neck while I lift you."

She obeyed, and he carried her over to the bed of grass and laid her down.

"Is that better?" She nodded. "Then I'll fetch you another drink. I'll have a look in the saddle-bag too. There may be some biltong left over from yesterday . . . the day before yesterday—I forget. It's twenty-four hours since either of us has tasted food."

The horse still stood in the stream luxuriously cooling his feet. It would have been kind, John thought, to off-saddle him and let him roll; but fear checked the impulse: though the danger might be remote, it was best to let him graze knee-haltered and ready to start at a moment's warning. He filled his hat again from the stream and drank the sweetest draught he had ever tasted. When he had slaked his thirst he searched in the saddle-bag. Not a shred of biltong was left in it, as he might have known. He remembered one of Jan Bothma's horrific stories—how he had boasted that once, half-dead with hunger, he had chewed his horse's reims.

He laughed at such an idea. They were surely too near the trek-paths now for them to come to that. But the reminder of Jan Bothma himself that the story brought to him checked his laughter. It was to Jan Bothma, the huge, intemperate braggart who had persecuted him and whom he had hated in return, that Lisbet and he owed their lives. The man had loved her —there was no doubt about that—and had willingly offered the double sacrifice of his hopes of her and his life. There was a splendour in this that awed John and made his own love, exalted and ecstatic as it was, seem poor and unsubstantial. This man whom, in his heart, he had always disliked and often despised, had a nobility, a magnitude of soul that made him feel humble. That last act had imposed upon him the heaviest obligation a man could bear. He was ready to acknowledge this; but what was the use? Such a debt could be acknowledged, but never paid.

The memory of that final, heroic scene, of the great buffalo-bull dragged down and broken up by the howling pack, lay heavy on him as he stumbled back through the dark with his hat full of water to Lisbet's side.

"There is no biltong left. We should have thought of that," he said; "but I've brought you another drink, if you think you can manage it."

She drank gladly. "I'm more myself now," she said, "if there is any self left. I begin to remember. . . .

Oh, John, shall we ever forget?" she asked pitifully.

He heard her draw a sharp gasping breath, and then she was crying. He put his arms round her and held her. She clung to him, burying her face in his neck; the sobs that shook her body shook him too and harrowed him. Yet he was utterly impotent. There was nothing to say—no word of love could have soothed her —and nothing to do but hold her and let the movements of her shaken body spend themselves and steady themselves, maybe, on his. He lay there, holding her close, with a set face, until the fury of the storm subsided, until the rhythm of her sobbing was broken into long, shuddering breaths, and at last she was still. Though she still trembled and caught her breath from time to time, he knew that the worst of the agony was over. He kissed her wet eyes gently and loosened his arms.

"Where are you going?" she cried.

"I ought to knee-halter the horse. If I don't, he may stray. I would light a fire to keep off the lions if I dared. But that is too great a risk. He must take his chance."

"You'll come back to me, won't you?" she pleaded.

"Of course I'll come back."

"And don't go far away. It's so dark."

"I'll be as quick as I can, and then I'll come to you."

He returned to the stream and led the horse up the bank and knee-haltered him. Then he returned to

Lisbet, and lay down beside her and took her in his arms. She pressed close to him. He kissed her dry lips.

"You must never leave me again, my dear love," she said. "I am so weak and so lonely."

"I will never leave you again by God's grace," he said, "so long as I live."

CHAPTER NINE

BLOOD RIVER

AT sunset on the following evening they reached the track that hundreds of wagons had worn bare in their descent from the pass called Van Reenen's. The new day had broken with disaster. In the night, a lion had found the knee-haltered horse an easy prey. They slept so heavily, out of sheer fatigue, that the sound of the brief struggle had not awakened them, and it was only when John rose at dawn to make sure the animal had not strayed that he came on its gnawed carcass, half-stripped to the bone by hyenas.

This was a cruel blow. They were both of them already so weakened by want of food that their drugged sleep had not refreshed them. Though he believed that he could force himself by sheer power of will to push on to the end, he had been counting on the horse to spare Lisbet's strength. As he gazed at the mangled carrion, he had half a mind to cut a few strips from it to stay their aching hunger; but the sight so revolted him that he shrank from the bloody task. Other gloating eyes were already fixed on the carcass. A congregation of vultures, which the busy hyenas and jackals had kept at a distance, sat perched on the thorn-trees encircling the spot where the poor beast had fallen. As he turned, they flopped down in scores, grotesquely waddling, and settled on it in triumph, fighting for what was left.

John walked back to Lisbet despondently and told her his news. She took the disaster more lightly than he.

"Why, then, now we are equal," she said serenely. "I couldn't have borne to ride when you were walking."

Her bravery gave him new heart; though it was of her strength that he had been doubtful rather than of her courage: in the morning light she looked so small and frail. Yet he need not have doubted. She came of a hardier stock, perhaps, than he. Many times during that endless day he was forced to confess that he would have been glad to halt when she was prepared to go on. If he had given her of his strength on the night before, it was her spirit, her resolution that now sustained him.

By the time they met the wagon-track, he was near the end of his tether. It was a moment of chilling bathos. All day they had driven themselves to reach this goal, and now they had reached it at last, it seemed as though they were in no better case than when they started. There was no sign of life or succour. East and west, the wide, dusty trek-path rolled away emptily. On either hand the thorn-bush burned in the gold of sunset, empty and silent. They stood and gazed at each other hopelessly. It was Lisbet who broke the silence of defeat at last.

"We can do nothing now but stay here till to-morrow," she said. "If the folk are driven back, some will surely pass this way, and others may be coming down from the Berg. Who knows? Let us lie here and rest and hope. There is nothing else."

"If we had to go on, I don't think I could do it," he said.

She took his hand. "Come, then," she said gently; "let us take off our shoes; and later, when we are rested, perhaps we will find some water and bathe our feet." She smiled tenderly, and spoke to him as if he were a tired child.

They sat down on the edge of the track side by side. The leather of John's *veldschoens* was stuck to his blistered feet; he winced as he moved them, yet the relief of easing their constriction was very heaven.

"Now let me take yours off," he said. He loosened the latchet and saw her set her teeth. Her feet were no more swollen or blistered than his, but the sight of them hurt him. "Your little feet, my darling, your poor little feet," he said. He fondled and kissed them, torn, swollen and begrimed as they were. Lisbet gently protested.

"Do you love me so much as that?" she said wistfully. "You make me ashamed."

He shook his head. "If I could say how I loved you!" There was no part of her body that was not meet for his service and worship.

They sat down, hand-in-hand, for a while and did

not speak. The shadow of the Berg crept over them, quenching the fire of the transfigured bush. John felt he must rouse himself.

"It will soon be dark," he said. "I must try to find water. It will be safe to fire now. If I take Hendrik's little gun I might shoot a small buck or a guinea-fowl."

He looked round, as though expecting to find it. It was not there. It came over them both together that the child must have dropped it when his dying fingers relaxed as he sat between Lisbet's arms. So confused were their minds that neither had thought of it.

"Oh, John!" she said. "Hendrik's little gun—and he was so proud of it!"

"I will go none the less," he said. "But I won't leave you for long. If we can't eat, we will drink."

He crossed the track barefooted: his feet were too swollen for him to force his shoes on again, and so pulped that they had no more feeling. He entered the bush and waved to her and Lisbet waved back to him. Then he stopped of a sudden and listened. A new sound broke the evening silence: the rumble of wagon-wheels jolting over the uneven earth. Then he heard a shout and the pistol-crack of a whip, and threw up his arms in joy as he ran to rejoin her.

It was a little *trekkie* of poor folk on their way to Natal from the Sneeuwbergen. They had come down over the Berg that morning and were looking for an open space in which to outspan. When they saw the two haggard, bedraggled figures in the track, the men came forward with guns in their hands. They were uncouth, half-savage folk who lived lonely, precarious lives and regarded all strangers with wary hostility. Their ramshackle wagons seemed hardly fit for the road; their cattle looked weedy, degenerate, and several of the men showed traces of Hottentot blood. They listened in grudging silence as Lisbet told them her story, and seemed disinclined to believe it.

"Andries Pretorius of Graaf Reinet has sent round the word that Natal is empty, and the Zulus friendly," their leader said. "That is why we have trekked."

"If what this young man says is true," a sallow half-caste muttered, "we had better turn back. There is good country beyond the Vaal."

"What is this you are saying, Dirk van den Berg?" a tall, gaunt woman, with a furrowed face like a man's, cried indignantly. "If the Zulus have fallen on the people there will be need of men; we must go on and help them. If you want to go back, we can do without you."

"My wife is right," the leader of the *trekkie* said. "We will not outspan. We will trek on through the night as far as we can. Give the young man a horse. His wife can ride in the wagon with the other women."

"Give us food, uncle, first of all," Lisbet pleaded. "We have tasted nothing for two days."

"I will see to that, never fear," the woman said. They ate ravenously from a pot full of shreds of mutton, swimming in grease and spiced with red peppers that pricked their throats. Before they had finished, the ramshackle wagons were under way. The gaunt woman took charge of Lisbet. Her manner was harsh and ungracious, but her heart was kindly.

"We must change your clothes," she said. "They are caked with dust and blood. You must have been wounded."

"It is my little brother's blood," Lisbet told her. "He bled to death as he lay in my arms and we buried him." Her voice broke on the words.

The gaunt woman's face hardened. "And that yellow-faced *schelm*, Dirk van den Berg, was for turning back! I am glad I made my husband go on. There is a heavy account to be settled."

John found himself slowly riding and sleeping by turns. He saw no more of Lisbet, but knew she was cared for. Now that the tension was over he suffered an intolerable reaction that obliterated all feeling. He was no longer capable of grief or of exultation. He rode on in a state of numbed nescience that was like a drugged sleep.

When they reached Maritz's great laager where those who had escaped from the scattered bivouacs on the Blauwkrans were concentrated, another blow fell on them. The news of the massacre at Dingaan's Great Place had just reached the camp by the mouth of its only survivor, a slave of Retief. They heard, too, the full story of the slaughter along the Blauwkrans. When the rescue parties had ridden out with Maritz it had been too late. In that night of blood and weeping, camp after camp had been beset and wiped out. Eighty men and women and twice as many children with more than two hundred and fifty servants had been slain.

The loss of life in that single night had been almost as heavy as that of the great Kaffir invasion of the Eastern Province in which Jacoba Prinsloo's sons had been killed. And this dark onslaught was even more terrible, not only in its swiftness but also in its savagery. On the eastern frontier the Kaffirs had spared women and children. On the Blauwkrans, there was no limit to the Zulus' lust for blood: there were stories of infants spitted in their cradles and mothers with children in their arms whose breasts had been sliced away before they were killed. All along the stream, where once the peaceful bivouacs of tilted wagons had stood, lay mounds of smouldering ash and strips of torn tenting, and wagons, overturned and smashed to matchwood, with their wheels in the air. Twenty thousand head of cattle had been driven away. But that was a matter of small importance. It was the voice of their owners' blood that called from the ground for vengeance. *In Rama was there a voice heard, lamentation and weeping and great mourning, Rachel weeping for her children, and would not be comforted, because they were not.* They called the place Weenen, Weeping. It is so named to this day.

But vengeance could not be yet. The Tugela flowed

swollen with rain and its drifts were impassable. The news of the massacre of Retief and his sixty men had stunned the community. They were leaderless now (for Gert Maritz was ailing and Piet Uys still refused to serve under him) and uncertain of their strength. Fierce rain persistently drenched the muddy laagers. Inaction and mourning weighed on folks' spirits. There were many, like yellow-faced Dirk van den Berg, who began to mutter the word that Natal was accursed. Better leave the Zulus to their victory, they murmured; better turn their backs on the Land of False Promise and recross the mountains to a country not bordered by shadows. It was only the steadfastness of the women that stiffened these fainter hearts. They were as stern in their attitude as the gaunt wife of the Sneeuwbergen, and nothing could move them. Vengeance was due. It was for their menfolk to take it. An eye for an eye. . . .

It seemed strange to John that a creature so mild as he had imagined Lisbet to be, should harbour such vindictive emotions. Yet so it was. Alone with him in their flight through the bush she had shown him, with all her courage, a gentleness that made her seem pitiable as a hurt child. There was nothing gentle or childlike about her now. She was a grown woman, as bright and hard as steel. He found it hard to fathom the causes which, in so short a time, could have changed the tender intimacy of those rapt and tragic hours into a remoteness of spirit that puzzled and almost intimidated him.

In his blind lover's impatience he failed to realize

how much greater than his her personal losses had been. In the numbness that followed the succession of cruel blows that had smitten her—first her father, and then Jacoba, and then little Hendrik—she herself had hardly been able to feel the extent of her desolation. In the wagon of the Sneeuwbergen's farmer's wife she had come to herself; the numbness had passed away; the power to feel and to suffer had come back. And then, as if this were not enough, on their return to the hurriedly improvised camp on the Bushman's River, where the sound of weeping and lamentation was still in the air, a heavier blow than any of these had fallen on her bruised spirit: the news of Sarel's death. It was this cumulation of woes, and the last the most bitter of all (for, from childhood, Sarel had been her second self), that turned Lisbet's face and heart to stone. Though she loved John none the less, it was beyond her power to show it. She knew that her frigid, unwilled remoteness hurt and bewildered him, but could not thaw it or bring herself nearer to him. There was a time to love, and this was not the time.

In their homelessness they had returned to the camp of Jacoba's friend Lenie Retief, who had lost her beloved son Pieter as well as her husband. Though John Oakley was willing and eager to play any part he could in that stricken household, though they treated him kindly, he found himself a stranger within their gates. These folk were Lisbet's own people, hers not only by common experience—and that of the most bitter—but by race and by language. She belonged to them more than to him. A barrier invisible but impassable like a wall of glass rose between him and her. It was none of Lisbet's making, he knew; but he could not pierce it as yet without doing violence to some part of her nature which he felt his love should respect. Only time, he told himself, could dissolve this barrier; and time is the lover's dourest enemy.

Yet another misfortune conspired to separate them. Though no living soul but one slave had escaped to tell the tale of Retief's disaster, rumours came to the laagers in plenty from the coast, and others were born of themselves in the idle camp. Folk would not be content to admit its true cause, Retief's mistaken confidence. The old prejudices rose from the graves in which, for a time, they had lain hidden. The English, of course, were responsible. After Retief's first visit to Dingaan, two Englishmen, named Garnett and Stubbs, had come from Natal. "What do you do with deserters who are unfaithful to their king?" they had asked. According to his laws, Dingaan said, such men must be put to death. "The Boers are just such deserters," Stubbs and Garnett had told him. Even Cane, who had lost his life in the cattle-kraal at Retief's side, and Owen, the missionary, were loaded with the same accusations. All four were emissaries of the Colonial Government, which had frowned on the trek and tried to spoil it from the first, and were determined, even now, to keep Natal for the British.

John Oakley, the only Englishman in the camp, felt the repercussions of these tales. However loyally he might have devoted himself to the trekkers' cause, however grievously he might have shared in their privations and dangers, he was known to be English—and that was enough to damn him and exclude him from being trusted. When he showed himself away from the Retiefs' encampment, black looks and whispers followed him.

There were many ways in which he could prove his willingness if not his fidelity. As soon as the rains began to decrease he borrowed a couple of boys and a span of oxen from the Retiefs, and drove them down to the Blauwkrans River to see what he could retrieve of the Prinsloos' belongings. There would be little movable property left in all probability; but such as there was, according to the Roman-Dutch law of inheritance, belonged now to Lisbet, Barend and Anna in equal portions.

He approached the ravaged camp from the south in a sombre mood, his mind steeled against the havoc and pathos he was prepared to find. One horror, at least, he was thankful to know, he would be spared: he would not be forced to set eyes on the mutilated dead; for on the day after the massacre, Maritz had sent out parties to collect the remains and bury them.

It came to him as a surprise when, rounding a bluff of the blue crags that gave the place its name, he found himself suddenly in sight of the Prinsloos' encampment. Seen thus from a distance the group of laagered wagons appeared to have suffered little from the enemy's violence. The tilts of the two new wagons shone white in the sun. The whole scene looked strangely peaceful. It was hard to believe that the camp was not still inhabited. As he rode towards it he almost expected to see old Adrian smoking his pipe on the wagon-seat and Jacoba, half asleep on her rest-bench, looking up to greet him with her slow, placid smile.

In the Blauwkrans raid, the Kaffirs had wrought less material destruction than usual. It had been planned, in fact, as an act of terrorism rather than depredation; its chief purpose was swift and indiscriminate slaughter. There had been no time for more; the Zulus had known what force could be mustered against them when once the surprise was over—so the flame of havoc had run like that of a grass-fire, leaping on from one bivouac to the next before its destruction was complete.

The Prinsloos' camp, which had not been one of the first to be attacked and, thanks to Daniel Bezuidenhout's warning, had been able to put up a fight, had come off more lightly than most. Only three wagons —the two that belonged to Jan Bothma and that which was packed with the heavier furniture from Welgelegen—had been overturned and burnt. The remaining five, though the three that stood next to Jan's had caught fire and were partially consumed, appeared little the worse for the onslaught, but the wagon-chests had been hurriedly rifled and their scattered contents lay sodden with rain amid the matchwood of splintered assegais. Only the tilts of the blue wagons from Graaf Reinet betrayed the numbers and fury of the attackers: John counted no less than two hundred holes in them through which stabbing-assegais had been thrust.

When he had surveyed the melancholy scene for a while, he set to work sorting the debris and then collecting it. Of that which was irreparably ruined, he made a great pyre in the midst of the charred remains of Jan Bothma's wagons which the rains had quenched before they had burnt themselves out. The two Hottentots worked with him at this task of salvage, picking out for themselves many pitiful damaged trifles that he rejected as useless. One of them, for some unfathomable reason of his own, had possessed himself of an object that looked like a wooden club. He whirled the ugly weapon round his head and seemed highly pleased with it. When John asked him what it was he handed it over reluctantly. It was a peg of hard oak, tipped with iron, expanded at the other end into a hollow boss to which strips of leather were nailed. John recognized it, with a shudder, as George Dicketts' wooden leg. The face of the man who had found it fell when he pitched it into the blaze.

The discovery of this grotesque relic shadowed his mind for the rest of the day; it moved him more deeply than any of the other reminders of mortality that he found Remorse tinged his grief. He reproached himself, remembering how often he had shown his impatience with the obstinate insularity of that brave little man. He remembered George's good humour, his staunchness, above all, his simplicity. When he came to think back over the hours they had spent together—in the *Minerva's* stinking 'tween-decks, during their flight through the bush, and the long days of trekking, and the nights when they had lain awake side by side gazing up at the pitiless, alien stars—he realized that in George he had lost (apart from Lisbet, who was more than friend) his only friend in the world. George Dicketts, he told himself, had been even more than that. He was the only tie that united him to his old English life, an unalterable symbol of the land to which he belonged and which he had so little cause to love—mere English in his kindness of heart, in the childish grumbling that masked his inherent cheerfulness, in his obstinacy, his stupidity, his indomitable courage. He remembered the rapt, the almost mystical devotion with which, as they lay in the dark, George Dicketts had babbled of the green fields of Grafton Lovett, of the cuckoos that called and the lambs that frisked in the growing grass of Tom Collins's field, Long Dragon. They seemed nearer and clearer now and of a more poignant sweetness than at the time when George Dicketts had spoken of them, and, in his present state of lonely frustration, more desirable. This was the first time since he had set foot in Africa that John had felt homesick.

It was with difficulty that he extracted himself from this treacherous mood. Its proper corrective was fierce physical labour. For three days he toiled incessantly at the work of salvage, driving his Hottentots till they dropped. By the fourth, when he returned to Mevrouw Retief's camp with the first wagon loaded, he had mastered it and become himself again. On the homeward journey he had made up his mind to talk seriously with Lisbet. He waylaid her that evening, and drew her aside. She seemed to him pale and unsubstantial as a little ghost. Her face was drawn and set; it had lost its alertness; her eyes looked as if they could never smile. She was thinner, too—and this was hardly surprising, for the laagers were short of any food but millet.

"I must talk with you, Lisbet," he said. "I never see you alone now. We always seem to have people staring at us."

"That isn't my fault, John. Mevrouw Retief is kind to have given us shelter, and we ought to be grateful. And how can I be with you more? There are so many orphans to be cared for, and wounded, too. That is a woman's work. I am helping the Italian woman Teresa, and glad to do it. I think you are impatient, John."

"Of course I am impatient. I love you. When I do not see you I might as well not be alive. I had thought

U

you would feel the same . . . but it seems you don't."

"And so you are angry with me?"

"I couldn't be angry with you, because I love you. But I think I have a right to be a little impatient. Now listen to me, my darling. Things are not as bad as they might have been: we have not lost everything. During the next few days I shall go down again to the Blauwkrans and bring back four more wagons. Then we must begin to think of the future."

"The future?"

"Our future, Lisbet. We love one another, and we are both of us alone in the world. Why should we go on living apart, as if we were strangers, not lovers? We can make a home of our own now. Why shouldn't we be married?"

She was silent for a moment. He saw the distress in her face. She loved him and found it difficult to make herself understood without wounding him. It was like explaining a complicated thing to a child.

"Oh, John," she said gently, "I know this is hard for you. I don't blame you for being impatient. But we cannot be married yet, my love. If you lived all day in the midst of so much pain and weeping, I know you would feel as I do. When I marry you, I must come to you with an open heart and a happy conscience. I must give you all of myself and feel it is right. But I cannot give myself now. Myself is not mine to give. It belongs, it ought to belong, in part, to those who have lost everything and have nothing more to look for. Can't we spare them a little of our happiness, John?"

"A little! I see you working yourself to the bone. There'll soon be nothing left of you. I have a right to protect you. You are giving your life to these people!"

"They are my people, not yours. No, no . . ." (For she saw she had hurt him.) "I don't wish you to think they mean more to me than you. My heart is all yours, and you know it. But I belong to them too, in a different way. We are a small people, hardly more than one large family. A quarrelsome family, you may say, for you've seen our quarrels; but when woe falls on us, it draws us closer together, the women even more than the men. I am a Boer woman: my loving you doesn't alter that. My blood tells me what I must do, and I must obey it. That is what my mother and Sarel would have said. Can't you understand?"

John Oakley was gloomily silent. Though he knew her strength, he had not foreseen this obstinacy. Jacoba and Sarel were dead, and he was alive. He was hungered beyond reason. He resented the domination of these imperious ghosts. "If she loved me as I love her," he thought, "there would be no talk of duty."

His silence did not discourage her. "And apart from that," she went on, "this is no time for marrying. Our hearts are too heavy. And the danger is not yet over. Remember the Zulus are not beaten yet . . ."

"Isn't that all the more reason why we should grasp our happiness while we can have it?" he cried.

Lisbet shook her head. "There is an account to be settled—we are all of one mind on that—and until it is settled we must not weaken our will by other thoughts. When Dingaan is beaten and you come back to me, my darling, then I will marry you."

He laughed harshly: "And if I should not come back?"

"Why, then, I think, my heart would be broken, and I would rather die."

With this confession he was forced to content himself. If it did not quench his impatience, it assuaged some of the doubts which, in the worst moments, had frightened him. At least one of the obstacles to their marrying seemed likely to be removed before long. Maritz had sent a party down to the Port in the hope of hearing more details of Retief's disaster and enlisting the Englishmen's aid in a combined movement against Dingaan. Other messengers had ridden back over the Berg to implore the help of the dissidents, Potgieter and Uys. It was no longer a question of Dutch against English or Uys against Maritz, but of black against white. For the moment, the black man was uppermost. The whole future of white settlement—not only in Natal, but anywhere beyond the colonial border—depended now on Dingaan's being defeated—and the sooner the better; for the Tugela's floods had fallen, and the initiative lay with the side that could use it first.

So Piet Uys, that fiery man, came sweeping down

from the High Veld over the Drakensbergen with his turbulent followers, and Hendrik Potgieter followed. John and Lisbet had half expected (and dreaded) that Barend would ride with the Potgieter clan to divide what was left of his parents' property and take his own portion and Anna's back with him. But Barend, it seemed from his wife's kinsmen's reports, was deep-sunk in domesticity and no longer adventurous. He had staked out six thousand acres of land on the grassy slopes of the Witwatersrand, the Ridge of White Waters, and built for his delicate wife a *pondakkie* hut in which, anxiously, they awaited the birth of their first-born.

John and Lisbet were glad of this news. Though Barend was softened by marriage, they could not believe that he had shed his old violent prejudices. They knew there would be the devil to pay when he found that his sister had taken up with a *verdomde* Englishman. There was conflict enough in the camp already without the gratuitous addition of a family quarrel.

The contest repeated itself with a slight permutation. At Winburg and Tafelkop, the Potgieters and Uys had been ranged against Piet Reticf and Maritz. Now Retief was dead, and a canonized hero; so, for want of a common enemy, Uys and Potgieter must needs fly at each other's throats, while Maritz, a tired man with little fight left in him, kept the ring. It was the old story of conflicting prestige. Potgieter, the older man, would not take his orders from Uys: Uys, proud of his daring (and not without reason), refused to serve under Potgieter. In the end, Maritz wearily gave Uys the nominal command. Potgieter, grumbling and hating both of them, could not turn back, for shame, when he had come so far and so much was at stake.

The two forces, three hundred and fifty men in all, rode out, together and yet divided, to the Tugela drifts. John, with little enthusiasm for either, attached himself to Potgieter's. He was sick of love for Lisbet, who still withheld herself, and could think of nothing else. His comrades were resolute men, determined on righteous vengeance; yet somehow, it seemed, the faith that was in them burned fitfully, beclouded by memories of the Blauwkrans massacres and Retief's death, and lacking the draught of a single leader's enthusiasm.

They followed the track John had taken before on the long reconnaisance, and crossed the Buffalo River into the country of tumbled hillocks from which the grizzled Zulu had turned them back; and there, in a stony defile, the battle broke. Dingaan's warriors held the hill-sides on either side of them. Potgieter's force rode up the slopes to the left, and Uys's to the right. Uys whirled through the black host with his native impetuosity, while Potgieter, cautious as usual, moved on more slowly; was checked and retreated. Piet Uys, his first fierce impetus spent, found himself trapped and encircled. His men fought their way out of the ring through the gap their slugs had blasted; but Uys and his son lost their lives.

The place was called Italeni, and a brave man died there.

So the *Vlugcommando,* as the people had boldly called it, rode back to headquarters, dispirited and defeated. Their return was a bitter blow to the waiting laagers. There was far less talk of speedy vengeance now. John Oakley had only one consolation in the wretched business: an assegai wound in the shoulder that would not heal and gave him a better excuse for Lisbet's company. But the folk were crushed in spirit, and even more discouraged when messengers from the Port brought the news that the English settlers, too, had been scattered and driven to take refuge in the swamps by the sea.

The old murmurs arose. There was a curse on this country, men said; the sooner it was abandoned, the better for all. The old quarrels, too. Potgieter was the villain of the piece; he had called back his men and retreated when victory was in his grasp, leaving all the spare horses and arms to fall into the Zulus' hands; he had left Piet Uys to fend for himself and to die, out of spite, out of jealousy. Maritz held his hand and let the storm hurtle about him. Perhaps he was not ill-pleased to see that Potgieter had hanged himself in the rope he had given him. He had never liked Blauwberg Potgieter, nor yet had Retief. If Retief could have heard how folk spoke of Blauwberg now, they would have laughed at the joke together. But his friend was dead and still unavenged, and Mariz himself a sick man.

Potgieter could not take these recriminations so easily. He was no match for his enemies in words, but deeds spoke louder. He gathered his men together and rode back sullenly over the Berg to the High Veld. The others could call him a traitor as loudly as they liked, but that was not an encouragement for him to risk his life for them. Let them fight their own battles and be damned to them: he had finished with them and with Natal. Many more would have followed him, if their women had let them.

He rode away; and then, once more, the rains broke.

Old Smit might thunder his three-hour-long jeremiads from the pulpits of all the scattered camps; the laagers themselves might be turned into permanent fortresses with turf walls and loopholed palisades; but the people inside them were hungry, and sad, and faint-hearted. They lifted their eyes to the hills, but no help came to them. They lived in a state of siege—beleaguered doubly by the unvanquished Zulu hosts and the sluicing rains. In September, Gert Maritz died.

Retief, Uys, and now Maritz. . . . Of the trek's first leaders only one was now left—and he, Hendrik Potgieter, the traitor, had washed his hands of them.

This was the Great Trek's nadir. It lay spent and helpless at the feet of the Drakensbergen, uncomforted by Father Smit's sermons and waiting for an angel to trouble the waters. It seemed little use sending appeals for more help over the mountains now. Since Potgieter's return to the High Veld with his own story of the scurvy manner in which he had been used, nobody even troubled to answer them. It seemed as though they were utterly forgotten, until, suddenly, in October, a ship dropped anchor in Port Natal laden with stores of all kinds, a gift from their kinsmen at the Cape. Besides flour and rice, she brought coffee, sugar, spices and tea: all the minor luxuries that might make tolerable the staple diet of millet-meal on which they had subsisted for months. Transport-wagons carried these up from the East; and now, from the West came a word of good cheer that was even more welcome: Andries Pretorius of Graaf Reinet was already approaching the Berg with plentiful reinforcements of men and arms and ammunition. Arms and ammunition were good enough; they had need of both; but what they needed still more was a leader of spirit to whom they could rally, and here, by the grace of God, was their man.

Andries Pretorius. . . . It was a well-sounding name for a builder of victory. John Oakley had seen him once and heard him speak when he had swung down over the Berg in his horse-wagon and visited Retief's laager: a tall fellow, heavily built, with a stolid face, who, for all his shrewdness and comfortable air of substance, appeared to lack Maritz's fire and the transparent goodness that had made Retief, in his simplicity, seem a great man. Yet one recommendation Pretorius had besides the material resources he commanded: he had taken no part in the tragic schisms which, more than all else, had wrecked the trekkers' enterprise. He was a new man, a strong man, the only man for that bankrupt hour. And the folk were sick of taking part in other men's quarrels.

The word of his coming was enough. Immediately the camps came to life with new hopes and new energy. Not only the men but also the women turned to, grinding flints, moulding slugs and bullets and cleaning gunbarrels. Gert Maritz's scrap-iron cannon was pulled out and remounted, though rumour said that Pretorius was bringing a bronze piece of his own. When, riding ahead of his force, he reached Maritz's old headquarters, Pretorius was greeted with flattering salvos and cheers. His confident humour bred further confidence. All his movements were business-like: there was no trace of Maritz's cavalier *panache* or Retief's quiet mysticism about him. As soon as the people had accepted him as Commandant-General, he made his hand felt. That was what they were wanting: they saw there would be no more bickerings over religion or precedence while he was in charge, and no more time wasted. This was a man who "deferred not to do."

During the week that followed his arrival his forces increased miraculously. At Italeni, Potgieter and Uys between them had disposed of three hundred and fifty men. Pretorius could rely on nearly five hundred, well-armed, in addition to a small detachment of Englishmen from the Port and a body of Zulu deserters. Five divisions he made, each counting a hundred guns, under five Field-Commandants. Behind them would move a train of fifty-seven wagons and the two cannon.

It was surprising, John thought, how the inspiration of a single man (and one who had not struck him as being remarkable) had changed the whole situation in so short a time. The whole camp was in roaring high spirits. Old Father Smit rose to the occasion with a stirring sermon. It did not even trouble him to know that, once out of sight, his lay rival, Sarel Cilliers, would be able to preach at his flock to his heart's content. Even the farewells of the departing commando were untinged with doubt or dread. They rode out on their righteous errand with a gallant air amid rattling salvos of musketry. For the first time in months they had powder to spare.

John said good-bye to Lisbet on the night before his departure. The wound in his shoulder was still unhealed, for Zulu assegai-blades were as foul as a lion's teeth; but the arm that lifted his gun and aimed it was whole, and nothing else mattered. He was amazed at the change the last few days had wrought in her. The shadows which had puzzled and even intimidated him were gone. She was gay and serenely confident, yet no less tender. Her eyes glowed; her mouth was no longer set and sombre.

"When you come back," she said, "we will begin our lives over again. You have been so good and patient, my darling, and I know you have suffered. But the bad days are over now and will soon be forgotten."

"If only I know you are happy," he said. "That is all I ask."

"Can't you see how happy I am to-night . . . and how proud?" she said.

Four of Pretorius's divisions rode out at daybreak. In a few days, moving northwards and inland, they had crossed the Tugela's tributaries near their sources. Here they waited for Landman's, the fifth. Then, turning seaward again, they approached the Buffalo River and laagered their wagons. The recent disasters had taught Pretorius that lesson, and he was taking no risks. He knew that he would not have long to wait. The presence of a force so powerful within his borders was a challenge which Dingaan could hardly refuse to accept. As yet the scouting patrols had encountered few of the enemy; but prisoners and deserters all told the same story: the Zulus were massing: if Dingaan wanted to keep them together the onslaught could not be delayed.

They moved forward again, more cautiously. These

were great days for Sarel Cilliers. There was no jealous official predikant to stop his preaching now. Every evening, when prayers were said and sung, he harangued the commando at unctuous length: Pretorius knew his own people, and gave him his way. They waited for Jacobus Uys, who still lagged behind. It was fitting that he should be with them, for Pieter was still remembered. When he had come, they kept the Sabbath at a deserted village which they had called Dancekraal. It was a solemn occasion. As soon as the prayers were finished Sarel Cilliers mounted on one of the gun-carriages and spoke to over four hundred men.

"My brethren and fellow-countrymen," he said. "At this moment we stand before the holy God of heaven and earth to make a promise, if He will be with us and protect us, and deliver the enemy into our hands so that we may triumph over him: that we shall observe the day and the date as an anniversary in each year, and a day of thanksgiving like the Sabbath, in His honour; and that we shall enjoin our children that they must take part with us in this, for a remembrance even for our posterity. And if anyone sees a difficulty in this, let him retire from the place. For the honour of His name will be joyfully exalted, and to Him the fame and the honour of the victory must be given." Then he lifted his hands to heaven in the name of them all. "Will you swear this oath with me, brethren?" he asked.

Four hundred and seven men raised their right hands in answer.

"We swear it," they said.

They rode on for another week, burning the winter-dry grass as they went, heading straight for Dingaan's Great Place, and encamped, ready to rest on the following Sabbath, in the loop of a stream that ran through a deep ravine. As they laagered their fifty wagons in a square, scouts rode up with the news that the hills on every side were black with all Zululand. Sarel Cilliers, exalted with prayer, was for an immediate attack, but Pretorius would have none of it. "Here we will keep the Sabbath," he said. So they interlocked and chained the wheels of their wagons, unlimbered their cannon, and lay down at their firing stations, waiting for dawn.

But the Zulus had less patience. They were seven thousand strong and full of fight. In faint starlight, just before daybreak, the first wave of attack swept down from the hills, the foremost rank armed with muskets taken from Retief. As they advanced, the side of the laager that faced them crackled into fire, the rapid, withering fire that the Matabele had tasted already, but the bulk of the Zulu army had never yet faced. The great wave leapt in the air, its crest torn away like that of a surge that is broken on jagged reefs. A new crest formed and rolled on, and that, too, was broken. Four times the ranks re-formed and swept forward over the swathes of dead. Four times the line was shattered. It was clear daylight now: the defenders could see the sights of their guns; but there was hardly need for sighting—they fired into the brown and saw the compact masses dissolve before them.

It was pure slaughter now. John Oakley could never remember how many shots he fired. He was no more than one among four hundred machines of destruction, pouring handfuls of powder and slugs un-rammed into the burning barrel and shooting point-blank at the sea of black yelling faces through the veil of powder-smoke that rose straight as a plumb-line from the ground in front of the laager. He only knew that the hair of his face was singed with heat, his hand blistered by the hot gun-barrel, his wounded shoulder bruised to pulp with the gun's recoil, so that each shot was an agony. But still, wondering when the heat of the gun would discharge it and blow off his hand, he poured in his charge of slugs and powder and fired.

He heard, above the tumult, a voice that roared: "Open the gates . . . both gates!" A hundred and fifty men who had been warned for the sortie leapt to their horses. The barriers were opened, and out they poured to converge in a crescent, firing from the saddle as they rode. Two thousand Zulus between them stood motion-less, stricken dumb with this new horror. The mass seemed to wilt as it stood. It wavered inward and broke and ran for the hills.

The victory was won, but the slaughter was not yet over. From the deep ravine which the river closed at its lower end there was no escaping. Here dead Zulus in hundreds lay on the ground like pumpkins on a rich soil that has borne a large crop. The wounded who fled plunged into the river or, fearing its depth, sank down in the rushes that fringed it and gave up the ghost. Like a pool of blood the river lay that morning. It is still called Blood River.

By noon all was finished. Not a living Zulu was in sight.

That evening there were high thanksgivings, with some boasting and self-laudation that troubled poor Sarel Cilliers more than a little. But next day there was no time for either. Pretorius, determined not to lose grasp of the victory, gave orders for the laager to be broken and the force to advance. John Oakley rode on in a dream. His ears were deafened by gunshots. His shoulder was stiff as though it were broken and the right arm useless. They moved onward steadily for three days till they reached the ridge where once Mr. Owen's wagons had stood, looking down on the oval kraal of Umgungundhlovu. The Great Place had been fired. The ringed huts and the royal house were mounded ashes, from whose smoulder a haze of smoke and fierce heat rose so high that not even a vulture could be seen in the quivering vault.

They rode silently past the great fig-tree where Retief had rested, the three gaunt euphorbias about which the horses had been tethered and the arms piled; they followed the track over which Retief's men had been dragged to the Hill of Execution; and there, on the noisome top, they found their scattered remains, their bony wrists still bound by thongs of untanned hide. Men moved from one to another, identifying their friends as best they could; and that was not easy, for the vultures had done their work thoroughly. That Golgotha had been strewn with all the carnage of Dingaan's bloody reign; and there is no great difference between a white man and a black man when each is stripped to the bone. Here and there, as they passed in silence from victim to victim, the shape of a head, the lack of a thumb or finger, or some remembered detail of clothing, brought them to a halt. John tried his best and failed to find Sarel Prinsloo's body; but Retief's impaled corpse, which lay apart from the rest, was recognizable by all. It still wore his glossy waistcoat, and, over the shoulder, the leather wallet into which he had stuffed the concession Dingaan had signed: the title-deeds of Natal. There they buried the bones of him and his men in a great pit dug for all on the crown of the Hill of Execution. There they lie to this day, remembered.

Andries Pretorius did not tarry. He rode on in pursuit.

CHAPTER TEN

FOUNTAIN OF WONDER

THE news of the fight at Blood River reached the anxious laagers on Christmas Day, but the *Wincommando*, as it was called, did not return till the end of January.

A month later, Elisabeta Prinsloo and John Grafton (as he was called) were married. Old Erasmus Smit married them (now that Maritz was gone, civil marriages were no longer the rule) and found time for a lengthy homily on the obligations of matrimony —particularly as they regarded the duties of a wife. Mevrouw Retief and her younger son Jacobus, who had returned with John from Blood River, were their only witnesses. When the rite was over they quietly returned to their camp.

There were no wedding-guests, and none of the usual dancing or fiddling or feasting. In the general stir of rejoicings over the victory, this minute individual happiness of two unimportant young people— an orphan girl and a friendless stranger—passed without notice. In any case, the Retiefs were in no mood for jollity: Jacobus had brought back with him from the Execution Hill the wallet in which the treaty with

Dingaan had been folded, the glossy waistcoat, and a leather-cased water-bottle—and the sight of these pitiful relics had reopened the wound in his mother's heart and renewed her grief. When the evening meal and the customary prayers were over, John and Lisbet left them and walked, hand in hand, through the dark to the wagon whose slashed tilt Lisbet had patched with canvas, that was to be their first married home.

Next morning they bade farewell to Mevrouw Retief and thanked her for all her kindness.

"There is nothing to thank me for," she said. "It is a blessing to have friends in misfortune, and you, Lisbet, have been a daughter to me. You are a good girl, and I love you for your own sake as well as your mother's. God be with you always, my children. You are starting your life in a happier world than was granted to me. And God be with you, too, young man," she said. "Be gentle with your wife. Remember that the first years of marriage are more difficult for a woman than for a man, and Lisbet has had her share of sorrow and suffering. But I need not tell you this. I think you have patience and understanding. Jacoba spoke well of you many months ago, and told me she knew that you and Lisbet would marry. She is finer-spun than most of our young women, although her spirit is so strong. That is why I tell you to be gentle with her. But I think you will be so, though you be a stranger. You have been with us long enough to learn our ways. My dear husband always spoke well of the

English to me, although he was forced to differ with them. But that was my Piet. He was like the Lord Jesus Christ. He never thought ill of men even when they were his enemies. Now go, and God bless you."

They had decided between them, as soon as the marriage was over, to follow the drift of the people moving south-east. The country of the foothills, in which they had starved and suffered so long, was too full of unquiet memories for comfort. They felt the need of escaping from these and from the creeping shadow of the Berg. There was already talk in the camp of the fine new capital that would be built before long in the smiling, open country between the hills of bitter memory and the hot coastal plain where the English stifled. It was to be called Pieter-Maritzburg, in eternal memory of the two dead heroes, Retief and Maritz. Here the Raad of the folk would sit and govern the Free Province of New Holland in South-East Africa; and here, in due time, the Church of the Vow would be built.

It was as well, they thought, that they should settle within reach of a centre of population; for Dingaan, although he had been defeated, was still alive and mischievous, the Zulu power crippled but unbroken; and they had learnt the lesson of Blauwkrans, the Place of Weeping. It was better, too, that John should have the chance of plying his trade and earning a living by it; for the *Wincommando* had brought back from Zululand a meagre part of the stolen flocks and herds, and the share that had come to Lisbet was hardly sufficient to stock a farm for their sustenance. There were not even enough trek-oxen to make full spans for five wagons. If they moved south with the throng, they would have to trek slowly, in stages, advancing no more than a few miles a day.

The prospect of this laborious journey did not trouble John and Lisbet. It made little difference to them whether they travelled five miles a day or thirty. Time had no significance to either of them in a delight that was timeless; one place was as good as another if only they were together. Much prodigal beauty unrolled itself before them as the slow train of wagons coiled downhill and the sinister bastions of the Berg sank below the horizon behind them; yet no beauty could equal in rapture that which they found in each other's eyes.

When they left the disintegrating headquarters laager, the heavens had opened themselves, as in spite; black clouds, ripped by the craggy Berg, had deluged the foothills; every brook that crossed their path was a foaming torrent; the wide track, already churned by the wheels of the wagons in front, became nothing but a series of slides and pools and morasses in which the diminished spans slithered, finding no foothold, and wagon-wheels sank. The road from the hills to the swollen Umgeni river was cluttered with scores of *trekkies* brought to a standstill. For seventy-two hours rain pelted down without ceasing. Men grumbled and swore and declared, once again, that Natal was no country to live in. Women and children, packed in the wagons, sat disconsolate, listening to the fury that drummed on the leaking tilts, staring out on the muddy waste in which they were marooned. In this brookland there was not even clear water for drinking.

Others shivered and suffered; but to Lisbet and John this untimely downpour, the last of the trek's second summer, was no more than an adventure of the kind in which children delight. For children they were, to themselves and to each other, and the warmth within them was enough to keep them from shivering. They sat in the wagon untroubled and conscious of a surpassing happiness, too rich for belief. They talked of themselves; nothing else seemed worth talking of, and the subject was endless. The deluge swept over them and had passed before they were aware of it. The turbid brooks sank; the mud-lagoons steamed and cracked in the sun. When, at last, an impatient *trekkie* moved up behind them, they beheld its impatience with wonder. It seemed to them strange that in such a miraculous world there should be any need for this urgency. So, laughing at the new-comers' grim faces, they hauled their wagons out of the fairway, and slept and loved for another night before they passed on.

They crossed the dwindling Umgeni and came to the site of the new Pietermaritzburg, a deep cup hollowed out of the grassy hills whose green the late rains had already faded to autumn's first pallid gold. On their heels, from the High Veld, came Andries Pretorius with all his people. The great victory had magnified his importance in his own eyes as well as in the eyes of others. He was determined to rule, to weld the people together, and confident of his power to succeed where Retief and Maritz and other leaders had failed. His head was swollen with grandiose schemes for the ordering of church and state; and so dazzling was the aura of victory that none dared to dispute him as yet.

He laid out the plan of the capital, on whose plots, with immediate optimism, folk were already running up huts of wood and rushes, hurriedly plastered with cow-dung. There were more than two thousand souls in the valley by now, and three hundred allotments of land were quickly granted. Five rix-dollars the tenants paid for each, on the condition that within two months a water-furrow should be made and the land sown with grain and fenced and, later on, a dwelling built to con-form with the lines of the future town. For folk who were used to the great loan-farms of the colony these *erven* of seven thousand five hundred square yards seemed meagre spaces; but the commonage that sur-rounded the capital covered no less than a hundred and twenty square miles, and to those who, like John and Lisbet, had few cattle left, yet were not devoid of other movable property or money, the prospect seemed favourable.

They chose their *erf* and drove their wagons into the midst of it to shelter them, while John raised a wall of sods about it and ploughed the fertile loam and sowed it with seed they had brought from Welgelegen. He unwrapped the carefully-lifted fruit-trees too, and found, without much surprise, that all were dead; but that, in a land so rich as this, where cuttings of all kinds, men said, took root immediately, was a matter of small importance. When they had sown their *erf* with corn and pumpkins they started building their house. It was no more than a wattle-and-dab *pondakkie* roofed with reeds, far too small, at first, to contain what was left of the heavy colonial furniture carried from Welgelegen; but to these two, as proud and busy as birds building their first nest, it seemed an important building. They worked at it together, through the brilliant dry winter months, radiantly happy and hopeful, if only because they were never more to be separated; and by June the need of finishing it became more urgent, for Lisbet was with child.

John was finding tradesman's work enough to fill any spare time that was left to him. After eighteen months of trekking, few of the women in Pietermaritzburg had shoes fit to be worn, and, at present, he was the only skilled cobbler in the town. The lines of mud hovels were already assuming an urban air; folk adapted themselves with relief to more settled conditions of life. Women called on each other and began to compete in the clothes they wore when they went to church and in the embellishment of their houses; while the men engaged themselves in politics, religious and civil, and took part in the deliberations of the Raad of Representatives over which Pretorius presided without dispute. The site of the Church of the Vow was chosen; its foundations were laid; new buildings, new institutions arose, as it seemed, overnight. But, though the new State took no heed of him, the fact remained that Dingaan was still alive, malignant and powerful. And the English were still at the Port.

The English were still at the Port—not the first band of traders whom Retief had found there living in sordid promiscuity and who, some still maintained, were the cause of Dingaan's treachery, but a detachment of troops, damned red-coats of the seventy-second, with a detachment of Royal Artillery and three guns, under Captain Jervis: a small detachment, it was true, of not more than a hundred men, but backed, if it came to a push, by the hated Colonial Government and, behind these again, by the armed might of the new Queen Victoria. Even before the *Wincommando* reached the Tugela, Pretorius had received an insolent dispatch from the English commander warning him to desist from his offensive plans of vengeance on Dingaan until measures could be taken by Her Majesty's Government. Pretorius had flushed with anger; he had torn the dispatch to pieces before the messenger's eyes and marched on to Blood River.

But the English were still at the Port. What was more, the new Governor, Napier, D'Urban's successor, had proclaimed that the Boers who had trekked from the Colony could not and would not be absolved from their rightful allegiance as British subjects; and Stockenstrom, their old enemy, had further advised him to refuse to acknowledge any bargain entered into by an emigrant British subject, or any right to an inch of land, unless obtained with the Government's sanction. The innocent Napier, people said, was already in Stockenstrom's pocket. An inch of land? Had not Dingaan himself signed the document that gave them all Natal from the Berg to the sea? And, if that were not enough, had not this land of Natal been paid for in the blood of the five hundred who had died at Blaauwkrans?

But the English held Port Natal. They had proclaimed martial law, and were arbitrarily seizing all ammunition on which they could lay their hands; they were also building a fort, called, after their queen, Fort Victoria. They also, alas, held the sea. There was another matter for concern: Dingaan was flirting with the English. He had even made overtures lately to Andries Pretorius: and that was equally sinister, for it meant that he realized the mutual hostility of English and Dutch, and was trying to play off one against the other. One thing only was certain: that trouble was bound to come.

It came first, as such troubles will, over a trifle: the case of a horse strayed or stolen from a boy named Piet Kemp, who lived at Congella, not far from the Port. Kemp saw the horse (or one not unlike it) with a tame

Zulu on its back. He fired and wounded the black man in the hand—since Blauwkrans there was no more talk of "friendly intercourse"—and was promptly summoned by the English to answer a charge of malicious wounding. The boy's father refused to acknowledge the court's jurisdiction. His son, he said, was no longer a British subject, and Natal, for that matter, was not a British possession. Captain Jervis tactfully referred the matter to Capetown, and the governor, fearing a clash for which he was not prepared, withdrew the summons. First round to Andries Pretorius and the Free Province of New Holland in South-East Africa!

This trifling success was sufficient to turn Pretorius's head. At the Volksraad's next meeting he persuaded the Assembly to demand not only the return of the ammunition the English had seized from Boer settlers, but also the summary removal of all troops from the Port, and to repeat the assertion that the emigrants were no longer British subjects. If the British seized any more powder or tried to prevent its import into Natal, the Raad would not be responsible for the consequences.

Jervis answered the dispatch with a tact that was born of his knowledge of his own weakness. If the Boers would give an undertaking, he said, that the powder he had seized would only be used for defensive purposes, he would order its release. The Assembly would do nothing of the sort. At that moment a new cause of irritation had arisen. The fever-stricken remnant of Louis Trigardt's forlorn trek had drifted down to the Port from Delagoa, and the soldiers, obeying routine orders, had deprived them of their arms. Indignation for this gratuitous cruelty stung the Assembly to fury. Refusing Jervis's conditions, they repeated their peremptory demand that the British should leave Port Natal, which they claimed as Dutch territory. No person, in future, would be allowed to settle in Natal unless he acknowledged the Volksraad's jurisdiction, and none should even land without its permission. If Jervis would not accept this decision he must face the alternative: war to the knife, without quarter.

Pietermaritzburg boiled up in its hot hollow like a cauldron of molten metal. The old doctrine of racial hatred revived, and Pretorius was its new prophet. John Grafton, busily working all day on his land, or out on the commonage, was unaware of this; but Lisbet, who stayed at home, was not so immune. Friendly neighbours, who came to gossip and advise her on her condition, talked of nothing else.

"What a pity," they said, "that you should have married an Englishman!"

She resented their sympathy, but, none the less, had to listen.

"There is trouble coming," she told him, "between your people and mine."

He laughed at her. "Why should you worry your

head over women's gossip? I have done no harm to anyone, so what need we fear?"

"I fear war," she said. "And I hoped we had done with wars."

John went on with his work; but in time even he was forced to realize that the position was growing serious. Men who once had been friendly avoided him. The neighbours who once had dropped in to chat with Lisbet came near her no more.

"That is all the better," he told her when she complained. "There is too much talk in this town. I wish to heaven we had stayed at the Mooi River with Mevrouw Retief."

In November—by now Lisbet was six months gone and apt to be irritable in spite of herself—a new access of fierce Anglophobia swept the community. A company had been formed in England, backed by the Liverpool merchants, to obtain a Royal Charter for the colonization of Natal. Pretorius, hysterical with anger and fear, harangued the Volksraad and sent down to the Port a dispatch with the wording of an ultimatum. Men took our their guns and cleaned them. The cannon were dragged into the new market-place and admired. Organized drilling began. The only question now was how soon the war with the English would begin.

"What are we going to do when it comes?" Lisbet asked. "Which side will you take?"

"I shall not take up arms against my own people,"

John told her. "After all, I am English-born."

"Yes, yes, I know that. But how can you possibly avoid it? If you will not fight, they will make you a prisoner; and what shall I do then?"

"They cannot fight the English," he said. "Pretorius may bluster as much as he likes, but he is not so foolish as that."

"But even supposing they do not fight," she persisted, "and the English send soldiers from the Cape and take Natal, where would you be then? They might find out who you are and where you came from."

He laughed at her fears. "That is ancient history," he told her. "John Oakley, if they remember that such a man ever existed, was drowned and buried nearly two years ago at Algoa Bay."

But she would not be comforted.

"I am frightened for you, my darling," she said. "Whatever happens, I can only see one end to it. If we wait too long, I shall lose you, John; I know it."

"Then what can we do?"

"We can trek."

"This is no time for you to talk of trekking, my love. This scare will blow over; you take my word for it. Let us go on with our work and live our own lives and pay no more heed to it."

"We cannot live our own lives, John. We are part of the world, and the world will not let us."

He went on with his work. This was the first time in his life he had felt himself his own master; he was proud of the turf walls he had built with his own hands, of the tilth, where the corn showed bravely, and of the little house he had built. But he could not content her. Through her lonely days, fear dwelt with her; and at night, when they lay side by side, she could not sleep. Though he used all his gentleness in comforting and humouring her, John knew there would be no peace for either of them until she had her way. And perhaps, after all, she was right.

At the end of November they trekked.

It was a sombre journey. The long anxiety had worn Lisbet to a shadow. Their backward path was full of ghostly memories of pain and ecstasy: the morass in which they had been marooned for three happy days on their honeymoon; the length of road where the Sneeuwbergen *trekkie* had picked them up battered and starving; the point where, more than a year ago, they had diverged from the trek-path to reach the Blauw-krans River. They did not speak of these things, though the minds of both were full of them. Lisbet had only one purpose, grim and dominant: to escape from the land of shadows, to recross the Berg, to find new life and new hope on the untroubled High Veld.

They scaled the high ridge of the Drakensbergen by the track over which they had descended. It was well worn now and free from its ancient terrors, for thousands of wagons had crossed and recrossed the range since last they saw it. As they mounted, down

came a shaggy cavalcade of armed men hurrying eastward. As they passed, they taunted Lisbet. "You are
going the wrong way," they said. "Make your man
turn back and help us to fight the English. We shall
drive them into the sea, and then all will be well."

They reached the highest point of the pass from
which, looking backward, their eyes might have seen
the splendours of Natal, outspread and falling, terrace
by terrace, to the invisible sea. But Lisbet would not
look back. She would not even consent to outspan on
the crown of the Berg where the neighbourhood of that
land of sorrows could be felt if not seen. They dropped
down over the gentler slopes of the Berg's western
shoulders and encamped for the night, tired out, on a
grassy plain that stretched, infinite and red as blood,
towards the sunset.

"Now I feel I can breathe again," Lisbet told him.

And, indeed, the lightening of her spirits (and therefore of his) seemed almost miraculous in its suddenness. It made him reproach himself for the suffering
his obstinacy had prolonged, and thank Heaven he had
yielded to her at last and put an end to it. That night,
though it froze, they slept soundly, serenely. At morning, when they awoke, John hardly knew her. The
heaviness had gone from her eyes, the anxiety from her
mouth; she was gay and childlike and tender. There
was no cloud in the peerless sky, no shadow in her heart.
Though he begged her to spare herself, she would not
ride in the wagon.

"I want to be near you," she said. "It seems to me as though we have been separated for years; but nothing shall ever separate us again, John, as long as we live."

They walked hand in hand as the slow spans moved without swerving over the veld. It was clad in the lush green of summer now, and there were few flowers to pick; but the crystalline air of the heights seemed purer and sweeter than that of the plains. There was new life and invincible hope in every breath of it.

Day after day, for weeks, they trekked slowly on without care or forethought. Life had never seemed richer or more untroubled to either of them than in that halcyon season. Before dawn they inspanned. In the heat of the day they bivouacked. An hour before sunset they halted, and John rode out with his gun to pick up a buck for the pot from the grazing herds that dappled the waste like slow-moving shadows of cloud.

When they had turned their backs on the pit of Pietermaritzburg, they had made no plans for the future: Lisbet had only known one anxiety—to trek, to escape. But now that they had escaped, it seemed (as Jan Bothma would have said) that some plan must be made. In less than two months her time would be upon her; and though, to soothe his fears, she treated the matter lightly, John was anxious that, when it came, they should be within reach of help. When he spoke of it with concern, Lisbet smiled at him—she had recovered her old, teasing ways.

"One would think," she said, "that this baby of ours

w*

was the first that had ever been born. I am well and strong. I feel better and happier now than ever before in my life. We are a tough breed, my darling: my mother bore twelve children and never thought anything of it. Why should you be more frightened than I am?" But she could not dispel his indefinite dread with her teasing.

"Very well, then," she said. "We will make a plan if you must. We will cross the Vaal and make for Potgieter's country where many folk have settled. There is another good reason for that. It is our duty to go there. We must not forget that we are not so rich as we seem. Two-thirds of our property belongs by right to Anna and Barend. We will find out where they are settled and give them their due, and then we shall really be free."

"I doubt if Barend and Anna will be pleased to see us," he told her.

"Who knows?" she answered. "Still, we ought to do what is just. And, after all, Barend and Anna are my brother and sister."

They crossed the Vaal and came to the Zuikerbosch Rand. The folk on the newly-settled farms were glad to welcome them and eager for news of Natal. When they heard of the Volksraad's strife with the English, they shook their heads and their faces grew grave.

"If the English attack our people," they said, "we shall have to ride over and help them; but pray God it may not be so. We have settled in this good country where nobody troubles us, and all we ask is peace."

Wherever they halted they asked for news of Barend. None knew where he was precisely, but all felt sure that he would be found among the Potgieters somewhere along the Witwatersrand, the great ridge that made their horizon to the north-west. There, Potgieter had founded a town called Potchefstroom, with a Volksraad and government of its own; but they themselves had little truck with the Potchefstroom people. Folk who lived in towns must always be quarrelling. It was better to abide in the back-veld and live one's own life. They were as tired of politics as they were of fighting.

John and Lisbet turned north and approached the long blue shape to which the farmers had pointed. From the Zuikerboschrand it had appeared as no more than a meagre fold in the uniform carpet of veld; yet, in fact, this Ridge of White Waters marked the dividing line between two great river-systems: the basin of the Limpopo, emptying into the Indian Ocean, and that of the Vaal and the Orange, flowing towards the Atlantic. Many streams ran southward to meet them as they advanced. Though the water was only white by comparison with the turbid content of other African rivers, the country through which they flowed was plainly well-watered and the grazing to the taste of their cattle.

They struck the ridge itself at its eastern end. Here the grass was scrubby and coarse and the land itself

stony with outcrops of iron-grey rock imbedded here
and there with quartzy pebbles. When he saw these
rocky outcrops John shook his head:

"A poor, thin soil," he said. "There is no wealth
for man or beast in it. If George Dicketts were here he
would tell us about Tom Collins's field, Long Dragon."

It was odd how often, in these days, the memory of
his friend returned to his thoughts.

They climbed the gradual slope and reached the
northern lip of the ridge. Here the ground fell more
steeply, and other streams had their sources in scrubby
kloofs beyond which the great plains of grassland rolled
on again, dun and endless, towards the north, but were
broken to westward by the humped shapes of mountains
called the Magaliesbergen: a landscape impressive not,
as that of Natal, in tumbled grandeur, but in its sheer,
vast monotony which, like that of the sea, was changeless yet ever-changing.

"What do you think of this country?" John asked
her.

"It rests the eyes," Lisbet said, "and rest is all we
are asking. It seems to go on and on for ever."

"Yes, on to Monomotapa."

"What is that strange word?"

"It means the City of Gold."

"Who told you that, John?"

"It was a story of Mr. Blair's. Somewhere there-
abouts, he said, lay the great Gold Country, where
Solomon sent the ships of Tarshish for gold for his

temple. *Mombaza, and Quiloa, and Melind, and Sofala, thought Ophir.* . . . He said that the Portuguese . . ."

But she was not listening.

"Poor Mr. Blair," she said. "I think he is somewhere in these parts. I should like to see him again. He was fond of you, John."

She did not say that poor Mr. Blair had been fond of herself.

They turned westward along the Rand. On the second morning, they fell in with a mounted man who was rounding up cattle and enquired once more of Barend.

"Barend Prinsloo?" he said. "You are not more than three hours from his place. It's on the south side of the ridge; you cannot miss it. He has called it Welgelegen, and it doesn't lie badly. Who are you, then, and where do you come from, and what do you want?"

They wasted an hour with him, telling him the news of Natal. He was as little inclined for war as the other farmers, and had no great opinion of Andries Pretorius, with whom he had served in the Marico campaign against Mozelikatse. "We have peace here at last," he said. "We want no more wars."

The wagons rolled on for four hours. The sun was declining—the halt had hindered them—when they saw, at a deceptive distance, a single low building, clinging close to the veld of which it seemed part.

This must be Barend's house, they decided, since there was no other. Lisbet approached it gaily, excitedly; but her gaiety was a little nervous; and John felt in his bones that the encounter would not be easy.

As they drew near, they saw a tall figure regarding them from the unsheltered stoep, and wondered if they were mistaken: this surely could not be Barend. The wagon rolled up in front of the house, but still he did not move. John walked towards him and wished him good evening.

"We are looking for Barend Prinsloo," he said.

"I am Barend Prinsloo," the tall man answered sullenly. "What do you want?"

Lisbet had heard his voice from the wagon. She ran forward eagerly.

"Barend, Barend, can it be you?" she cried. "But how you are changed! And Anna. . . . Is she still with you?"

"No, Anna is no longer with us," he answered. "She has married a Kruger. I thought, when I saw the wagon in the distance, that it must be you."

"But you didn't welcome us, Barend?"

"Why should I?" he said. "You are English now, I've been told; and no English are welcome here."

He stood scowling heavily at John. As Lisbet said, he had changed. The sanguine, ardent boy they had known was no longer. In his place stood a tall, hungry man with a shaggy black beard and heavy brows beneath which the old hot eyes smouldered.

"No, I don't wish to see any more of you or your husband," he said.

John saw Lisbet go pale with anger in his defence. Her gentle eyes were as hot as Barend's now. He laid a hand on her arm to steady her, but she shook her head as though she resented the suggestion of restraint.

"We have brought five wagons as well as the sheep and cattle," she said. "One-third of them is now yours, and another third Anna's. You may take what you want, and then we will go our way."

"Anna may take what she likes," Barend said. "She is farther west with the Krugers. But my father gave me half of my portion at Winburg: that you know. The wagons I do not need, but I will take my sixth part of the beasts, and one or two wagon-chests."

"Do it now, then," Lisbet said. "We are not folk who like to outspan where we are not welcome."

"I speak the truth," Barend said. "That was always my habit. I will look to the cattle while the light lasts. Your Englishman can go with me if he likes."

"Stay with me, John. Don't move," Lisbet whispered. Barend heard her and laughed.

He stalked to the back of the house and called out his natives. They were naked Kaffirs, people of the conquered tribes. He jumped on his horse, and, between them, he and his men picked out a sixth of the cattle and drove them to a mud-walled kraal. He rode back to the wagons and dismounted.

"I have counted the beasts," he said. "You can check the number if you wish."

"No, Barend; you speak the truth," Lisbet said. "That was always your habit. Is there anything more?" she asked stonily.

"Ay, the wagon-chests, as I told you."

"You may choose for yourself."

"I will take the first I see; but I do not want women's clothing: we have no use for finery here."

"Our mother's chests are in the first wagon," she said.

"Then I will take mine from the second."

The natives hoisted and hauled the three chests from the second wagon and carried them into the house.

"That is all?" Lisbet asked.

"That is all."

Barend turned his back on them.

"It is over, Heaven be thanked," Lisbet said. "Now let us move on."

The western levels of sky were already blood-red and night was at hand. They trailed on, with the ridge on their right, until darkness fell and they could see their way no further. Lisbet walked beside her husband clutching his hand, but no word was spoken until they lay down for the night.

"You have suffered for me to-day, my love," he told her.

"I have suffered nothing I cannot bear," she said. "What does it matter? Are you not worth it?"

When they awoke next morning her face showed how deeply her pride and her love had suffered. It was a brilliant winter day, the air cold but windless. Rime whitened the veld; the great plains were as pure as the sky.

"I can see you are tired," he said. "Let us stay here a day or two. I will laager the wagons."

She smiled at him. "There is no fear in this country," she said, "and no need to do that. Not even fear of Barend: he is three hours behind us."

In the gold of afternoon they walked out over the veld to the place where the cattle were watered. It was the source of one of the streams that fell to the Vaal. Clear water gushed icy-cold from the stony slope to feed it. Lisbet knelt and drank.

"It is beautiful water," she said. "So sweet and so cold."

"And a wonderful spring. It flows freely even in winter."

"A wonderful spring. Yes, I like to hear you say 'wonderful,' John. Let us give it that name. We will call it Wonderfontein."

He laughed. "We can call it Wonderfontein if you like; but that will be our secret. When we pass on and leave it behind, it will lose its name."

She was silent awhile, her far gaze resting dreamily on the great sea of golden veld. He wondered what she was thinking.

"Why should we pass on, after all?" she said. "Why

shouldn't we stay here? We have wandered so far, you and I. If we wander farther shall we find greater peace than this?"

"You are tired?" he asked anxiously.

"Yes, I am rather tired. I can't walk very far now, and the wagon jolts me."

"We will stay here and rest for a while, then."

"If we stay here after to-morrow," she said, "I think we shall stay for ever. And then our spring's pretty name will not be lost after all."

Next day he brought their wagons nearer the fountain. The peace of the vast expanses of veld it commanded began to grow on them, and the beauty of the High Veld too—a beauty that does not reveal itself to casual eyes.

"This place makes me strangely happy," she told him. "The air is so bright and the water so sweet. There are no shadows on it but those of clouds, and shadows of cloud are hardly shadows at all. It seems to me a good place to live and die in."

"To *live* in . . ." he said.

"Yes, I should not have spoken of death. That was wrong of me. I think I should like to stay here at Wonderfontein. There is no reason why we should not stay. The land is all free."

"If you are happy here," he said, "that is all I ask."

"I am happy enough. I suppose I shall soon be happier. It cannot be very far off."

"You think it as near as that?"

She smiled at his anxious face. "I think I would rather not move. Don't look so frightened. You watch me too closely, my darling. You are always near me, and that is bad for you. Now listen: To-morrow you will take your horse and ride out the land, half an hour in either direction with the fountain as centre. You will take a spade with you, and when you have made your marks you will set up beacons. Turf will do to begin with. There will be no rain to wash them away till the spring, and by that time we shall have found stones. Later on we will go to the Drostdy at Potgieter's town and take out the lease to put all in order. And then Wonderfontein will be ours, and we will live happily ever after. Now be good, and do what I tell you," she said. "To-morrow . . ."

"I don't like leaving you, Lisbet," he said.

"How suspicious you are! Let me be alone for one day. It will be good for us both. Promise me not to come back till you've finished."

He promised reluctantly.

At dawn he fetched water from the spring and boiled their coffee.

"You are all right this morning? Look, you have spilt your coffee."

"How stupid of me!" she said. "Of course I am all right. You needn't stay with me now. You have a day's work before you. Now kiss me, and go."

She was glad when he waved her good-bye. In the

middle of the night, as she had foreseen, the first crawling pain had set its teeth in her. It was another spasm that had made her spill her coffee. When he was out of sight she resigned herself to the pangs, returning with slow steps to the wagon, whose tilt would hide her till they were over. She climbed up to the floor of the wagon laboriously. Half-way, another pain took her. She clung to the rail until it had passed; then lay down to her lonely struggle. She was not afraid. In the laager at Dorenkop after the Blauwkrans massacre, she had watched and helped many women in labour with Mevrouw Retief and the Italian, Teresa Viglione. She knew something of their desperate business, and believed she could bear it provided that she were left alone to go through with it. Her greatest anxiety was lest John should return to the wagon before her child was born. It was enough that one should suffer. She lay on the floor of the wagon, gripping the rail, as she had seen other women do, while pain after pain remorselessly tore her.

John rode out the bounds of Wonderfontein in a sombre mood. Though he had obeyed Lisbet's word, he could not be happy about her. In the back of his mind he reproached himself for having let her have her way and halted until it was too late to go further. If he had been within reach of the new town at Potchefstroom, where there were women who understood these mysteries, he might have been happier. In an emergency, he comforted himself, he could still ride there in a day—it was not more than sixty miles—and bring a woman back with him. At the very worst, he might even appeal to Barend's wife, Alie. But Lisbet's pride would fight against that, he knew.

He rode his half-hour and dismounted. It struck him that the pasture was poor. On that side, the outcrop of iron-grey stone lay in a broad band. They would have been better off, he told himself, had they chosen land farther from the ridge; though, in that case, they would not have possessed their wonderful fountain. The day was brilliant, of a dry, glistening clarity such as only the true High Veld at its best can show. As he bent to his work, cutting turf to make his beacons, something of the beauty which Lisbet had seen from the first, but which he had been late to discover, dawned upon him. It struck him, with the suddenness of a conversion, that God was good, and the gift of life surpassingly sweet. The labour engrossed him and made him forget his preoccupation. He looked on the land that was to be theirs, appraising its possibilities. They were endless, it seemed to him. Here, at last, was elbow-room and more scope for his energy than in the cramped *erf* at Pietermaritzburg. In this noble space a large family of sons could find work for their hands in a strong air that would make men of them.

It was only when he rode back to the wagon in mid-afternoon that the old anxiety, from which labour had freed him, returned. He looked at the bivouac from afar and saw no sign of Lisbet. The fire he had kindled at dawn had gone out, for none had fed it. He jumped off his horse and ran towards the wagon, calling Lisbet's name. No voice answered him. The blood rushed to his head and an awful terror seized him. If she were alive she would surely have answered. With limbs that shook beneath him, he hoisted himself to the tail-board and stepped under the tilt. She lay there motionless. Her eyes were open caverns of darkness, her face ivory-pale.

"You are there," he gasped. "Thank God you are there. I could not see you. I called, and you didn't answer. I thought . . . oh, Lisbet."

"I heard you," she whispered. "I tried to call back, but my voice wouldn't carry." She smiled wanly. "Oh, I feel so weak!"

"It has begun, then?"

"Begun?" She gazed at him wonderingly. "No, no, it's over. Thank Heaven it's over at last. Oh, more than an hour ago. A boy. He is here at my breast. So strong. He is sucking already."

"I can only think of you. You are all that matters to me, my poor, poor love."

He knelt beside her and took her hand and pressed it to his lips. Tears blinded his eyes. It was hard to keep from sobbing. Her hand pressed his feebly: she had strength for no more.

"You needn't worry about me any longer," she said. "I told you I was strong and healthy and all

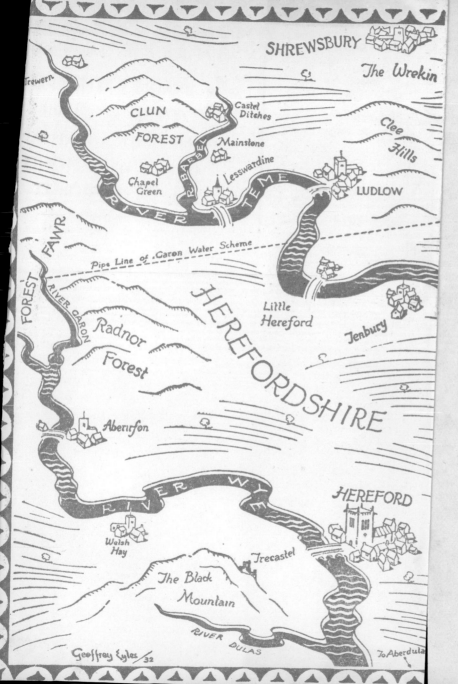

would be well, but you wouldn't believe me. And the baby is as strong as a little lion, too, John. All I need now is to rest for a while."

"Is there nothing I can do?"

"Nothing . . . nothing. I was in hell, and now I am in heaven. Perhaps a cup of water. I drank all there was, and I'm thirsty."

He held the cup to her lips and she drank.

"Such sweet water, so sweet and cool," she murmured. "Yes, that is better."

He still remained kneeling by her. For a long while she was silent. She lay with closed eyes, content and exhausted.

Many hours later she spoke.

"Are you there, John?"

"Of course I am here, my love."

"I have been thinking. As soon as I knew he was a boy, I said to myself: 'We will call him Adrian. Do you think that sounds well: Adrian Grafton?"

"It's well enough. Any name you choose will do for me. It is a mixture: half Dutch and half English. And so, after all, is he. So call him that if you will."

"Half Dutch and half English. . . . Yes, you are right," she said. "But he will be neither one nor the other, I think. When he grows to be a man he will call himself a South African or an Afrikander. Some day, perhaps, that will be a name to be proud of."

Craycombe. 10.xii.36—23.v.37

AUTHOR'S NOTE

Since this novel has a historical setting and some readers of fiction are (as Sheridan complained of Fox) "damned surly about facts," it is as well to mention the sources to which I am indebted for most of the historical detail. In the First Book I have gratefully availed myself—and not for the first time—of the works of J. L. and Barbara Hammond, to whom I owe a particular debt for their kindness in reading the manuscript. The picture of working-class life a hundred years ago, terrible as it is, is not overdrawn, as any reader can judge for himself if he consults their admirable 'Village Labourer' series, and the report of the Royal Commission on Transportation. In the African part of the book I have relied on the histories of Theal and Cory, on Bird's *Annals of Natal*, and on the collected personal narratives of the Great Trek published under the title of *Voortrekkermense*; and I must acknowledge a particular debt to Professor E. A. Walker, whose admirable book on The Great Trek, in the Pioneer Histories Series, is a model in style, poise and accuracy of what such a work should be.

F. B. Y.